IT *Always* LEADS TO *You*

TAMMY SUBIA

*For anyone who hears "'tis the damn season"
and thinks of their high school love*

CHAPTER ONE

NOW

*A*MHERST, MASS 70 MILES

Montana frowns as she passes the highway sign. Because it means she'll be arriving in Hartley—a town so small it doesn't merit its own sign—in less than two hours, and the final nail in the coffin of her formerly successful life will be nailed in.

Up until a few months ago, she was working her dream job. A full-time travel writing position for a hugely popular magazine that covered expenses. The Holy Grail of travel journalism. But budget cuts led to her getting laid off, and while she hoped she could sell some freelance articles to scrape by until she found something more stable, it turns out that L.A. is *not* a place where you can just scrape by.

Losing her job was devasting. But having to admit defeat and move back into her parents' house in the hometown she ran away from the first chance she got?

Well. The closer she gets to the town line, the more that proverbial coffin is feeling like a better option.

As she's contemplating turning the car around and making the three-thousand-mile trek right back to California—or, you know, driving into a ditch somewhere—her phone rings through the car's sound system, abruptly cutting off one of Taylor Swift's best bridges.

Grudgingly hitting accept, she attempts to keep the melancholy out of her voice as she says, "Hi, Mom."

"Honey! Are you driving?"

"Yes. You know that. I'm almost there."

"Good. I wanted to make sure you didn't change your mind at the last minute and do something crazy."

Montana rolls her eyes. Her mom knows her too well. "Only if you count shaving my head, tattooing my face, and joining the circus crazy."

"Don't forget the key is under the frog," her mom says, completely ignoring her joke.

"I know."

"Are you sure you want to stay in the house alone? You could still come live with us, you know."

"I know," she repeats, fighting exasperation. She's well aware of her two options, and neither are ideal.

Resorting to asking her parents for help, after six years of making it on her own, was a huge blow to her self-esteem. But she should probably be grateful that the timing worked out the way it did. Ever since her parents bought a condo in Florida, they've been renting out their house in Hartley. And when Montana made the dreaded phone call to tell them she was being evicted from her apartment, it just so happened that their last tenants had moved out and they hadn't found new ones yet.

She has a few minor reasons—and one major, guy-shaped one—for not wanting to come back to her hometown. But it was either move into her old, empty house rent-free, mooching off her parents, or move to Boca Raton and live *with* her parents in their tiny condo. She actually briefly considered the latter but decided it would be even more humiliating.

This is fine. She'll survive. She has to.

For all she knows, Austin may not even be living in town anymore. Although, if she's being honest with herself, she can't imagine him living anywhere else. Nor can she imagine the town of Hartley without him in it.

But it's fine.

"Well, your father and I will come visit when we can," her mom goes on. "His knee's been bothering him, but I don't think it's anything serious."

Desperately needing out of this conversation—she'd rather be left to wallow in her misery alone—Montana says, "Hey, I'm coming up to the exit. I'd better go."

"Okay, I'll call you tomorrow after you're settled."

"Oh, no, you don't have—"

"Bye, honey," her mom cuts off her protest and ends the call.

The music comes back on, but she's not in the mood to sing. As she takes the road heading into town, it's like she's being sucked backward through a time vortex. Suddenly she's a teenager again. The future wide open in front of her. Torn between love and her dreams.

No.

She's twenty-eight years old. She made her choice a long time ago.

And then Austin made his.

♦

AFTER PULLING HER battered Ford Fiesta into the driveway of Seventeen Peachtree Lane, Montana lets out a long-pent-up sigh. She's here. No turning back now.

With nothing left to do but face the suburban music, she gets out of the car and drags all she has with her—her laptop and the small suitcase she packed for the five-day drive—toward the house. She ducks down to snag the key hidden not so cleverly underneath Wilson, the small frog statue that's sat in front of the porch for as long as she can remember. Then she makes her way up the porch steps, but that's as far as she gets. She needs a minute before unlocking the door.

Maybe two.

Three minutes, tops.

Sitting down at the top of the steps, she takes in the familiar view of the street. Two rows of modest two-story homes painted neutral colors facing off against each other. White mailboxes posted dutifully on the tree belts. Stately maple trees looming over front lawns. Furry gray squirrels scurrying from tree to tree with their tiny treasures tucked safely between their teeth.

It's not like she hates it here. She never did. It's only that she thought she'd moved on long ago.

Being back now is making her feel itchy, somewhere deep underneath her skin where she can't scratch. For all the years she spent on the West Coast, she never submitted to all the spiritual, hippie, meditation culture that's so popular there, but maybe she should have. Because she could really use some zen right now.

She does zone out, though, three minutes turning into almost twenty without her realizing. Going inside probably can't be stalled any longer. She has no idea if Mrs. Coulter still lives across the street, but if she does, the old woman is sure to be as nosy as ever. Montana wouldn't put it past her to call Montana's parents a thousand miles away and snitch on her for lurking suspiciously in front of the house.

Reluctantly, she gets up to unlock the door, wheels her suitcase over the threshold, and steps inside. It's bizarre. She's stepped through this doorway a million times before, but it's been years.

After she graduated college and moved to L.A. permanently, she rarely came home to visit her parents. Mainly because she was afraid of running into Austin, but also because she couldn't really afford the plane tickets. Even with her magazine job, rent and food and semi-regular manicures were pretty much all she could manage. With the occasional luxury of treating herself to an eight-dollar latte instead of the sludge that came out of the coffee pot at the office.

So she made excuses, claiming she was too busy with her writing and travel for work. And it wasn't a total lie. She *was* busy. For a while, she was living the dream. Regular paid trips around the country, and even the handful of trips around the world. She had what she always wanted.

And now . . .

Now all she has is an alarming heap of credit card debt and an empty two-bedroom house, built in the eighties, that isn't even technically hers.

It looks the same as she remembers, albeit without any of her family's belongings inside. A shell devoid of anything to actually make it a home. But peering into the space of the living room, she can see the ghosts of her former life here. Her dad in his ratty T-shirt and sweatpants on the couch, swearing loudly as the Red Sox lose a game on the TV. Her mom off in the kitchen cooking spaghetti for dinner, begging him to calm down. Daisy, their black lab, circling a spot on the rug before she plops down, perfectly content.

And herself, everywhere. Doing homework at the dining room table, up in her bedroom bouncing around to the newest Taylor Swift album, inexpertly applying eyeliner in front of the bathroom mirror.

With Austin.

Almost always, with Austin.

She shakes her head to clear the memories. Again, she has to tell herself that was a long time ago. This is now.

Going into the living room, she lays her suitcase on the floor and unzips it, searching for her last clean shirt. When she hit the road this morning, she stopped for an Egg McMuffin, and she's been wearing a greasy splotch of it on her chest all day long. She changes quickly, then does another scan of the empty room. *What now?*

Her stomach growls, a reminder that the tiny breakfast sandwich isn't enough to sustain her for the rest of the day. The movers aren't scheduled to arrive for another couple hours, and just sitting on the floor waiting for them would be sad, so she might as well venture downtown for something to eat. Even if that idea almost makes her lose her appetite.

She pops into the bathroom before she goes, finding only half a roll of toilet paper and no soap in there. *Wonderful.* Better add a stop for some essentials too.

As she drives down Main Street, she feels a bit like a fugitive, slouching down in her seat at every red light to avoid being spotted. Though her bright purple car is about as conspicuous a vehicle as you can get. When she passes the red brick façade of Alan's Place, she experiences a heartbreaking pang of nostalgia. That's obviously off limits. Austin always planned to help his father run the restaurant one day. And even if he's not there, going in and seeing his parents would be equally as awkward.

She keeps driving, trying to think of a safe place to go. The diner's out too. And *damn*, pancakes sound great right about now, but there's always the chance he could be there. Even if it's slim, her luck hasn't been the greatest lately, so it's best not to risk it.

Finally, she spots a café. Something new (or new in the last six years, at least) with big glass windows out front. The painted logo in one window says BREAD & BREW, accompanied by an illustration of a coffee cup and a bagel. As she parks the car, she realizes she has no way of knowing if Austin comes here or not. But since *she's* never been here, she can almost let herself believe he hasn't either.

At least she has no memories of him here.

And let's be real, if she refuses to go to any place he's ever stepped foot in, she'll need to find somewhere else to live. A different house. A different town.

The inside of the café is as charming as the outside, with a handful of small round tables and a few squishy looking armchairs. It smells divine, like bread and sugar and cinnamon. She peruses the chalkboard menu on the wall before approaching the counter to order a turkey avocado BLT on one of their fresh-baked specialty breads and a hazelnut iced coffee. Then, quickly scanning the glass display cases, she adds a raspberry turnover, happily accepting the cashier's offer to warm it up. After she pays, the woman hands her a little number placard stuck in a metal holder, and she brings it over to a table that's far off to the side.

The turnover arrives before her sandwich. Immediately biting into it, she moans in both pain (*hot!*) and pleasure (*sooo good*). She takes a long sip of the iced coffee to soothe her burnt tongue, and then forces herself to wait for the pastry to cool before finishing it. Even with that appetizer, when she gets her sandwich, she scarfs it down pretty quickly. Guess she was hungrier than she realized. Wanting an excuse to linger, though, she takes her time with the rest of her drink.

Three separate people walk in while she idly stirs the straw around her cup, and she briefly thinks each of them is Austin. Considering how the third person is a woman with shoulder-length hair, she probably needs to relax. Turning her focus to scrolling social media on her phone, she tries in vain not to feel jealous of her friends back West with their In-N-Out burgers and their beachy vibes.

Her guard is finally down when it happens.

Some instinct tells her to look up. A man stands at the counter, his back to her. And this isn't her imagination anymore. It doesn't matter that it's been six years—she'd recognize the back of that dirty blonde head anywhere.

Austin Adler.

She sucks in a breath, stuck in a moment of disbelief and another moment of fight-or-flight. Then he turns, paper coffee cup in hand, and his green eyes lock on to her brown ones.

"*Ana.*"

Not a question, but so quiet that if she wasn't staring right at his face, she may not have caught it.

He's the only person who's ever called her that, and only in their most intimate moments. Hearing it now jolts her back in time once again. He appears frozen in place, giving her a chance to recover. But right as she opens her mouth to say something, he abruptly jerks his gaze away from her and bolts out the door.

Well.

Okay, then.

THEN

*T*hat was amazing."

Montana rolled onto her side to face Austin, the covers still bunched down by their feet, and slipped one of her legs between his. "Mmhmm," she replied, too sated to form coherent words yet. Placing her hand against his chest, she drew invisible circles through the light smattering of hair there.

"I can't move," he said, contradicting it by inching his fingers out to twirl around a wavy strand of her long, light brown hair that was splayed across his pillow.

She smiled lazily. "That's okay."

It was the middle of the afternoon, and the sun shone valiantly through his bedroom window. Even though a layer of snow blanketed the ground outside, his bed with the plaid flannel sheets was one of the warmest places she'd ever known. The January chill would creep into the room eventually, but for now, they were good.

They were more than good.

His dad was at the restaurant, and she didn't know where his mom or his sister were, only that she and Austin had the house to themselves, which they'd taken full advantage of. She *could* come around when his family was home. But the change in their feelings toward her was obvious, and it hurt. In high school, his family was her family, and vice versa. Now things were different.

Though she couldn't exactly blame his family. She'd broken up with Austin, after all. And this arrangement they'd found of getting together whenever she was home on break from college, enjoying their limited time as best they could, didn't seem to make sense to anyone other than the two of them.

Actually, if she was being honest with herself, it was starting not to make much sense to her either. If they fell back into each other like this, so naturally, every time they were in the same place, did they ever really break up at all? Was this the long-distance relationship she hadn't wanted to have?

No.

Not exactly.

They were only together when she was here. When she wasn't . . .

They didn't promise each other anything. During her semesters at UCLA she was free to see other people. And she did, occasionally. A few dates and a few hookups here and there. But nothing serious.

He was free to see other people too, of course. She'd be foolish to imagine he didn't do it. But if he did, she didn't want to hear about it.

As he continued idly playing with her hair, she wondered if maybe she was wrong for ever believing she'd had to give him up. Maybe it hadn't needed to be a choice between college and him. Maybe they could have made promises to each other and kept them. But she didn't have the luxury of changing the past. All she had was this, right now. The pleasure of knowing that he still wanted her, that he still cared, four years after she'd left him.

And she had the future in front of her. She was graduating after next semester, and she'd have choices to make. Again. After high school, she'd chosen the opportunity to attend her dream college and study journalism. She'd chosen it over him.

California was everything she'd hoped it would be.

Except it was three thousand miles away from the warmest bed and the most wonderful boy she'd ever known.

She'd always had a plan for after graduation. Stay in California, pursue her dream career. But was it worth it if it meant she only got to have this with Austin on the rare occasion she could make it back here to visit? And how long would she be lucky enough to find him still waiting, happy to let her slip back into his arms? If she stayed in California, surely that would mean eventually giving him up for good.

So what if she was considering a different decision now? Leaving him the first time had torn both of them in half. She didn't want to do that again, but she couldn't figure out how to navigate a path that would let her keep everything she wanted.

They should discuss it, she knew. Instead of making the decision on her own like last time, trying to decide what was best for the both of them, she should let him be a part of it.

"Hey." His soft, intimate voice drew her gently out of her own head. One of his hands covered hers over his chest and squeezed. "What are you thinking about?"

She sighed softly, taking in his green eyes that, in this moment, seemed to hold all the secrets of the universe. He might have answers for her, but she was scared of what they would be, so she said, "Nothing."

He brought his hand to her face, thumb gently tracing her cheekbone. "Your flight leaves tomorrow."

Leaning into his touch, she said, "I know."

CHAPTER TWO

NOW

*A*fter Austin runs out of the café, Montana remains there stunned, glued to her seat for so long she starts to worry she's become that sad girl Taylor Swift sings about in "Right Where You Left Me," with dust collecting on her hair.

Fuck, it's been six years since the last time she's seen Austin. And god, she hadn't even known that last time was going to *be* the last time. And now . . . nothing.

Is it really a surprise he didn't want to talk to her though? She may be the one who originally left him, but he's the one who ultimately cut things off. Cut her out of his life without another word.

During her last semester of college, he stopped answering her calls, stopped responding to her texts. It took her many months to admit to herself that was it. She wasn't going to hear from him again. And it took a hell of a lot longer for his absence from her life to not feel like a huge gaping hole threatening to swallow her up at any moment.

Over the years, she's thought up the craziest explanations for why he did what he did. She's fantasized a hundred different scenarios of what would happen if she ever saw him again.

In her head, it never went like that.

The ring of her phone snaps her out of a daze. It's the moving company letting her know the truck will be arriving in thirty minutes.

Oh, right. That prompts her to grab her stuff and make her own hasty exit from the café.

On the way back to the house, she stops at the gas station and fills up her car before running inside. A slight odor of cigarettes lingers in the air. She grabs a single roll of toilet paper in that crinkly paper wrapping and a bottle of generic brand hand soap that only costs a dollar. Who cares if the ambiguous "BERRY" scent will probably smell more like chemicals, right? There's no food in the house either, so she should probably get some stuff to tide her over until she goes grocery shopping.

Three minutes later, she's stumbling over to the register, arms laden with the toilet paper, soap, a hand of bananas, a bag of Cool Ranch Doritos, a pint of Haagen-Dazs Rocky Road, and a bottle of the cheapest chardonnay they had. She carefully deposits her bounty onto the counter and gives the teenage cashier a warm smile when he doesn't even bat an eye at the odd assortment.

She beats the movers back to the house, but it's not long before they're pulling up. They unload her stuff while she stays out of the way, and in no time at all they're heading out, leaving her alone with her furniture and cardboard boxes all piled in the middle of the living room.

It would have been nice if her parents had sprung for the full packing and unpacking service when they hired the company for her, but beggars can't be choosers.

So where to attack first?

Locating the boxes labeled KITCHEN, she gets started by moving them there, then repeats the process with the BATHROOM and BEDROOM boxes. Muscle memory has her bringing her bedroom stuff into her old room. Before heading back downstairs, she goes to the end of the hall and peeks into the master, sizing it up, but . . . no. It's too weird, sleeping where her parents used to sleep. The room's not that much bigger than hers anyway.

Next, she handles her TV. It's covered in bubble wrap—reminding her that the cable company is supposed to be stopping by later to install internet—so she carefully unwraps it and sets it up on the low rectangular stand that she's carried over to one wall. The couch isn't so easy, but after clearing some other stuff out of the way, she manages to slide it across the floor and up against the opposite wall in front of the windows.

The formal dining room feels unnecessary, since all she has is a small square table, which she sets up in the kitchen. Her bookcases might look good in there, but they're heavy, and quite possibly the nicest things she owns. Trying to drag them might damage them or the wood floors, so for now they're going to remain in the middle of the living room.

While she waits for the cable guy, she accomplishes a bit more, like unpacking her towels and attaching the shower curtain. Then after he leaves, she sets to the task of carrying the metal pieces of her bedframe upstairs. When she goes back down for the mattress, though, the idea of pulling it up the staircase is too daunting. It's been a long day.

She grabs the chardonnay out of the fridge, the ice cream out of the freezer, and the bag of chips for good measure, and then plops down on the couch. She'll finish setting everything up tomorrow. There's a new crime drama series calling her name. (Even if her life is in shambles, at least no one's getting murdered.)

After streaming three episodes and downing a third of the wine, her eyes are starting to close, so she shoves a pillow under her head and lies down across the couch. It's comfortable enough.

In the quiet, the house creaks like it's talking to her.

Welcome back, Montana.

THE HARSH MORNING sun beating in through the windows assaults Montana's eyelids, waking her up. And that's when she realizes she doesn't own curtains. Her apartment in L.A. came with blinds. Groaning, she gets off the couch and stretches as she makes her way to the kitchen. She might not own curtains, but she certainly owns a coffee maker.

She locates the box where she packed it and pulls it out, setting it on the counter. But—*Shit.* There's no coffee.

Okay.

This is fine.

She's an adult, and she knows how to handle setbacks.

Opening another box, she finds her wine glasses and pours herself some chardonnay instead, then eats two bananas. She really needs to go to the grocery store.

After a quick shower and unpacking a pair of leggings and a light UCLA sweatshirt to change into, she heads out. Lenny's Market is still the only real grocery store in town as far as she knows. When she walks through the automatic doors, she yanks a shopping cart free from the corral and wheels it toward the produce section from memory.

She grabs more bananas and a few Granny Smith apples as she starts making a mental list of what she needs. Everything, obviously. But just some staples will be good for now. Coffee, milk, cereal, pasta, pasta sauce. Probably a good idea to load up on Ramen, too, since it's about the cheapest meal you can buy.

Taking a sharp turn down the pasta aisle, she almost rams her cart into someone. She opens her mouth to apologize, but the words are swallowed by a gasp, and a spike of adrenaline shoots through her system.

Austin.

Again.

There must be some deity out there that she's royally pissed off somehow, because this is ridiculous. Yeah, it's a small-ass town, but still.

She's freshly showered, at least. But she didn't bother to blow dry her hair, so it's undoubtedly frizzing up by now, her sweatshirt is baggy, and she's pretty sure these leggings have a small hole in the butt. And here he is. Facing her with wide eyes, holding up a box of penne.

It looks like he's about to bolt again, and she should probably let him. But due to a gross miscommunication between her brain and her mouth, she instead word vomits, "Please don't run away."

His mouth gapes open like a fish. Then—"Me? Isn't running away your specialty?"

She frowns. "That's not fair."

Or maybe it is. But he shouldn't get to throw it at her now, after all this time. When she looks like a mess, under harsh florescent lighting in the middle of the grocery store, with Blake Shelton twanging in the background.

His jaw twitches. "Sorry."

"It's okay."

"I just . . ." he starts, but he doesn't seem to have anything to finish with.

"I know," she says anyway.

He just stands there, not saying anything else but not walking away. He looks unfairly good. A little older in a way that's filled out his muscles and the scruff on his face. But he still looks like the first and only boy she's ever loved.

"How've you been?" she asks. Then she mentally grimaces, because really? After six fucking years, she finally has the chance to ask him the most important question of all. *Why did you disappear?* But instead she goes with the politest and blandest of small talk questions.

Oh well. Guess they've got to start somewhere.

He's still holding the box of pasta, making no move to either put it in his cart or place it back on the shelf. "I've been . . . good. You?"

She shrugs. "You know." He doesn't know, but she has no desire to elaborate on the current sad state of her life, so she asks how his sister is.

"Good. She's married."

"Wow."

He runs his free hand through his hair. "I know."

She's at a loss for what to say next. Then she spots another familiar face strolling down the aisle toward them. Blake Hansen, Austin's best friend. And he's got a little boy in tow.

Woah, she cannot imagine Blake having a kid. In high school, he could barely be trusted to keep himself alive.

He looks shocked when he sees her, eyes widening and his step faltering for a second before he keeps going. So Austin must not have told him about running into her yesterday. But she doesn't know if that's a good thing or a bad thing.

The boy's short little legs are working hard to keep up with Blake's long strides. He's gripping a plastic package carefully with two hands, and when he reaches them, he holds it out to Austin hopefully. "Daddy, Uncle Blake said we could get Oreos."

DADDY?

Montana's stomach drops out of her ass.

No. Absolutely not.

Except now that she's looking closer, she sees the uncanny resemblance. Same dirty blonde hair, slightly wavy, same green eyes.

Austin recovers first and says, "Sure, bud," taking the package from his son. *His. Fucking. Son.*

The boy beams up at him, and *damn.* Same freaking dimples.

Montana blurts out, "I've gotta go," and pulls a wild U-turn with her cart, nearly taking out the kid, but thankfully only nudging Austin's arm when he throws it out like a shield. With quick *parental fucking instincts*.

She books it until she's safely a few aisles away before squeezing her eyes shut for a moment, as if that will somehow erase what she just saw. Then she guiltily abandons the cart with the fruit in it and speed walks to the doors, probably looking like a shoplifter.

It's not until she's in her car, and her heart rate has begun returning to normal, that she realizes she proved him right. She's the one who ran away again.

THEN

*M*ontana had been nervous about calling Austin when she came home for the first time since leaving for college. Would he want to see her? Would he even want to hear from her?

But being back in town for winter break and not seeing him felt all sorts of wrong. So she'd made the awkward phone call and now here they were, sitting across from each other in a red vinyl booth at the Goldleaf Diner, which was decorated garishly for the holidays. Multicolored lights were strung up behind the counter, garland wrapped around the rotating pie display case, and the vinyl decals of Santa Claus and his reindeer were affixed to the windows.

Their plates had been cleared a while ago, and they were both on their third mugs of peppermint hot chocolate.

"How's Andrea?" Montana asked, her knee bouncing idly under the table. They'd already covered how much she'd enjoyed her first semester at UCLA, how she'd driven down the coast to explore San Diego, and up it to Santa Monica, and how he'd reluctantly attended a few classes at the local community college at his dad's insistence.

"She's great. Finally made varsity cheerleading."

"That's awesome."

Austin smiled, wiping a bit of whipped cream from the corner of his mouth. "Yeah, I went to the homecoming game to watch her."

"Was it weird being back at school after you graduated?"

"Kind of. It's like we just barely left there, but somehow I felt like the thirty-year-old creeper trying to hang out with high schoolers."

She laughed.

"It was cool though. I took Blake with me, so I wasn't the only creep. And nothing's changed there. Everything looks exactly the same."

"Everything looks the same in town too," Montana mused.

Of course it did. She'd only been gone a few months. Not enough time for anything to really change. Except . . .

She and Austin were being friendly enough, but this wasn't *them*. Not the intimate couple they had been for almost three blissful years, navigating in each other's space like they were actually one person. If this had been last year, their feet would've been tangled together under the booth, or she would've had her legs stretched out over his lap.

Now they were broken up. It was her choice, and she'd accepted it. But seeing him again, it was so hard not to reach out and touch him, set her fingers on warm skin which felt as familiar as her own.

And she didn't know if he was feeling the same things. She used to be able to tell everything he was thinking, but some cartoon thought bubbles over his head would've been helpful now. He'd been sitting here with her for hours, though, so that was something.

This was the only place in town open twenty-four hours. And somehow, they'd long overstayed their welcome. Their original waitress had left, passing on their table to the incoming overnight waitress, and now even that girl was eyeing them with annoyance.

Montana figured they should leave, but right when she was about to voice that, Austin said, "I could go for some pie." His raised eyebrows suggested that he also felt guilty about them sitting there not ordering anything, but he wasn't ready to go yet.

Okay, so maybe she could still read him a little bit.

Even though her stomach was full of the pancakes she'd eaten, she smiled and told him, "Me too."

So they flagged down the waitress for a couple slices of cherry and stayed for another hour.

Inside his old red truck, after they'd finally left, Austin turned to her. "Do you want me to take you home?"

No.

"I don't know. It's late," she hedged.

"It is," he agreed. "But I'm not tired."

"Me neither."

His green eyes held her gaze a few moments, as if trying to read her, and then he said, "We could drive around? For a little bit?"

Yes. Anything.

"Sure," she said, hoping not to sound too eager.

A light dusting of snow coated the empty roads, but he navigated them with ease as they continued talking about anything and everything. Well, not everything. There was still the fact of her crushing his heart when she broke up with him after graduation—the awkward elephant squished onto the bench seat between them. They didn't talk about that.

The heater in this truck, passed down from his dad when Austin got his license, didn't work the best anymore, and she was starting to get cold. But when he pulled into the empty parking lot of their old high school, she tugged her jacket sleeves over her fists and didn't object.

He was right. It was exactly the same. At least from the outside.

"Are you excited for Christmas?" he asked, turning in his seat to face her.

"Yeah, I guess."

Truthfully, when she'd flown home for break, she hadn't really been thinking about the holidays at all, or even seeing her parents. She was only thinking of him, him, him.

"I actually got you something." He reached across her to open the glove box and pulled out a thin rectangular package covered in Boston Red Sox wrapping paper.

"You didn't have to," she said, but she was already carefully peeling off the paper to reveal a black leather journal. She ran her finger over the embossed gold letters of the word WRITE in the bottom corner. "Wow, this is beautiful. Thank you."

"I figured you could use it to write about all the new places you visit." He sounded unsure of himself, maybe wondering if this was stupid and cheesy, or if he was revealing too much.

"I—" She stopped, looking down at the gift in her hand. Something thoughtful that he'd bought for her, even though they'd made no plans ahead of time to see each other over this break.

It was like he knew she'd come back to him.

When she looked up, their eyes met again. A zing of electricity passed between them. And then before she could talk herself out of it, they were kissing.

Fuck it. 'Tis the damn season, right?

He kissed her with so much sudden heat that she dropped the journal to her lap and reached for him to hold herself steady. He blindly groped for the gift and set it on top of the dashboard. Then, hand much gentler, he cupped her cheek, tucking her hair behind her ear.

Montana wasn't cold anymore. And soon, the windows were so fogged you couldn't see anything out of them. The truck could've been beamed up by aliens, now parked on another planet, and she wouldn't have noticed. Or even cared.

After what might have been minutes, hours, days, or years, Austin pulled away, catching his breath. "What are we doing? Are we really doing this?"

"Do you want to?" she asked, her voice coming out a little raspy.

He gave her thigh a light squeeze. "You know the answer to that. But what exactly are we doing? What does it mean?"

"It means that you're here, and I'm here, and we . . . I . . ."

"Yeah," he agreed, pulling her in again. "Yeah," he repeated in between the kisses he was leaving down her neck. "Yes."

CHAPTER THREE

NOW

Fueled by shock, anger, and adrenaline when she gets back, Montana drags her mattress up the stairs. *There.* Now she has a bed.

How could this be happening?

A kid? A freaking kid?

Austin has a son. He made a baby. With a woman. How old did he look?

A ball of sludge fills her stomach as she wonders if this is the reason he stopped speaking to her years ago. The last time they were together . . . was he already sleeping with someone else and didn't want to tell her?

She's terrible at judging children's ages, but the timing must have been close.

Needing to do something with her hands other than throw things, she starts to unpack her clothes, hanging them in the closet until she runs out of room. *Great.* There's nothing stopping her from using the closet in the master bedroom—except that it still feels weird. She almost expects to find her dad's old bowling league shirts still hung up in there next to her mom's cashmere sweaters.

Abandoning the rest of the clothes, she manages to get a lot more done before she runs out of steam. Rage works for her, apparently. Though she's not even sure who she's mad at—Austin or herself.

It's not like she has any right to be mad at him, does she? *She. Broke up. With him.* She never expected him to stay single forever. She'd be a hypocrite if she had, because it's not like she hasn't dated anyone since him. But a *kid?* You'd think that news would at least merit a phone call.

Oh, who is she kidding? He hasn't spoken to her in six years. Obviously, she should have gotten the memo that she was no longer a part of his life, and therefore didn't need to be updated on any developments, no matter how momentous.

Her phone does ring then, but it's not the call she wanted. She goes to the kitchen and pours herself a glass of chardonnay as she answers. "Hey, Mom."

"Hi, hon. I'm just calling again like I said I would, to see how you're settling in. Nothing was damaged in the move, I hope."

"No, everything's fine. I'm fine." *Not at all losing her shit over finding out that the person she loved went on to love someone else after her.*

"Good, good," her mom says, and then Montana can hear her dad in the background saying something. "Your father wants you to know that all the utilities have been transferred into your name, but if you need help—"

"I don't need help."

"I know. But if you do—"

"Mom," Montana cuts her off again.

Her mom sighs as if she's being difficult. "Okay, so how do you like being back in town? You'll have to send us pictures of what's different."

"Everything's the same," she tells her. "I mean, not everything, I guess. There's a new café I went into yesterday that was good. I don't remember what used to be there before. But I really haven't gotten out much yet. I'm still unpacking."

"Right, of course. Nothing too exciting is happening down here either."

Despite that statement, an unnecessarily long update follows, in which Montana learns about a dispute her mom had with the neighbors over playing their music too loud at night, as well as all the gross details of her dad's recent problems with acid reflux.

Before she knows it, she's finished off all the chardonnay. But then mercifully, as she's frowning into the empty bottle, there's a knock on the front door.

"Mom, I gotta go. Someone's at the door."

"Who'd be coming to see you already?"

"Bye!" she says, jamming her finger at her phone screen to end the call.

Her mom's right—it's weird for someone to be knocking—but she'll gladly take the excuse to get off the phone. Even if it's somebody trying to recruit her into their cult-like religion. Is that still a thing? Do people still go house-to-house like that toting Bibles?

In her haste to get to the door, she bumps into the half-wall jutting out from the entryway. Weird how she forgot it was there. Guess she still needs to adjust to being back in this house.

She opens the door, then stumbles back a step as her brain struggles to compute. There's a slight chance her mind is playing tricks on her again, but she's about ninety-five percent sure Austin is standing on her front porch.

He's wearing the same thing he wore at the grocery store. Light blue jeans that are slightly ripped at the knees, and a dusky purple Henley that clings to him in a way she wishes she could.

Nope. No. She doesn't wish that. Absolutely not.

"You know," he says, "when you answer the door, it's customary to greet the person on the other side." His flat tone doesn't give away whether he's teasing her or actually accusing her of being rude.

"How'd you know where I was?" she asks, rude or not.

"Where else would you be?"

Okay, right. Sure. "But what are you doing here?"

He shoves both his hands in his back pockets and glances down at his sneakers before looking back up at her. "Can I come in?"

"Um, well, uh . . ."

Her mouth isn't exactly mouthing properly, but she opens the door wider as an answer. As if she has any real choice. In no universe could she turn him away. Even if her last self-preserving instinct is telling her she should. She moves to the side, sweeping out her arm in a *go ahead* gesture and accidentally bashing her knuckles on the door frame. *Ouch.*

A whiff of something clean and woodsy and familiar hits her nose as he passes by her. He takes a few steps into the living room, then stops, surveying the furniture and boxes still strewn about. "So you're living here now."

"Yup!" she chirps from behind him, hoping he won't pick up on the entirely false enthusiasm.

When he abruptly turns to face her, she sways a little in surprise. He eyes her suspiciously. "Are you drunk?"

"*What?* No!" she cries indignantly. But she feels herself start to sway again, and s*hit*, she's barely eaten anything today. Couple that with her emotional instability, and the alcohol she consumed rather quickly might be affecting her a little more than it normally would. She hastily tries to straighten herself up. "Anyway. What are you doing here?"

"I felt foolish for running out of the café when I saw you yesterday. I was shocked, but that was uncalled for. Then earlier this morning . . ."

He trails off, scratches the back of his head. "I know you must be shocked too. And I guess I came to see if you were okay."

She frowns. He hasn't wanted to know anything about her well-being in the last six years, so why start again now? "I was shocked. Yeah. But a lot can happen in six years, so . . ." She shrugs, going for casual.

"Montana."

"Well, thanks for stopping by!"

Ignoring the clear dismissal, he turns back to the mess of a living room. He crosses to the middle of the room where her bookcases are standing, quite obviously out of place. "Where are these going?"

"Uh, the dining room, I guess."

He sizes one up, running his hand over the wood.

"You don't have to," she says. But he's already attempting to pick it up by himself, so she runs over and grabs the bottom.

As they walk it to the dining room, it's obvious he's carrying most of the weight while she's basically making sure it doesn't knock into anything. She can't help but notice his biceps flexing under the tight sleeves of his Henley.

They silently repeat the process with the other two bookcases, Montana trying hard not to let her slight inebriation trip her up. Then, once again, they're standing awkwardly in the living room.

She should thank him for his help, but instead she says what she really wants to say, unable to hold it in any longer. "So you just went and got married and had a kid without telling me?"

"We weren't speaking by then," he responds immediately. As if he knew this was coming.

"*You* weren't speaking to *me*!" she argues.

He rubs at his temple like she's giving him a headache. And he *so* doesn't get to do that when he's the one who showed up here uninvited. "Yeah . . . well," he says. Pauses. Then—"I didn't."

"Didn't what?"

"I didn't get married. I just, uh, had a kid."

Oh.

She doesn't have time to analyze the rush of relief that washes over her. "And his mom?"

He shakes his head. "We didn't last too long after Kalen was born."

"Nice name," she muses. *Did that sound stupid?* She doesn't know any kid-related small talk.

"Why'd you move back?" he asks, before she can think of something else to say.

Her first instinct is to lie. Come up with something to make it sound as if she actually *wants* to be back in Hartley. But what's the point? She's never been able to lie to him, and she doesn't have the energy to try now. So, feeling like the world's biggest loser, she explains about the magazine she worked for cutting back on full-time staff, and how she couldn't find anything else fast enough to keep up with her living expenses in L.A.

"I'm sorry," he offers when she's done.

"It is what it is. I'll figure something else out. I can still submit freelance pieces to different places." She should end the conversation here, send him politely away, and remain with some of her dignity still intact. But. "Why did you cut me off?"

He shifts his weight, slipping one hand into his front pocket. "Come on. Can't we forget about it?"

Oh, not a fucking chance.

"Forget about it? Is that what you wanted me to do back then too? You thought you could magically erase yourself from my life, and I'd forget you ever existed?"

"No, of course not," he says.

"Because I didn't forget about you. I remembered. I *still* remember!" Cutting her eyes to the floor, Montana forces herself to take a calming breath. Then, softer, she says, "I remember every moment."

"Me too."

Looking back up, she finds him watching her intently. "It wasn't fair," she tells him. "You disappeared like that without a word. You really hurt me."

"Hurt you?" His hand flies out of his pocket to rake roughly through his hair. "Montana, you *destroyed* me!"

She flinches when he yells, and he looks apologetic, but only for a moment. Then he shakes his head.

"I tried to hide it whenever you came back, but you had to know that. Don't try to make this all about what I did to you. If you remember everything, then you remember what you did to me. Don't act like you weren't the one to end things first. I guess I just did a cleaner job of it."

Wow.

"Yeah, I guess you did." She can't let him see her cry, but she can feel the tears coming. "You'd better go then. You're messing up your clean break."

"No, wait," he says. "I'm sorry. I didn't mean to bring this up."

"I started it."

"It's in the past."

She doesn't know what to say to that. Because, yes, technically it is. But since she got back to town yesterday, the past doesn't feel so much like the past anymore. The past is all around her. It's right in front of her now, staring her in the face with gorgeous green eyes.

"You're right, though," she admits. "And I *am* sorry. For hurting you."

"Me too."

Sighing in defeat, she asks, "So what now?"

"Well, you're here now. For a while, at least." He hesitates, looking as lost as she feels for a moment. Then he gets a determined look in his eyes and says, "There's no reason for us not to be friends, right?"

She flounders for an answer. *Isn't there?*

They've never been just friends. They were everything, right from the beginning. Is it possible to go from that to friends?

"Sure," she says, finding her voice. "Friends."

Guess they'll find out.

He finally makes his way toward the door with her trailing behind him. But then he turns back. "Call me if you need anything."

"I don't know your number," she tells him.

"It hasn't changed. Unless you deleted—"

"I didn't."

"Okay, then," he says with a slight nod.

"Okay, then," she repeats. "Well. Thanks."

He chuckles softly.

"What?" she asks.

"Maybe there's really no such thing as a clean break, huh?"

She shakes her head. "Probably not."

THEN

*F*reeeeduuuuuum!"

Montana turned to see Blake running to catch up with her and Austin as they made their way across the football field. He slapped Austin hard on the back when he reached them.

The boys still had their graduation caps perched on top of their heads, but Montana had taken hers off the moment the ceremony ended, because her hairline had been starting to sweat under it. All three of them had taken off their gowns. Blake's was slung over his shoulder and Austin had neatly draped both his and Montana's over his arm.

For weeks, Blake had been threatening to go naked underneath his gown and flash the principal right after he received his diploma. So it had been a relief when he'd shown up earlier and was in fact wearing a button-up and black slacks.

Though, truth be told, Montana did find it kind of pointless how they were expected to dress up for this. People only saw what they were wearing underneath their gowns for the fifteen minutes after the ceremony when everyone had lingered on the field, navigating awkwardly around the rows of metal folding chairs to mingle with family and friends.

Still, she'd picked out her favorite daisy-print sundress for the occasion. This day was supposed to be special. Happy. She could at least look the part, even if she couldn't entirely feel it. Even if the dress material was starting to feel itchy against her skin in a way it never had before.

As they walked, the boys started talking about Safe Grad. One last school-sanctioned event, even though technically, they were no longer high school students. Everyone was supposed to change into comfortable clothes they could sleep in and head over to the hotel the school had booked for the night.

Montana could feel the euphoria exuding off the two of them. But with each careful step she took, her heels sinking into the grass, her sense of apprehension built.

The boisterous sounds of their classmates celebrating rang through the air. Someone's wireless speaker was blasting an upbeat party song that was a huge hit a couple summers ago. But to Montana, it may as well have been a funeral march. Because something other than school was ending today.

It was time.

Out of the corner of her eye, she caught Austin's wide, easy grin, his shining dimples. She hated that she was about to ruin this day for him, but she'd been putting it off for too long. First, she didn't want to ruin prom night. Then she didn't want to upset him before finals. Now she was running out of excuses, and she knew with absolute certainty that she could not allow herself to be locked in a hotel ballroom with him and every one of their classmates until morning. The words she'd been holding in would end up exploding out of her in a disastrous public fashion.

She'd felt the tension between them these last few months. Surely, he'd felt it too. She'd been excited from the moment she'd opened her acceptance letter to UCLA, but he was bitter about her choosing a college all the way across the country. He tried to hide it, tried to act like everything was okay, but she knew.

He didn't want her to leave, and she understood why. He loved her. He'd loved her for years. And god, she loved him too. But this was her dream.

Even though she was leaving, he expected them to stay together, do long distance. No other possibility had seemed to even occur to him. And again, she could understand, in a way. It felt like there'd never been a time when they *weren't* together.

But that was the point, wasn't it?

They were adults now. Set free to make it on their own. And that's how she needed to do it—on her own. They couldn't both stay here forever, living in the safe bubble of what they'd always known. He was content here in Hartley, but she wasn't. There was an entire world out there for her to explore. And it wouldn't be fair to expect him to wait for her.

He kept saying, *We'll make it work,* but their relationship had never been work before. It'd been as easy as breathing. Until now. She couldn't let the wonderful thing they had with each other turn into something that would eventually make them both unhappy.

Blake was rambling on, something about his plan to sneak alcohol into the hotel, until they got to the parking lot and Austin stopped him.

"You know the whole point of Safe Grad is to keep us from drinking, right?"

"No," Blake argued. "It's to keep us from drinking and getting hurt. But we'll all be perfectly *safe* because we're locked inside!"

Austin huffed a laugh. "Tell that to about a hundred different horror movies."

"Come on, man."

Montana just stood there, biting the inside of her cheek, not participating in their conversation at all. Her own heartbeat sounded so loud to her now, she was surprised neither of them heard it.

"You're gonna get caught," Austin warned, shaking his head.

Blake scoffed. "Have some faith! I'll see you guys in a bit."

As Blake jogged over to his car, Austin led Montana to his truck. But when they reached it, she remained frozen behind him by the driver's door instead of moving around to the passenger side. She couldn't climb in there. She'd done it a million times, let him take her anywhere they needed to go. Worry-free drives where he kept one hand on the wheel, the other on her thigh, as they hummed along to whatever was on the radio.

But she couldn't go with him this time.

"*Wait.*" The word came out weak, like the tiny squeak of a mouse, but he heard her. He paused with his hand on the door handle, shooting her an enquiring look over his shoulder. "I need to talk to you."

He turned around fully. "Okay, but can we talk on the way?"

"No." They should have talked way before this. Now it really couldn't wait another minute. Her nerves were starting to make her feel lightheaded.

"What's wrong?" he asked, frowning.

Everything.

She swallowed the lump in her throat. "Austin. Listen to me."

"I am listening."

"I love you."

"I love you too—"

"I'll probably always love you," she continued, talking over him. Because if she stopped now, she may never do what she needed to. "But I need to see what else is out there. And so do you. We need to let each other go."

He stared at her, unblinking, for a few agonizing moments. Then— "I don't understand."

"I'm breaking up with you."

"What? *No*. You—"

"Yes. I have to. Please understand. I never thought I'd have to do this and it's killing me. But it's the right thing to do. I don't want to feel like we're holding each other back from living our lives."

His face hardened, twisted up into something she'd never seen from him before. "I'm holding you back?"

She shook her head hurriedly. "No, I didn't mean it like that. But think about it. We need to focus on our futures."

"I thought our futures were together," he said.

"I'm sorry," she told him, meaning that word more than she'd ever meant it in her life. She was so incredibly sorry she had to hurt him, the kindest boy who'd done nothing to deserve this. But she wouldn't apologize for what she wanted. "I don't think they can be. We want different things."

"I want *you*."

Montana nearly sobbed at that. She knew this wouldn't be easy, but nothing could have prepared her for it—the hardest thing she'd ever fucking done. There was still a tiny part of her that wondered if she was making a huge mistake. But she'd already made the decision, already started it. And she had to finish it.

"I know," she said as gently as she could. "But someday you'll want more."

"No." His voice was sharp now, cutting. "You don't get to tell me what I'll want. Where is this coming from? It didn't just hit you today that we should break up. How long have you been thinking about this?"

"A while," she admitted.

He kicked at a small rock, sending it skittering across the pavement. His eyes followed it until it came to a stop a few feet away. When he looked back up at her, the green of his irises blazed. "You never mentioned anything," he said accusingly. "You didn't think if you were unhappy, I deserved to know? That I deserved a chance to fix it?"

She shifted her weight. The strap of her heel dug into her ankle uncomfortably, but it was nothing compared to the aching pain in her heart. "There isn't anything to fix. This is where we are in life. I don't want to do this, but I have to."

"You *don't*."

"Austin, please." She was going to cry. She was going to cry at any moment, and she couldn't do that with him in front of her, because he would try to comfort her, and then this would never be over.

"So that's it?" he asked after a minute. His eyes had dimmed, and she almost wished the fire back into them, even if it was aimed at her.

She nodded, biting her lip hard enough she tasted blood, but she had to make sure she didn't take it back.

"Are we . . . still going to Safe Grad together?" He sounded so small, so defeated, confused. Now she wanted to comfort *him*, but she couldn't.

"I'm gonna skip it," she told him. "You should go though." She wasn't foolish enough to think a party could salvage this day, but he should be with his friends. Maybe it would help if Blake did manage to sneak in that alcohol.

He let out a stilted bark of a laugh. "I think I'll pass. Do you want me to drive you home?"

"I can call my parents to come back."

"Okay," he said, the finality in his tone a punch to her gut. He held out her graduation gown to her. "Bye, then."

Her fingers dug tightly into the material as she took it. "Bye."

With only one final sad glance, he hopped in his truck, yanked it into drive, and sped out of the parking lot, leaving her standing in the dust in her sundress, clutching a silly gown she would never wear again. She remembered belatedly that her bag with her change of clothes was in the truck. But it didn't matter, really. That wasn't why she was crying.

CHAPTER FOUR

NOW

*M*ontana really needs to get her shit together. She may have lost her job and her apartment, but she's not this much of a mess, damn it.

So she adults really hard, and eventually all her boxes are unpacked, and the fridge is stocked with groceries. She even drove forty-five minutes to the nearest Target to buy curtains for all the windows. And she's managed to avoid thinking about Austin for a whole twenty-four hours now.

Okay, that's a lie. But she hasn't completely fallen apart while thinking about him.

So.

Progress.

With the house all set, though, she could use a new distraction. Sloane, her old friend from high school, isn't in Hartley anymore, but she's still in Massachusetts. Maybe Montana should see what she's up to, ask if she feels like getting together to catch up. They've tried to remain in touch over the years, but it's hard to keep a friendship going when you never see each other.

She grabs her phone and finds Sloane in her contacts. She can't remember the last time they actually talked on the phone, but they do exchange messages on social media every so often.

It rings so many times she's about to hang up, but then Sloane answers with a, "Hey."

"Hi. It's Montana."

A laugh. "I know. What's up?" Sloane's tone is casual, if maybe a bit surprised.

"Why didn't you tell me Austin had a kid?"

"What?"

Montana facepalms, glad this isn't a video call. That is *not* what she meant to say. "Sorry." She swings her legs up onto the couch, tucking her feet underneath her. "I ran into him in town, and to say I was shocked to find him with a child would be an understatement. I just figured, something like that . . . maybe someone could have given me a heads up."

"I didn't know," Sloane says. "I've only seen him a handful of times since high school, and not at all after I moved."

"Oh, right. Of course."

"Why are you in town?"

Keeping it simple, Montana says, "I moved back." She doesn't feel like getting into the long, agonizing explanation over the phone.

"So you called to ask why I didn't keep you updated on the life of your high school boyfriend," Sloane says, "but you didn't even bother to call and tell me when you were moving across the country?"

"Shit. No, I'm sorry. That's not why I called." Actually, she called to *stop* herself from thinking about Austin. Clearly, it didn't work so well. "The move hasn't exactly been my proudest moment, so I wasn't eager to advertise it." She picks at a loose thread on the end of the couch cushion and sighs. "Look, I know we haven't really talked in a while, but I've been busy with work. Until I got fired, that is. And you—"

"You got fired?"

"Laid off, technically. Anyway, I know you've been busy, too, since you moved in with Jeremy. But I was hoping we could grab coffee or something and catch up. Whenever you can. I can totally drive to you if you want. I'm currently jobless and friendless, so I have nothing but free time."

Well, that didn't sound pathetic or anything.

Sloane coughs. "Sure, we can do that. Let me check my schedule and get back to you, okay?"

"Okay, that's great. Thanks."

As they end the call, Montana hopes Sloane really means what she said, and that it wasn't just a polite way of blowing her off.

If she's being honest with herself, the two of them were never extremely close to begin with. She didn't have one of those almost-like-sisters best friend relationships with any girls in high school. It wasn't intentional—simply a result of her spending practically all her time with Austin. When Blake dated this girl Marisela for a while, Montana was friends with her, but when the two of them broke up, she barely ever spoke to Marisela again. Sloane was at least the closest thing she had to a best friend back then.

She made good friends when she was living in L.A., but she wonders if those friendships will fizzle out too, the way hers and Sloane's did, now that she's moved. Is that the accepted cost of adulthood? Losing people along the way?

That's depressing.

Not wanting to dwell on it, she tries to find her next task. Now that she's got the house taken care of, she should work on her job situation.

Or lack-of-job situation. So she makes herself a turkey sandwich (yay for groceries!) and sits down at the kitchen table with her laptop. She still has a couple banked articles she needs to send out for freelance. But it's going to be hard coming up with ideas for new travel articles when she doesn't have the money to travel.

There must be something out there she can do for now, even if it's not her dream job. She has a degree in journalism, for fuck's sake. That must qualify her for plenty of things.

After two hours scouring the internet, though, she hasn't found much. Only a bunch of listings for technical writing jobs that would bore her to tears, and they don't pay nearly enough anyway.

Very reluctantly, she switches over from Indeed to Craigslist. She only needs something steady to pay the bills and hold her over until she can find another full-time writing job. Who cares what it is? But the listings here are even more depressing. Feeling defeated, she closes her laptop and stands up to stretch. She needs to get out of the house.

Even though she has no money to blow, she hops in her car, deciding to take a walk around Main Street and check out the shops. If she and Austin are friends now (*ha!*), at least that means she can go places in town without the abject fear of running into him. Although she'd still prefer to keep their encounters to a minimum if she can help it.

After parking and grabbing a takeout coffee from Bread & Brew, she starts wandering, popping into a few places to look around. Then, before she realizes where she's headed, she finds herself approaching Alan's Place and stops abruptly.

Okay. Going inside to eat is out of the question, but she can walk past the damn restaurant, can't she? She doesn't need to cross to the other side of the street like a part of her brain is telling her to do. Still, she quickens her pace as she keeps going. No need to linger.

Except, hold on. Her eyes flick inadvertently to the building's façade as she walks by, catching a sign posted in the window. BARTENDER WANTED.

Hmm.

She waits until she's a safe distance away before taking out her phone. Then she hesitates. Is she really doing this?

Yes. She has to. She cannot ask her parents for more money.

Austin answers on the first ring. "Hello?"

"Hey, it's me," she says awkwardly. She may have kept his name in her phone all these years, but she has no clue if he did the same. Though he'd recognize her voice either way, right? "So um . . . you know how you said I could call you if I needed anything?"

"What do you need?"

"Um." *Stop saying that, damn it.* "I was walking past Alan's Place, and I saw the sign looking for a bartender. I've had plenty of bartending gigs in L.A. to supplement my income, so I have experience. And I really hate to ask this, because I know it'll be super awkward for all parties involved, but I'm kinda desperate, honestly, until I can start selling some stuff freelance again. So anyway, do you think, uh, you could ask your dad to give me an interview?"

She has to take a deep breath after all that babbling.

"No."

"Oh." *No?* "Okay, I'm sorry. I know it's a lot to ask, I just—"

"Montana, I meant . . ." He clears his throat. "My dad doesn't own Alan's Place anymore. I do."

"Woah, since when?"

There's a long pause. Then—"Since my dad died two years ago."

Oh god. Fuck. What?

She has to say something.

Anything.

Something.

"I . . ."

"Come by tomorrow at two-thirty," he tells her. "Wear sneakers." And then he disconnects the call.

She stares down at a crack in the sidewalk for far too long before her feet remember how to move.

◆

HER HEART STILL HURTS the next day when she steps inside the restaurant looking for Austin. She can't believe his dad is gone. He hadn't been that old, and as far as she knew, he'd been perfectly healthy. She spent last night in a state of shock and grief, drinking wine until, after her third glass, she called her dad just to say hello. Because, well, you never know, do you?

"Can I help you?" the girl at the hostess stand asks.

Montana stops, realizing she almost walked right past her, following muscle memory. She and Austin used to treat this place like another home. "Yes, sorry. I'm here to meet with Austin. Montana Sinclair?"

It sounds like she's not sure of her own name, but the hostess smiles and says, "Oh, sure. Let me go get him for you."

"Thanks."

Left alone, she takes a glance around. How many meals did she eat here as a teenager? How many nights did she and Austin spend up on the roof, looking out over the town?

From where she's standing, she can only see the main dining room with the booths and low tables, but she remembers the second room off to the side with the bar and the high-tops. Everything seems the same. It's strange and sad, though, to be standing inside Alan's Place with Alan Adler gone.

"Hey." Austin's voice startles her.

"Hey."

He's wearing black pants fitted snug over his hips, and a long-sleeve, mint green button-up with the cuffs rolled up a bit. It's a look she's only seen on him a handful of times when they were younger, for formal occasions, but he looks as comfortable and good in the outfit as he does in his casual jeans and T-shirts.

"Why don't we go over here?" He cocks his head to indicate the other room, and she follows him there.

This side has a fairly large bar and a dozen or so high-top tables. It's the middle of a Sunday afternoon, so the restaurant isn't packed, but every bar stool is taken. All by men. There's a baseball game playing on the TV that seems to have everyone's attention.

Austin snags a laminated menu off the corner of the bartop and then leads her to a table up against the wall. Something feels different. It takes a few moments before she realizes that some tables at the far end of the room are missing, replaced by a small stage.

Before she can comment on it, he opens the menu and says, "A lot of this is the same, but I'll go over it with you, and then you can take it home to study on your own. Landon looks a little busy, but the lunchtime bar crowd is easy, so he should be able to show you how to use the computer and teach you the specialty cocktails. I'm sure you'll pick it up fast."

"Oh."

"What?"

"I thought this was going to be an interview," she tells him, nervously pressing her index finger into the tip of her thumbnail.

He rolls his eyes, but really, she didn't expect him to give her the job without any kind of discussion first. "Should I ask you what you would say your greatest strengths and weaknesses are?"

That's probably a joke, but she cringes anyway. Surely, he has a few opinions on the weaknesses that she'd rather not hear. "No, let's not do that."

"Okay then." He taps on the appetizer section of the menu and starts to go over the relevant details of each item.

He goes through the whole menu like that. Most of it really is the same—lots of fried pub foods, plus comfort foods like meatloaf and pot roast—but he's added some things. She'd love to try the jalapeño and cheese stuffed pretzel balls.

When he finishes, she motions to the stage. "Do you have live music now?"

"Oh yeah. I guess you don't know, but on Friday and Saturday nights I've turned the place into more of a straight up bar. We close the dining room at nine, and then at ten o'clock it's twenty-one and over. And yeah, we have bands play."

"Wow. Cool."

"Is that okay for you?" he asks. "It means a couple late nights, but you'll make really good money. I don't know what you were making as a staff writer, of course, but I think this will be enough to get you on your feet again."

She hates that phrase. It makes her sound like a toddler, stumbling as she tries to take her first steps. He isn't wrong though. "This is great. Thanks."

He just nods in response. And it hits her then, what she's gotten herself into. She's going to be working for her ex-boyfriend. He'll be her boss. Yeah, this shouldn't be awkward at all.

Taking her over to the bar, he introduces her to the bartender, then tells her to come find him in the office at four if she doesn't see him. When he walks away, she's a little relieved.

Landon looks a bit older than her, maybe mid-thirties, and he's clearly a good bartender. He moves effortlessly between his own customers and filling drink tickets for the servers. The whole time he keeps up a running commentary for her, explaining things as he goes. She absorbs as much as she can while also trying not to get in his way.

The hour goes by fast, and then, since she doesn't see Austin around the dining room, Montana heads toward the back by the kitchen where she knows the office is. She knocks.

"Come in."

"Hey." She steps inside, leaving the door open behind her.

He's sitting at a slightly cluttered desk but gets up when he sees her, crossing over to a metal shelving unit against the wall. "Here," he says, handing her a stack of folded black T-shirts with the Alan's Place logo on them.

"Thanks."

He turns again to the shelf and then holds out another stack. "We have women's scoop necks now too. Only for the Friday and Saturday bar hours."

At this, he scratches the back of his neck, looking a little awkward when she takes them from him. But Montana almost smiles. She remembers Blake complaining one time about how the servers here didn't show any skin. (They did wear shorts in the summer, but what he really meant was boobs.) Austin told him his dad liked to maintain the position that this was a family place.

The urge to smile slips away.

"Austin?"

"Yeah?"

She clutches the pile of shirts to her chest like they can keep all the emotions inside her. "I'm really sorry about your dad."

He lets out a quiet sigh. "Thank you."

She should end this here.

Instead, she takes a step forward, like there's some invisible string tied around her middle that's tugging her closer to him. "You could have called me."

"I wanted to," he admits after a few long, agonizing moments. "But it had been a long time, and I didn't know if you'd answer. I . . . couldn't have handled it if you didn't."

She shifts her pile into one arm, then reaches out tentatively with the other until her fingertips graze the back of his hand where it's hanging down at his side. "I would have answered."

He doesn't say anything, but he holds her gaze and doesn't pull his hand away. When he nods, she blinks as if coming out of a trance and moves backward, out of his space.

Explaining he needs her to fill out some paperwork, he sits back down at the desk and gestures for her to take the chair opposite. She fills out the forms he slides to her as quickly as possible. The air still feels thick in here. It's hard to breathe.

They go over what kind of schedule she can expect to work, although he warns her it won't always be the same, and then that's it. She's got a job.

As she stands to leave, she notices the small framed picture of Austin's dad hung on the wall beside his desk. In it, Mr. Adler is standing behind the bar, grinning at whoever took the picture.

Before slipping out of the office, she says, "He'd be really proud of you, you know."

Austin smiles sadly and simply nods again.

THEN

I'm sorry we have to go back to my house for more pictures," Austin said, turning the truck onto his street. They'd already posed for countless ones for Montana's parents when he'd picked her up.

His hand was on her bare thigh, right below the hem of her dress. She placed hers on top and squeezed. "It's fine."

"You know how my mom is."

She did. And she also knew how Austin was, which was equally as sentimental. But it was prom night, after all. Sentimentality was natural. So she'd let him have all his straight-out-of-a-Netflix-teen-romcom cliches.

Although if this were really a teen movie, they'd probably be sneaking off afterward to have awkward sex for the first time, but that ship had sailed a long, long time ago. It was probably in Tahiti by now.

Still, she wanted this night to be perfect as much as he did. Not just for him, but for herself too. They didn't have many more nights like this left together, so they might as well make every last memory while they could. Because come September, she'd be gone, and they'd only have the memories to hold on to.

She should've already ended things. It wasn't fair, not saying any-thing each time he talked about how he'd call her every day while she was at college. He didn't understand that when she left, she wouldn't only be leaving for college—she would be leaving him.

Thinking about that hurt so much, but she had to do it. It was the only way to give them both the chance to fully experience their lives. A long-distance relationship at eighteen wasn't healthy.

She wasn't strong enough to let him go just yet though. There was no way she could handle seeing him at school every day for the last six weeks and not being with him. But the longer she waited, the more it had started to feel like she was lying to him.

He pulled into his driveway and cut the engine. When she grabbed her door handle, he said, "Wait. Let me help you."

"I know how to step down from your truck," she said with a sarcastic laugh.

"You're in a tight dress and heels. Act like a damsel in distress for once and let me be a gentleman."

Laughing earnestly at that, she waited for him to hop out and walk around to her side. Once he'd helped her land safely on the ground, he laced his fingers through hers and led her to his house. In her heels, she was almost as tall as him, which made it easy to sneak a quick kiss onto his cheek right as he opened the door.

He grinned and started to say something to her, but his mother was already running into the foyer to greet them.

"There you are!" she exclaimed, arms out wide as if to give them both a hug, like her son hadn't left here only forty-five minutes ago to pick up Montana. Before reaching them, she gasped, staring at Montana with wide eyes. "Oh, dear! You look beautiful!"

Montana felt herself blush. "Thank you."

Mrs. Adler did go in for a hug now, one arm around Montana and

Austin each, knocking their shoulders together.

"Okay, mom," Austin said. "Let's move this along."

"Right, right. I'll go grab my phone and find your father."

After she rushed off, Austin and Montana made their way into the living room. Then he turned to her. "You really do look beautiful. Have I said that yet?"

"I think about five times," she teased.

He shrugged good-naturedly. "Well, you do."

"You don't look so bad yourself."

"We all knew I'd clean up nice. *You*, on the other hand . . ."

She shoved him in the side just as his sister rounded the corner out of the kitchen carrying a large bowl of popcorn. "Don't kill each other before Mom gets her pictures," Andrea said.

"Oh my god, I'm starving!" Montana reached out to snag some popcorn.

With quick reflexes, Austin grabbed her wrist. "Don't you dare."

"Why not?" she whined.

"Because I know you, and as soon as you touch all that butter and grease, you'll end up with yellow stains all over your dress."

"He's got a point," Andrea agreed. "White is a bold choice for you."

Austin laughed and Montana stuck her tongue out at the pair of them.

Then Andrea appeased her by saying, "Open your mouth." And when Montana obeyed, she fed her a giant handful of popcorn.

"—ank you," Montana said, mouth full.

Andrea smiled. "You do look like a freaking princess in that dress, though. I can't wait for my prom."

"You'll have one next year," Austin told her.

"Junior prom's not the same." She took her bowl over to the couch and sat down. "Did you guys get a hotel room?"

"Why would we do that?" Austin asked.

"So you could bang someplace where your poor sister doesn't accidentally have to hear it."

That made Montana laugh, but Austin cringed dramatically. "That happened *one time*! And could you keep your voice down?"

Andrea threw a piece of popcorn, which landed on the carpet, not even coming close to hitting him. "Mom and Dad obviously know you guys have sex, doofus. They're not stupid."

"Who's not stupid?" Mr. Adler asked, walking into the room.

"Nobody!" Montana answered quickly. "Hi, Mr. Adler."

"Am I ever going to get you to call me Alan?"

Smiling shyly, she shrugged.

"Where's Mom?" Austin asked impatiently.

"She ran up to our room, she'll be right back."

"We're gonna be late."

Montana elbowed him in the ribs. "We're fine."

"Do you want to miss the food?" he said, turning to her. And at her widened eyes, he added, "That's what I thought."

"I'm here, don't worry," Mrs. Adler announced, hurrying over with something shiny clutched in her hand. "I was looking for this. I thought it would be perfect with your dress."

Montana realized she was talking to her. "Huh?"

Mrs. Adler stepped closer to hold up a necklace against Montana's chest. It was covered in diamonds. Like seriously. She wasn't sure she'd ever seen that many diamonds outside of a jewelry commercial. Yet somehow it didn't look gaudy. Just expensive as hell.

"See how nice it goes?" Mrs. Adler asked, beaming.

"It's lovely," Montana told her honestly. "But I don't think I can wear it. What if something happens to it?"

Mr. Adler moved in now. He smiled at Montana, his brown eyes warm and kind. "We're not worried about that, sweetheart. You're family."

Mrs. Adler hummed in agreement.

Taking the necklace from his mom's hands, Austin said, "Let me."

He looked at Montana and tilted his head, waiting for permission. He looked so much like his dad. But his bright green eyes, he got from his mom. And with those eyes shining hopefully at her, it was impossible to say no.

When she turned so her back was toward him, he carefully swept her hair over one shoulder and fastened the jewelry around her neck. His fingers trailed delicately over the top of her spine before he spun her to face him, moving her hair back into place. It looked like he wanted to kiss her right there in front of his parents.

They wouldn't have minded, Montana was sure, but she turned to his mom instead. "Thank you."

"Of course, dear."

She felt the weight of the necklace against her chest, heavier than it should have been, and swallowed down the ball of guilt in her throat. "Are we ready for pictures?"

"Yes," Mr. Adler said, "come on." He waved them over to stand in front of the fireplace, where Austin promptly put his arm around her waist.

Mrs. Adler held up her phone, then lowered it. "Oh my gosh, they look so wonderful together!"

"Yeah, yeah, we know." Andrea pretended to gag. "Just take the pictures so they can go."

"I can't help it! My baby's all grown up, and they're such a perfect couple."

"Mo-om," Austin warned. "Don't start crying. We don't have time for that."

Montana laughed, but really, she felt like crying herself. Although for much different reasons.

Mrs. Adler got herself under control and started snapping pictures like the paparazzi, ordering them to move this way and that. She kept muttering things like, *"Beautiful,"* and, *"Oh my,"* but she managed to hold herself together.

Angling her body one way as directed, Montana caught a better look at Mr. Adler's face. He was wearing the same proud and adoring expression as his wife. But *he* was the one with tears welled up in his eyes, threatening to spill over.

You're family, he'd said.

Montana was the worst person ever.

CHAPTER FIVE

NOW

*T*wo weeks in and Montana already feels like she's gotten the hang of things here. The bartending part, anyway. The being around Austin part? Not so much. Every time they have to navigate around each other in the busy space as they're both working, or she messes something up and needs him to fix it, she still thinks this might all be some type of cruel punishment for her past sins.

It hurts. Being around him now after everything that's happened between them. They're coexisting fine as employer and employee—or *friends* if she's going by what he said to her. But seeing him all the time and not being able to talk to him, *really* talk to him, like before, fucking hurts.

She's not sure if this is better or worse than the six years of not seeing him at all.

At least, they don't have to work together every shift. Blake is also a manager. A fact that surprised her when she found out, but she realizes that's not fair. She's grown as a person since high school, so she should give Blake the benefit of the doubt and assume he has too.

But it's hard to get a gauge on Blake at all, because when he works with her, he seems to avoid her more than Austin does. Which is silly. They're not the ones with the crazy complicated and painful history, but whatever. Montana's just trying to focus on doing her job well so that Austin doesn't regret helping her out.

Landon is cool with her. He trained her on a few more shifts and seemed interested in getting to know her. She told him about some of the most fun places she's traveled, and he proudly showed her pictures of his older boyfriend who's a Cultural Studies professor at UMASS, and their two French bulldogs, Freddie and Mercury.

She and Landon work together on some of the night shifts, but for lunch, there's only one bartender. This was her first solo shift, and as she stands at the edge of the bar counting her tips at three-thirty, she feels pretty pleased with herself.

After Sabrina, another bartender Montana hasn't gotten to know as well, arrives for the night shift, Montana's gathering up her things to leave when she notices Austin pacing over by the doorway between the bar side and the dining room side. Kalen is with him, but he wasn't when Austin came into work earlier.

Going over to them, she asks, "What's wrong?"

Austin looks at her, his eyes a bit unfocused. "Oh, uh. Just a little bit of a problem."

"And again, I ask, what's wrong?"

"Kalen's mom had to drop him off. Some kind of emergency at work and she got called in. I texted Blake to ask if he could come in and cover for me or take Kalen to his place, but he hasn't responded." He glances from Kalen into the dining room, which is starting to fill up. "I'm gonna call him."

He turns away to do that, holding the phone up to his ear. Blake must answer now, because Austin starts talking frantically.

Montana shifts her gaze in time to see Kalen about to walk right into the path of a server carrying a large tray of food through the doorway. On instinct—an instinct she wasn't aware she had, quite frankly—she sweeps him up out of harm's way.

When Austin turns back to see her holding him, his eyebrows shoot upward.

"Um. Sorry," she says, just as surprised to find herself with an armful of child as he looks at seeing it.

"No, don't be! Shit." He reaches out to take his son from her. "I shouldn't have been distracted, I can't—"

"It's okay," she interjects. "He's fine. Is Blake coming?"

"Yeah, he's gonna cover the night shift for me, but he can't get here for a couple hours. And one of the cooks called out, so they need me in the kitchen. Fuck." He grimaces after he swears, eyes casting down to Kalen guiltily.

Her fingertips graze his arm as she says, "Hey, it's okay. I can stay and watch him for a while." Then she quickly pulls her hand back, realizing that both the touch and her offer might be unwelcome. "I mean, if you'd be okay with that."

"Yes!" he blurts out. The tension seems to drain from his shoulders as he puts Kalen down. "Thank you. That's . . . I mean, you don't have to."

"It's not a big deal."

"No, it kind of is."

She shrugs. "Well, if it's too—"

"You can take him back to my place if you want."

"Oh." Now *that* is too weird. "Maybe it would be better if we stayed here? I can keep him occupied in the office."

He nods. "You're probably right. But let me run home real quick and get some toys and stuff for him. I don't want him throwing a tantrum for you when he gets bored."

"You sure you can leave?"

"It won't take long, and the dinner rush isn't going to hit yet. Tony can handle front of the house too if anything happens."

"Okay. So . . ." She glances at Kalen, unsure what to do now.

"Right." He kneels down so he's closer to the boy's eye level and explains to him that Montana's going to hang out with him for a bit while his dad works.

Kalen eyes her suspiciously, but when Montana gives him her best attempt at a confident smile, he seems to buy it. "Cool," he says, reaching out for her hand.

Relieved at how easy the transition was, she leads him to the office, her palm cupped around his much smaller one. As she closes the door, she realizes it was a good idea for Austin to go get some stuff for him though, because what the heck are they supposed to do in here?

"Do you like to draw?" she asks hopefully.

Kalen nods. "I can make trees."

"That's awesome! Let's see if I can find you something to draw on."

She pulls a few sheets of blank paper from the printer and grabs a pen out of a coffee mug on Austin's desk. After carefully moving aside some files, she sets him up at the desk, letting him sit in Austin's nice office chair while she takes the hard one on the other side. He immediately gets to work on his drawing while she just watches him.

Has she ever really been around kids? Some of her coworkers in L.A. had kids, but she wasn't attending birthday parties or anything. And she certainly never babysat them.

For the time being, at least, Kalen seems content as he scribbles away, and Montana starts to think this will be easy. Until five minutes later when he pushes the papers aside and declares, "This isn't fun. I need colors."

"I'm sorry, bud. We don't have any colors here. But your dad is coming back with stuff for you to play with, okay? He'll be here soon."

Please let him be here soon.

Kalen lets out a dramatic sigh like his life is extremely rough. (Which is totally not fair.) Then, mercifully, he picks up the pen again and continues to draw.

Montana breathes a sigh of relief. She isn't equipped to be a babysitter. What the hell made her volunteer for this?

Well, *duh*. She couldn't bear to watch Austin panicking like that. He'd been her person—back then when she was still developing as a person herself. And now, no matter how much he hurt her years ago, she still doesn't want him to be anything but happy.

It would be so much easier if she could hate him. But then she probably wouldn't have this job.

Somebody enters the office without knocking, and she jumps, her body angling itself in front of Kalen. A protective reflex that, again, she wasn't aware she had.

"Sorry," Austin says, "I didn't mean to scare you."

She laughs awkwardly. "It's okay. It's your office."

"Did you bring me colors?" Kalen asks.

Austin steps forward, holding out a small rainbow-printed backpack. "Sure did. And books and Spiderman."

"Good," the boy says, making tiny grabby hands. Austin gives him a stern parental look that both disturbs Montana and turns her on a little. *Fucking hell.* "Thank you," Kalen offers grudgingly, and his dad relents, giving him the bag.

"You guys gonna be okay in here?" Austin asks, addressing Montana. Kalen has already unzipped his backpack and started pulling things out.

"We'll be great, don't worry."

His fingers brush across her shoulder so lightly that, if she didn't see his hand move, she would've thought she imagined it. "I really appreciate this."

She manages a smile and a nod before he turns to go. Then it's just her and the kid again, but now he has more to keep him entertained. He's piled a couple picture books, a coloring book, and a large box of crayons on top of the desk, but his attention is focused on the large plastic Spiderman action figure in his hands. He shoots invisible webs across the small room and then swings Spiderman around, landing him on a shelf, then back on the desk, then bouncing him off a wall.

As she watches him play, she thinks about Austin. About the fact that this child is his *son* whom he's raised for however many years. (*Four? Five?*) She and Austin are the same age, but suddenly she feels decades behind him in maturity. Sure, she had her own apartment in L.A., and she always managed to pay the rent on time, and usually, there was a fair amount of groceries in the fridge. But he was here that whole time, keeping an actual tiny human alive.

That's way beyond her realm of capabilities—just ask any houseplant she's ever had. *Oh, wait.* You can't, because they're all dead.

There's also the fact that he owns what she assumes is still the most successful restaurant in town. So if life is a contest, he's probably winning.

Kalen eventually loses interest in Spiderman, dropping the toy carelessly onto the floor. He examines his two books, then holds one out to Montana expectantly.

"You want me to read to you?"

The head tilt he gives her reminds her instantly of Austin. "Do you know how?"

She laughs. "Yes. I know how."

"Then yes, please."

She complies, laying the book out sideways on the desk between them so they can both see it as she reads. Halfway through the story about a dog and a cat who learn they don't have to be enemies and become best friends instead, she realizes Kalen is frowning slightly. "Something wrong?"

"Daddy does the voices better."

Sheesh. Another way she's losing.

"I'm sorry, I'll try to do better," she promises.

Thankfully, he lets her finish the book without any more performance critiques. After that, he moves on to coloring, and Montana sits there a few minutes, bored, until he generously offers her a page from the coloring book and shares his crayons.

That's how Austin finds them some time later. "Hey, you two," he says, smiling softly. "Did you have fun?"

"She's not very good at the voices," Kalen proclaims without looking up from his activity.

Austin laughs. "Maybe she just needs some more practice." He moves closer and gives Montana's shoulder a squeeze. And she *definitely* didn't imagine that one.

"I'll get right on that," she says sarcastically, using her arm to cover her picture of mushrooms that she totally didn't color in to look like dicks.

"Blake's taking over for me," he tells her. "I was going to feed Kalen here before we head home. You should stay and eat with us."

"Oh, it's okay. I already had my shift meal earlier."

"Montana. That was lunchtime. Have dinner with us." He's smiling at her so openly now it's hard to refuse.

And why is she trying to refuse?

Oh yeah. Because it would be we-eird.

His smile falters when she doesn't respond right away. "I mean, unless you have something else to do. Sorry, I shouldn't assume you're free. You've already given up part of your evening to help me."

"I can stay," she says quickly.

He smiles again. "Okay. Good."

And that's how she ends up in a comfy black booth in the far corner of the dining room, sitting across from father and son. When she threw on her T-shirt and jeans for work this morning, this is not where she pictured her day going. She's already interacted with Austin way more today than any previous day she's worked, and it's left her a little emotionally drained.

But it's Austin.

As weird as it is to be sitting here with him after all these years—and with his son, no less—it also feels sort of right. The push-pull of being around him but basically estranged has been exhausting. Maybe it would be easier if they could actually be friends like he said.

Maybe.

He grabbed a menu for her before they sat down, and even though she's memorized it by now, she flips through it idly for a distraction.

"You should have the pot roast," he suggests. "You used to love it."

"Is it still your mom's recipe?"

"Of course."

She smiles at him, nodding her agreement. Then he leaves to go tell the kitchen what they want, and in his brief absence, she tries to relax.

Friends. They can be friends.

"Thank you again for watching Kalen," he says, sliding smoothly into the booth when he returns.

"You're welcome."

Kalen has resumed playing with Spiderman, climbing the toy up and down his father's arm now. Totally unfazed by this, Austin asks her how she has settled in and adjusted to being back. He makes the small talk seem effortless.

But is it really so easy for him to put aside everything that's happened between them and do this? Montana remembers all too vividly him showing up at her house only weeks ago and saying she destroyed him. Clearly, he's moved on from that though.

"I'm sorry I've had you working so much," he tells her, after she reports that she's doing fine.

"Don't be," she says. "I could use the money. And anyway, it gives me something to do. When I'm not working, I'm sitting home bored." *Ugh.* Does she really need to remind him how alone and pathetic she is? "At least I finally unpacked my books," she forges on, "so I can read on the couch instead of zoning out on TV. I think my brain was starting to melt from Netflix."

"What about reading out on the porch?" he asks. "That was always your favorite spot."

She shakes her head. "I don't have any porch furniture. My apartment in L.A. didn't have an outdoor space."

"So go get some furniture."

"I guess I could eventually," she allows, shrugging noncommittally. "It just feels sort of like buying more stuff to fill up the house is admitting defeat. Like that proves I really do live here now. I mean, I guess I already admitted defeat when I packed up my stuff and drove across the country, but . . . I don't know."

Buying furniture feels *permanent*, even porch furniture.

He looks at her thoughtfully but doesn't say anything.

She needs to change the subject. "You said Kalen's mom had to run into work unexpectedly?"

"Yeah, it happens occasionally, and it's not usually much of a problem. But Brittani's parents are out of town for the week, and my mom wasn't home. I've normally got it together better than this, I swear."

Brittani.

"Seems like you're doing a pretty great job to me," she says honestly. "What's Brittani do?"

"She's a nurse."

Of course she is.

"That's nice."

Someone dependable with a steady career. Sounds like a good fit for him—unlike Montana with her constant urge to run off and travel the world. So why aren't he and Nurse Brittani still together?

She can't ask him that in front of his kid. Actually, she probably shouldn't ask him at all, so it's good timing when their food arrives at that moment.

They all dig in, and Montana moans after the first forkful of her pot roast. It's as good as she remembered. Austin laughs quietly and cuts off a chunk of his steak, setting it on the edge of her plate. She smiles her thanks.

When Kalen dips his grilled cheese into a pile of ketchup, she tries not to laugh, because she remembers how Austin used to hate it when she did that. Said it was gross. But he doesn't even flinch at it now.

This is nice, she realizes. It's been a while since she's eaten a good, home-cooked dinner. True, this doesn't technically count as home-cooked, but it sure feels like it. Because of the familiar atmosphere and the familiar presence of Austin in front of her. Anyone looking at the three of them would assume they're a family.

In another life, this *could* have been her family.

Montana tries not to let that thought hurt.

THEN

*D*o you ever think about kids?"

"Kids?" Montana asked.

She and Austin were in her room, sitting sideways on the bed with their backs against the wall, listening to The Neighbourhood. An easy, relaxing Sunday afternoon.

Daisy nudged open the door with her nose and wandered in. Austin patted the bed for her to jump up and lie down, and then started scratching behind her ears when she rested her head over his knees. "Yeah. I want kids. Three, I think. Maybe more."

More?

"I . . . I haven't really thought about it," Montana told him.

She didn't know if she could imagine herself having kids. It wasn't that she *didn't* want them, but she was barely more than a kid herself. College was about as far into the future as she could see. And then, hopefully, she'd get to travel. Where would having kids fit into that?

"You don't think it would be nice to have a big family?" Austin asked. "After growing up an only child? I know you wanted a sister."

"I have Andrea."

He smiled and wrapped his arm around her shoulder, pulling her in tightly. "Yeah, you do. But what about building your own family?"

She placed her hand on his stomach, curling her fingers into the soft material of his sweatshirt. "I don't know. When do you plan to have all these kids?" The *three or more.*

"Not until after you get back from college, obviously. We'll wait until we're both ready."

He was planning to wait for her for four years. Kids or no kids, he expected them to stay together while she was gone. Was that fair to him? To her?

College was supposed to be about meeting new people, having new experiences.

And what if, after she finished those four years, she didn't want to come back here? There were so many places to see out there.

Montana needed to figure out a lot of other things about her life before she would even start to consider whether or not she wanted to have kids. And yet, not wanting to disappoint him, she said, "Maybe. Kids might be nice."

CHAPTER SIX

NOW

*N*ow that Montana's working instead of sitting around in the same comfy tee and leggings every day, she needs to do laundry. It's been weeks of managing to avoid it, but the situation is getting desperate. Carrying her overflowing basket with both hands, she carefully makes her way down the basement stairs. But when she hits the bottom, she finds herself staring at the empty space where the washer and dryer used to be.

Shit. She expected them to still be here. Was that dumb?

Groaning, she lugs her laundry back up the stairs and drops the basket onto the kitchen floor. A couple rebellious articles of clothing escape over the sides.

She finds her phone to make a call.

"Hi, hun!" her mom answers brightly. "How are you?"

"Where's the washer and dryer?"

"What?"

"In the basement. They're gone."

There's a pause before her mom answers. "Well, yes. We took them with us when we moved. The tenants are responsible for supplying their own."

"I'm a tenant?" Montana snarks.

Her mom sighs deeply. "No, of course not. But what would you like us to do?"

"Warn me, at least." She hates that she sounds like a child, but this is so frustrating.

"Have you really gone this long without doing laundry?"

Montana rubs her temple, feeling a headache coming on. "That's not the point."

"Do you need money?"

"No!" She's doing fine now. She doesn't need any more help from her parents. "I can just go to the laundromat."

"How has it been working at the restaurant?" her mom asks her fourth question in a row. "Not too weird for you, I hope."

Ha.

"No, it's good," she says. That may not be entirely true, but she's not in the mood to get into a discussion about her and Austin's relationship. Friendship. Whatever it is. "Anyway, I'm gonna head out. I need to get this laundry done."

"Okay, but you can call us if you need some money."

"I'm fine, Mom, thanks, bye!" She abruptly ends the call, then gives her laundry a contemptuous glare. "All right. Let's go, you pile of filth."

She leaves the escapees on the floor. They've earned their freedom.

◆

MONTANA'S NEVER BEEN to the laundromat in town, but she remembers where it is. She brings her laptop with her to try to get a little bit of work done while she waits, hoping to find places to submit the articles she has banked. By the time she's loading her wet clothes into the dryer, though, she's done about all the work she can for now.

A nail salon sits a couple spaces down in the strip mall, and her nails are looking pretty rough, so she decides to head over there. It's nice knowing she has a steady enough job now that she can afford this one indulgence for herself. But she should definitely start saving for a washer and dryer, because having to use the laundromat is a pain in the ass. Maybe she can find a used set online.

Driving home with clean clothes and perfectly rounded cobalt blue nails, she feels good. A little more like her put-together old self before everything went to hell.

She even goes up to her room to put away the clothes, rather than living out of the basket for the next two weeks and tossing the dirty stuff on the floor. Not everything fits in the closet, but she does good enough with some things folded and piled on the nightstand.

She's just barely gotten back downstairs when there's a knock on the door. Opening it, she's only slightly less shocked this time to find Austin standing there on her porch.

"Come help me with this," he orders.

"With what?" she asks. But he's already turned and is striding down the steps, motioning over his shoulder for her to follow him.

He leads her to a black Jeep Grand Cherokee parked in the driveway behind her Purple People Eater. At some point he must have traded in his old beat-up truck for this nicer vehicle. It makes sense. More responsible. With his *kid* and everything. Even after spending the evening with him and Kalen, it's still hard to wrap her mind around the concept of him being a father.

When he opens up the back, revealing a bunch of white wicker furniture, she says, "What's this?" Even though it's fairly obvious as he pulls out a chair and passes it to her.

"Porch furniture."

"I can see that."

"So why'd you ask?"

"Austin."

He stops moving—a long two-seater maneuvered halfway out of the SUV—to look at her.

She tugs at the hem of her ratty, cut-off shirt, wishing she'd changed once she had clean laundry. "Why did you do this?" she asks, voice coming out a little softer and more awestruck than she liked. She meant it to sound angrier. Like, *Why are you meddling in my life?*

"Look," he says, propping the furniture up with his chest. "I know you said buying more furniture is like admitting that you live here now. But you *do* live here now. So why force yourself to live in this sad limbo where you try to pretend your life isn't what it is?"

That's a good question. One she doesn't want to think too hard about right now. Not when he's here, standing in front of her, a living embodiment of all the good things this town has to offer. Making her wonder if being here isn't actually so bad.

But she can't afford to think like that. She can't get stuck here when there's still so many places to see and articles to write.

They continue their brief stare-off until she relents and thanks him. Then together they finish unloading before carrying the loveseat, two small chairs, and a low rectangular wicker table onto the porch. When everything's set up, Austin plops himself down in one of the chairs, stretching his legs out long in front of him.

"Let me pay you back," Montana says.

He gives her a look. And yeah, he knows she's kind of broke.

"Or . . ." she tries again, "let me get you a drink?"

"Sure."

Running inside, she grabs two bottles of Coors Lite from the fridge.

She's not sure why she even bought beer the last time she was at the grocery store. If she's at a baseball game or something, she'll drink it. But she's really more of a wine and hard liquor girl.

When she steps back outside and offers him a bottle, though, his pleased grin makes her think, *Oh. Maybe this was why.* But that's crazy because she never expected he'd be here, relaxing on the porch with her.

Tucking her legs up underneath her as she settles on the loveseat, she gazes out over the porch railing. The suburban view feels less oppressive than it did on her first day. When she looks back at Austin, he's rubbing his thumb up and down over the label of his bottle, the only indication that their situation might make him uneasy. That she's not alone in it.

"This was really nice of you. Thanks," she says again.

"You should be happy here. I don't like to think of you alone and miserable." He takes a long pull of his beer, not meeting her eyes. And then—"Your lawn needs to be mowed."

"I don't care about the lawn."

"Everyone can see it. It looks unsightly."

Well, okay. Apparently they're done with the nice moment.

"I don't have a lawn mower," she tells him.

He rolls his eyes. "Of course you don't."

She huffs, annoyed now. "I didn't exactly have a yard to worry about in L.A."

"You keep doing that."

"Doing what?"

"Talking about what you had or didn't have in L.A. But you're not in L.A. anymore, Toto."

Her foot is starting to tingle, on its way to falling asleep, but she's suddenly too self-conscious to move. "Trust me, I know that."

He gives her a conciliatory smile. "I'm only saying. You're *here.* So focus on what you have here."

There he goes making her think dangerous thoughts again.

She takes him in—his comfortable posture, jeans hugging his thighs delightfully, his kind green eyes. Could it be possible that *he's* something she has here?

THEN

"Hold still," Austin said, one hand wrapping around Montana's ankle. "I'm almost done."

She resisted the urge to wiggle a bit more as she flipped a page of the book she was reading from. They were on the porch, sharing the loveseat, her bare feet across his lap as he painted her toenails neon orange.

The sun had already gone down, and the porch light was barely bright enough for either of them to see properly, but she didn't want to go inside yet. This porch was their place. Out here in the evening, with nothing to disturb them but the quiet rustling of the leaves, they could simply savor each other's presence. It's not like her parents would really bother them in the house, but sometimes when she was with him, she wanted Austin all to herself. To be the sole focus of his warm, careful attention.

They only had two chapters left of *Of Mice and Men* for their English class, so she continued to read out loud, ignoring the strain on her eyes. When he finished her pedicure, she turned herself around, lying with her head in his lap and bending her knees so she could set her feet up on the arm of the furniture to dry.

He began playing with her hair, smoothing it back away from her face and twirling his fingers slowly through the strands. She transferred the book to one hand so she could reach down to rub his knee with the other. This was the definition of contentment.

Austin wasn't a reader like her. He didn't hate it—just wasn't the best at it. He had trouble concentrating. But when she read to him, he could listen to her for hours without getting bored.

Her voice had grown hoarse now, but she wouldn't quit until they reached the end. She'd already gotten into college, and he wasn't interested in going, but still, she wanted him to do well in his classes. They had a system. She helped him with English, talking over the themes of the books they read and proofreading his essays, and he explained math to her in a way that made much more sense than when her teachers did it.

Next year, though, they wouldn't have this. Wouldn't have each other to lean on anymore. She'd be on her own in California, and he'd be here without her.

It seemed inconceivable, the two of them ever being apart. But that was what happened after high school, right? You grew up. You moved on.

Would they break up? They hadn't talked about it yet, but the thought of it made her heart clench.

His hand fell to the back of her neck as she finally closed the book and set it aside. With gentle fingers, he rubbed circles against her nape, and she wished she could burrow herself right into him.

It would be okay. They still had the rest of the year to figure things out. To be together like this, happy.

"That was the worst ending ever," he said.

She laughed softly. "I know."

CHAPTER SEVEN

NOW

Somewhat surprisingly, when Sloane said she'd get back to Montana about meeting up, she meant it. Their schedules rarely align, since Sloane teaches fifth grade and Montana works on the weekends and some weeknights, but they finally have the chance to meet up for coffee on Memorial Day, when schools and Alan's Place are both closed.

Sloane picked a place that was closer to her, and this is definitely earlier than Montana would've chosen to wake up, but it's fine. She doesn't mind making the drive. It's high past time for her to put some effort into rehabilitating this friendship.

As she pulls up to the shop that's simply named Java, she vows not to talk too much about Austin. She could use a friend, someone who knows their past history, to talk through all of the mixed emotions she's been feeling ever since he stepped back into her life, but she's not going to make everything about her.

She spots Sloane inside, seated at a round table with a paper coffee cup already in her hands. Approaching the table, she prays for this not to be too awkward. She's dealt with enough awkward lately.

Sloane stands when she sees her, saying, "Hey! You look great," and leaning in for a hug.

Montana suspects she would say that even if she looked like a mess. But she did put extra effort into getting ready this morning, using the curling iron to enhance the natural waves in her long hair. She wore capri jeans instead of leggings, and even opted for the strappy sandals rather than her preferred flip flops. Honestly, she kind of felt like she was getting ready for a date, complete with a slight case of nerves.

She's glad she didn't just roll out of bed to come here, though, because Sloane looks as put together as she always did in high school. Though her dark hair is cut shorter now, hanging an inch above her shoulders, which makes her look more mature.

"Thanks, so do you," Montana tells her.

That nervous, jittery, first-date feeling comes back when Sloane says, "I wasn't sure if you'd want to sit inside or outside, so I just grabbed a table to wait. After you get a drink, we can move if you want."

"It doesn't matter to me."

"Me neither."

Montana bites the inside of her cheek. "Let's go outside. The weather's great." Yup, she's already mentioning the weather. "I'll be right back."

Heading to the counter to order, she's grateful for the moment to regroup. Why is this so hard? She should have been better about keeping in touch, but it's not like Sloane was calling her all the time either.

They'll just have to start over, get to know each other again. If she and Austin can be friends after all the hurt they've caused each other, surely, she and Sloane can do the same. It's not like *they* broke up—they only lost touch.

When she returns to Sloane with her double shot iced latte, they head outside, snagging a couple empty chairs in front of the building. The weather really is nice today. It's probably way nicer in California, but she'll take what she can get. Very soon it'll be warm enough to wear shorts.

"So how are things with Jeremy?" she asks. She's never met Sloane's boyfriend, just knows that he's a financial advisor. Not that she truly understands what that means, since she's never exactly had enough finances to be advised on.

"We're great." A wide grin spreads across Sloane's face. "Actually, we've been talking about getting married."

"He proposed?"

Sloane shakes her head. "No. Not yet. We just wanted to make sure we're on the same page about where we are with our lives and what we want our futures to look like."

Montana hums. "Remind me how long you've been dating?"

"Our two-year anniversary is next month."

Two years doesn't seem like enough time to be considering marriage. Montana and Austin were together for longer than that. But it's different when you're older, isn't it?

It hits her then, her sore lack of experience in actual adult relationships.

"That's wonderful," she forces herself to say, fiddling with the straw in her plastic cup. "I'm happy for you."

Sloane is beaming now, and Montana takes a long sip of her latte, trying not to let her tepid feelings about this news show on her face.

She *is* happy for her friend. It's just . . . She felt more mature than half of her classmates in high school—the one with a big plan for her future, making the decisions that would get her there. And she did get there. But now she's *here*, essentially right back where she started. Meanwhile, it seems like everyone else has managed to develop both their careers and their personal relationships.

How did she end up with neither?

Apparently, having things figured out at eighteen doesn't mean you'll still have them figured out at twenty-eight. Taylor Swift warned her about this.

"Okay, spill it," Sloane says after a moment.

"Spill what?"

"You and Austin. You said you ran into him, and I know there must be drama there." She holds up her cup, tipping it a bit toward Montana. "I may not be drinking tea, but I'm ready. Give it to me."

Montana laughs. "There's no drama."

"Oh, please."

"Well, okay, I mean, there *was*. When we first saw each other. But we got over the shock of it, and now we're okay, I guess. I'm even working for him."

Sloane gasps exaggeratedly. "You are not."

"Yup. It was awkward as hell at first. But we're trying to be friends."

Giving her a deeply imploring look, Sloane asks, "Do you *want* to be his friend?"

"Why wouldn't I?" she says. And is she slightly evading the question? *Yes.* Yes, she is. Because the answer to it is so incredibly complicated.

"You guys were, like, madly in love. I know it's been a long time, but I imagine it must be hard to spend time with him without some of those old feelings creeping back in."

"No. No feelings. No creeping." She shakes her head vehemently. "He just . . . He keeps being nice to me, and I don't know how to handle it."

"Do you expect him to be mean to you?"

"No. Well. Maybe." Shrugging, Montana adds, "I'd kind of deserve it."

Sloane smacks her palm against the table. Not hard, but it makes Montana jump, nonetheless. "No, you wouldn't. You broke up with him, but you still wanted to be his friend back then. He's the one who cut you out of his life without another word. So if you're not ready to be friends with him now, that'd be understandable."

"I . . ." She sighs, watching a couple holding hands as they cross the street while she gathers her thoughts. It feels oddly good to hear someone else acknowledge the fact that she's not the only guilty party in that relationship. "I do want to be his friend. I want to let the past go. It's just hard."

Sloane offers her a small, comforting smile and says, "I'm sure it is." Then her smile morphs into more of a conspiratorial grin, a spark of mischief reaching her eyes. "But I'm still waiting for details."

Montana swipes a lock of hair out of her face before grinning back at her and launching into the whole story of every interaction she and Austin have had since she's been back. Sure, she told herself she wasn't going to do this, but Sloane asked.

And the more she talks, the more natural things start to feel between them. By the time there's nothing but ice left melting in her cup, she could almost pretend it was senior year of high school and they were hanging around after school while she waited for Austin to get out of baseball practice.

"Okay," she says, knowing she's babbled enough, "no more of the Austin saga. New subject, please."

"How's the writing?" Sloane asks. "I know you're working at the restaurant, but what happened to journalism?"

She tilts her cup, twirling the bottom edge against the table idly. "Nothing happened to it. It still exists. The magazine I worked for just had to cut back on staff. I can still do freelance, but I haven't written anything new since my move." She sighs, not sure if she's ready to admit this out loud. But this is the first time since she's been back on the East

Coast that she's really been able to let her walls down, so she forges on. "It's starting to feel like I failed. I've had so much published, I know, but now it's like all the doors have slammed in my face and I don't know how to get back in."

"So that's it? You gave up Austin to chase after your dream, and now you're going to give up on your dream because of one setback?"

Fucking *ouch.*

"In my defense, it was a pretty major setback. And I'm not *giving up* on it. Unfortunately, there's not much I can do in that department while I'm here. I don't exactly have the money to travel anywhere." She doesn't need the reminder that none of the magazines or sites she's sent out pieces to recently have responded, or that she doesn't have any ideas for new ones to write. She's already stressing about it in every free moment that she's not stressing over Austin. "Can we change the subject again? Let's go back to you."

"Sorry," Sloane says guiltily, clearly realizing she upset her. "It's just, I always thought it was cool that you went after what you wanted and made it happen. Not to mention you got to roam all over the world. It's weird to see you back in Massachusetts talking about bartending."

"It's weird for me, too. But the bartending thing is only temporary. I'll get back to doing what I love eventually."

At least, that's what she keeps telling herself so that she doesn't have a complete mental breakdown.

"Cheers to that," Sloane declares, knocking her empty cup against Montana's.

Montana only wishes she truly believed what she said. The longer she stays here without any job prospects in the writing field, though, the more her doubts grow. There is the possibility that her career is simply over. But dwelling on that thought too long will have her tempted to jump from her seat and run into traffic.

So she forces a smile and says, "Cheers."

HIT WITH A STRANGE urge to be domestic that afternoon, Montana mixes up a pitcher of Country Time lemonade. When she was younger, her mom made this all the time, and Montana used to wonder why she bothered with the powdered stuff when she could simply go to the grocery store and buy pre-made lemonade. But finally, she thinks she understands. Having the plastic pitcher of it in the fridge feels homey.

The fridge is also loaded up with plenty of produce right now, making it a perfect day to have a salad. She's proud of herself for the money she's saved by skipping takeout and cooking at home more. She won't be competing on *Top Chef* any time soon, but she gets by. And it's kind of relaxing, listening to music while she seasons the chicken and cooks the diced-up pieces in a pan.

This kitchen lacks a fan, though, except for the one over the stove, which does nothing to cool off the room. So she opens up a window when it gets too hot.

The loud, steady sound of a motor immediately filters in, disrupting her peace. Someone must be mowing their lawn. She cranks up the volume on Taylor Swift to compensate and serenades herself to a chorus of "Betty" while she idly keeps the chicken from sticking.

Turning the heat down when the meat is almost done, she leaves it in the pan and runs to open the living room windows too. It will feel good to get the fresh air circulating. As she's about to open one at the front of the house, her eyes catch something outside, and she freezes.

Austin freaking Adler.

He's out there in a white T-shirt and tan fitted shorts *mowing her damn lawn.*

She flies out the front door and onto the porch, shouting to get his attention. But his back is to her, and he obviously can't hear over the mower. As he turns it her way, she waves her arms overhead like an air traffic controller. Finally noticing her, he pauses and cuts the motor.

Then he just stands there in the middle of the grass with an annoyingly innocent smile.

"What are you doing?" she yells.

Smile not faltering, he says, "What does it look like?"

"You don't have to do that."

"I told you. It's unsightly."

Leaning over the porch railing, she starts to protest. "But—"

"Open your gate so I can do the back after," he interrupts her in the most casual tone possible. Like this whole situation isn't ridiculous.

She crosses her arms defiantly. "No one sees the back! I don't even go out there."

"But you could. If it wasn't such a disaster."

Well, ouch. For some reason that actually stings. Like maybe he thinks *she's* as much of a disaster as her lawn. "I-I've got food on the stove," she stammers awkwardly.

As she's turning to go inside, he shouts, "Unlatch the gate!"

She huffs, throwing her hands up in surrender. Then she walks straight through the house, out the kitchen door, and into the backyard to do what he says.

Her chicken looks a tad overdone when she returns to it, but it's fine. She sets it aside and starts pulling vegetables out of the fridge, placing them on the cutting board. As she chops, it's possible she may be taking some of her frustrations out on the peppers.

Who does he think he is? She asked him for help when she needed a job, sure, but that doesn't give him the right to waltz over here acting like he can fix everything in her life. Like she's only a silly girl, incapable of handling a task like that on her own. She survived in California on her own for six years, for fuck's sake. Ten, actually, counting college.

But . . . despite the way he framed it, this *is* a really nice thing he's doing. Maybe he needs to make it feel condescending in order to justify it. Because he's already done plenty of nice things for her since she arrived, and this one might tip the scale from *he's just a nice guy* over to *he still really cares about her.*

And she's not sure either of them can handle that yet.

He's in the back now; she can hear it. But she's facing away from the window, so she tries to ignore him as she cuts up enough vegetables for two salads. Soon everything is prepared and divvied up into large bowls, just waiting to add the chicken and dressing.

That's when she makes the mistake of turning around. Right as he's pulling his shirt over his head and tossing it aside in the grass.

Fuck, why does he have to look that good after all these years? He looks even better now than he did in high school, damn him.

She tears herself away from the view and goes to the fridge for the lemonade. She should take some out to him. That's the nice thing to do, right?

As she's moving to the back door with a cold, refreshing glass in her hand, he changes direction. Now he's walking away from the house, which puts his back to her. The muscles there are just as delicious as the ones on his front, but her focus is drawn to a black and gray tattoo on his shoulder. That's new.

She steps forward, squinting to get a better look. It's . . . *a rose.*

The glass falls out of her grip, and she only vaguely registers the sound of it smashing to the floor.

THEN

*M*ontana was watching a movie on Austin's couch, something ridiculous with Kevin James in a mall, but she wasn't really paying attention to it. Her mind kept drifting to the thick acceptance packet sitting on top of her desk at home. She couldn't believe she'd actually gotten into UCLA.

It was really happening. She was going to California.

She'd always wanted to live there, despite never having set one foot inside the border. The only downside was that it was three thousand miles away from where Austin would be next year. Which was right where he was now. Here in Hartley.

She didn't understand how he had no desire to go to college. It was cool that he wanted to help his dad run the restaurant, and she wasn't elitist enough to believe everyone needed a formal education. But didn't he want to go somewhere first for the experience, at least?

He'd always been content with where he was and what he already had. Unlike her. Because no matter how happy she was, she always yearned for something else. The desire to travel was like an itch under her skin, and it seemed the only way to scratch it would be to get out there and see everything the world had to offer.

Sometimes she wished she was more like him though. It would be easier, maybe, to be satisfied with a simple life. But Montana wanted more.

Austin laughed at something on the screen, bringing her attention back to where she was.

"What happened?"

He gave her arm a gentle shove. "Are you not paying attention?"

"Not really," she admitted. "It's kinda dumb."

"Well you vetoed my first suggestion."

"You know how I feel about Will Ferrell."

He chuckled. "Yes, you've made that extremely clear every time you've said that just looking at his face makes you want to punch something."

She shrugged. "I know it's irrational. I can't help it."

"Do you wanna turn this off and do something else?"

"Are you enjoying it?" she asked.

"Yeah."

Shaking her head, she said, "We can finish it. And then you owe me a massage. A full one. Not just shoulders."

He laughed as he slid his arm around her, pulling her up against his chest. "Yes, ma'am."

She tried to focus on the movie, but a few minutes later she was distracted again. This time for a different reason. He'd slid her cardigan off her shoulder and was now kissing the exposed skin beside the strap of her tank top. Soft kisses that warmed her body pleasantly.

"If you want to finish the movie, you'd better stop," she warned him.

"Eh. Screw the movie." He turned her a little so he could see her face, and his hand came up to wrap around the side of her neck, his thumb against her jaw, guiding her to look at him. "I love you, Montana Rose Sinclair."

"Of course you do," she said. Though she'd meant it to sound teasing, her words came out a little breathless. Not wanting to give him the smug satisfaction of knowing how his simple ministrations had affected her, she attempted to double down with the humor. "It's like I own you. I should make you get a tattoo."

He smirked. "What, like your name?"

"Give me some credit. It'll be a little more subtle than that."

"Like what then?"

"Hmm . . . maybe just a rose." She gazed down, drawing a vague flower shape with her finger on his forearm. "Yeah. A rose."

"I could live with that."

Her eyes flew back up to meet his. He really meant it. She could tell.

And that was . . . not something she was comfortable with. They belonged to each other; they both knew it. She didn't need to brand him to make him hers.

Not knowing how to respond, she angled herself back toward the TV.

A minute later, he said, "You didn't say it back."

"Huh?"

He turned her head his way again. "I love you."

"Oh, duh!" A nervous giggle escaped her, though she didn't know why. "I love you too. I thought that was obvious."

Satisfied, he kissed her.

And she did love him. She really did.

But she loved the idea of California too.

CHAPTER EIGHT

NOW

*I*t is most definitely *not* subtle.

But it doesn't mean anything. It doesn't.

It doesn't mean anything *now*, anyway. Montana is a huge part of his past, no one could deny that. She was his first love. And maybe he doesn't want to forget that, even if it ended badly. It doesn't mean he still . . .

No. That's crazy.

Looking down at the broken glass and puddle of sticky spilled lemonade at her feet, she groans. She only had four drinking glasses to begin with (not counting wine glasses, of course). This leaves her with three. Good thing she doesn't have enough friends to be hosting dinner parties anytime soon.

With a broom and dustpan, she gathers up the pieces of glass and deposits them in the trash. She's on her hands and knees, blotting up the liquid with a fistful of paper towels, when Austin casually strolls in through the back door.

"What happened?"

Springing to her feet, she squeaks, "Oh, you know me."

He laughs. "I do, in fact."

She tosses the paper towels in the trash and tries to school her face into a neutral expression before turning back to face him.

Pointing at the two salad bowls on the counter, he asks, "Are one of those for me?"

"No." She inwardly facepalms, then outwardly sighs. "Yes."

"Sweet." He grabs a bowl and tosses some chicken from the pan on top. "The game's about to start."

She feels disoriented. It's lucky he put his shirt back on before he came inside. If she was confronted with the sight of his bare chest up close, she might have fainted. But still, even though he's covered up, she can't unsee that fucking tattoo.

"Are you okay?" he asks. And she realizes he's already dressed his salad and is now staring at her expectantly.

She shakes her head. "No, yeah." When he looks pointedly from her empty hands to the other bowl on the counter, she says, "I'm not hungry."

"Then why'd you make it?"

"I mean, I am, but—"

"Seriously," he interrupts her. "Are you okay?" His expression is split between concerned and amused. The bastard.

Trying to get it together, she says, "Um, yeah. I am. We can watch the game."

"Great."

With that, he takes his lunch into the living room where she hears the TV turn on. She takes a moment to compose herself before fixing her salad. Then she grabs two of her precious remaining glasses from the cabinet, pours each of them a lemonade, and carefully carries everything over to join him.

"You don't have cable," he states as she passes him a glass.

She glances at the TV. *Oh, right.* "No, I don't. Sorry."

"It's okay, I have an app. I'm downloading it for you."

"Okay."

Taking a seat beside him on the couch, she begins to pick at her salad. Within minutes, he's got the game on. He played baseball in high school, which accounts for the sport being the only one she can stand to watch.

They eat and watch in companionable silence, but Montana's head is still spinning.

He got a tattoo.

He's buying her furniture and mowing her lawn and *hegotatattoo.* For her.

Maybe it's to remind him what a horrible bitch she is, and how she broke his heart. But then why would he be here right now?

Even though he was just outside undoubtedly sweating, she can still smell his cologne. The scent is too familiar—crisp and clean, the tiniest bit woodsy. Has he really not changed colognes in the last six years? She's smelled it on him briefly a few times since she's been back, but now the prolonged exposure is taking over her senses. It's driving her crazy and unearthing a deeply buried instinct that makes her want to lean into him. Which she absolutely. Cannot. Do.

How is it that everything feels so different—that *he's* different, with a son and responsibilities—while at the same time, in these random moments, it feels like nothing has changed at all? He still feels like he belongs to her.

But he doesn't.

And she needs to remember that.

Out of the corner of her eye, she watches him eat while staying totally focused on the game. His legs have fallen open so that one knee is barely an inch away from hers. And suddenly, this is too much. It feels like an invasion. On her senses, her mind, her heart. She can't take it.

"You can't just keep showing up like this," she blurts out. "I do have a life, you know."

He turns from the game and quirks an eyebrow at her playfully.

"I do!" she insists. "For your information, I was out having coffee with Sloane this morning. So there!"

"I didn't know you and Sloane were still friends."

"Well, we are." That might be a bit of an exaggeration, but they're on their way to being friends again, so whatever.

He frowns. "Do you want me to leave?"

She shrugs like she doesn't care one way or the other. Like she didn't just attack him for coming here to do her a favor. Because while she *should* want him to leave for the sake of her sanity . . . when faced with the question, she can't bring herself to give him an answer.

"Where's Kalen?" she deflects. "I thought you always had him on Mondays because it's your only guaranteed day off." She doesn't know when she learned that, but apparently, she's been absorbing new information about him without even trying.

"Blake's watching him for me."

"And you don't want to get back to him?"

"He loves hanging out with Blake. Probably because Blake lets him have whatever he wants. When I pick him up, there's a very high chance he'll be so hopped up on sugar he'll try to climb the walls pretending to be Spiderman, but oh well."

There goes that excuse for him to leave. No others come to her, and well . . . That's the answer to the question, isn't it? *No.* She doesn't want him to leave. Actually, she really wants him to stay, her sanity be damned.

He takes the last sip of his lemonade and sets the empty glass back on the table.

"Do you want a beer?" she asks.

"Definitely," he says.

So she gets up, going to the kitchen to get him one. It's only a beer, no big deal. And sanity is overrated anyway.

◆

OPENING THE BAR for lunch on Tuesday, Montana finds there's absolutely no fruit cut. She silently curses the bartender who closed Sunday night and left the place barren before remembering that, *oh yeah*, it was her. Grudgingly, she goes to the walk-in at the back of the kitchen to grab the lemons, limes, and oranges, then swipes a cutting board and knife from the dish room. The restaurant doesn't open for thirty minutes, which is plenty of time, but this is still an annoying task.

She finishes the lemons and is starting on the limes when she notices Blake slide onto a stool at the other end of the bar. She mutters a greeting, and he responds in kind, then she returns to the fruit, proceeding to ignore him. He's eating a sandwich, something one of the cooks probably made for him. With the restaurant empty, the sounds of his chewing seem to echo loudly throughout the room, slowly grating on her. She could go ahead and turn on the music, but that might be too obvious.

As she works, she swears she can feel his eyes burning into her. Eventually, unable to stand it anymore, she turns her head to confirm her suspicions. He's done with his sandwich and just sitting there watching her. "Something you need?" she asks, not in the mood for this weirdness.

He shakes his head. Then—"Were you with Austin yesterday?"

The question jolts her, but she tries to play it cool. "He came over to mow my lawn."

"Is that a euphemism?"

She narrows her eyes, raising the knife in her hand a couple inches in a subtle threat. "Seriously?"

"Okay, sorry," Blake says. "He asked me to watch Kalen. Which is cool, I don't mind. But he was being cagey, wouldn't tell me where he was going. He's never cagey. So I put two and two together."

"And came up five. You were never very good at math."

"Neither were you. You just said he was with you."

Which he tricked her into admitting. She didn't know it was a secret.

"Like I said, he only came over to mow my lawn. And *no*, that's not a euphemism. So if that was all you wanted to know . . ." She gestures at her sidework, ready to get back to it.

He grabs his plate and stands, taking the hint. But then, with an annoyingly determined look on his face, he puts the plate right back down again. "I'm just wondering what's going on with you two."

"Nothing's going on."

Well, not exactly *nothing*. But Blake isn't a person she should be having this conversation with. He's on Austin's side. Not that sides need to be taken. But if they did, he'd be sporting the TEAM AUSTIN jersey, that's for sure.

"There better not be," he says.

"Excuse me?"

He moves down the bar until he's right in front of her. "Austin's in a good place now. I don't wanna see him go back to being that pathetic dude who did nothing but pine over the girl who left him."

Her posture goes rigid. "That's not fair. I left him so he could move on."

"But then every time you came back you let him think there was still something between you guys."

"There was. I didn't stop having feelings for him. But he knew it couldn't be more than a temporary thing while I was home. I didn't promise him anything."

God, why is he making her rehash this? If Austin wants to move past it, that's all that matters.

Blake shakes his head. "Maybe he was actually waiting for you to make a promise. But you were too selfish to do that."

"Okay, enough," she says, voice hardening. She drops the knife onto the cutting board and wipes her hands on her jeans. "You've barely said two words to me since I've been here. How can you expect me to stand here now and listen to this crap from you?"

"I'm your boss."

She scoffs. "Oh, is that what you are? Weren't we friends before? I thought we were."

"Of course we were. But Austin's like my brother, and I can't let you treat him like crap again."

"Get off your high horse, Blake. Didn't you cheat on Marisela and then try to lie your face off when you got caught?"

He crosses his arms over his chest. He's filled out like Austin has, but his muscles don't do it for her in the same way. Thank god. "Sure, I made some mistakes when I was younger," he admits. "We all did. But some of us have grown up."

Slamming her palm down on the bar and shaking the whole thing, Montana stares him down. Her body is vibrating now—with anger or guilt, she doesn't know. He shouldn't be able to get to her like this, but she wasn't prepared for a full-frontal assault at the start of her day.

"Screw you," she says, managing somehow to keep an even tone.

Then she turns her back to him before he can see her lose the false bravado. She pretends to occupy herself with straightening the liquor bottles, but her hand is still trembling a little. She's not sure if she's mad at him for being a jerk to her or upset because some of what he's saying may be right.

Yeah, she's already had the thought that she didn't deserve Austin being so nice to her. But she's tired of feeling guilty for a choice she made when she was eighteen. And Austin was twenty-two when he decided to ignore her calls, block her on all social media, and never give her an explanation as to why. How is *that* okay?

She hopes Blake will leave, but no such luck. Instead, he comes behind the bar and puts a cautious hand on her shoulder. "I'm sorry."

Praying she can keep her eyes from watering, she turns to him as his hand falls away. "You realize he hurt me too, right? I'm not some heartless bitch screwing with his emotions. I *loved* him. And these last six years . . . do you think I forgot about him completely and moved on? Because I didn't. Ask me how many successful relationships I've had in L.A."

"No, I—"

"None," she continues, on a roll now. "I've had plenty of hookups. But my longest relationship was four months before it imploded." She shakes her head furiously. "God, I don't know why I'm even telling you this."

He shifts his weight. His eyes are much softer now, but she doesn't want that, because she's still trying not to cry. "Montana. I'm sorry. I'm just worried about him."

"I'm not going to hurt him."

"Maybe not intentionally, but—"

"No," she cuts him off again. "I *have* grown up, Blake. I can see now how me and him hooking up while I was in college wasn't really good for either of us. We should have had a clean break, and he was smart enough to finally do that. I won't let the lines get blurry between us again. He gave me a job because I was desperate. We're friends, that's it. And even that's only barely." She sighs, thoroughly exhausted with the conversation. "Nothing's going to happen, okay?"

He nods. "Okay. I believe you." He puts his hand on her shoulder again, more confidently this time, and adds, "And hey, we *are* friends too. So if you need anything . . ."

It's the same offer Austin made when she first got back to town, though Montana knows she'll be even less likely to take Blake up on it. Still, she supposes this is better than the way he's been avoiding her since she started here, so she thanks him.

A minute ago, all she wanted was for him to leave her alone, but now when he ducks out from behind the bar and starts to walk away, she finds herself opening her mouth and spilling out a confession to his back. "I don't know why he keeps doing all these things to help me."

He turns around, his expression unreadable. "Yes, you do."

"I swear I don't."

"Well, you've always been a smart girl. You'll figure it out. I just hope you don't take advantage of it."

With that final parting shot, he leaves before she can parse his words. She manages to finish up everything she needs to right before the restaurant opens, but she has a hard time shaking off the conversation.

It's a welcome distraction when her first customers take seats at the bar barely five minutes after the doors are unlocked. Two retirees, who she's learned meet here every Tuesday afternoon to talk about sports and gripe about their wives. She mixes their Manhattans according to their exact specifications, and then tries to appear busy while she eavesdrops on their conversation.

But she still can't get Blake's words out of her head.

Don't take advantage of it.

She's not taking advantage of Austin's kindness. She just told him yesterday to stop showing up at her place and doing things for her. But what was Blake even implying? She *doesn't* know why he keeps doing so many nice things.

Okay, it's clear at this point that he cares about her. But if he cares about her, then why was it so easy for him to cut her out of his life six years ago? He didn't care about her then, did he?

No.

He didn't care that he left her feeling confused and empty and heartbroken. Composing long, sad text messages that she would eventually delete rather than sending, because she knew he wasn't going to respond, and it was too pathetic to keep trying.

She forces herself to smile at the old men when she offers them another round.

Blake was just talking out of his ass like usual. He doesn't know anything.

THEN

*M*ontana slid her lunch tray over to Austin. "Do you want my fries?"

He grabbed a handful and dropped them on his own plate. As she slid the tray back, Blake reached across the picnic table and snagged some fries for himself. She shot him a look, but then offered him the rest.

Scooting a little closer to Austin, Montana tried to leech some heat from him. They'd finally made it through winter, so it was warm enough to eat outside. Just barely, though. They still needed their jackets, but she'd take it. She hated the months she spent cooped up inside. While she didn't mind participating in occasional sledding or a spontaneous snowball fight, she definitely preferred the sun over anything.

"Did you guys see Marisela got her nose pierced?" she asked, as the two boys continued to scarf down their food. "It looks badass."

When neither of them answered, she glanced at Austin, and his eyes were flashing warning signals. She turned her gaze to Blake, who looked stricken.

Oh geez. Was he still upset about the breakup? She honestly thought he would have moved on already. Maybe to the girl he cheated on Marisela with. Except that poor girl was a freshman, so Montana was honestly glad he hadn't.

"Sorry," she said, grimacing.

Blake pushed his lunch tray away, a surefire sign he was about to have a meltdown. He never left food on his plate uneaten. Or on anyone else's, for that matter. "I can't believe she dumped me!"

"You cheated on her," Austin reminded him.

"But it was an accident!"

"Oh, no," Montana jumped in. "No, no. I do *not* want to hear these excuses again."

"But—"

She shook her head vehemently. "Nope."

"I wish you hadn't gotten him started," Austin said.

"I wasn't thinking."

Blake let out the world's most dramatic sigh. "Whatever. She's planning to move to Puerto Rico for at least a year after graduation to be with her extended family anyway."

"So?" Austin asked.

"So it wasn't gonna last much longer. We weren't going to get married or anything like you two freaks. It's fine."

Austin sent a fond look Montana's way, but Blake's words made her feel weird, even though he wasn't being serious. She and Austin didn't talk about getting married. Sure, there was that one time he'd mused about her having his last name, but that had been an offhanded remark. More of a joke, really.

Anyway, Blake didn't seem fine. He was slumped over the table, chin in one hand, the other hand idly picking up fries and dropping them back onto his plate. Apparently, he'd actually cared more about the relationship he'd screwed up than he'd let on. Who would have guessed?

Montana looked to Austin. He shrugged. She cut her eyes pointedly to Blake, then back to him.

Getting the hint, Austin threw a fry at his friend and said, "Frisbee?"

Blake shrugged unenthusiastically. "Sure."

As they wandered off into the grass, Montana turned sideways on the bench, pulling her knees up to her chest and wrapping her arms around them to keep herself warm. She watched the two of them flinging the Frisbee back and forth for a bit, and when they came back to sit down, Blake seemed a little less mopey.

He reached for some fries, which were surely cold by now, and shoved them in his mouth. Without fully swallowing, he announced, "Oh hey, I got into UMASS."

"Dude," Austin said. "That's great. Congrats!"

Montana smiled and congratulated him too.

She was still waiting to hear from UCLA. And the other three schools she'd applied to, but UCLA was her white whale. Her grades were great, and she was pretty sure she'd rocked her essay, but they only accepted less than twenty percent of students.

Even though she was trying not to get her hopes up too high, she could already imagine herself on campus, fifteen minutes from the beach, twenty minutes from the Hollywood sign, cruising up and down the 101 on the weekends. (Her discovery of *The O.C.* last summer and subsequent binge of all four seasons *may* be responsible for some of her California fantasies.) The letter needed to arrive soon before she drove herself too crazy. One way or the other, she needed to know where she would be next year.

"What do you want to major in?" she asked Blake.

"Hmm . . ." He tapped his finger to his chin as if he was contemplating. "I'm thinking beer funneling."

Austin laughed and Montana rolled her eyes. "You're an idiot," she told him fondly.

"What about you?" he asked her. "What do you want to be when you grow up, Montana Sinclair?"

Nervously, she glanced at Austin, not wanting him to feel left out of this conversation, since he had no interest in going to college. But he smiled at her, so she said, "I'm majoring in journalism. Hopefully. I wanna be a travel writer."

"That's sick!" Blake held up his hand for a high five, which she gave him, despite it being silly. "You'd better send me postcards when you're off exploring the world and shit."

She laughed. "Okay, I will. Lots of postcards. From Ireland, Spain, Greece . . ." She trailed off.

When she looked at Austin again, he wasn't smiling anymore.

CHAPTER NINE

NOW

*B*y the time Montana announces last call on Saturday night, she's so wiped out that she's about ready to lie down on the sticky rubber mats behind the bar and close her eyes. But she's still got fifteen minutes before she can kick everybody out, and then she has to do all the cleanup and restocking.

Sabrina should have been working with her, but the other bartender got a phone call around eleven and had to leave for a family emergency, so Montana's been on her own for the last three hours. Well, not exactly alone. Austin's been jumping behind the bar to help every time he noticed she was a handful of people deep.

Sharing the small space with him is a lot easier now than it would have been a month ago. They work well together. She's been able to handle most of the crowd, but he seemed to magically sense when someone was about to order a complicated drink—rather than just a beer or a vodka soda—and he'd be there to say, "I've got it," so she was free to grab the next customer. When he wasn't making drinks for her, he was filling the ice bin, washing glasses, running to the walk-in to grab more cases of High Noon, or out on the floor bussing tables.

She feels guilty about him having to do all this, even though she's not the one who left two hours into her shift, so it's not her fault.

When two a.m. finally arrives, Austin turns up the lights and begins herding everyone to the door. The band's already packing up their gear, and the kitchen closed a while ago, so the cooks are gone. Pretty soon it's only Austin and Montana left.

It feels eerily quiet now after how loud it was all night, so she turns the music on. Scanning the empty room, she's not even sure where to start with all the closing work. Before she can make a decision, Austin grabs a rag and begins wiping down the tables.

"You don't have to do that."

"I'm not going to make you do everything yourself," he tells her. "Take your credit card tips out of the drawer so I can count it."

He's the boss, so she does what he says, tossing the money into the bucket with her cash tips to count later. Then she wipes down the bartop as he finishes a quick sweep of the floor. When he goes to the dish room and comes back with the mop bucket though, she shakes her head. "Okay, you really don't have to do that."

"Just worry about back there, would you."

Well, fine. She's not going to argue anymore. Mopping sucks.

While he does that, she caps the pour spouts on the liquor bottles and then checks the coolers, making a list of what she needs to restock. Then she carries the boxes of empty beer bottles into the back and grabs the six-packs she needs from the walk-in.

As she's putting those away, Austin comes to take the cash drawer out of the register and sets it on the bar. Rather than going to sit down with it, he grabs two shot glasses and turns to her. "What are you drinking?"

She shakes her head. "I'm good, thanks."

"Oh, come on." His sparkling green eyes goad her playfully. "You deserve a shot after working that hard. Jack Fire?"

A minute ago, all she wanted to do was finish her work so she could go home and pass out, but now this feels like a challenge. One she can't back down from, though she's not sure why. So she says, "Sure."

Smiling triumphantly, he uncaps the bottle and pours out two shots, passing one to her. He holds up his own, and they clink the glasses together before throwing them back. It burns going down, but in a good way. A freeing sort of way.

She sets the shot glass down, ready to return to the restocking, but he's already pouring them each another. He raises his eyebrows until she picks hers up and they do round two.

"All right," she says, shuddering through the aftershock, "count the drawer before you're too drunk."

He laughs and moves around to the other side of the bar, taking a stool. As he's counting to make sure the money matches up with the sales report, she finishes her sidework. Then she comes around and grabs a stool two down from him, dumping out her tip bucket onto the bartop to count the cash. She made a killing, but grudgingly, she divvies out half and slides the pile over to him.

He glances at the money and rolls his eyes. "I'm not keeping your tips."

"But you did half the work."

"I really didn't," he argues. "Besides, I'm the owner. It would be frowned upon for me to take that."

"But—"

"Put the money in your purse," he says, cutting her off, "and then will you grab me a Coors Lite, please?"

Maybe she should push the subject, but she could use this money, so fuck it. She scoops up all the cash, then goes to stash it in her purse behind the bar. After grabbing the beer for him, she pauses, peering into the open cooler. She could go home now. She's freaking exhausted. But . . .

What the heck.

She grabs another one for herself and pops the caps off both before setting them on the bar.

Austin eyes the two bottles, then smirks. "Drawer's even. I'm gonna go put this in the safe, be right back."

In his brief absence, she has enough time to realize this might be a bad idea. Those two shots are starting to hit her. Only enough to make her tipsy, but she does have to drive home. And if she keeps drinking, she runs the risk of getting drunk and doing something foolish around Austin that she'd be too smart to do sober.

It feels rude to leave him here alone after all the help he's given her with closing though. Plus she can't waste an open beer. So she'll drink this one, thank him, and that's it.

When he returns, he takes the seat right beside her, his arm brushing hers briefly as he squeezes in. He picks up his beer and knocks back half of it in one long gulp.

She reaches for the stack of small, laminated late-night menus on the bar beside her, tapping them straight in her hands. Running her finger over the Alan's Place logo on the top one, she says, "You ever think about changing the name?"

"Hell no."

"Good."

He smiles and then jumps up and runs behind the bar again. He grabs the bottle of Jack Fire and the two shot glasses, ignoring her protest as he pours. When he goes back to sit down, he leaves the bottle on the bar in front of them.

She eyes the amber liquor warily. "This is my last one."

He flashes her his infuriatingly adorable dimples. "Whatever you say, babe."

The endearment makes her pause. But he's teasing her, so it doesn't count. She holds up her glass reluctantly, and they clink again before taking the shots. Then her favorite Janis Joplin song starts playing over the stereo system, and an excited, "Oh!" slips out of her. The alcohol is certainly to blame for the way she sings along, unabashedly off-key, about taking another piece of her heart.

"I've gotta say," Austin starts, tipping his Coors Lite her direction, "I've missed your terrible singing."

Her mouth drops open. "*Hey!*"

"And that false indignation thing you do when you know I'm right."

She smacks him on the arm, which only makes him laugh, and tells him, "If you missed me so much, you could have answered my calls."

Ohhh. Shiiit.

Regret immediately floods in after the words are out. *This*, damn it. This right here is why staying and drinking with him was a bad idea.

His face is serious now, and with a flat tone, he says, "Montana. Don't."

It sounds like he's chastising her, and even if that's only in her head, it rubs her the wrong way, flipping her switch from mortified to a little angry. Because that's all he's going to give her? Maybe she should've kept her thoughts to herself, but she can't put the words back in her mouth now. And you know what? *Fuck it.* She deserves some answers.

Snatching the liquor bottle off the bar, she pours herself another shot for courage and takes it quickly, slamming the empty glass down a little too hard. "Why did you cut me off?" she demands.

He avoided the question when she first got to town, but she needs to know.

For an excruciatingly long time, he's silent, gazing down at the freshly wiped bartop. Then, just when she thinks he's going to ignore her, he says, "I had to."

"But why?"

He raises his eyes to meet hers, and in the few seconds it takes him to speak, she has time to worry if finally knowing might somehow be worse than not knowing. "I met Brittani after you went back for your last semester at UCLA. She asked me to get coffee, and then we went out a couple times more."

Yup. She's changed her mind. She doesn't want to hear this. But she can't manage to voice that, so she just sits there, picking at the label of her barely drunk beer as he continues.

"I liked her. She was nice, and fun, and it was obvious she was into me. It had been so long since I'd felt that rush of getting to know someone new. The flirting and the excitement of wondering what's going to happen next."

Please stop talking.

He pours them both another shot. They don't bother to clink this time. And after they set the empty glasses back down, he sighs. "But even though I liked her, I felt like I was doing something wrong. Like I was cheating on you."

"You weren't," she says. Because really, he wasn't. Not technically. Still, if he just stabbed her in the chest, it might be less painful than hearing about this.

"I know I wasn't, but it felt like it."

Good, she thinks savagely.

"I almost ended things with her because I didn't want to ruin what I had with you. Then I realized what I had with you wasn't ever going to be what we had before you went to school. I didn't think you were coming back. You loved California."

She opens her mouth to tell him that she *was* thinking about moving back to Hartley for him after she graduated. But the words stick in her throat. And as much as she hates this, he looks like he needs to get it all off his chest, so she stays silent and lets him go on.

"And I remembered what you said to me when you broke up with me. That we both needed to see what else was out there. I was never going to do that as long as you were still in my life. I was going to keep waiting for you, taking whatever you could give me while you were here, and then letting you leave me again. Over and over."

The music has changed to something slower, more depressing. And she wishes she could skip whatever this stupid song is, but she can't move. His intense eye contact has her frozen.

"It was killing me, holding onto the silly fantasy that we were going to get back together someday." His mouth turns down at the corners before he finally looks away from her, wrapping his hand tightly around his beer bottle. "I had to let you go for real."

She doesn't know what to say. So she just continues to sit there, heart pounding in her chest, while he drains the rest of his beer.

He eyes the liquor bottle, and there's no way she can do another shot. But luckily, he seems to think better of it himself. He does get up, though, to grab himself another beer from the cooler. When he sits back down, he turns sideways in his seat, mirroring her so their bodies are facing each other. Slotting one of his legs between hers, he rests his foot casually on the bar at the bottom of her stool.

She should tell him the truth—say that she would have come back for him.

But what good will it do now?

The stereo is still playing that slow, moody song. And damn, one of them really needs to say something. But he seems content to sip his beer, letting everything he revealed fill up the room around them until they're both drowning in it.

"I should go," she finally says, though without much conviction.

"Don't go."

"Okay."

He rests his arm on the bar, his hand close enough to grab her shirt sleeve if he wanted to. "Tell me about your job at the magazine. All the places you've been. I want to know everything."

She tells him about some of the coolest places she's traveled— Alaska to see the Northern lights, Reykjavik for the hot springs and then over to Vatnajokull National Park to explore the ice caves. She shares fun stories, like the time she was interviewing artists at Burning Man and somehow got talked into stripping down to her underwear and letting people draw on her body with Sharpies. Austin laughs loudly at that, and the memory makes her grin too.

She tells him how she picked up a hitchhiker outside of Reno—"It was a sixty-five-year-old woman," she clarifies when his eyes darken— but then her car broke down on the side of the road, and the woman ended up walking with her six miles into town, the two of them singing "Don't Stop Believing" every half hour to keep themselves entertained.

The next time Austin hands her a shot, she takes it without really thinking. And a minute later, she realizes how dumb that was when she almost falls out of her seat. His arm flies out to catch her, a few drops from the beer in his hand sloshing onto her jeans as she slurs, "*Nomoreshots.*"

"That's probably smart," he says, setting his bottle on the bar.

The alcohol has warmed her insides and caused an oddly pleasant buzzing in her head. She's glad she stayed. They're talking, laughing, joking. Everything is good. His fingers have fallen to the top of her leg, but she doesn't think he notices. That's okay. She likes them there. She shouldn't. But she does. If she inched forward, his fingers would reach a little higher.

No, stop.

He's just being nice. Friendly. The shots have loosened their limbs, but that's all it is.

"Did you ever make it out to Montana like you wanted?" he asks, thumb pressing into the side of her knee.

Smiling brightly, she leans in closer. "Yeah, I did! It was beautiful."

"Of course it was."

He's looking at her.

His hand comes up to tuck her hair behind her ear.

She's lost the thread of the conversation.

"What's your absolute favorite place you've been to?" he asks, voice lower now.

"*Austin.*" She says the word with reverence, without thinking.

Then he's quiet, and it just hangs there like a heavy truth between them.

She tugs her bottom lip between her teeth. It *is* the truth. She loved that city, with its energetic live music scene, the hipster coffee houses, and the fancy cowboy boots on everyone's feet.

But she was destined to love it, wasn't she?

Suddenly, Austin's eyes flood with heat and he's off his seat, crowding into her space, both hands pressed down on her thighs. She sucks in a breath, and before she can let it out, his mouth is on hers.

Her response is automatic, kissing him back greedily, taking, taking, taking. Their lips slot together perfectly like they've been doing this all their lives. Because they have, haven't they? His fingers dig into her thighs, and she scoots closer, half off her seat, but she can't fall because his body is right there up against her.

The warmth in her blood has ignited into a fire.

His tongue is seeking, searching, exploring. And now she knows he still tastes like cinnamon. Except it's the alcohol, of course, not the sticks of Big Red he used to chew all the time.

She's clutching his shirt in one hand, because she'll die if he moves away. But he's not going anywhere. One of his hands slides over her hip, traveling up the side of her ribcage. She can't catch her breath, but who needs to breathe when everything is finally, blissfully right.

It was inevitable. This moment. Inevitable as soon as she drove her car over the Hartley town line. Inevitable from the time they first kissed when they were fifteen, really.

They were always going to come crashing back together.

In one swift movement, he picks her up and spins them, setting her ass onto the edge of the bar. Then their mouths eagerly reunite. His hands have rucked up her shirt, fingers setting off sparklers against her skin.

She rubs over the spot on his shoulder where the tattoo is. A rose. *Her.* He infused her into himself with permanent ink.

He groans hungrily into her mouth like he knows what she's doing. Except he doesn't even know she saw it that day. When he pulls back a little, she whimpers at the loss of contact. But then he's hiking her leg up so he can run his hand slowly down it, squeezing her thigh again, finger teasing at the back of her knee, feeling the curve of her calf with his palm.

She cards her fingers through his hair, tugging once with fervor, relishing in the surprised gasp he lets out. He hasn't stopped his exploration, and now his fingers wrap around her ankle. They stare at each other, breathing heavily. She feels his finger push up underneath the hem of her jeans and run over the tiny, raised scar right above her ankle bone.

He pauses, tearing his gaze away from hers to study it. Running his finger over it again, he laughs softly.

"What?"

"Nothing." He shakes his head. "It's just . . . I remember how you got this."

Her mind is fuzzy, and her eyelids drop closed when he brings her leg up higher to kiss over the white flesh of the scar. She's only half listening as he says, ". . . another casualty of Blake's drunken antics."

Oh shit.

Blake.

Her eyes fly open as regret slams into her chest.

Shit shit shit.

She scrambles to push his hands off her, her leg falling back down like a lead weight. "We can't do this."

"Wait, what?" Austin looks so confused, coming out of the haze of lust much slower than her.

And it's crazy how badly she wants to disregard what she said, reach out, pull him back in, and keep fucking everything up. But she promised. She told Blake nothing was going to happen, and she hates that she made herself a liar.

This was a drunken mistake. When she came back to town, she never dreamed Austin would welcome her back into his life in any way, but he did. They were in a good place.

So what the hell is she doing? She's going to ruin everything.

"Montana, what . . ." He raises his hand to touch her face, but she grabs his wrist, stopping him.

"I'm sorry," she says, shaking her head. "This isn't—We shouldn't cross the line."

"Don't you think it's a little late for that?"

"No. I mean, yes, but. We have to end it here." She nudges him back a step so she can slide down from the bar top. Her sneakers smack the floor with an echoing finality.

Maneuvering around him, she runs behind the bar to get her purse. And to put more distance between them. "I was a mess when I first moved back here. And this job and your friendship have really helped me. Austin, it means everything to me that you were willing to let me back into your life. We can't fuck this up."

She can't fuck it up. She can't hurt him. She told Blake she's grown up, and she thought that was true.

"So you're saying you just want to be friends?" he asks.

She clears the empty beer bottles off the bar, setting them into the box on the floor as she explains, "I'm saying I don't think either of us were thinking straight. And yeah, I can't lose you as a friend."

Very slowly, he starts to move. He picks up their shot glasses and hands them to her to put in the sink. "I don't want to lose you either."

"So we're good?" she asks, slinging her purse over her shoulder and hoping he can't see how much she really doesn't want to leave this room.

Which he can't, because he's not quite meeting her eyes now. "Sure, we're good. Are you okay to drive?"

"Yeah." That's probably not true, though the last five minutes have certainly helped sober her up. But she needs to get out of here.

"Okay. I'm gonna lock up," he tells her. "Drive safe and text me to let me know when you get home."

"I will. Goodnight."

He nods once. "Bye."

Fuck fucking fuck.

THEN

*M*ontana leaned back against Austin's chest as they watched the fireworks show from their private rooftop view. She was sitting between his legs, his arms loosely around her. The few sips of whiskey she'd taken made the colors seem even brighter. Or maybe everything was just brighter when she was in his arms.

She giggled to herself. Guess the alcohol had made her cheesy too.

"Why do you think our parents named us after places they've never even been?" she asked, thinking out loud.

Austin chuckled. "I never thought about it. But my name's a lot more common than yours. I doubt my parents were really thinking about the capital of Texas."

"I should ask my mom what she was thinking."

Tugging her in closer, he rested his chin on her shoulder. "I love your name though."

"I didn't say I didn't like it." She wrapped her hand around his forearm, one finger tracing the prominent vein there. "But I feel like I have to go there someday. Like maybe it'll reveal to me some big secret about myself."

"Can I come with you?"

"Definitely. And then we'll go to Texas too."

"Sounds like a plan."

She craned her neck to look back at him. "You know those aren't the only places I want to go, right?"

They'd talked before about her desire to travel, but she wasn't sure he realized how serious she was. It wasn't just a dream, a *maybe someday*. She was going to make it happen.

"I know," he said.

"I want to go everywhere," she insisted. Then she hesitated, feeling like everything rested on her next question. "Are you coming with me?"

He placed a soft kiss at the bottom of her jaw. "I sure hope so."

"Good."

She settled back into place to enjoy the fireworks, humming happily when he took one of her hands in his, his thumb stroking along the back of it. As he slid one of the silver rings off her middle finger and onto her ring finger, idly twisting it back and forth, she didn't think anything of it.

Until she heard, so quiet it was almost as if he was speaking to himself—"*Montana Rose Adler*. It sounds good."

"Stop," she said, laughing nervously.

"But it does, right?"

She glanced at the ring on her finger, his hand holding hers. "Yeah. It does."

"Okay, you two are so cute you're gonna make me puke," Blake complained loudly, yanking Montana out of the silly fantasy.

"No, I think that's the ten ounces of Jack Daniels in your stomach," Austin said. He picked up a small piece of gravel and threw it at his friend. "Would you sit down before you fall off the roof? My dad will kill me if your parents sue."

Montana laughed.

Blake contemplated the liquor bottle in his hand (which they'd stolen from the storeroom), then eyed the roof ledge. "Nah, I'm good, dude. Don't worry. Go back to your nauseating little love fest."

Austin turned Montana in his arms, leaning in for a kiss. She shook her head, fighting a smile. "Come on," he urged. "He told us to."

Giving in, she let him kiss her. Only for a moment though. She wasn't too keen on having an audience.

But when she turned back around, Blake had already wandered off a few feet, a little closer to the edge, watching the fireworks as he sang something to himself and danced clumsily in place. He'd definitely drunk more of the whiskey than her or Austin.

"Uh, Blake," she called out, "maybe you want to come back over here?"

He gave her a put-upon look, but then stumbled his way back to where Montana and Austin were sitting. "Relax, you two. I'm just enjoying this perfect summer night. We're gonna be seniors soon! One more year 'til we're outta here."

"If you don't sit down," Austin said, "you might not make it to senior year."

"Live a little!" Blake encouraged. "Have another drink."

As he moved to offer Austin the bottle of Jack, he slipped, and it flung out of his hand, smashing to the roof by Montana's feet.

"Ow!" she exclaimed, more surprised than hurt, really, when she was hit by a ricocheting shard of glass. Then she looked down at her foot. "Oh. Crap." It was more than a shard of glass. A large piece of the bottle was sticking out of her skin, right above the ankle, blood slowly trickling down from the gash.

Springing into action, Austin reached out to hold her leg still. "Don't move." He carefully disentangled himself from her and moved around to crouch in front of her. "Do I take it out?"

"*Fuuuuck*," Blake said slowly, looking down at the mess he'd made, his reaction speed clearly dulled. "I'm sorry."

Montana shrugged, giggling a little. Maybe it was shock, or the slight buzz of alcohol, but she wasn't terribly concerned with her predicament at the moment.

Austin gave her an exasperated look, which only made her giggle more. "We need to call your parents and bring you to the hospital."

"But the grand finale's starting!" she protested, as fireworks shot off rapidly, bangs echoing over their heads.

"Are you drunk too?" he asked.

"It's fine," she insisted. "Just take it out."

While Montana *oohed* and *aahed* over the beautiful explosions, he carefully removed the piece of glass from her skin, seeming only mildly annoyed. Then he quickly shrugged out of his plaid overshirt and tied it tightly around her ankle to stop the flow of blood.

"See?" she said. "All better."

"You get two minutes," he told her. "And then we're taking you to get this checked out. You might need stitches."

"Yes, sir." She gave him her best attempt at a solemn nod, but it was ruined when another giggle slipped out.

"Blake, sit your ass down," Austin demanded. "Now."

Blake obeyed, and the three of them watched for another minute as the fireworks lit up the sky, bathing them in vibrant colors. Her ankle did hurt a little, Montana realized now. But it was fine. She didn't want to be anywhere else.

Like Blake had said—this was a perfect night.

CHAPTER TEN

NOW

*I*t's fine.

Everything is fine.

Montana has *not* lit a match and tossed it into the dumpster that currently is her life. Austin's not going to fire her.

Really.

It's fine.

Or it will be. Eventually. Once the embarrassment has worn off and they give it maybe a week or two of awkwardly avoiding each other at work. Then it will be fine. They'll forget about it and—

Oh, who is she kidding?

She's not forgetting about last night any time this decade. Even through this morning's hangover headache, she can still feel his lips on hers, his hands pressed into her sides, his hair between her fingers.

Fuck.

Trying to be his friend was hard enough before. How the hell is she supposed to do it now?

One small mercy is that she doesn't have to work today, so at least she can put some more space between the incident and seeing him. He still seemed confused when she left him at the restaurant, but when he woke up today, surely, he would have remembered all the reasons why what they did was a horribly bad idea. She hurt him. Then he hurt her. And starting something again would risk them repeating that pattern.

She's in the middle of drinking her coffee out on the porch, while working on the Sunday crossword on her iPad and trying in vain not to think about him, when her phone rings.

And it's him.

You've got to be kidding.

Didn't he get the avoidance memo? Or is he calling to tell her she needs to find a new job because she made things too weird?

No. This isn't her fault. It's not like she jumped him out of nowhere. She's pretty sure he initiated it, in fact. He's not allowed to be upset with her now.

She takes a deep breath before accepting the call. "Hey." That sounded calm, right?

"Hey," he says. "Hope I didn't wake you."

"It's eleven thirty."

"But I know you were up late."

She wants to tell him he's the one who pushed her to stay and drink last night. But that would lead him to the thoughts of what happened *after* they started drinking, so she just says, "So were you."

"Brittani dropped Kalen off before eight so she could go to work. I don't usually get the chance to sleep in."

Damn, how can he function on only a few hours of sleep?

"Oh, well, I'm awake," she says. "Are you calling for a reason? Not that you can't call just to call. I mean, it's fine." *Mental facepalm.* Why is she babbling?

He clears his throat. "Sorry, yeah. So the library over in Brewer does this Sunday evening movie-in-the-grass thing during the summer. Kalen and I had plans to go see *Shrek* tonight, and I was actually wondering if you wanted to come."

Seriously? So much for space.

"If you don't want to, it's okay," he rushes on when she doesn't respond right away. "If you think it's lame or whatever. But ever since you babysat him at the restaurant, he's been mentioning you. He keeps asking when he can play with Miss Montana again."

She laughs, despite her nerves. "Okay, that makes me sounds like a Miss America contestant."

"As long as your talent's not singing."

"Hey!"

"So what do you say?"

Her head is spinning. This proposition is the last thing she expected after last night, but if the goal is to not screw up the tenuous friendship they've been building, then maybe it would be weirder to refuse. And she can't disappoint a child. "Sure, I can go. Sounds good."

"Great," he says, voice not hinting at any of the mixed emotions she's currently experiencing. "Kalen will be excited."

"Tell him I'm excited too."

Excited may be the last thing she feels, but she supposes it's in there, way deep down. So she's not exactly lying.

"Will do," Austin says brightly. Then he gives her the time he'll pick her up and lets her go without so much as a reassurance that the two of them will be okay. Almost as if they don't even need reassurances because nothing monumental happened.

How can he be so unaffected by last night? He kissed her. *He. Kissed. Her.* And then she told him they should just stay friends, and he's wholeheartedly going along with that like it's easy for him. Or maybe it's not.

Maybe he's only trying to make this seem normal because Kalen wants to see her.

Frankly, she's surprised her babysitting efforts were that much of a hit with the kid. She was bad at the voices, after all. But if she and Austin are ever truly going to be friends, it's important that Kalen likes her. So this is a good thing, right?

Right.

They'll forget about the ill-advised kissing and the groping, and everything will be fine.

Before Montana realizes it, her coffee has turned cold. And she's pretty sure she's read the same crossword clue about ten times without her brain connecting any dots. Giving up, she heads inside.

She needs to shower. What do you wear for a play date with a five-year-old and his father who's your ex-boyfriend-turned-sort-of-friend anyway?

◆

FLIP FLOPS, LEGGINGS, a loose-fitting tee, and a lightweight cardigan. That's a casual, not-trying-too-hard outfit. And if it took Montana three tries to look like she's not trying too hard . . . well, nobody needs to know that. Especially ex-boyfriends who are probably going to look hot legitimately without even trying.

When she climbs into Austin's Jeep, Kalen immediately engages her in conversation from the backseat. "Are you excited for the movie? Daddy says it's about an ogre, and I don't know what that is, but it sounds cool."

"It *is* cool," she tells him, twisting around to smile at him. "But the best part is the donkey."

"Actually, the best part is going to be the popcorn," Austin says.

"We went to a couple of these last year, and they make the best popcorn. Seriously. I don't know what they do to it, but it's better than the movie theater's."

Montana relaxes into her seat. Okay, this isn't too weird. "I didn't know there'd be snacks."

"Of course there are snacks," Austin informs her. "You can bring your own, too, but it's more fun to get them there."

"If you're good," Kalen pipes up, "Daddy will even let you have the nuts!"

This makes Montana snort in the most unattractive way, her hand flying to her mouth to try to cover it up. Her eyes are wide and tearing up with the laughter she's holding in when she risks a look at Austin. His cheeks are flushed, and she can't help but derive a small, savage pleasure from this.

"He, uh . . . means these cinnamon sugar roasted almonds they sell there."

She fights her grin. "Right. Of course. Sounds delicious."

Austin shoots her a dirty look, though he's clearly struggling not to smile too.

"Daddy doesn't like the nuts," Kalen says, "but I think that's crazy."

"It's nuts!" Montana agrees, quirking an amused eyebrow at Austin.

He shakes his head. "Nuts shouldn't be sweet."

Her eyebrows attempt to climb her forehead now, and she has to bite back her laughter again.

"You know what?" Austin says, gaze shooting to Kalen through the rearview mirror. "Why don't we play the no talking game for the rest of the way?"

"That's not a game," Kalen complains.

"It is now. Whoever can go the rest of the ride without saying a word wins."

Montana can't help but smirk. It's fun seeing him flustered like this.

The no talking thing lasts maybe two minutes before Kalen announces, "I don't like this game."

"Yeah, it's boring," Montana agrees. And she's fully pleased with herself for earning the exasperated look Austin sends her way.

By the time they get to the library grounds, she's feeling much more at ease. Maybe she should feel a little bad that her ease came from Austin's discomfort, but hey, it was *his* kid chiming in with the inappropriate comments. Totally not her fault.

When Austin takes a large blanket out of the back of the SUV, she's hit with a small wave of nostalgia. They've never done a movie on the grass together, but they used to grab blankets for outdoor seating at plenty of other places, like the lake.

It's not until they've picked their spot and spread out the blanket that she starts to feel unsure again. How close is she allowed to sit to him? The blanket's big, but not that big. And his kid is here. How does she keep a respectable distance without looking like she's scared to go near him?

The dilemma's solved for her when Austin sits on one side of the blanket, stretching his legs all the way out in front of him, and Kalen plops down right beside him, leaving Montana to take the boy's other side.

There. Now they have a buffer.

"Oh my god, I can smell the popcorn!" she says, craning her neck to find the refreshments stand set up in a large tent behind them.

"Yeah, but I usually wait to get it until right before the movie starts," Austin tells her. "Otherwise Kalen will eat it all right away."

Kalen shakes his head. "Not uh. Daddy eats it way faster than me."

Shrugging guiltily, Austin admits, "I *may* be the one who eats it all."

When Kalen spots a few kids playing tag off to the side of the seating area, he asks if he can join them, and Austin tells him to make sure he stays close by. Which suddenly leaves Montana and Austin alone. On a blanket that seems to be shrinking by the second.

And she was right about him looking hot. He's wearing a deep purple short-sleeved shirt, with a slight v-neck and a pocket that both draw her attention to his well-defined chest.

"So . . ." she says when she can't take the silence any longer.

He angles himself to face her. "Thank you for coming with us. I know you probably weren't expecting to hear anything from me so soon after . . . uh." He glances down, running his finger over the blanket. "But I completely agree with what you said about not wanting to lose this friendship. I hope you meant it."

"Of course I did."

"Good. So. Friends."

"Friends," she repeats. And when he extends his hand to shake hers, she complies, ignoring the tiny jolt when their palms press together. Then, still holding on to her hand, he leans forward and pulls her in for a hug. The way her body thrums with pleasure as she settles against him is a little harder to ignore.

She still maintains that their collision last night was inevitable. And it didn't kill her. But now she has to live among the wreckage, with the knowledge that his lips are still the softest she's ever kissed. Sitting here with him and knowing he's not hers is starting to feel like penance yet again.

Before the movie starts, Austin offers to go grab the snacks, wrangling Kalen on his way. The two of them return to the blanket loaded up with a giant cardboard bucket of popcorn, a paper cone filled with nuts (insert smirk emoji), a tray of nacho chips with cheese sauce, and two large drink cups.

Kalen has the popcorn wedged between his side and the crook of his elbow, with the nuts grasped carefully in his other hand. Montana rises to her knees to take the bucket before he drops it. With a hand free, the boy starts pulling multiple bags of candy out of the pocket of his hoodie, dropping them one by one onto the blanket. "You must really like snacks, because we never get this much."

"I didn't know what you'd want," Austin says, "so I kind of got everything."

"You didn't have to do that," Montana tells him.

He passes her one of the cups and the nachos so he can kneel down. They arrange everything in the middle, in front of Kalen's crossed legs, and then Montana takes a sip from her cup, smiling at the taste of Cherry Coke.

Austin reaches into his back pocket and hands her a bag of Starbursts. "Figured these were a must-have though."

Running her fingers over the plastic, she's unable to meet his eyes, touched he remembered both her favorite candy and her favorite soda. "You were right."

Didn't know what she'd want, her ass.

The three of them settle in to enjoy the movie together. During which, Austin entertains not only Kalen, but Montana as well, with his impressions of Donkey. And Kalen's totally right. He's better at the voices.

They all make themselves more comfortable as the movie goes on, and by the time Smashmouth sings "I'm a Believer," Austin is lying on his side and Kalen is on his stomach, his head at the bottom end of the blanket. In the absence of their buffer, Montana and Austin still maintained the child-sized space between them, only at some point Austin's arm crept out far enough that his knuckles were brushing against her thigh. The contact was minimal, but when the credits end and he abruptly sits up, she misses it fiercely.

Nope. Stop that.

Just friends. There was a fucking handshake and everything.

Kalen falls asleep during the ride back, and as they pull into Montana's driveway, he's snoring much louder than any five-year-old should have the right to snore.

Montana takes a glance into the backseat and laughs softly. "This was fun," she tells Austin truthfully. "I'd invite you in, but . . . you've gotta get him home."

"He's totally conked out," Austin says. "I can bring him in and put him on the couch."

"Oh." She didn't think she'd actually have to follow through with the half-hearted offer to let him inside. Not like he hasn't been inside her house a million times before, but that makes this feel more like a date.

So far she's survived the evening with only minimal awkwardness, and she doesn't want to risk it. But he's looking at her expectantly, so she says, "Yeah. Sure. We could have a drink." She glances again to the sleeping child and cringes. "Or not a drink. I mean—"

"Let's get inside," he gently cuts her off.

"Okay."

They hop out of the vehicle and Austin opens Kalen's door, leaning in and pulling him from the backseat, carefully cradling him in his arms. Montana shuts the door for him as quietly as possible, and then walks up the porch, unlocking the house and letting Austin in first. He settles the boy on the couch, head propped on a cushion, and then pulls a blanket off the back of it to cover him with.

Montana motions for Austin to follow her into the kitchen. There, she sets her purse on the counter and pulls out the almost empty bag of Starbursts. Selecting a pink one, she unwraps it and pops it in her mouth, savoring the sugary sweetness on her tongue.

"I'm surprised you didn't finish those already," Austin says, keeping his voice low.

"I was trying to save some." At his outstretched hand, she wrinkles her nose before peering into the bag and taking out one little square, setting it in his palm. "You can have an orange one. Nobody likes orange."

"Hey, I like orange!" he protests.

She gives him a wise-ass smirk. "I know."

He lunges for her, lightning fast, his arm winding around her middle to tickle her side.

"*Eep! Stop!*" she squeals, trying to wriggle away. "You'll wake up Kalen."

His solution is to clap his other hand over her mouth as he resumes the attack. She twists away, but he follows her until he's managed to crowd her against the counter, effectively trapping her. Her laughter dies away, and she's starting to catch her breath when she realizes their position. His proximity. His body heat. His green eyes, laser-focused on her.

For a moment, he doesn't move, other than his eyes darting down to her lips and back up. He tightens his grasp on her waist, bunching up her cardigan. Gazing at her lips again, he inches in closer.

"What are you doing?" she whispers.

He pauses but doesn't let her go. "Listen, I'll respect whatever you decide. If you're really only interested in being friends, then we can just be friends. But I'd be lying if I said I'm not dying for a repeat of last night. Minus the you-walking-out-on-me part."

As he smooths her hair away from her face, she holds her breath, waiting, waiting.

"Being near you," he goes on, "but not able to touch you . . . It feels wrong. Like my body still thinks it belongs with yours."

The confession punches the air out of her lungs.

She's not the only one feeling these things then.

"I—" she starts.

God, what are they doing?

"Can you honestly tell me that what happened last night didn't feel good?" he asks.

"We were drunk."

Cradling her face, he says, "We're not drunk now."

No, they aren't.

And the kiss last night may have been inevitable, but *this*, right now? This is a choice.

When she slowly leans in, he meets her halfway. The hand on her face moves to tangle in her hair, and then he's using his grip on it to tug her head slightly to the side, exposing her neck. The edge of the counter digs into her lower back, but she doesn't care because he's kissing and licking and sucking all down the column of her throat. Little noises start escaping her, half gasps, half moans.

"*Shhh,*" he murmurs into her skin before resuming his work.

"I can't help it when you're doing that!" she hisses quietly.

He pulls away only enough to look at her. "Upstairs?"

She considers it. She wishes she could say it's a hard decision, but it only takes her a second to nod in agreement.

Wasting no time, he lifts her under her ass, hiking her up so she can wrap her legs around his waist. And *fuck. Yes. This.*

He carries her back through the living room, shushing her again, and then up the stairs. Holy hell, how is he making this seem easy? He could pick her up when they were young, but she's certainly not the same size as she was back then. But he isn't either. *These muscles. Damn.*

When he walks them down the hall, he passes her bedroom door, clearly on his way to her parents' old room since it's the master.

"Wait," she tells him, tugging on his sleeve. "I'm in there." She jerks her head behind him.

He looks confused for a moment before turning around and carrying her into her room, where he deposits her not so gently onto the bed, letting her bounce a little as he lets go. She doesn't complain, because suddenly he's standing between her legs, whipping off his shirt. She hums her appreciation at the sight and reaches out to touch his abs, but he grabs her wrist to stop her, laughing at her whine of protest.

He slides her cardigan off her shoulders and pulls her shirt over her head, and then his hands are on her breasts, cupping them over her magenta bra, his thumbs dipping down under the lacy material to swipe at her nipples. They harden instantly, aching for more attention.

She needs to get her hands on him before she goes crazy. As she begins exploring the hard panes of his stomach, he somehow shifts her so that she's lying on the bed properly with him hovering over her.

It's all happening fast, but that's okay, because now he's grinding his pelvis down into hers and she's pushing up to meet him. And this, right here, is everything. The years have melted away and everything is centered on the two of them, as they should be, in this bed together.

He's sucking what is sure to become a large hickey at the top of her breast, squeezing it with one hand while his other hand works to get his jeans undone and shoved down his legs. He pulls away from her long enough to get rid of them completely and toss them to the floor.

His hands are tugging on her leggings now, peeling them down, when a loud wail comes from downstairs.

"*Daddy?* Daddy!" Kalen shouts.

Austin is off of her and running out her bedroom door before she can even sit up, stumbling into his jeans and yanking his shirt over his head as he goes.

The moment he's out of her sight, the guilt hits her. They weren't supposed to do this. And with his freaking kid asleep downstairs? What is wrong with her?

No.

No, she didn't start this. He did. Again. She's not going to shoulder all the blame.

She takes one more moment to compose herself, then quickly locates her shirt and gets dressed before going downstairs.

By the time she reaches the living room, Austin is standing there holding Kalen on his hip, uttering soothing noises into the boy's hair. He doesn't look at all like he was just ravishing her thirty seconds ago, but Montana's willing to bet that she still looks thoroughly ravished. And good god, he didn't even get her pants off. Imagine what he could've done with five more minutes.

"He got scared when he woke up and didn't know where he was and couldn't see me," Austin explains.

"Of course."

"We should go."

"Yeah, of course, I understand." She follows them to the front door, with Kalen watching her over Austin's shoulder. He seems calmer already, but she still feels like this was a colossal fuck-up.

Austin doesn't look mad when he turns at the door to say goodbye though. He just gives her a sympathetic look and says he'll see her later.

As soon as his SUV leaves the driveway, Montana goes back up to her room, sinking onto the bed in frustration. She tries to avoid mentally replaying what just happened, because somehow, despite the abrupt panicked ending, she's still a little turned on.

But it's impossible to keep Austin out of her head.

The memories are all around her, and not only of tonight.

This certainly isn't the first time they've hooked up in this bedroom. Not even close.

Ignoring the lingering sense of guilt, she slowly slips her hand down the front of her leggings, beneath her underwear, and starts rubbing in tiny circles. She'll never be able to fall asleep otherwise.

THEN

*M*ontana was half asleep when a *taptaptap* startled her eyes open. *What was that?*

Hearing the noise again, she sat up in bed, looking around. "Holy sh—" She clapped a hand to her mouth, not wanting to wake up her parents.

Austin was outside her window, perched on the porch roof, grinning at her.

"Are you crazy?" she hissed as she opened the window.

"I climbed the tree," he said matter-of-factly. As if the explanation for *how* he got up here was more important than *why* he was here. "Are you gonna move so I can get in?"

She shook her head but moved back anyway, urging him to be quiet as he crossed over the windowsill and landed on the floor. He was allowed in her room, but she doubted that allowance extended to middle-of-the-night-while-everyone-else-was-asleep visits.

"Well?" she asked, as he sat on the edge of the bed and pulled off his sneakers.

"I needed to see you."

"I was supposed to see you tomorrow."

He shrugged. "I couldn't wait that long."

She wanted to ask him again if he was crazy, but then he smiled, turning the full force of his dimples on her, and she suddenly didn't care if they got caught. Getting back in bed, she held up one end of the covers, inviting him to slip in and join her. When he did, she rolled onto her side so she could rest her head on his chest. His arm wrapped around her, and he began rubbing circles against her hip over the thin material of her silk shorts.

"How was vacation?" she whispered.

"Boring."

"Don't even tell me Cape Cod was boring, you spoiled brat."

"Okay, fine. Some of it was fun. But it would've been better if you were there."

He'd come close to convincing his parents to let Montana go with them on their annual trip, but in the end, his mom had said it was supposed to be family time. Montana wasn't sure her own parents would have let her go anyway.

She'd missed him while he was gone, but it gave her more time to spend with Sloane. They'd binged *The O.C.* for days on end after Sloane's older sister told them about it and they realized that Rachel Bilson from *Hart of Dixie* was in it. Montana had subsequently started saying, "*Ew!*" at any opportunity and then laughing about it.

Austin had apparently handled the two-week separation worse than her, judging by the way he was currently sniffing the top of her head.

"What are you doing, weirdo?"

"Your hair smells good," he whispered. "I missed the way you smell."

"*Ew.*" She scooted up to kiss him, then settled back down with her head on the pillow, facing him. "Now tell me about your vacation."

He reached out, going for the thin strap of her camisole and sliding it down her shoulder. "My dad and I went paddle boarding, which was pretty sweet. And Andrea spent every minute on her phone texting her friends and ignoring the rest of us. So much for family time, right? We did play a lot of games of Setback in the cabin at night, but Andrea and I kept losing because, again, she wasn't paying any attention."

"Did you come over here as soon as you guys got home?"

"I had to wait until I was sure my parents were asleep so they wouldn't hear the truck start."

"You're crazy," Montana told him fondly.

Rolling on top of her, he got to work removing her clothes. "I had to see you. I *needed* this." When he pressed himself against her, she could feel him already hard through his shorts. His hand snuck down to touch her as he kissed her.

Once they were both naked, she told him regretfully, "We can't have sex. The bed will squeak."

He groaned into her mouth. The way he was acting like he'd die if he couldn't be with her right now was a bit dramatic, but also endearing.

She pushed him onto his back and then slid down his body, taking him all the way into her mouth in one fluid motion. After a few seconds, she pulled off and told him, "You need to be quick."

He nodded vigorously, mouth dropped open slightly, and she went back to work. It was really up to her to make it quick, but she knew all the tricks he liked. When she pressed her tongue to the sensitive skin behind his balls, he started leaking. And soon after, as she swirled her tongue around the head of his dick, his whole body shuddered, and he shot off like a rocket into her mouth.

As she came back up to lay beside him, she thought of her first time trying this and how uncertain she was. She'd had a lot of practice since then, but it still always felt satisfying to be able to make him lose control like that.

Breathing heavily, he said, "Just give me a minute."

"You don't have to."

"*Ana.*" He rolled over, his hand cupping the back of her head to draw her mouth to his, dipping his tongue in briefly before he pulled away. "*Let me.*"

She nodded, and the next thing she knew, she was the one gently being pushed onto her back. She should have reminded him to hurry up, but her sense of urgency was forgotten as he began to trail featherlight kisses down her neck, her collarbone, over her breasts, and down her stomach until he reached her thighs. There, he set his attention on the creases of her inner thighs, sucking harder and nipping at her skin. By the time he reached his main target, she was already in a blissful haze.

If she knew all the things he liked, he knew her and her body just as well, maybe even better. He knew if he dug his fingers into her ass, she'd arch up into him. And he knew that when she got close to coming, she wouldn't stay quiet, so now he covered her mouth with his hand to block her moans as he finished her off.

They lay there together afterward, both fully sated, his fingers tracing patterns over her stomach. She was so tempted to ask him to stay, but there would be hell to pay if her parents found him in her bed in the morning. So, reluctantly, she nudged his shoulder and told him it was time for him to go.

"Five more minutes," he said.

Letting out a contented sigh, she gave in. "Five more minutes."

CHAPTER ELEVEN

NOW

With the restaurant closed yesterday, Montana hasn't had to face Austin yet. And Blake's here with her for the lunch shift today, so he probably won't be coming in until later when she's headed home. She kind of expected to hear from him yesterday, though. Not that she has any idea what he would say.

Does he regret it? Does *she* regret it?

Honestly, at this point, she's not sure. But it's probably good they got interrupted. They really need to think this through with their brains, instead of letting their hormones think for them.

He said his body wanted hers, but did *he* want *her*? That's an important distinction. If this is only about sex for him, she's not willing to risk their friendship for it. No matter how badly she wants his hands on her body again.

And she's absolutely *not* thinking about his hands as she cuts lemons to get ready for her shift. She's not thinking about his hands as she makes the two retirees their Manhattans. She's not thinking about them when she passes a younger guy his blackened chicken alfredo. Not thinking about them when she inputs orders into the computer, when she counts out change, or when she's washing glassware.

She's especially not thinking about his hands when her phone buzzes with a text message and it's his name on the screen.

Why aren't you sleeping in the master bedroom?

Confused, she just stares at her phone a few moments. This is what he has to say to her? Really? She glances at the customers sitting at her bar to make sure they're all happy before typing a response. It would feel weird taking my parents' room.

That's silly. All the rooms are yours now.

So I can use whichever one I want. She sends a shrugging emoji to highlight how she doesn't see an issue here.

Your bed has a metal frame and no headboard.

So?

You should get a nicer bed and take the master bedroom and act like it's your house. Leave the smaller room for a guest room if your parents want to visit.

But they wouldn't be guests. It's their house.

The dots to indicate he's typing go away and come back. Go away and come back again. Then a message finally comes. You're ridiculous.

Grinning at her phone, she sends another shrugging emoji. Maybe she should be offended, but she can picture him on the other end, shaking his head with that small smile he uses when he doesn't understand or agree with her but still loves her anyway.

Likes. Still *likes* her anyway. Not love. Not anymore. Just because she can still catalogue all his facial expressions doesn't mean things are the same as they were before.

When she sets her phone back on the counter, she realizes Blake is standing over at the service end of the bar, watching her. At first, she thinks he's going to say something about her being on her phone, but the rules are pretty relaxed here and she wasn't ignoring her customers. He clearly wants to say something though.

She gives him a questioning look, and he just raises his eyebrows in response.

Then it hits her. *Duh.* Austin must have mentioned something to him about the kissing Sunday night. Or Saturday night. Or both. Blake is his best friend. Of course they'd talk.

As she moves over to him, he opens his mouth to say something, but before he can, she says, "Don't."

He frowns. "You promised me."

"I promised I wouldn't hurt him. I'm not hurting him." For what it's worth, she keeps trying not to give in to him so that she won't end up hurting him.

"I hope you know what you're doing," Blake says with a sigh.

No, Montana has no idea what she's doing. What she and Austin are doing. She needs to talk to him about it and find out.

She tries to come up with something to say to assure Blake she's not fucking up, but she may, in fact, be in the process of doing just that. Thankfully, he lets her off the hook for now, giving her a curt nod and walking away.

The rest of her shift goes smoothly. Austin shows up as she's finishing her sidework and getting ready to leave. He waves at her in greeting as he's passing through the room but doesn't stop to say hi.

As much as she's tempted to duck out of here with no further interaction, she has to be more mature about this. So after she grabs her purse, she goes to find him. She catches him as he's coming out of the storeroom carrying a large box of receipt paper. "Hey."

"Oh, hey," he says.

"Can we talk?"

"About what?"

She gives him a pointed look. "You know about what."

"Yeah, ok. Um . . ." He glances around, looking a tiny bit nervous.

"I mean, not here, obviously," she says.

He readjusts the box in his arm. "No, not here. We can talk tomorrow."

"Okay, good."

"I'll pick you up at eight a.m."

She starts to nod, but then—"Wait, what? Pick me up for what?"

"Just trust me."

"Ohh-kay . . . See you tomorrow then."

The smirk he gives her is a little concerning. "Yes, you will."

◆

FORCING HER TO be up and ready by eight a.m. is bad enough, but when Austin rolls into her driveway at seven fifty, Montana's tempted to make him wait in the car for ten minutes just out of spite. Instead, she heads out the door in a cropped Beatles tee, ripped jean shorts, and flip flops, and hops in his passenger seat.

His eyes widen when he looks at her, but if her outfit isn't appropriate for whatever it is they're doing, she doesn't care. Maybe he should have offered her some details instead of insisting on being mystery man. Anyway, he's wearing a simple white tee and fitted plaid shorts, so she's probably fine.

"Do you even listen to The Beatles?"

"All you need is love," she says brightly before pulling a *so there* face.

He grabs a paper bag from the center console and drops it into her lap. "Breakfast."

She thought they might be *going* to breakfast, but she unrolls the bag and peers inside, pleased to find four glazed donuts. "Thanks."

"They're not all for you," he says, prompting her to roll her eyes. Then he points at the two paper cups in the holders. "One of those is yours."

She reaches into the bag for a donut and takes a big bite. The glazed icing melts deliciously in her mouth. It also tastes incredibly familiar. She takes another bite, chewing thoughtfully. "Hey! These are from Dave's!"

"You know it."

Dave's Donuts is technically in the next town over, right on the border, but Montana considers it a Hartley staple anyway. She's glad to know it's still there.

The two of them used to drive fifteen minutes out of their way to pick these up before school at least once a week. It's not as fancy as all the newer coffee shops nowadays, but the place had been around forever even back when she was a teenager, and she imagines it hasn't changed at all. They only served regular and decaf coffee, no lattes, no flavors. And iced coffee, technically, but those always tasted weak and watered down. She was pretty sure they just poured the regularly brewed coffee over a cup of ice when you ordered one, so she stuck with hot coffees, even in the summer.

Grabbing hers now, she takes a tentative sip. It's loaded up with extra cream and sugar, way lighter and sweeter than she takes her coffees from anywhere else. But this is the best way to order it at Dave's.

"Good?" Austin asks, eyes flitting over to catch her smiling down at the cup before he looks back to the road.

"So good. I can't believe how long it's been since I had this, but it tastes exactly the same."

"You might be disappointed to hear this, but they serve bagels now."

"Bagels? They can't do that, it's Dave's *Donuts*!"

He laughs at her overreaction and sticks out his hand for a donut. "At least they still serve the best glazed in the state."

"Amen."

She's already on her second one by the time he merges onto the highway. "Are you going to tell me where we're going now?"

"Don't worry about it. We've got almost an hour to talk."

The childish urge to pinch him for continuing to withhold their destination comes over her, but she doesn't do it. They do need to have a serious conversation about where they stand with each other. "Right. So." She might as well come out and say it. "What the hell's going on with us?"

When he hesitates, she thinks he's going to make her spell it out further. Then—"I don't know, but I'm certainly enjoying it." His grip tightens on the wheel. "Aren't you?"

"Yes, of course, but—"

"Do we really need to analyze it? If we're both enjoying it, can't we let whatever happens happen?"

That's what they did while she was in college. No strings, they didn't try to define it. And she thought it was working, that they were both happy—up until the day he decided it *wasn't* working for him and he ended it just like that, with no warning, no discussion.

They're more mature now. They need to make sure they're both on the same page.

"But if it's just sex—"

"Stop," he says, cutting her off again. It would annoy her that he isn't letting her finish a sentence, except she's not sure where she's going with any of them anyway. He turns to stare intensely at her for a couple beats before cutting his eyes back to the road. "You know it's not just sex. It could *never* be just sex with us."

Oh.

Well then.

She takes a big gulp of her coffee, stalling while she tries to figure out how to settle this conversation. She appreciates his admission that this is more than only a physical attraction, but they still need to be careful. Like wear-a-helmet-and-kneepads careful. If feelings are involved, then that means feelings can get hurt.

She's not exactly a *que sera, sera* person. Neither is he.

But how well does she really know him now? Maybe he's changed. If he's willing to take a chance and see where this goes, then she is too.

"Okay," she says finally. "Good to know. So . . . we're doing this."

"I sure hope so," he says. He runs his hand briefly over her thigh, eliciting a shiver from her.

She smiles. *Que fucking sera, right?*

Rolling down her window, she kicks off her flip flops and props her feet on the ledge with her knees bent. His quiet laugh makes her ask, "What?"

The fond look he gives her warms her skin even more than the sun's gentle morning rays. "Some things never change."

♦

THEY GET OFF the highway in a town Montana doesn't recognize, driving a few more minutes until Austin finally pulls into a large strip mall. He parks in front of the very last store, which is at least three times the size of all the others. The sign reading ROSIE'S CONSIGNMENTS is painted with red flowers.

"What's this?" she asks.

"It's a consignment store."

"I can read the sign." Has he always been such a smartass? "What are we doing here?"

"Getting you a bed," Austin says, before promptly hopping out of the Jeep and striding off.

She scrambles to put on her shoes so she can follow him. Catching up, she grabs onto his wrist. "I don't need a bed."

"You need to move into the master bedroom. And you need more than a double bed." He doesn't slow down, but he shakes free of her grip only to take her hand instead.

Her annoyance slips away as their fingers entwine. "What's wrong with a double bed?"

"There's no room for me in it."

When she gapes at him, he just smirks back at her until she eventually breaks down and starts laughing. She smacks his arm for good measure as they enter the store, but truthfully, she's always wanted a bigger bed.

Her old apartment was a shoebox, so she didn't have enough space. But Austin told her to stop using her life in California as an excuse, and he's right. She has the space now. She should take advantage of it.

Still, she feels the need to state, "You can't just make decisions for me."

He squeezes her hand, leading her through the maze of furniture and décor. "I would never try to make decisions for you."

That's probably true. He hated her decision to go to college all the way across the country, but he never attempted to change her mind. Which was probably for the best, because if he had, she would've been furious, and their breakup likely would've been messier than it was.

"But I know you," he continues, turning them down an aisle toward all the bedroom stuff like he knows exactly where he's going. "I think you'll be happier about your living situation if you're not sleeping in your tiny childhood room."

She doesn't respond.

She's skeptical about finding anything she actually likes among the sea of random junk. But then she spots a slatted wooden headboard with a subtle curling pattern carved along the top. "This is nice," she comments, running her finger along one of the grooves.

Austin points to the matching dresser. "It's a set."

"I don't need a dresser," she says, even though she knows he's going to argue this point. But she's starting to suspect they're both arguing for the sake of arguing now. Like a game.

Sure enough, he says, "Half your clothes were piled on the night-stand."

"*Half* is an exaggeration. And that's because I'm a slob." She's surprised he even noticed the state of her bedroom that night, since all *she* was focused on was the fire igniting between them.

"No, you're not. And you'd be even neater if you had a place to put everything."

She eyes the dresser contemplatively. It has the same curling pattern as the headboard. And if she's moving into the bigger room, it'll look depressingly empty without some more furniture. She sighs, cranky that she's losing the game. "Fine."

He grabs the headboard and most of the other pieces of the bed-frame, only handing her a couple thin, long boards to carry. Then they head to the front of the store and send an employee to handle the dresser.

While they're waiting, she notices a dark purple area rug. She reaches out to see if it's as soft as it looks, smiling to herself when she discovers it is. "This might look good in the living room." Really, she's considering less how it will look, and more how it will feel to squish her toes into it.

"Get it," Austin says. So she does.

When it's time to pay, he's quick to take out his wallet, but she bats him away. "Absolutely not."

He frowns. "This was my idea. I planned to buy it for you."

"I appreciate everything you've been doing for me," she tells him sincerely, taking the wallet from his hand and tucking it back into his pocket. "But I can afford this. Remember, you gave me a job? And now I use my boobs to rake in the tips from horny drunk dudes on the week-ends."

The young cashier laughs, and Austin shoots him a menacing look. Then he watches as Montana fishes out her own debit card. "Okay, fine. But I'm buying the mattress."

She only agrees to this because he looks so determined to do something nice for her (as if his good deed list isn't long enough already). It's not until they're at the mattress store that she realizes the mattress costs way more than the bedframe. But she doesn't say anything, because she really doesn't have that much extra money to spend. She's still working on saving for the washer and dryer.

Damn, she should totally bake him a cake later. Or five of them. Maybe throw in a foot massage.

They're quiet on their way back to Hartley, but it's a companionable quiet. The sun is shining high in the sky now, Austin's tapping his fingers on the steering wheel and humming along to the stereo, and Montana's life is really starting to look up, huh?

Right after she thinks this, the sky darkens, and not even a minute later, it's pouring. She's going to try not to take this as a sign. "Everything will get soaked when we unload it," she says worriedly.

"Nah," he says, "it'll pass. Rain's moving the other way."

Grabbing the donut bag, he takes out the last one he saved, tearing it in two and wordlessly offering her half. He really is too good to her. He deserves ten cakes, a full body massage, and so much more.

She just hopes she can give him everything he deserves. Hopes she doesn't screw this up.

Because this, right here, is wonderful.

As they take the exit that will lead them back to Hartley, the rain has already cleared, and for the first time since she moved back, Montana actually feels like she's headed home.

THEN

*T*he cool night air tickled Montana's bare feet as they hung out the window of Austin's truck. From this position, her emerald green prom dress wasn't giving her too much modesty, but she didn't care. Maybe because she'd had quite a few drinks at the afterparty.

It was hard to believe she'd just gone to her junior prom. She'd been a little surprised that Austin even wanted to go. Neither of them had ever cared much about school dances. But he'd been all for it, buying her a fancy corsage and everything.

He'd even danced with her. He didn't like to dance in public, but he'd held out his hand, all Prince Charming style, and led her to the dance floor. His movements were a bit stilted and awkward, but so what?

It had been a wonderful night.

Glancing over at her now, Austin smiled fondly. He didn't seem to mind that she was a little drunk while he wasn't. Whenever they went to parties, they took turns with who got to drink, and tonight he'd been the responsible one. He'd spent the last hour keeping an eye on her, making sure she didn't do anything too embarrassing, like fall over and flash everyone.

She smiled back at him, the smile only growing as a scattering of raindrops began landing on her feet. It tickled in a delightful way. But very quickly, the rain was coming down much harder, and Austin said, "Okay, close the window."

"But it feels good!" she protested.

"You're gonna get soaked. And the seat's getting wet."

"Oh, *fine*." She swung her legs back into the truck and rolled up the window, but she made sure to pout about it. "You're no fun."

"Excuse you," he scoffed. "I'm very fun. You're drunk."

Giggling, she said, "Maybe juuuuuuust a little."

He rolled his eyes. "Uh huh. And when Blake wanted you to take a belly shot off him, you guys did that because you were both sober, right?"

"Oh god." She facepalmed, hit with an image reminding her that yes, she did in fact do that. Remembering something else, too, she turned accusing eyes on him. "You took a video, didn't you?"

"You bet your sweet ass, I did."

She groaned but laughed at the same time.

It was really pouring now. They were on a fairly deserted back road and Montana could barely see a few feet in front of the truck. She was glad she wasn't the one driving. Actually, Austin was starting to look a little stressed as he squinted past the windshield wipers that were working rapidly to keep up with the rain.

"Pull over."

He shook his head. "No, it's fine."

"Just pull over," she insisted.

He complied, carefully maneuvering off to the side of the road and setting the truck in park.

"Come on," she said.

"Come on, what?"

She was beaming at him now, absolutely zealous, as she gestured out the window.

"No way! Are you crazy?"

She laughed. "No, I'm drunk, remember?"

"Not happening."

"You said you were fun." Dramatically, she stuck out her lower lip and gave him her best impression of puppy dog eyes.

He stared at her a few moments, then sighed in resignation. "If you get pneumonia, I'm making sure your parents know it was totally your own fault."

With a drunken glee, she clapped her hands a few times before flinging open her door and hopping down to the pavement. She was still barefoot, but there was no way she would bother putting on those strappy heels ever again. Despite being cold, the rain felt so good.

When Austin got out, he came around to the front of the truck, in the beam of the headlights. He shook his head exasperatedly, but as she stood on her tiptoes to kiss him, he leaned down to meet her.

Montana could still hear the faint music coming from the stereo, so she spun in place, singing to herself and reveling in the moment. Suddenly, Austin grabbed her hand. She thought he was going to make her get back in the truck, but instead he pulled her in close, his free arm winding around her waist. And then they were dancing. In the middle of the night, in their formalwear, on the side of the street, in the pouring rain.

They probably *would* get pneumonia, but she never wanted this to end. She could blame her temporary insanity on the alcohol. But he couldn't. He was totally sober. Or maybe he was drunk on her.

Pushing the limp, wet strands of hair out of her eyes, she leaned in to kiss him again as raindrops ran down both their faces. When she pulled away, he grinned, twirling her out then back in again. She laughed as he repeated the move, and soon they were dancing wildly, without any real rhythm.

He looked so different dancing out here where they were all alone.

Freer and more relaxed. Neither of them was ever self-conscious about anything if it was just the two of them. They'd been entirely comfortable with each other for a long time.

She wished it could always be just the two of them.

Everything was better when they were together.

Montana had no idea how long they stayed out there, enjoying their own private universe, but they were both completely soaked through by the time they climbed back into the truck.

Austin held her hand the rest of the way home. And he didn't say a word about his wet seats.

CHAPTER TWELVE

NOW

*B*ack at the house, they work together carrying everything inside. Montana follows Austin's instructions, and in no time at all, she has a queen-sized bed set up in the master bedroom, complete with a set of new sheets. For the finishing touches, she grabs the pillows off her old bed and tosses them on the new one, and then they step back to take a look.

Austin places a hand on the top of the headboard, giving it a tiny shake. "See? Nice and sturdy."

"Looks it."

He eyes her pointedly up and down before raising an eyebrow. "Wanna try it out?"

God, yes, she thinks.

But despite what she *wants*, an annoyingly responsible voice inside her head—which sounds an awful lot like Spencer Hastings—urges her to take it slow. So she hesitates.

He's given her so much already, and it's like all she's doing is taking.

She doesn't want this to end up like before. When she took too much, not realizing it was hurting him.

"Hey," he says, reaching for her hand. "I don't want to push you for more than you're ready for."

Shaking her head, she tells him, "You're not pushing. I'm afraid of taking more than you should give me, that's all."

"You don't have to worry about me. I'm a big boy, Montana."

"Oh, I *know*," she says.

And it's probably her tiny smirk that does it.

One moment they're standing there facing each other. The next, she's being shoved down roughly onto the bed, her gasp of surprise swallowed up by his mouth on hers.

He's everywhere all at once, not letting her catch her breath. Sliding his hands up the bottom of her cropped tee to grope her breasts, sliding them up the bottom of her shorts to cup her ass and make her arch into him. Pressing her into the mattress and sucking hard on the side of her neck, ignoring her protest about him leaving a mark.

Her shirt is gone, tossed to the floor. Then her bra, flung carelessly across the room. Her shorts and underwear come down together. As he's pulling them off her legs, he only slows down for a moment to bite at her calf and lick—*lick!*—over the scar on her ankle. And that shouldn't be hot, but it is.

Everything is hot. She's already naked, but it feels like she's burning up. They should have turned on the overhead fan, but there's no way she's getting off this bed. Not like she has a choice. He's not letting her up. He's kissing her hard, his tongue plunging into her mouth, and he's the one taking now.

When he grinds down against her, she can feel how hard he is. Inexplicably, he's still fully clothed, and the roughness of his jeans against her nakedness is the most delicious contrast. She moans, reveling in the harsh friction on her softest parts.

But he should be naked too, she realizes through the lust-filled haze in her brain. Her hands move under his shirt, but they're ineffective at accomplishing her goal. She doesn't seem to have control over her own body at the moment. All she can do is hold on, gripping at the muscles of his back as he continues his assault on all of her senses.

Then he sits up on his heels, thighs bracketing hers, and yanks his shirt over his head.

Finally.

She's aching to get her hands all over him. But suddenly he rips at the bottom of his tee, tearing it all the way up to the collar. Her eyes widen, and before she can ask what he's doing, he's got her arms raised over her head. The next thing she knows, her wrists are tied together against one of the slats of the headboard.

Giving an experimental tug, she finds there's not much give. Her eyes grow impossibly wider at the predatory grin he fixes on her. Then he cradles her face in both hands and kisses her softly, melting her into the mattress. But *what, where, when*. When did he learn to do this?

For a moment, she wonders if he's trying to tie her down in more ways than one. To make sure she doesn't leave him again.

But then her nipple is between his teeth and her brain stops working, and her body's shouting, *yes, more, there, please, yes!* He bites down on it, just shy of too hard, and his fingers are pinching and rolling the other one, and her whole body is a live wire.

There's no turning back now. There was no turning back, really, since the day in tenth grade when he said, "*Be my girlfriend?*" and she said, "*Yes.*" But there's no one to interrupt them now, and all rational thought has flown out the window, and she's whining pathetically because she needs more, needs it all. She *needs needs needs*.

Thank fuck, he gets that. He can read her like her every desire is spelled out across her skin. Ceasing the delicious torture on her nipples, he begins to kiss and bite his way down her stomach. When he gets low enough, she jerks up, eager, but he laughs quietly and holds her down by her hips. She's whining again, so he says, "*Shhh*, I've got you."

And he does. He really does. He has her in ways he doesn't even know, but right now this is the only way that matters. The way he settles between her thighs, spreading them open under his large, capable hands.

She's straining her neck trying to watch him, which means she catches the evil twinkle in his eye when he bypasses the place she most wants him to go and focuses his attention instead on her inner thigh. His lips latch onto the sensitive skin and *ohhh. Yes. He remembers.* He remembers how to bliss her out on sensation so that she's wet for him before he even really gets started.

The noises she's making might not be considered human anymore. She's mewling like a cat, like *pleeease.* His mouth is kissing, licking, nipping, and his hands are massaging, squeezing, kneading. And then finally, finally, he takes pity on her.

His mouth zeroes in on the goal, and his tiny hum of pleasure when he tastes her is almost enough to make her come undone right then. He sets a steady pace, working her over until she's practically panting.

Her toes curl and her fingers squeeze into fists. She tugs once at her makeshift bonds, not really wanting to get free but fighting the desire to run her hands through his hair, to pull, and twist, and tug. The only thing she can do is wrap her legs around his shoulders, grinding her pussy up into his mouth. And she can't see it, but she knows he must be grinning at the way she's so greedy for more.

He pulls back a bit, and she huffs out a protest. But then he slides two fingers inside her, crooking them just the right way, and his mouth latches onto her clit, sucking hard, and *there, that's it, yesfuckyes, yes!* Intense waves of pleasure roll over her.

She rides out her orgasm, and he doesn't let up until she becomes too sensitive, groaning for him to back off. Then he's hovering above her, his chin slick, and she needs to kiss him right now. So she leans up, as far as she's able with her arms still tied over her head. As if reading her mind, he leans down, his mouth meeting hers. And when she relaxes her head back onto the pillow, he goes with her.

They kiss for what might be an eternity while she comes down from her high and things start coming back into focus.

"Untie me," she says once she's able to form words. When his happy expression morphs into a worried frown, she quickly shakes her head, wanting to assure him she's okay. She's great. "I just need to touch you. Please."

He complies at once, undoing the knot and whipping his ruined T-shirt to the floor.

As soon as she can get her hands on him, she doesn't know where to start. She slides her palms up the hard planes of his chest, loving the feel of the light coating of hair that wasn't there when they were younger. Then she delicately drags her nails back down over his nipples, and he shudders, eyes falling closed.

Reaching for his hip with one hand to tug him down closer, she wraps her other hand around his cock, which is still hard as a rock. Giving her pleasure turns him on. She's known this before, but to know it still, to have the proof in her hand, makes her chest ache a little. She wants to make him feel good too. Always.

She works him up and down, slowly at first, twisting her wrist on the upstroke. When her ministrations get faster, his hand shoots down to cover hers, stopping her. Wordlessly, she lets go, and he guides himself toward her entrance.

That's when he pauses, eyes brimming with heat and emotion. "Are you on—"

"Yes. We're good. Please."

It's hard for her to form coherent sentences with how badly she wants him, but that must be enough for him, because in one smooth thrust, he's filling her completely.

When he pulls out, it's only to slide back in agonizingly slowly. And Montana's not having that. Sometimes slow is wonderful, but that's not how she needs it right now. So when he tries to do it again, she thrusts up quickly to meet him, and thankfully he takes the hint, speeding up his pace.

They find a rhythm from there. A sweet, hard, steady rhythm that soon has her on the brink of another orgasm.

Surely, he can tell by her moans, by her leg wrapping around his waist to keep him close, by her nails digging in below his shoulder blades. His eyes stay locked on hers as he sucks his thumb into his mouth and then brings it down between their bodies to rub smooth circles over her clit. She clenches around him as she comes, and he groans, giving a few more frantic thrusts before he's spilling inside her with no barrier.

His forehead collapses gently onto her shoulder, and she twists her neck to kiss his temple. They stay like that a minute, connected, their breathing working on returning to normal. Then, with a look of reluctance, he pulls out and rolls onto his back beside her.

"What do you think?" he asks softly. "Did it meet your standards?"

"You're talking about the bed, of course."

He props himself on his elbow to face her. "Of course."

Grinning, she says, "I'd give it an exceeds expectations."

"Good."

When she rolls to her side too, he kisses her softly. If only they could stay in this bed for the rest of their lives where everything is warm and easy and happy. He's got one hand on her hip, fingertips grazing her ass, and he's looking at her like there's nowhere he'd rather be either.

Then her stomach growls loudly, and he laughs, flopping onto his back again.

"Shut up."

"Are you hungry?"

"Mayyybe," she admits. It's been a while since those donuts this morning.

"You want your favorite?" he asks, sitting up. And as she gazes at him questioningly, he adds, "Banana chocolate chip pancakes. Are they still your favorite?"

Her stomach grumbles again at the prospect. "Yeah, but I don't feel like getting dressed and going out right now."

"We don't have to go to the diner. I can make them for you."

"I'm sorry, you can *what*? You cook now?"

He scoffs. "I am an adult, you know."

So is she, theoretically. But she certainly can't cook pancakes. Unless microwaving those little frozen ones counts. "I don't have anything here to make them."

"I'll run to the store."

"You don't have to do that," she tells him, though the offer is so sweet.

"It'll take me fifteen minutes." Peering down at her, one side of his mouth ticks up. "Take a nap. It looks like I wore you out."

"Oh, fuck off." She forces herself to sit up so she can give him a shove. And also to prove him wrong and wipe that smirk off his face.

He looks around at the mess of clothing strewn across the floor and wrinkles his forehead. "Although Lenny's might frown on me walking in half naked."

Spotting his torn shirt, she laughs heartily. "That's your own fault you had to go all caveman." The question nags at her again of when he discovered he's into the whole bondage thing. Of *who* he discovered it with. So she says, hoping to sound casual, "I've never seen you like that before."

"I know." A hint of pink appears on his cheeks, which is unfairly adorable. "I'm sorry. It's just been so long."

"Since you've—"

"No," he cuts her off. "I mean, yeah, actually, it's been a while with anyone. But I meant since *you* and I . . ."

"Oh. Yeah."

He shrugs sheepishly. "Guess I couldn't help myself."

"I'm not complaining," she assures him. She's *not* going to ask who he's been tying to bedframes while she was gone. Not going to ask if it was Brittani. She's not, she's not, she's not. She's just going to appreciate his admission that it's been a while since he's been with anyone.

Leaning over to kiss her, he nudges her onto her back again, his weight settling comfortably on top of her. They kiss for a minute, and she could totally go for round two, but then suddenly he's off of her and standing. She stares unabashedly as he bends down to grab his boxers and pulls them on, then does the same with his shorts.

"I'll find something of yours that's big enough for me to wear to the store."

"What the heck do you think you're gonna find?" she asks, jumping up and throwing on her shirt and underwear. She skips the bra and shorts in her haste to follow him out of the bedroom and into the other one where her clothes are still hung up.

He's already got her closet open, pushing aside tank tops. The rose tattoo on his shoulder is impossible to miss, like a homing beacon calling to her. Coming up behind him, she rubs her thumb over the black ink before pressing a kiss there.

He stiffens. He knows she's seen it now.

She wraps her arms around his waist and turns her head to the side to let her cheek rest against his back. "Why?" she whispers.

His body relaxes as he places one of his hands over hers. "I . . . It was . . . It's not a big deal."

Yeah, right.

"Austin."

"Our relationship was important to me," he tells her, giving her hand a squeeze. "Being with you helped shape who I am. And I guess I wanted to honor that."

She sighs happily against his back. What can she possibly say to that to let him know she gets it and feels the same way?

Damn, this is too meaningful of a moment to have while she's not wearing pants. But he doesn't seem to expect a response from her as he gently steps out of her grasp to continue his perusal of her closet.

"I'm telling you, nothing will be big enough to fit you."

"Oh, come on. You wear giant baggy tees to bed sometimes. Or there's got to be a large hoodie in here somewhere."

As he says this, he's nearing the far end of her closet, and Montana's heart jolts. Because she suddenly remembers. There *is* something in there that will fit him. A super soft and worn dark gray zip-up hoodie with the word VARSITY on the front and HARTLEY HORNETS BASEBALL on the back. And she knows it'll fit him because it's his. Or rather, it was. She's had it for so long that sometimes she forgets how he gave it to her to keep her warm one night and she accidentally kept it.

"Um," she starts to say, hoping to divert his attention somehow. But it's too late.

"What the—" He whips around to face her, the offending article clutched in his hand. "You dirty thief!"

She reaches for it, but he holds it up too high. "I can explain."

"I always wondered how I lost this! But now I know I didn't lose it. It was stolen! This is a crime."

"You're being a little dramatic, don't you think?" she says, as he puts the hoodie on over his bare torso and zips it up halfway.

She knows they're joking around, but something inside her makes her want to demand he take it off and give it back to her. It doesn't belong to him anymore. It's a part of her past that she's not willing to let go of.

"I'm calling the police," he says, moving over to the full-length mirror to check himself out. It only barely fits him now. His arms have gotten too big, his biceps strain against the fabric. But he still looks good. *Damn him.*

"I'm sure the moratorium on the crime has passed, so you can't take me off to jail."

He turns to her again, a playful glint in his eyes. "Too bad. Because I do have the handcuffs."

"You do not."

"Wanna bet?"

She gulps. "Um."

God, he probably does. And that means he's used them with someone, which brings up all kinds of irrational, unpleasant feelings again that she tries to shove back down.

His smile is blinding as he shrugs. "Believe me or don't. You'll find out someday."

Jesus. She doesn't know if she should consider that a threat or a promise, but a shiver runs down her spine that has nothing to do with the fact that she's only half-dressed.

He leans in to kiss her forehead, tells her he'll be back quickly, and then walks out, leaving her in a daze.

◆

BY THE TIME Austin returns, Montana's put her shorts back on but chosen to remain braless. And she has a pot of coffee brewed, because yes, the smug bastard tired her out. The physical exertion wasn't the only thing that did it though. It was also the comfort of being tangled up in his arms. How is she supposed to continue on with her day when all she wants to do is crawl back into bed with him and cuddle up until they both fall asleep?

It's been so damn long since she's had this intimacy with him, and now with the fresh reminder of how great it is, how great they are together, concentrating on anything else is almost impossible.

While he gets to work in the kitchen, she sits at the table watching him. This kitchen has got to be one of the most familiar rooms in the world to her. And yet, it doesn't feel the same. One Mother's Day, her dad bought her mom a painting of cows drinking coffee at a kitchen table, and it used to hang on the wall by the window. Her mom claimed it was ridiculous, but she never failed to smile whenever she caught sight of it.

The room's also missing the seasonal dish towels hanging over the oven handle that her mom swapped out for each holiday. There are a few overripe bananas on the counter, but no fancy glass bowl, which was always stocked with a cornucopia of different fruits. And, of course, it's not her mom at the stove cooking, while her dad wanders by to kiss her cheek and tries to swipe a bit of whatever food is in her pan.

Montana may be back here in her childhood home, but this house is something different now. Is this what they mean when they say you can't go home again? You can return to a physical place, but it's not the same home anymore. You leave, and the world inevitably moves forward without you. Nothing truly stays the same forever.

Neither do people. *Especially* people.

But maybe that's a good thing, because Austin is here, and he's making her pancakes.

"What else can you cook?" she asks.

He's sprinkling chocolate chips into the batter in the pan, but he glances over his shoulder to give her a ridiculous wink. "What else do you want?"

She shakes her head. "I can't believe this. If your parents didn't feed you, you used to just eat anything that came out of a box from the freezer."

He turns around, leaning against the counter while the first pancake cooks. "I have a son now. I want him to be healthy. And I needed to know how to cook for the restaurant so I can jump on the line to help."

"Oh, right. That makes sense."

"My parents never really taught me to cook when I was younger. They were usually busy at the restaurant cooking for everyone else. But when I wanted to take on more responsibility with the place, I knew I needed to learn from my dad. Luckily, he was able to show me a lot before he . . ."

Montana rises and walks over, wrapping her arms around him for a tight hug. He strokes her hair, and they stay like that a minute. Eventually she pulls away, but she doesn't go back to her seat.

"I'm trying to teach Kalen already," he says, flipping the pancake. "I know he's young, but he loves feeling like he's helping whenever I give him the simplest task."

"That's awesome," she says. But it hits her then, the image of father and son together in the kitchen. Kalen playing around joyfully while Austin makes him breakfast.

She could have had that. She could have had Austin making her breakfast every morning for the last six years, her wrapping her arms around his waist while he stands at the stove. If only she never left him.

And great. Now she's jealous of a five-year-old.

For the umpteenth time since she came back to Hartley, she reminds herself that she can't change the past. But she has him here now, and maybe that's all that matters. With Austin in this kitchen, and the smell of banana chocolate chip pancakes wafting through the air, the house truly feels like a home again.

THEN

"Oh, thank god," Montana said, shoving her textbook aside as the waitress arrived at her and Austin's table with their food. They'd only been waiting less than fifteen minutes, but her rumbling stomach seemed to think it was much longer.

When the woman set the stack of banana chocolate chip pancakes in front of her, Montana removed her feet from Austin's lap so she could sit up properly. She dug in before the plate with his burger even hit the table, shoving a large bite of pancake into her mouth, and then getting to work slathering the rest with butter as she chewed.

"You're lucky you're pretty," Austin said, shaking his head.

"That's a misogynistic thing to say," she informed him around her mouthful of food. But okay, she sort of understood what he meant.

He actually looked contrite when he mumbled an apology. Something she loved about him was how he always heard her when she pointed out things like that.

Barbeque sauce dripped off the sides of his burger as he took a bite. While his hands were occupied, she stole a fry off his plate. Then she went back to her pancakes, eating more slowly now.

She and Austin had their routines, and doing their homework at Goldleaf Diner was one of her favorites. It was amazing how even something like schoolwork was more fun when she had greasy food and him for company.

If you told the awkward bookworm, middle-school-version of her that she'd spend her high school years with a serious boyfriend—and she wasn't even embarrassed scarfing down food around him—she wouldn't have believed it. She was still a bookworm, of course. But after a year and a half with Austin, she didn't feel awkward anymore.

He let her be herself, and he kept showing her that he loved her for exactly who she was. Thanks to him, she was more comfortable showing who she was to everyone else now, too.

Every day, she still felt lucky that he'd somehow noticed her at the beginning of last year. That he'd made an effort to get to know her. That they were learning from each other, growing together.

Maybe it was silly because they were so young, but she couldn't imagine going through the rest of her life without him by her side.

CHAPTER THIRTEEN

NOW

*M*ontana's at the grocery store stocking up when she spots a familiar face headed her direction down the cereal aisle. It's been ten years, but Mrs. Gray was her favorite English teacher. Favorite teacher ever, really. Even her college professors weren't that tough but fun at the same time.

Torn between wanting to say hi and wanting to avoid any interaction where she has to explain what she's doing back in Hartley, Montana pretends to be deep in concentration debating Cocoa Krispies versus Cocoa Pebbles. Pebbles is the clear choice though.

It looks like Mrs. Gray is going to pass right by her, but then— "Montana?"

Turning her head to the woman, she feigns surprise. "Oh, hi!" It sort of feels like she's been caught cheating in class. (Which she's never done, obviously.)

At least the obnoxious hickey Austin left on her neck the other night has finally faded completely. She's never been very good at covering them up with makeup. In fact, she remembers one unfortunate incident where she asked Andrea to help her, and Austin's sister pretended to gag the entire time, muttering things like, "my doofus brother's dirty fucking mouth."

"It *is* you!" Mrs. Gray exclaims. "Montana Sinclair! My gosh, it's been so long."

Montana's pleased her teacher even remembers her, considering she must have taught so many students in the last decade. "I know. How are you?"

"Oh, I'm fine. Are you visiting or . . . ?"

Cringe. "No, I'm here for a while at least."

"Oh! I didn't know you moved back. Last I heard, you were at UCLA, but I haven't seen you here since, so I figured you stayed in California."

"I did," she explains, "but I'm back now."

Mrs. Gray maneuvers her shopping cart to the side so it's not an awkward metal barrier between them. "What made you decide on this? Surely there must be more writing opportunities in L.A."

Montana fights back a sigh. Leaving California to return to Massachusetts wasn't so much a decision as it was desperation. She can't believe her teacher even knew what she was doing after she graduated, but this is why she didn't want to stop and chat. Admitting her failure isn't fun. Especially to the woman who wrote in her yearbook, "*You have such a talent for writing. Use it.*"

"I'm figuring out my next career move," she says finally.

"Whatever it is, I hope you keep writing. Journalism really suits you." Mrs. Gray lightly sets her hand over Montana's where she's still clutching the top of the cereal box. Only for a moment, but Montana feels the warm ghost of it when she pulls away. "I've come across your articles from time to time. I really enjoyed them, and it's nice to get a little glimpse of what my students are doing after I send them off into the world. Especially my favorite students. And from the looks of it, you've sure done a lot."

"Thank you," she says, her voice welling up embarrassingly with emotion. "I have. And I'm still writing." *Sort of. In theory.*

"That's good to hear, because you can't let your gift go to waste."

Swallowing the lump in her throat, Montana agrees, "No, I can't."

"Well, it was good to see you, dear. I'd better go so my husband can have his roast beef sandwich for lunch. Heaven forbid he handle the grocery shopping himself some time."

Montana laughs. "It was good to see you too."

And it was. But it makes her realize how little effort she's been putting into trying to get writing work. Ever since she started making good money bartending at Alan's Place—and, frankly, spending so much time with Austin—her writing career has gotten pushed further to the back burner.

Well. No more.

Mrs. Gray's words still echo in her head when she's back home. *You can't let your gift go to waste.*

So she gets on her laptop and spends a couple hours searching magazine sites, hoping to find somewhere that may be interested in one of her articles, or to be hit with inspiration for something new she could write based on her past experiences. But despite her renewed determination, she's not having much better luck now than she did when she first got back to town.

Something's not clicking. Writing used to come easy for her, article ideas spilling out of her brain constantly. But maybe her well has run dry.

Maybe her days of exploration are really over, and from here on out, it'll be nothing but the same old, same old. Same regular customers on their bar stools. Same scenery she looked at every day for the first eighteen years of her life. Same Austin.

No. That's not fair.

She can't drag him into her defeat. None of this is his fault. He's basically the only thing keeping her from wanting to crawl into her closet and hide there for the rest of her life.

And he's not the same. He is in all the best ways, but he's different, too, in even better ones.

As if he can magically tell she's thinking about him, he chooses that moment to call her. He might be one of the only people left who still prefers talking on the phone over texting. Besides her parents, of course.

"Hey, what's up?" she answers.

"Hey. I was wondering if you're free on Wednesday."

"You write the schedule, so you know I'm not working."

"Yes," he says, "but as you've reminded me, you do have a life, so."

When she said that, she was only trying not to sound too pathetic. In reality, though, her life now basically consists of work and him. "I'm free."

"Good. Then would you be interested in spending the day at the lake? It's supposed to be hot and sunny."

Beaming, she asks, "Is this like a real date?" It's lucky he can't see how happy she is at the idea of spending more time with him. Over-eagerness isn't exactly a turn on, especially when this thing between them is supposed to be casual.

"Well, I'm not just using you for sex, you know." He clears his throat awkwardly. "But it'll be with Kalen, and I don't know how I should explain this to him yet."

"Oh. Right."

"I think I'd rather he keeps thinking we're friends for now, if that's okay with you."

Disappointment edges in, even though she probably has no right to be disappointed. They agreed on seeing where things go. It's not like he's going to be introducing her as his girlfriend to anyone any time soon, since nothing is even close to official.

But still. Hiding whatever they are could get complicated.

"He's your son," she concedes. "I'll go along with whatever you feel is best."

"Thank you," Austin says. "But if you want me to take you on a real date . . ." Her heart speeds up a bit as he pauses. "I drop Kalen off at his mom's that evening. We could do dinner somewhere besides the bar. Where we actually have to pay for the food."

"Technically, you're still paying for the food even when you give it to me for free."

He laughs. "You know what I mean."

"I do." She presses her hand to the spot on her neck where that hickey has faded, flashing briefly to how they made out furiously up against the desk in his office when they were the only two left in the restaurant after closing. With his busy schedule at Alan's Place and shared custody of Kalen, they haven't had time for much else since they started this thing, so an entire day and night with him would be amazing. "It sounds great."

When they get off the phone, Montana tries to get back to her research, but her mind keeps drifting to images of Austin in swim trunks, his bare chest glistening in the sun. She hasn't been to the lake here in forever, and she hasn't really thought about it in years. Now she can't wait.

She and Austin may not be able to define what they're doing, but they're definitely doing *something*. And she's pretty damn sure it's something great.

◆

THE LAKE IS ONLY thirty-five minutes out of town, and they manage to make it there without any inappropriate comments from the backseat.

Montana was pleased when Austin let her play *Red* (Taylor's Version, of course) on Spotify for the whole drive. She was even more pleased when Kalen joined her in shouting along to "22."

"Good job teaching him the classics," she told Austin.

He mumbled something about not knowing where Kalen had heard it. But then when she jumped ahead to the ten-minute version of "All Too Well," she caught Austin out of the corner of her eye mouthing the words. *Ha!* This version wasn't out back when they were dating, so he can't even blame it on her for why he has it memorized.

By the time they get out of the Jeep at their destination, Montana is in the best mood. Group sing-alongs while driving will do that to her every time. (For the record, she totally skipped right over "We Are Never Ever Getting Back Together.")

The three of them trek down the short path through the trees that leads to a large open area by the water, and they're pleasantly surprised to find no one else here. They pick out a nice flat spot to spread their blanket, then set down the cooler Austin packed for them with drinks and snacks.

Montana pulls her black cover-up dress over her head, revealing her neon orange strapless bikini. The dress was mesh in the middle, so it wasn't actually covering up much, but she can almost *feel* Austin's eyes now raking slowly over her body before he turns away.

Trying to hide her smile, she stuffs the dress into her beach bag and takes out her towel and a book. She unrolls the towel on top of the blanket and sits, leaning back on her palms with her knees bent out in front of her.

Kalen's already stripped down to his superhero swim trunks and thrown his clothes wildly to the ground, where Austin now dutifully scoops them up.

When Austin removes his own T-shirt and shorts, she tries to avoid staring. He pulls a bottle of sunscreen out of his bag and quickly slathers up Kalen before starting on himself. It's even harder not to stare as he slowly rubs the lotion over his arms and stomach.

Then he sits down right between her legs and says, "Can you do my back please?"

She takes a deep breath before squeezing a large dollop of lotion into her palm and bringing her hand to his upper back. This might feel like the opening to a cheesy porno if there wasn't a small child sitting two feet away. Focusing on the task and not on the smooth muscled skin under her palms, she makes sure to cover every inch and really slather a lot over his tattoo.

"You're good," she tells him when she's finished.

He twists around to look at her. "You need to put some on too."

"I don't burn easily like you," she says, sticking out her tongue, because she's in a playful mood.

The stern look he gives her in response is kind of hot. "You can still get skin cancer, so cut the sass and do what I tell you."

"Oh my god, you're such a dad," she teases.

"Here, I'll get your back." He repositions himself to sit behind her, bracketing her in now with his legs. She tries not to react as his hands firmly spread the lotion across her skin. But then he leans closer and whispers in her ear, "And don't you dare stick that tongue out at me unless you're prepared to put it to better use."

Certain parts of her body clench tightly, but she recovers quickly and says, "Oh, I am. Later."

"What's later?" Kalen asks.

"Nothing," Austin says, voice noticeably strained. "Do you want to go play by the water? I'll be over there in a minute. Don't go in without me."

After Kalen runs off with his plastic pail and shovel, Austin takes longer than necessary to finish her back, until his thumb is simply massaging the nape of her neck. Montana feels as melty as the lotion, but as her body starts to sag against him, he props her back up with one hand and drops the sunscreen bottle into her lap with the other.

"Make sure you do your front."

With that, Austin stands and goes to join Kalen where the boy is trying fruitlessly to build a sandcastle, probably not understanding that the sand here isn't like sand at the beach.

Letting out a quiet whimper, Montana flops backward onto her towel. She counts silently to ten, focusing on the sounds of the water gently hitting the shoreline and the wind rustling calmly through the trees, as the arousing effects his hands had on her wear off. Then she sits back up to follow his order, spreading the damn lotion over the rest of her body.

While Austin and Kalen laugh and dip their toes into the water, she grabs her book and stretches out on her stomach, head pointed toward the lake.

The hot sun feels lovely beating onto her back as she reads. In between pages, she lifts her head up, peering over the top of the book at the two of them having fun. Austin kneels so Kalen can climb onto his shoulders, then he grips the boy's legs as he walks farther out. Soon the water's up to his chest and Kalen's ankles, and Kalen is laughing and squealing with glee.

Looking up and catching her staring, Austin yells, "Hey, nerd! Put the book down and get out here!"

Montana rolls her eyes at the insult. He loves her nerdy side.

But she's starting to sweat now, so she gets up and makes her way to the water. Avoiding a small floating piece of driftwood, she carefully wades in, so as not to splash herself too much as she gets used to the chill. After a minute, it feels good.

Austin and Kalen come closer to the shore to meet her. When Austin sets Kalen down, Kalen runs into the sand to grab his toys and then brings them back to the edge of the water, crouching down to dig up sand and scoop it into his pail. Austin tells him he can play there, but not to go in any deeper on his own. Kalen waves him off, already absorbed in his task.

Austin shakes his head, then he and Montana start to swim a bit farther out. It's sweet, the way he keeps turning back to check on his son. And once they're submerged up to their shoulders, he faces the shore to keep Kalen in view.

"This is nice," Montana says, watching a dragonfly expertly skimming the surface of the water a few feet away. "I've missed this place."

"See?" he says. "Massachusetts isn't all boring."

"I never said it was."

It's obvious what he's getting at though. The fact that, in high school, she was so desperate to leave Hartley. But she was never unhappy here. There was just the whole rest of the world out there she needed to see.

To deflect from this topic, she sends a small splash of water his way. He retaliates with a much bigger splash, and she screams as the cold water hits her face. Diving forward, she grabs at his shoulders and uses her entire body weight to try to dunk him, but he's too strong for that.

He laughs when she gives up, lulling her into a false sense of security. Then he reaches out, lightning quick, and dips a hand into one of the cups of her bikini top, pinching her nipple hard.

The unexpected jolt of pain makes her hiss. But after a second, he eases up a bit, rolling the bud between his fingers instead, and a more pleasurable jolt travels all the way down to settle between her thighs.

While he works over the one nipple, his actions hidden just below the water, he stares at her intently. She tries to give him an annoyed look but ends up biting her lip at the sensations instead.

Then he suddenly withdraws his hand, causing her to let out a choked whine. From the way he's smirking, he's clearly pleased with himself. And *oh, no way.*

Two can play this game.

She wades in even closer. Before he can react, she snakes her hand down the front of his trunks, wrapping it around his semi-hard cock.

His lips part open but no sound comes out.

Smirking triumplantly, she strokes slowly up and down, bringing him to full hardness. She can't kiss him because Kalen might see. But doing it this way, without the kissing? It's unbelievably hot watching his face as she drives him closer to the edge.

She could make him come with only her hand. Despite the glances he keeps sending Kalen's way to make sure the kid is safe, it's obvious he's very much into this.

Good. That makes the revenge sweeter as she releases him and starts swimming away on her back.

A curse slips from his lips, and then he catches up with her, grabbing her ankle as she tries to kick away faster. Next thing she knows, her head's being dunked under the water. She comes up sputtering and fixes him with a dirty look as she swipes messy strands of wet hair out of her face.

Laughing at her unremorsefully, he says, "You deserved that."

"You started it!" she argues.

He shrugs innocently, but he's totally not innocent. And it's the presence of *his* child that's keeping them from taking things any further, so it's really unfair that he started turning her on like that.

She makes her way back to shore, squinting at the bright sunlight glistening off the water, and sits down in the shallow area with Kalen. As he plays, he tells her a story about the mermen who live in the lake and how he's collecting treasure for them, but she's only half listening.

Her mind wanders dangerously to the blanket in the dirt as she imagines letting Austin lay her down right there, in this open space where their privacy could be interrupted at any moment by other lakegoers. She'd risk it. She's never had any exhibitionist tendencies before, but for some reason now, the idea of getting caught actually gives her a tiny thrill.

Damn him. He's driving her crazy.

Joining them a minute later, Austin asks if everyone's ready to dry off and eat lunch.

"No," Kalen says, not even looking at his dad.

Austin laughs. "Okay, you can have five more minutes and then you need to eat."

Kalen sighs dramatically. "Fine."

Montana follows Austin out of the water, and they grab their towels, patting themselves dry a bit before they lay the towels out on the ground to sit, not wanting to get the blanket wet.

After rifling through the cooler, Austin holds out a plastic-wrapped turkey sandwich for her. But when she goes to take it, he yanks his hand back. "*You. Are evil.*"

She pouts until he hands over the sandwich, then starts peeling off the cold plastic. "Like I said, you totally started it."

"I didn't do . . . *that!*"

"You did enough."

As she takes a bite of her sandwich, he leans in and says right in her ear, "You'll pay for that later."

She doesn't know if it's the words themselves, the low, dirty tone of his voice, or his hot breath hitting the shell of her ear, but the promise sends a tingle down into her bikini bottom again.

He pulls back and smiles casually, grabbing something else out of the cooler. "Apple?"

"I'm not worried," she tells him a few beats too late as she accepts the fruit.

Smiling wickedly now, he gets himself a sandwich and leaves his response unspoken, but she hears it loud and clear. *You should be.*

The sexual tension is so thick, she's almost relieved when Kalen runs over to join them, his boisterous energy cutting right through it.

While they're eating, a woman and two young children emerge from the path behind them and set up a small distance away. When the kids run over toward the water, Kalen asks if he can go play with them.

Austin surveys Kalen's food. He's only eaten half of a sandwich, but most of an apple. "Finish your apple first."

Kalen does this quickly and then jumps up, sprinting away.

"Make sure you ask them if it's okay to join!" Austin shouts after him.

The kids look more than happy to include Kalen in their fun as they chase each other around the shore. Soon the mom joins them and crouches down to talk to Kalen. She tells him, loud enough to be heard from where Montana and Austin are sitting, "We're going to go in the water, but if your parents say it's okay, I'll take you with us."

Montana's heart does a weird thing she can't explain at the word *parents*, but Austin just calls out, "It's fine! He can swim, he's just not completely confident, so he shouldn't go in too deep. Thank you!"

The four of them wade around in the shallow part of the lake, and suddenly Montana's picturing Kalen coming here with both of his actual parents. Surely, they must have done it at some point when Austin and Brittani were still together. She's wondered about Brittani before, torn between wanting to know everything and wanting to pretend the woman doesn't exist.

The nosy side winning now, she asks, "Why did you and Brittani break up?"

"What?" Austin says, clearly caught off guard.

"I'm curious what happened between you guys. She sounds perfect for you."

Ugh. Montana doesn't mean those words. Brittani was probably good for him, but perfect? What possessed her to say that? Maybe she's hoping he'll contradict it.

"You don't know anything about her."

It's not exactly a contradiction, but the weird look Austin gives her is something.

"Just that she's a nurse," she says. *And that she was willing to have a baby with him while Montana was busy chasing after her career.*

He sighs. "I'm not sure what that has to do with her being perfect for me, but our relationship was . . . fine. I mean, it was pretty easy. We got to know each other, spent a lot of time watching movies, ate a lot of dinners at the restaurant. My parents said she was nice, although Andrea thought she was boring."

Montana feels a small sense of smugness, since she and Andrea get along great. *Got* along great. She hasn't seen Andrea in forever. But still.

"And I dunno," he goes on. "It wasn't that she was boring, but it was kind of like we were boring together. She never challenged me in any way. And then when we had Kalen, things weren't so easy anymore, and I realized there wasn't enough there between us to make it worth sticking out the hard times together."

Unsure if he's done yet, Montana holds her breath as he looks at her. She doesn't know what to say, because it would certainly be awful to tell him she's glad he wasn't passionately in love with Brittani. But she is. *So glad.*

He trails his fingers down her bare shoulder and leans in briefly to press a kiss there. "I guess I needed the girl who jumps out of trees."

"What?"

His gaze shoots farther down the shore, and she follows it. There are more trees down there, less beach. As soon as she spots the giant tree, close to the water's edge, its one very long, thick limb hanging out over the lake, she remembers.

It's hard to believe she was once brave enough—or foolish enough—to jump from that tree limb into the water.

THEN

"You losers are going down!" Blake taunted, charging through the water with Marisela on his shoulders.

Montana yelped, trying to dodge when Marisela came at her and almost tipping backward off Austin's shoulders. Thankfully, he gripped her calves tighter, and she was able to right herself. She managed to give Marisela's shoulder a push, but she didn't know Blake's girlfriend that well yet, since the two of them had just started dating, so she didn't want to be too rough.

Marisela, however, had no such qualms. As soon as she got the chance, she knocked into Montana's chest, shoving her hard. When that didn't work, she clutched Montana's forearm and tried to yank her forward with Blake cheering her on.

Once Montana freed herself from Marisela's grip, Austin gave her leg a squeeze, then lunged forward. The movement almost made her lose her balance again, but she held steady long enough to reach out and pinch at Marisela's side. When the girl instinctively squirmed away, Montana took advantage and shoved her shoulder as hard as she could.

Marisela screamed as she fell backward, and Blake couldn't hold on to her. Montana's momentum sent her falling off Austin a second later, but that was okay. They won. She swiped her wet hair out of her eyes as Austin pulled her in for a victory kiss.

"Rematch!" Blake shouted when Marisela popped up from the water laughing.

"Maybe later," his girlfriend told him. "Let a girl catch her breath, babe."

"What if I don't want to let you catch your breath?" Blake asked, before tugging her closer and promptly shoving his tongue down her throat. Montana couldn't help but watch in a mixture of amusement and horror as he appeared to try to eat the girl's face.

Austin sent a large splash of water their way. "Could you cool it, dude? Geez!"

Blake released his suction on Marisela's mouth and flung himself into a backflip, almost kicking her in the head.

"Dios mío," Marisela muttered. And when Blake reemerged, she told him, "You need to get out your energy a safe distance away before you hurt someone. Go swim down there."

He shrugged and swam off in the direction she pointed him. Austin went too.

Now that they were alone, Marisela turned to Montana and said, "I'm gonna get out and rest for a bit."

"I'll come with you."

The two of them made their way back to the shore and grabbed their towels, securing them around their waists. Austin and Blake were already pretty far away.

"Wanna meet them down there?" Montana asked.

"Sure. I should make sure Blake doesn't drown."

"How's he going to drown?"

Marisela shrugged. "Sheer stupidity, probably."

Montana laughed as they trudged barefoot down the shoreline. "You know, I love Blake as a friend, but I don't get how you put up with his hyperactivity and all the nonsense that comes out of his mouth."

"He's super cute. And he's really sweet when we're alone, like a cuddly golden retriever." Marisela smiled fondly. Then a wicked spark grew in her eyes. "Plus his dick game is strong as hell."

Montana gaped at her before they both burst out laughing.

Reaching the area where the boys were, they stood there watching them try to dunk each other, and Marisela said, "You and Austin are perfect together, though."

"Thanks. I guess."

"You don't think so?"

"No, I do," Montana said. "I dunno, I've been hearing stuff like that for a while now, and I never know how to respond. Like is it a compliment, or is it a fact that doesn't require appreciation?"

Marisela laughed. "It's just an observation. An obvious one. I think everyone can see it. You really love each other, and that's kinda rare in high school, ya know?"

"I guess," Montana told her. Although, *no*, she didn't really know, because she didn't have any other relationships to compare hers and Austin's to. There was Blake's and Marisela's, of course, but she didn't think they'd even been together long enough for it to count.

The boys were making their way out of the water now. As soon as Blake hit the sand, he ran at Marisela, grabbing her around the middle and knocking her over. At least he managed to twist them as they went down so that she landed on top of him.

"Fucking hell, you're insane," Marisela said. But still, she leaned down to give him a quick kiss.

Then Blake jumped up and took off again, heading for the trees.

There wasn't as much shore here, so the trees were much closer to the water.

"What are you doing?" Austin asked.

"Look at this tree!" Blake called out.

"What about it?" Marisela said.

"I'm gonna jump!"

Marisela threw her hands on her hips. "Excuse me?"

Blake turned back to them to say, "Yeah, look. That limb goes way out over the water."

They all watched in disbelief as he climbed the tree trunk and shuffled his way ever so slowly across the giant limb. Montana held her breath when he wobbled a bit on the end of it where it was thinner, but he caught his balance.

"Blake!" Marisela shouted. "Get back down here before you die!" Glancing at Montana, she added, "See? Sheer stupidity."

"I'm not gonna die!" he yelled back. "The water's much deeper over here."

"Are you sure about that?" Austin asked.

"Pretty sure!"

Montana turned to Austin. "Shouldn't you try to stop him?"

"Probably. But I don't think I can. You know how he is when he gets a dumb idea."

"Ay Dios, he's gonna die," Marisela cried, covering her eyes.

Montana gently pulled the girl's hands down. "He'll be okay. I've seen him survive a lot of stupid stuff." She definitely had her doubts about this one, but Austin was probably right in that there was no use trying to talk him out of it.

"All right, here goes!" Blake yelled.

"Fuck," Marisela said.

And then suddenly, Blake jumped out as far as he could, and they watched him sailing through the air for a moment before he fell down, down, down and hit the water with a terrifyingly loud splash.

Holding her breath again, Montana gripped Austin's hand until finally, what seemed like an eternity later, Blake's head broke up through the surface.

The three of them all let out a relieved exhale.

"Holy shit," Blake said, swimming back toward them. "That was awesome! You've got to try it."

"Did you touch the bottom?" Austin asked.

Blake stood as the water got shallow and trudged to the shoreline. "Yeah, but it didn't hurt. I told you it was deep enough. Hitting the water stung for a second though. But it's so worth it!"

Austin visually scanned his friend up and down when he reached them, assessing for damage. And then, apparently satisfied that there was none, he started walking over to the tree.

Montana's eyes widened. "Are you kidding?"

"I'll be fine. Love you."

"If you'll be fine, why are you saying you love me? That's totally an *in case you die* thing!" There was an edge of panic in her voice now.

"No," Austin called back, already shimmying his way up the tree trunk, "it's just an *I love you* thing."

Resigned, Montana sighed and watched her boyfriend climb the branches of the tree until he reached the upper limb. If Blake could do this without getting hurt, surely Austin could too, but she was still nervous as he made his way out across it. If he fell off before he was far enough over the water, it would be bad.

He made it to the end and let out a whoop as he jumped, no hesitation.

It felt like her heart stopped, only resuming its beating once she finally saw him reemerge from the water in one piece.

When he got back to the shore he gave her a tight hug, dripping water onto her and the mostly dry towel around her waist. "Blake was right," he said, pulling away to kiss the top of her head. "That was awesome."

She took in his exhilarated smile, then turned her head, eyeing the tree critically. *Well, if they can do it.* She undid her towel and let it drop to the sand before marching away.

"Woah, woah, wait," Austin called, catching up with her and wrapping his fingers around her wrist. "I didn't mean for you to do it."

Shooting him a glare, she said, "So it's okay for you and Blake to do it, but not me?"

"Well, no, I'm not saying that, but—"

"But what? But I'm a girl?" She held his eyes, challenging him.

With a sigh, he let go of her wrist. "Please be careful."

That deserved an eye roll. He hadn't said she shouldn't do this because she was a girl, but it was what he'd meant. Gripping the tree as best she could, she tried to find a good indentation for her foot. She was having trouble pulling herself up, because she couldn't reach the first branch as easily as the boys could.

Her cheeks heated, and she was starting to feel foolish. But then Austin was there, his linked hands forming a foothold. She stepped into it gratefully, and he boosted her up until she could stand on the branch. From there, she didn't have much trouble climbing up the rest of the way.

She wasn't scared until she stepped out onto the limb. There, she made the mistake of looking down and almost panicked. But she forced herself to stay calm. Instead of walking across the limb like the boys had done, she sat down and straddled it, scooting her way along on her butt. She looked out across the water to the other side of the lake, taking in the view. This was really freaking cool.

Taking a deep breath, she very cautiously got to her feet. And then she jumped.

It was incredible. That sensation of flying before gravity pulled her body down toward the water. Right before she hit it, she held her nose and braced for the impact. Slamming into the water felt like a hundred stinging slaps all over her body, but she forgot about the pain as her feet hit the bottom and she started fighting her way back up. She was still buzzed on the adrenaline and grinning when she reached the surface.

Her eyes found Austin immediately, and the relief on his face was evident. He ran into the water to meet her as she swam, and as soon as she was within reach, he grabbed her face and kissed her. She was still trying to catch her breath, but she kissed him back enthusiastically while her brain spun with thoughts of other thrills they could experience together.

The kiss went on until Blake mocked, "Could you cool it, dude? Geez!"

They broke apart laughing, then held hands as they made their way over to rejoin him and Marisela.

Montana turned to Marisela. "Your turn?"

"Oh, *hell* no."

Everyone laughed.

Heading back with the group to where they'd left their stuff, Montana was still dreaming up new adventures. If any other view could beat the one at the top of that tree, she wanted to find it.

CHAPTER FOURTEEN

NOW

*B*y the time Austin drops Montana off at home, she's sun-drunk and her stomach's full enough to burst. He was probably right about her not needing that chili cheese dog, but she couldn't resist. When they left the lake, she remembered one of the best ice cream places in the world, Dream Cream, was only five minutes out of the way. So obviously, they had to go. And it was so worth it for the adorable pictures she took of Kalen sitting on top of the cheesy cow statue out front.

She didn't exactly *need* the hot dog in addition to her black raspberry soft serve waffle cone right after they'd eaten lunch, though, even if she shared a couple bites with Kalen. When Austin reminded her they were having dinner later, she shrugged him off. But now she might be regretting her decision just a tad. Only because she wants to look good tonight.

This is going to be their first real date. Or . . . second first real date? Their first real date as adults, anyway. It's kind of a big deal.

Even if Austin made it sound so simple, not a big deal at all. Like, naturally, they'd go on a real date. But has anything with them really been simple since high school?

Sometimes Montana overthinks things. She knows that. But dating Austin again isn't something she can take lightly. The stakes feel higher this time. If the whole thing blows up in their faces, she might not recover.

She survived losing him once, but barely. She doesn't think she'll survive it twice.

They're adults now, with separate lives they've built for themselves. (Granted, hers crumbled this year, but she's building it back up.) They need to figure out if their lives can meld together without any damage. Nothing's going to be as easy as when they were fifteen and hanging out after school. When their only worry was getting their homework done with enough time to makeout afterward.

Austin said there wasn't enough between him and Brittani to make it worth sticking out the hard times, but Montana prays it's different with them. They have years and years of stuff between them to make it worth it. Then again, some people might call that stuff baggage.

Okay, that's it. She's going to take a nap to clear her head and digest her food, and hopefully she'll wake up refreshed.

It works pretty well. She gets up with plenty of time to shower and get ready, and she's no longer exhausted from being in the sun all day. She picks out the sexiest dress in her closet, one she used to wear to clubs in L.A. It's dark purple, shows plenty of cleavage, and hugs her hips just right. Granted, it's so tight she needs to go commando to avoid panty lines showing, and dancing in it would always put her on the verge of exposing herself to the entire club. But she doesn't expect that'll be an issue tonight. Dancing was never Austin's thing.

Pairing the dress with tiny black heels, she gives herself a once-over in the mirror and smirks in satisfaction at her reflection. She wants Austin to know she's not a teenager anymore, doesn't live in T-shirts and leggings and draw-string shorts. Those are still her go-to choices when she's home alone, of course. But tonight she needs to look hot.

Maybe she even wants him to regret it a little. The six years he chose not to be in her life.

She's feeling confident until the moment she opens the front door to find him standing on the porch in sandals, distressed jean shorts, a white tee, and a short-sleeve plaid button-up. He looks really damn good, but it's a standard outfit for him and totally fucking casual.

Shit.

"You look . . ." he starts but can't seem to find an appropriate word.

She cringes. "Overdressed?"

"Fucking amazing."

"But overdressed."

He shakes his head, tugging her closer. Then, with a hand splayed possessively on the side of her face, he gives her a kiss that quickly deepens. After being with him all day and not being able to kiss him, this is almost enough to make her want to skip the dinner and drag him up to her room right now.

But he pulls back before they get too carried away and says, "No, seriously. You look amazing. It's just a little fancy."

"Well, you didn't tell me where we were going."

He frowns. "Nowhere that fancy. I'm sorry."

"No, it's okay. I wasn't expecting . . . I dunno what I was expecting." She squirms, the material of the dress now feeling too constricting. "Should I change into jeans?"

"Absolutely not," he says adamantly. And the way his eyes keep scorching over her is enough to settle her doubts. "But you should probably bring something long-sleeved to go over it in case you get cold," he adds.

She runs upstairs and considers grabbing a nice cardigan, then opts for a black zip-up hoodie instead. It might help offset the dress so that she doesn't look too out of place wherever they're going.

Which is a fish fry stand.

That's where he ends up taking her. To a place called Fred's Fish.

And yes, she's way overdressed compared to everyone else. But you know what? She doesn't even care. They both love fish and chips, and it's actually kind of beautiful here. There's a large expanse of grass beside the wooden shack, where rows of delicate string lights hang over picnic tables, with a nice view of the mountains in the distance.

They don't need to go to a fancy restaurant for this date to be special. It's special because it's them, and they're here together now, after all this time. And when they bring their food and beers over to a table and Austin sits right beside her, under the soft glowing lights, with a slow ballad playing from a speaker, it suddenly feels really fucking romantic.

Until a glob of ketchup from her fries drops right down Montana's dress and lands in between her boobs. Austin laughs at her mercilessly as she grabs a handful of napkins and tries to wipe it up without flashing anyone.

"Shut up."

"I can't take you anywhere," he says, jabbing her playfully in the side.

"Eat your fish."

He does, cutting into it with his plastic fork and taking a big bite. She does the same, and man, this is the best fried fish she's ever had. They're not even by the ocean. This little place in the middle of western Massachusetts is such a hidden gem. Even the beer they're drinking—some kind of fruity IPA from a local brewery—is great.

She holds up her plastic cup to him. "Thanks for taking me here. I love it."

Smiling, he taps his cup against hers. "I figured you would."

They eat their meals, humming along occasionally to the music, and then Austin goes back to get them each a second beer. Halfway through these, he sneaks his hand over to the bare skin of her thigh and squeezes. She leans in for a quick kiss in response.

Soon, though, his hand inches up underneath the hem of her dress. He sucks in a sharp breath, probably at the discovery that she's not wearing underwear, and her eyes dart around to see if anyone's watching them. It doesn't look like it, but still, the picnic table doesn't provide much cover. The last thing either of them needs is an indecent exposure charge. And yet, she doesn't object when he starts stroking her gently with one finger.

He keeps his face neutral, sipping his beer with his free hand. But even though his eyes barely flit to her, she knows he's paying attention to her reaction. While for her part, she's trying hard *not* to react. Calm, cool, and collected. That's her. Not at all turned on, needy, and desperate.

She only lets him torture her a minute, and then, as she catches herself biting back a moan, she decides that's enough. Grabbing his wrist, she tugs his hand back down to a more respectable position on her leg.

He laughs softly. "Ready to get out of here?"

"Definitely."

They finish off their beers and then head to his truck. On the drive back to Hartley, Montana's buzzing with anticipation. They've been engaging in foreplay all day, and she's totally ready to get to the main event.

Apparently, he's ready too. He asks if she wants to see his apartment, but when they get there, he doesn't offer a tour. Instead, Montana finds herself shoved up against the door the second it's closed behind her.

He kisses her roughly, with hands roaming underneath her dress. "Can't believe you're not wearing any underwear," he rasps out, his lips barely leaving hers.

Before she can respond, he lifts her by her ass. Instinctually, she wraps her legs tightly around him, and he adjusts his grip so he's only using one arm to hold her up, pressing her into the door for support. His other hand reaches down between them to resume the delicious stroking he started at the picnic table.

The fire is building inside her, so when he abruptly sets her back down, she starts to pout. But then he growls, "Bedroom. Now."

Leaning against the door, she tries to catch her breath. Even though that sounds like a terrific idea, as he turns and begins walking away, she cries out indignantly, "You can't just order me around!"

Already down the hall, he yells, "You'd better get that hot ass in here right now!"

She kicks off her heels, but she's still unsteady on her own feet as she goes to find him. *Dear god.* That tone of voice is doing things to her. But she can't simply obey him without a little sass, so stepping into his bedroom, she says, "Or what?"

He grabs her by the wrist, yanking her forward until he can bend her over the edge of the bed. She falls onto her forearms, letting out a huff of surprise. Then—*Slap!*

She jumps, startled by the impact of his palm hitting her ass. "*Wha—*"

"I told you you'd pay for what you did to me earlier."

Oh god. He did. But she thought that was a joke!

"Ow!" she yelps as his hand smacks down again on her bare skin. Her damn dress is too short to offer any coverage in this position. Although it doesn't really hurt. In fact, with the third and fourth spank, she starts to feel a pleasant heat spreading across her ass.

Guys have smacked her ass before, but never with intent like this, so focused. Maybe she should try to get up. She knows he'd stop if she did. But surprisingly, she doesn't want to. Her brain's a bit fuzzy already, though, so it's hard to say if she actually likes being spanked, or if she just likes it because of who's doing it to her.

This is Austin. And he's never shown her this side of himself before. She's kind of dying to know where it goes.

He spanks her a few more times, then lets her up.

As she stands, she hopes he doesn't notice how her legs are shaking. Turning to face him, she manages to joke, "I think I learned my lesson."

He smirks, and the playfulness mixed with the heat in his eyes goes straight to her core. "Hmm, I don't think so. Not yet."

Her entire body clenches in anticipation of what else he has in store for her. Whatever it is, she'll let him do it. She trusts him more than she's ever trusted anyone. Even after all this time.

With a gentle care that contrasts the way he was handling her thirty seconds ago, he pulls her dress over her head and removes her black bra, his hands caressing her back and shoulders as he goes. Eyes heated, he greedily takes in the sight of her fully naked before him, then finally strips himself out of his own clothing.

He pushes her firmly onto the bed and goes with her, shuffling them up by the headboard, his hands gliding along her sides now. She buries her fingers in his hair as he kisses her. Then suddenly, he's pulling away and leaning over her body to reach into a drawer in his nightstand.

Handcuffs. He pulls out a pair of handcuffs, and she gulps. Guess he wasn't lying when he said he had some. They're leopard print and fuzzy, but still.

"Can I?" he asks, and she nods without having to think about it. "I should have asked last time at your house. I'm sorry. I got caught up."

"Don't be sorry. I would have told you if I didn't like it."

Smiling, he urges her to put her arms above her head, which she does. She twists her head to watch him wind the cuffs behind one of the slats in the headboard before attaching each to her wrists. The click as they lock into place sends the best kind of chill through her. She can move her arms up and down a bit, but she can't go anywhere.

When he reaches over to the nightstand again, she can't move to see what he's digging for, and he comes back up with his hand wrapped around the handle of a black leather flogger. As the strands hang tantalizingly a few inches above her body, and her eyes widen with the tiniest bit of fear this time.

Not of him. But of what this will feel like. She likes to think she's been fairly adventurous in bed, but he keeps making her question that assertion.

He leans down to stroke her hair with his free hand, kissing her forehead, her temple, her cheek, the tip of her nose. Then finally, softly, her lips. How does he keep switching from aggressive to sweet, and why is it insanely hot?

Pulling away before she has the chance to really kiss him back, he whispers, "Only if you want to."

Wants to isn't exactly it.

More like *needs* to.

She needs to know how far this new dominant streak of his goes. Needs to know if she'll like it—if they're still in sync with their desires. So she nods, holding her breath.

"Breathe," he instructs gently, as he starts by running the leather strands along the skin of her upper body, teasing her. She shivers at the feel of it.

Then he grins devilishly. He scoots down the bed, giving himself more room, and raises the flogger higher above her before flicking his wrist and letting it come down lightly on the top of her thighs. She gasps, the sensation new but not unpleasant.

He strikes there again, then quickly ducks his head down, kissing over the spots on her skin where the tips of the flogger landed, where it stings the most. He licks the same spots before blowing cool air against them, making her gasp again.

As he moves up to her stomach, the hits sting a little more, but he follows them up with the same treatment from his mouth. Then it's the tops of her breasts. Striking, kissing, licking, blowing. The mix of sensations is deliciously overwhelming.

The next strike lands across her nipple, and she hisses, because *fuck*, that hurt. She's not sure she likes it, but then his mouth is there sucking, and you know what? Suddenly she wants him to do it again.

And he knows. He fucking knows, because he grins before striking across her other nipple, and *holy shit, fuck, dammit, hell*. She needs—She just *needs*. More. Release. *Something*. She's a mess. She must be dripping between her legs at this point. And she can't do anything to take control because he's got her handcuffed to the freaking bed.

She's not sure if she's relieved or disappointed when he drops the flogger to the floor.

Quickly, he brings his hand between her legs, fingers touching, testing. His grin is fucking feral. "Look at you. So wet and ready for me already. I don't need to do anything else. I can take you right now, can't I?"

Whimpering and squirming, she offers a nod of consent, but he still uses a couple fingers anyway. They slide right inside her with no resistance, and he moans, watching in awe. As he pumps them in and out, she bends one leg, digging her heel into his lower back to urge him on. To go faster, to give her more. To *do something. Please*.

She can't take it anymore. She's going crazy. She needs him now.

And they *are* still in sync, because he removes his fingers and grips her knee, hiking her leg higher as he lines himself up and then slams into her, knocking the breath out of her lungs.

As soon as he's settled fully inside her, she feels calmer. Her body is still on fire, burning up with desire, but her heart is content. This feels so right.

It's where they belong.

Together.

The forms of foreplay might be new, but they're still them. Montana and Austin. They still fit.

He's gentler now, but his pace isn't quite slow. Wanting to kiss him, she goes to reach for his face but realizes belatedly that she's still handcuffed to the headboard. She groans in frustration.

"What?" he asks. She pointedly tugs at where she's restrained, but he shakes his head. "Nah."

Her mouth drops open, and he smiles. He's still teasing her. Torturing her. *The bastard.* The unfairly hot bastard.

She doesn't care though. She can let him have full control, let him take care of her. Because she knows he will.

The rhythm of his thrusts becomes stilted, which means he's getting close. She's close too, but she needs more to make it happen, and he hasn't touched her since he's been inside her.

Right as she's about to ask for what she wants, he suddenly pulls out. Smirking at her confusion, he slowly reaches down, wrapping his hand around his erection. He's jerking off above her now, staring into her eyes, his pupils blown so wide there's almost no green left, and she's too surprised to say anything.

Then to her total astonishment, he lets out a groan and releases himself all over her stomach. She makes a nonsensical noise, a little grossed out, and yet also turned on by how animalistic this is.

They stare at each other a few moments longer—until Montana comes back to her senses and realizes she's still *very* much on edge. She whines, jerking her hips up toward him.

"What's the matter?" he asks smugly.

"I haven't . . ."

"Haven't what?"

"You know!"

He tilts his head. "Do I?"

God, he's torturing her on purpose still. She opens her mouth to demand he do something about the state he's left her in, but then she closes it again and just growls. *Words. Difficult.*

Chuckling, he says, "Oh. You need me to take care of you?"

The bastard. The absolute bastard.

All she can do is nod and whimper pathetically.

"Say please."

She growls again. Fuck, now she's the one who's feral.

"Well, if you can't ask nicely . . ." he says, getting off the bed and turning to walk away.

"Please!" she screeches, begs, pleads.

He turns back, totally smug again. "As you wish."

Montana can't even properly appreciate the *Princess Bride* reference because she's such a fucking mess. She might actually lose her mind if she doesn't get to come soon. That's a thing, right? Maybe.

He bends down, reaching into that infernal nightstand again, and then holds up a slim pink vibrator. Because he's a crazy, wonderful, total effing bastard.

The idea of him with other girls crosses her mind again—because he's got a whole damn treasure chest of toys, and he must have used them with someone before her—but then he's on the bed and using the vibrator on her, pressing it firmly to her clit, and she has no rational thoughts left.

Little by little, he turns up the speed, until the buzzing sound is almost loud enough to drown out her moans. She's thrashing around wildly, and the pull on her shoulders from the cuffs hurts a little, but she can't control herself. Then something—Austin's arm—presses across her hips, holding her down. And from there it only takes a few more seconds until she's coming so hard she actually screams.

He turns off the vibrator, discarding it onto the bed somewhere beside her, and they stare at each other, both a bit wide-eyed, as Montana's brain and body slowly return to Earth. Did they really just do all that?

There's still a faint heat on her skin from the flogger, so *yes*, they definitely did.

After a few more moments, her breathing evens out, so she should be able to move now. But she's still bound and hasn't regained control of her voice yet, so all she can do is continue to stare at him, waiting to be set free.

He smiles. "All right. See ya."

Before she processes the words, he's gotten up and left the room.

"Austin!" she yells, finding her voice and not caring if his neighbors hear her. "Get back here or I will murder you!"

When he reappears in the doorway a minute later, he's holding a washcloth and a bottle of lotion.

"Okay, this was fun," she says, "but you can unlock me now."

"Don't worry." He leans over to give her a brief kiss. "I've got you."

Perched on the edge of the bed beside her hip, he brings the washcloth to her stomach. It's damp, making her squirm. But then she realizes he's cleaning her off—cleaning *himself* off of her—so she stills, letting him take care of her.

She thought she understood intimacy, that the two of them reached the height of it as teenagers. But this whole thing has been something more.

Finished, he tosses the washcloth to the floor, and then he finally produces the key to the handcuffs. He frees her wrists, but when she tries to lower her arms to a normal position, it's a little difficult because of the soreness in her shoulders. But he helps her, carefully moving her arms down by her sides and then shifting her body so that she's sitting up.

He grabs the lotion and begins rubbing it ever so gently over her wrists where the skin is a little red. Apparently even fuzzy handcuffs can really do the job. After he's satisfied with the aftercare, he moves to sit beside her, leaning against the headboard and wrapping an arm around her shoulders. He presses a kiss into the hair by her temple.

"That was . . ." She still can't find the words.

"Yeah?" he says, getting it anyway.

"Yeah."

She feels like a puddle. Like she might slip back down onto her back and then seep right into the mattress, disappearing. But the weight of his arm around her reminds her that he won't let that happen.

"I didn't take it too far, did I?" he asks.

Turning her head to look at him, she says, "Oh my god, no. It was intense, really fucking intense, but no. It wasn't too much."

"Okay, good. That's good to hear." He sounds almost nervous now, which is laughable, considering how confidently he'd taken charge an hour ago. "I mean, I figured. It definitely seemed like you were into it. But we've never really done something like that, so I'm glad to have verbal confirmation."

"We certainly haven't done that before," she agrees. And she doesn't want to go here, but she has to. She needs to know. "Uh, it made me wonder, though . . . who you've done it with before me."

"Do you really want to know?"

She nods cautiously. "You obviously learned how to do all that from someone. Or with someone. Was it with Brittani?"

His hand moves, caressing up and down her arm. "Actually, it was just sort of a random hookup. After Brittani and I broke up. This girl was super into it, and I said I'd never tried it, but I was open, so she showed me the ropes. Um, metaphorically. She explained exactly what she wanted me to do to her."

He squeezes her forearm lightly now, his fingertips providing a comforting pressure as he goes on. "I liked it, so I tried some of it again with someone else a while later, but I wasn't entirely comfortable doing it with anyone I didn't know really well. I didn't want to accidentally do something they didn't like."

"How did you know I would like it?" Montana asks, trailing her fingers over his bare thigh.

"I didn't. But I know you like I know myself. I knew I'd be able to read you. Every time you seemed into something, I felt like it was safe to take it a little further."

He can read her, all right. And she understands what he means. She doesn't think she'd be as willing to try something like that with a random hookup. Hearing that he wasn't doing all this stuff with a girlfriend makes her feel better too. She likes that it's something he can explore further with her.

They're quiet for a little while. Just sitting, touching, soaking up each other's company. A part of her never wants to leave this bed.

As she glances around, fully taking in his bedroom for the first time, she realizes something. She's living in her childhood home, but he's not in his. This is his own place. A new place. Somewhere she's never been before today, and they've never been in together.

It's proof that they're no longer eighteen. Time has passed. They've gotten older.

But she's here in this apartment with him now.

They're choosing each other all over again.

"Okay," she says finally, the urge to stretch her legs growing stronger. "You asked if I wanted to see your apartment, but so far all I've really seen is the bedroom. And I guess I got pretty well-acquainted with the inside of the front door."

He laughs. "You're right, c'mon."

They get up and dress, Montana a little slower than him because her legs still feel a tiny bit shaky. Then he takes her back out into the living room, sweeping his arm around at the couch, the armchair, the coffee table, the entertainment center. There's a plastic bin with some of Kalen's toys in one corner. And a guitar in a stand on the floor.

"You still play?"

Following her gaze, Austin's lips quirk up in a shy smile. "I guess. Not as often as I used to. And just for myself." He shrugs. "Well, sometimes for Kalen. He likes when I do the kids' songs from his TV shows."

"Play something for me?" she asks, placing her hand on his waist and looking up at him imploringly. "Please?"

He takes her hand briefly, giving it a squeeze, then crosses the room to remove the guitar from the stand. He brings it over to the couch. "Any requests? I'm assuming you're not interested in hearing the theme song to *Paw Patrol*."

"Hmm." She sits down in the armchair, ready to watch her private concert. "Something classic."

He thinks for a moment before he begins strumming chords. Although Montana is mesmerized by the deft movements of his fingers on the strings, she recognizes the song right away. He's playing "Landslide."

Her eyes lock on his as he sings about taking his love, taking it down. It feels like he's trying to tell her something. She's not exactly sure what, but it feels like something important.

Something good.

When Sloane and Montana came out of the bathroom—where Sloane had been trying to get spilled bean dip out of Montana's top so it wouldn't stain—it looked like most of the party had moved outside. Montana wrapped her thick cardigan tighter around herself, attempting to cover the wet spot as they wound their way through the living room and kitchen, then out the back door and onto the deck.

She wasn't even sure whose house this was, some senior on the baseball team with Austin. And speaking of Austin, she'd kind of lost him. Scanning the crowd on the deck for him, she came up blank. As the sounds of a guitar being played reached her ears, though, she looked out over the backyard and—*Bingo.*

A small circle of Adirondack chairs surrounded a fire pit, and he was leaned back playing in one. He hadn't brought his guitar, so it must be someone else's. Maybe the guy sitting in the chair next to him. The other chairs were occupied by girls who all seemed entranced as they watched her boyfriend.

"Uh oh," Sloane said. "You better get over there before someone tries to swoop in on your territory."

Montana smiled and rolled her eyes. "First of all, he's not my territory. And second, I'm not worried."

Sloane studied her face. "You're really not, are you?"

"Nope."

If this was fall of sophomore year, maybe she would have been. But she was a junior now, and she and Austin had been dating for almost a year. She was no longer insecure enough to think she might lose him just because another girl batted her eyelashes at him.

A couple of those girls were doing more than that though. They were practically falling out of their chairs for him. They looked ready to climb into his lap.

Well, it sucked for them, because they couldn't have him.

She stayed where she was, resting her arms on top of the deck railing, content to listen from afar.

He didn't usually play in front of this many people, but he looked comfortable. He looked fucking beautiful, truthfully, with his light denim jeans, black T-shirt, and gray baseball hoodie, the guitar cradled in his arms. His head was bent down so his hair fell slightly over his eyes.

When the song ended, he looked up, finding her right away. How did he always do that? Like he could just sense her presence. He grinned at her.

Sloane gave her a shove. "Go. Fawn over him. At least make those girls jealous, it'll be fun."

Montana laughed, then made her way down the deck stairs and out into the yard, leaving Sloane to mingle.

Austin passed the guitar to the guy next to him and stood. The girls started to protest. Three of them even jumped up and surrounded him as he tried to walk away. He smiled at them, but as soon as one stepped closer and put her hand on his forearm, he apologized and twisted out of her grasp.

"Don't let me keep you from your groupies," Montana joked when he reached her.

Shaking his head, he leaned in to kiss her on the cheek. "They were just being nice."

She gave him a small smile. He acted like he didn't know what he looked like or sounded like. It wasn't as if he was the world's best singer. But a hot guy with an acoustic guitar? As long as his voice wasn't nails on a chalkboard, he'd be drooled over.

"You know if you wrote your own songs," she said, "you could become famous and have all the groupies you wanted."

He wrapped his arms around her waist, pulling her into him. "Screw groupies. I only want you."

She gave him a chaste kiss for that. Then she said, "What about the getting famous part?"

"I don't want that either. You know I only play for fun. And I *have* tried to write my own songs."

"You have?" Montana couldn't believe she didn't know that. "Why haven't you played them for me?"

He crinkled his nose. "Because they're terrible. If I don't have anything important to say, I'd rather say nothing at all."

"That was deep."

"Shut up," he said, laughing.

When he leaned in for another kiss, she couldn't help but smile to herself at the knowledge that some of those girls were probably watching. And if they were, they were undoubtedly jealous.

As they should be.

Because her boyfriend was the best.

CHAPTER FIFTEEN

NOW

*M*ontana's sitting on the front porch, feet up on the table, enjoying her morning cup of coffee in the warm sun. She's pleasantly full from the eggs and toast she ate inside, and she's just completed the crossword on her iPad. As she looks out across the street, Mrs. Coulter waves to her from her front yard, where the old woman is kneeling in the grass, tending to her flowers.

Waving back, that's when it hits her. She's happy. Like genuinely happy to be here, not merely trying to make the best of things. She never thought she'd feel this content being back in this house, this town.

A few months ago, she was a miserable mess, bemoaning her bad luck. But maybe it wasn't bad luck at all. Maybe it was fate. It sure feels like fate, her and Austin getting back together after so many years.

If only it didn't take her losing her dream job in order for her to find her way back to her dream guy.

Yesterday was a perfect day. The sex was amazing, but everything before it—the lake, the ice cream, the fish fry stand—was wonderful too.

She's glad she got to enjoy some of the best stuff this area has to offer with Austin and Kalen. She's spent years reveling in the California sunshine, the palm trees, the sight of the Hollywood Hills. But she'd forgotten how beautiful New England is too.

Holy crap.

That's it.

All of a sudden, her oversight becomes glaringly obvious.

She's spent all this time in Hartley thinking her career might be over. Because being stuck here in Massachusetts without a magazine footing the travel bill, how would she ever have new experiences to write about? But nothing's stopping her from writing *about* Massachusetts. About all of New England.

She has a car. She has a job that affords her enough to cover day and overnight trips. There's so much to offer here, so many beautiful places to visit without her ever needing to get on a plane.

How could she be so blind? Writing about New England never crossed her mind before, because this is where she grew up. After spending her first eighteen years here, all she wanted to do was get away to see new things. But for people living in other parts of the country, all these charming New England towns *are* great travel destinations.

People come here to see the leaves change to experience snow for the first time. People want to go to the Berkshires, Newport, Acadia National Park. The want to eat lobster on the Cape and go skiing in Vermont.

Invigorated by the sudden rush of inspiration, she runs inside to swap her iPad for her laptop. Then she settles back onto the cozy loveseat Austin picked out for her, and she pictures his warm easy smile as she types a title: "A Charming Massachusetts Summer Day." From there, the words seem to fly out of her. She's typing as fast as she can, her fingers working to keep up with her stream of thoughts.

Her favorite kinds of articles to write are the ones where she gets to make it a little bit personal. They're not simply listings of great places readers should check out. She relays her personal experiences there, what these places made her feel. Readers aren't only looking for the best flavored soft serve in the state. (Dream Cream's, obviously.) They're also looking to feel something.

Being at the lake yesterday with Austin and Kalen definitely made her feel things. Things she never would have felt if she'd gone alone. And maybe that's another piece she's been missing too?

The years she worked for the magazine were spent taking solo trips. Experiencing things from the point of view of a single woman in her mid-twenties. Drinking moonshine and riding mechanical bulls in Nashville. Skydiving in Utah. Smoking hookah and strolling down the red-light district in Amsterdam. Those were all incredible, fun ex-periences, and she's so grateful for them. But not all travel readers are young single women.

Yesterday she got to experience cool places from a romantic lens. A family one, also.

There are people looking to find the most romantic bed and breakfasts in New Hampshire, or the most exciting, kid-friendly activities on Nantucket. There's so much to do here, to see, to explore. And she can even do some of it with Austin and Kalen too.

She hasn't run out of things to write about.

She was just looking too far away, from the wrong perspective.

Being with Austin helps her see things in new ways. It's always been like that, even when they were young.

She doesn't regret the choice she made at eighteen. She'll never regret all the things she got to do and see. But maybe this time she doesn't have to choose between her career and him.

Maybe she can have them both.

A WEEK LATER, the article sells. Not to a huge magazine, and it doesn't pay much, but neither of those things matters. It's been forever since she's actually sold an article.

Now she really feels like she can do this. Leaving L.A. will *not* be the end of her career.

Montana shares her good news with Austin when he shows up for the dinner shift at the restaurant. She wanted to text him right away this morning when she got the email, but she decided to wait so she could tell him in person. By the time she sees him, she's jittery with excitement.

It's worth the wait, though, because he hugs her tightly, lifting her off her feet and spinning her around right in the middle of the dining room. "Congratulations! That's awesome!"

"Thanks, I know!"

"We need to go out to celebrate," he says, setting her down.

"It's not like it's my first article ever."

He gives her an incredulous look. "So what? Let me take you out. Somewhere fancy this time. You deserve more than fried food on a picnic table."

"That place was amazing," she argues. "And I don't want to go somewhere fancy."

"Okay, fine. Where do you wanna go then?"

The answer comes to her right away and she smiles. "Goldleaf."

He laughs. "Seriously? But we've always gone there."

"Exactly."

◆

MONTANA DOESN'T order her usual. It's been so many years since she's had the chance to order banana chocolate chip pancakes from Goldleaf Diner, but she passes them up, because now she knows that Austin Adler's pancakes are better.

Maybe she could convince him to add them to the weekend late-night menu at Alan's Place. That way she could have them every Friday night as a reward for working her butt off. And what drunk person doesn't crave pancakes at midnight? They could be a big hit.

She's about to suggest it when he says, "So when do I get to read this article?"

"It won't be out for a couple weeks, probably."

"And there's no way for me to read it early?" He reaches across the table and strokes the back of her hand. "After all, I *do* know the writer."

She laughs. "I can send it to you."

"Good." He gives her hand a little squeeze before letting go.

It makes Montana happy to know he's interested in what she writes. But it makes her a tiny bit nervous too. What if he thinks she sucks? Surely, he won't, because she knows she's a good writer. She's made a career out of it, hasn't she? But she values his opinion more than anyone else's. Plus, he's kind of in the article. Will that be weird for him?

Still. She's happy.

Now that she has Austin and a plan for her career, everything in her life seems to be falling into place.

As she eats her Rodeo Burger and fries, wiping the dripping barbeque sauce from her chin after each bite, she tells him about her plan. Traveling around exploring New England, writing freelance articles, hoping to eventually land a new full-time job with a magazine.

Her cheeks start to hurt from grinning too much. "I'm excited to check out new places. There's so much to see and do here, you know? It's such a relief to be inspired again."

"That's great," Austin says. "I'm happy for you." He smiles at her before taking a sip of his water, but . . . He doesn't *sound* happy. Which is weird.

She shifts in her seat, attempting to unstick the backs of her thighs from the vinyl booth. "And it's thanks to you that I've been inspired," she says. "So . . . thank you."

He nods and smiles again, then takes a bite of his own burger without saying anything.

What's going on here? His smiles aren't quite reaching his eyes, not big enough to really show off his dimples. He took her out to celebrate selling her article, but now he's acting almost upset while she's trying to share her excitement.

Is her talk about continuing to pursue her writing career triggering some old resentment for him? Because she knows it's what sent her away from him all those years ago, but things are different now. If he still doesn't understand what getting to make a living from traveling and writing about her experiences means to her, then that hurts. He's supposed to understand her better than anybody.

"Something wrong?" she ventures to ask when it grows a little too quiet.

He shakes his head, dragging a fry through his pile of ketchup. "No, nothing. Hearing you talk like this reminds me of before we graduated, when you were so excited to get to college. I'm . . . happy you're writing again. I know how important it is to you."

Okay. That doesn't feel like exactly the truth, but she's afraid to push him.

"Thanks. It is," she agrees, running her finger over a chip at the edge of the tabletop. Then she changes the subject to Kalen starting school in the fall, and Austin's mood seems to brighten a bit.

But as he talks, she still feels this weird disconnect between them, and finds herself more focused on the setting around them than on him. Distracted by the suddenly overpowering smells of bacon and onions frying, the scrape of silverware against plates, and the yells of a few children impatiently waiting for their food.

The diner is supposed to be one of her happy places. And this is supposed to be a celebration. So why are all these little things grating slightly on her nerves?

It isn't until she's alone again at home—Austin claimed he couldn't come in because he had to pick up Kalen—that she's hit with an uncomfortable thought. *Is he worried she's going to leave him again?*

Because she's not trying to go back to L.A. She made that clear, right?

THEN

*I*f you could go anywhere in the world, where would you go?"

Austin, his arm wrapped around Montana's shoulder, squeezed her even closer against him. "To visit or to live?"

Her head was resting on his chest, and she could smell the cinnamon gum he was chewing. She curled her hand into his shirt, her thumb stroking lightly over his stomach. They'd spent practically the whole summer together like this, minus when he took his annual family trip to the Cape.

The sun was setting, and the bugs would soon chase them from the porch, but right now in this moment, there was no place on Earth she'd rather be.

It was just that the idea of traveling had been on her mind a lot lately. Maybe because she was about to be an upperclassman, and her parents had asked her if she'd started thinking about colleges yet. She hadn't, really. She hadn't given much thought to what she wanted to major in or what she wanted to do for a career, because that stuff had always seemed so far away until now. But she did know that traveling was something she wanted to do the first chance she got.

"To visit. Or maybe both."

He brought his free hand up to the side of her neck, his fingers spanning out to brush her jaw and collarbone at the same time. "I never really thought about it."

She lifted her head to gaze up at him. "Seriously?"

"Yeah. Traveling sounds fun, I guess. But I've never given much thought to any specific places." His thumb swept ever so softly over her jawline. "Why? What about you?"

"I've been dreaming of going to Austria since I saw *The Sound of Music* when I was ten."

He laughed.

"What?" she said.

"Watching a movie about a war-torn country made you want to visit the country?"

She rolled her eyes. "Well, the war's no longer going on, you know."

His thumb stilled, and he asked, "You want to visit, or you want to live there?"

"Oh, just to visit, I think. I'm not sure I see myself living in a different country. But that's probably because I don't know enough about any other country." She thought a moment. "I could see myself living in California though. No more snow."

"You don't hate snow. You like sledding."

Shrugging against his chest, she said, "True. But maybe I'll trade it in for surfing."

"How is that the same thing?"

She sat up, reluctantly moving away from his touch so she could look at him properly. "It's not the same thing. That's the point."

"Okay . . ." His brow furrowed. "I don't know if I can see myself ever living anywhere but here."

"Here, meaning Hartley?"

He nodded.

"That's because you've always lived here."

"So have you," he reminded her. "And so what? I like it here."

"You're just comfortable here."

He frowned. "And what's wrong with that?"

She shook her head and then settled back against his chest. "Nothing. Never mind."

CHAPTER SIXTEEN

NOW

Sliding a small, cheap-looking wooden bowl filled with pretzels across the bar top, the young male bartender asks with a flirty smile, "What can I get for you ladies?"

"Just water for me, please," Sloane requests.

Montana fixes the guy with a flirty look of her own. "What's your specialty?"

His smile falters slightly. "We don't really have a specialty drink menu here. It's not that kind of place."

She takes a quick scan of the room. It's clearly a dive bar, with dim lighting, just a few tables, and the only décor being garish neon signs advertising brands of beer and liquor. Turning back to him, she says, "Yeah, I can tell. But what's the drink that *you're* best at making? That you have fun making."

"Probably an old fashioned," he says.

"Sold." She slaps her hand down playfully on the bar top. "With your best bourbon."

The bartender's smile is back in full force when he tells her, "Coming right up."

Truthfully, Montana can't exactly afford to order the best bourbon, but this is for an article she plans to write, so she'll let herself splurge. She's sold a few more freelance pieces, and this quest to find the best cocktails in Amherst seemed like a fun, easy idea.

But maybe it would have been more fun five years ago, because now she's already imagining the hangover she'll have in the morning when she's supposed to hang out with Austin and Kalen. It's the sweet drinks that kill you, and she's already been served a few overly sugary concoctions with rum and vodka and too many juices at the last two places she and Sloane checked out. Which makes this guy's choice a relief.

Sloane takes a sip of her water as they watch the bartender muddle the fruit for Montana's cocktail. She had two drinks at the first bar, but then she switched to water since she's playing designated driver tonight. "Not that it wasn't amusing for me," she says, "to watch you try not to cringe as you took a sip of that last bubblegum pink monstrosity, but why didn't you ask your ex-boyfriend-slash-again-boyfriend to accompany you on this little ill-fated adventure?"

"It's not ill-fated!"

"You won't be saying that in the morning."

Montana reaches for a pretzel. "True. But I wanted to do something fun with you." She and Austin haven't had many free nights together lately, because Brittani's had to pick up extra hours to cover for a sick coworker, so Austin's either been working or with Kalen. But she would've asked Sloane anyway. "And he's not my boyfriend."

Sloane raises one eyebrow pointedly.

"He's not!" she insists. "I know what you mean, but we haven't put that label on it yet. We're keeping it casual."

The bartender slides the old fashioned in front of her and waits for her to try it. She takes a sip, then smiles. After she tells him it's excellent, he wanders away looking pleased with himself.

"I'm sorry," Sloane says while Montana munches on the pretzel, "but there's no way in hell that Montana Sinclair and Austin Adler are just keeping it casual. You two have never been casual. You've been in love with each other since you were fifteen, for crying out loud."

"Maybe."

"Maybe?"

Fiddling with the tiny black cocktail straw in her glass, she thinks about it. "We were in love when we were fifteen. But we're adults now. It's not the same. It's . . . scarier. It makes more sense to be cautious and take things slow."

Sloane nods thoughtfully. "You're absolutely right. It does make sense to take things slow. But I bet you're lying to yourself if you think you didn't fall in love with him again the first moment you saw him when you got back to town."

She shrugs. Maybe she did. But that's not something she can *let* herself feel. The whole thing between them is overwhelming enough without going there. There's too much for them to work out before she can fall too deep.

But Sloane's probably right.

Whether it's the smart thing to do or not, she's probably already fallen.

"How's Jeremy?" she asks, changing the subject. "Did he pop the question yet?"

"No, but he better do it soon, because the other night I let him pop something else."

"Excuse me?"

Sloane glances toward the bartender, who appears busy a few feet away. But there's no one else sitting at the bar, and Montana knows from experience that he's probably listening to every word they say. Leaning in closer, Sloane whispers, "We tried anal for the first time."

Montana lets out a shocked, "*Oh!*" and immediately gets shushed by her friend. Lowering her volume, she asks, "How was it?"

"Not that bad actually," Sloane admits, grabbing a small handful of the pretzels. "But I don't want him to know that. Let him think I'm making this big sacrifice by allowing him to go there."

Laughing, Montana tells her, "You're awful. But you did like it?"

"I mean, not at first. But by the end, once I got used to it,"—Sloane shrugs—"yeah, kind of. I think it could get better if we try again."

"Interesting." Hopefully Montana doesn't sound too scandalized by this information. She doesn't want Sloane to feel awkward telling her stuff.

And it's not like anal sex is all that wild. Some of the stuff she and Austin have tried in bed lately might be considered wilder. But Sloane's always been . . . not *uptight*, exactly. Traditional, maybe?

Then again, it's been a decade since high school, since Montana really knew her. A lot can change in ten years.

"Have you done it?" Sloane asks.

"Nope." She's never been all that curious about it. After high school, she was never in another serious relationship, so there wasn't anyone she would have considered trying it with. But thinking about trying it with Austin now . . .

Well. Consider her interest piqued.

When she and Sloane are quiet for a minute, the bartender takes the opportunity to sidle up to them again. He suddenly produces a deck of cards from behind the bar and says, "You ladies wanna see a magic trick?"

"Sure," Sloane says agreeably, wiping her hands of pretzel dust.

As he shuffles the deck, he's eyeing them with more interest than before, and he seems to be holding back a grin. *Oh yeah.* He definitely heard what they were talking about.

Montana sips her drink and watches in amusement as he fans out the cards and asks Sloane to pick one. With another guy, this could feel sketchy, but luckily with this one, it only feels a bit cheesy. And after a few complicated maneuvers that she can't quite follow, when he successfully identifies Sloane's card, Montana is sufficiently impressed.

She asks him his name because she definitely wants to include him in her article. He provides a great cocktail, plus entertainment. What more could you need?

After finishing her old fashioned, she's tempted to order another, but there are still at least two more places she wants to hit, so that's not a good idea. Instead, she pays for the drink and tips generously, then she and Sloane leave and make their way down the street to their next location.

It's great that Sloane agreed to come with her. They've been talking on the phone more often, but this is the first time they've hung out since the coffee shop. Already, though, it feels more natural. Like old times.

Except in old times, they never talked about their sex lives in quite as much detail. Montana shared with Sloane when she lost her virginity to Austin, of course. But back then, when she talked about sex, it was more about the feelings involved. The graphic details, she kept to herself.

Maybe now it's different, since Sloane doesn't see Austin every day at school. It doesn't feel as wrong to overshare.

So when they take their seats at the bar in a joint named Minnie's, and Montana is served something in a martini glass called a Tipsy Flamingo off of the specialty cocktails menu (which she inwardly groans at), she spills all about the kinky sex she and Austin have had.

"It's so fucking hot when he takes total control like that."

Sloane smirks. "Damn. I'm surprised lover boy has it in him. He definitely seems more like the gently-worship-you-with-his-tongue-for-hours type."

Montana can't conceal her grin. "Oh, he does that too."

"Cheers," Sloane says, holding up her water glass.

Clinking her martini glass clumsily against it, Montana sloshes a few drops of bright pink liquid onto the bar. She grabs a cocktail napkin to wipe it up, not sparing any remorse for the wasted alcohol.

By the time Sloane drops her off at home, she's the giggly, giddy type of drunk. Hopefully tomorrow she'll be able to make sense of the notes she took on her phone.

Feeling loose and happy when she goes upstairs to her bedroom, she grabs her vibrator out of her underwear drawer and takes it to bed with her. *Why not?* Imagining new things to try with Austin has her finishing in no time at all.

But before she falls asleep, she's thinking about what she said to Sloane—she and Austin aren't anything official. She wonders how long that will continue to work for both of them.

She doesn't want to rush him, but she doesn't want to risk not giving him enough either.

And what if *she* needs more?

◆

IN THE MORNING, Montana curses her alarm. Silently, though, because she's too groggy to speak. It takes every ounce of her willpower not to hit snooze, and instead to roll herself out of bed and stand up. She probably should have made her cocktail research a multiple night thing. But hindsight, right?

She groans and then stumbles downstairs, sans pants, to make coffee. She, Austin, and Kalen are getting breakfast before going to the park, but she's not going to make it over to their place without caffeinating first.

Not wanting Austin to witness her hangover, she made sure to give herself plenty of extra time this morning to wake up and work on feeling normal before she has to leave the house. But she might have overdone it by drinking almost a whole pot of coffee. So now that it's time to go, she's moving with an unnatural amount of pep in her step, while also cringing at the cymbals that keep crashing inside her skull.

The caffeine gets her to Austin's apartment fifteen minutes early, dressed in flip flops, capri leggings, and an oversized, peach-colored tank top that she tied in a knot above her hip. But when he opens the door, his eyes widen at the sight of her.

"What?" she asks, hand reaching up to smooth her hair. Does she still look hungover? She thought she hid it pretty well.

"Nothing. You're early."

"Is it that surprising?"

He smiles teasingly. "Kind of. But no, I just thought you were going to be Brittani."

"Oh."

"She's running a little late, so she hasn't dropped off Kalen yet," he explains, moving aside to let her in.

She kicks off her flip flops and leaves them on the mat by the door. "That's okay, I won't starve." She's really not sure her stomach can even handle food yet, honestly. The hangover combined with all that coffee already isn't the best combination.

Austin gives her a strange look before he says robotically, "Right. It's fine."

Why is he being weird? Her head can't handle this right now.

Rising onto her toes, she kisses him, hoping to dispel whatever weird energy he's got going on here. He returns the kiss, one arm wrapping around to the small of her back, but he still seems distracted when he pulls away.

"She should be here any minute," he says.

"Okay."

He gives her another nervous look, and that's when she finally gets it.

"*Oh.* You don't want me to be here."

"What?" His eyes flash with panic. "Of course I do!"

She puts her hand on his forearm, squeezing reassuringly. "You don't want me to be here when Brittani comes."

A tiny wince of guilt, and then—"I'm just not sure how awkward it'll be introducing you."

"Does she know about me?"

"Sort of. I mean, I told her all about you when she and I first started dating years ago. And I mentioned it when we started doing"—he motions awkwardly between their bodies—"*this.*"

"And she's okay with it?" Montana presses, even though she's dreading the answer. "Me spending time with Kalen?"

"Yeah, that's why I told her. We agreed to always be open with each other if it affects Kalen. But I didn't know exactly *what* to tell her. I said we're being careful and taking things really slow."

Yup. Careful and slow. Like freaking turtles.

That's what she told Sloane. But in this moment, standing in Austin's apartment having this discussion, Montana has the urge to be reckless, even if she doesn't know what that would mean. Demanding a commitment from him right now? Staking her claim by pushing him down on the couch and straddling him so his ex can walk in and find them like that?

Ugh. The clanging still going on inside her head is probably what's egging her on. She really shouldn't have drunk so much last night. Rationality is eluding her today.

Lifting one heel, she presses the ball of her foot down into the material of her cushy flip flops, searching for something to ground her. "Well. If she knows, then I think it'll be fine. But I can wait in the car if you want."

Austin reaches for her, pulling her in against his chest. "No. The situation threw me off guard, but you're right. It'll be fine."

She melts into him, running her fingers down his pecs as the pounding in her skull seems to ease. He's magic, isn't he? Sighing contentedly, she lets her forehead rest against the soft material of his T-shirt.

This is good.

The pace they're going is fine.

She can be a turtle. She can.

A couple rapid knocks on the door break them apart.

Ah, shit.

Despite both of their assurances that this will be fine, she isn't emotionally prepared to meet Austin's ex and the mother of his child. Especially since her headache comes back the moment she loses physical contact with him. She tugs self-consciously on the knot at the bottom of her tank top as Austin goes to open the door.

Kalen comes barreling through, wrapping his arms briefly around Austin's legs before sidestepping his dad and running at Montana. "Hi!" he squeals excitedly.

"Hey, little man!" She bends down to hug him, her heart warming at the enthusiastic greeting.

Then she straightens again to find the woman who must be Brittani staring right at her. She's blonde, petite—short and thin enough that Montana can't imagine how she ever pushed a baby out of her body—and looking unfairly pretty even in scrubs.

"Uh, hi. I'm Montana."

Brittani nods. "I figured. I'm Brittani."

"I figured."

Well, this is going great.

Austin clears his throat. "We're gonna grab breakfast, then hang out at the park for a bit."

"Sounds nice," Brittani replies, her eyes lingering on Montana an extra beat before she turns her head to him. "I've got to get to work."

"Have a good day," he tells her.

"You too." Her eyes cut to Montana again. "Nice to meet you."

Montana forces a smile. "You too."

"Bye sweetie," Brittani says to Kalen, getting a wave in return, and then she turns to leave.

Austin shuts the door behind her and takes a deep breath. Montana's still holding hers.

"Can I get chocolate chip pancakes with whipped cream?" Kalen asks eagerly.

"Sure, bud," Austin says, scooping the kid up in his arms.

The tension drains from the room and Montana smiles for real. "Have you ever tried them with chocolate chips *and* bananas?" she asks Kalen.

His eyes grow as big as saucers. "You can do that?"

"Sure can!"

"What about strawberries?"

Austin laughs. "You want strawberries, bananas, and chocolate chips?"

Kalen nods. "Mmhmm. And blueberries."

Austin shoots Montana an amused look. "You've created a monster."

Montana only shrugs in response, not feeling bad about it at all.

At the diner, Kalen does get all four in his pancakes, and he loves it. Montana gets banana chocolate chip, even though Austin's are better. And Austin has to make the two of them look like pigs by ordering an egg-white spinach omelet. *Blech*. Why does she even like him again?

When they get to the park, Montana and Austin settle on a bench where they can watch Kalen as he climbs the jungle gym on the playground. The comfortable quiet they sit in for a few minutes is nice, but she wishes Austin would put his arm around her shoulders. He can't, though, because they agreed to let Kalen think they're just friends for now.

She scoots closer and presses her shoulder into his anyway. Subtle rebellion. "So. Brittani seems nice."

Austin raises an eyebrow. "She is."

"She didn't, uh . . . appear to like me very much."

"She doesn't know you."

Watching a jogger go past them, Montana makes a noise of agreement. "She knows *about* me though."

Which begs the question—how bad did Austin make her sound way back then?

And what about *now*?

He presses his finger comfortingly into her leg, right above her knee. Just a brief touch, and then it's gone. "I promise she doesn't have a problem with you. She's naturally going to be protective of Kalen, that's all. And me too, I guess. I mean, we have a kid together. We still care about each other."

"Right. I know."

Of course they do. That's nothing to be jealous about. And yet . . .

Her hangover has subsided by now, but Montana's going to blame all her grumpy feelings on it anyway.

She needs to rein it in—all the jealousy and insecurities that have been spilling out of her this morning—and be in the moment. Enjoy this for what it is. Getting to relax and spend a lazy day with a man and a boy she cares about. What more does she need right now?

On the playground, Kalen is climbing down from the jungle gym. He's almost at the bottom when his foot slips and he falls to the ground. It's only the tiniest drop, so he lands on his butt looking more shocked than hurt. But then he scrunches up his face and starts to cry, and Montana springs up and runs, reaching him before she realizes what she's doing.

Austin's only a step behind her, but Kalen holds out his arms for Montana, so she picks him up and asks, "You okay, bud?"

"No," he whines, though he's already stopped crying.

"You sure? You look okay, but you let me know if we need to take you to the doctor."

Kalen resolutely wipes the tears from his cheek. "You're right. I'm okay."

"Good."

"You don't have to put me down though," he says matter-of-factly.

"Okay." She hefts him up a little higher to get a better hold on him. Then she looks up to find Austin staring at her, a sort of dumbstruck an expression on his face. Like he never expected to be standing here in the park with her while she holds his kid in her arms.

Well, she never expected it either. Yet here they are.

Montana loves traveling, loves adventures. She's never had too much desire to become a mother. But suddenly she knows, with absolute certainty, that if the rest of her life is filled with lowkey days in Hartley spent with this man and this boy—at the park, swimming, relaxing on the porch, eating pancakes, reading stories out loud and doing the voices—she'll be more than okay with that. She'll be so fucking happy.

Hopefully her face is conveying all this to Austin, since she can't say it out loud right now.

"Dog!" Kalen suddenly yells, causing her and Austin to break their intense eye contact.

He's squirming in Montana's arms, so she sets him on the ground, and he immediately takes off running toward a woman with a big dog on a leash. Austin catches him before he gets too far, scooping him up like he weighs nothing.

He scrunches up his face like he's about to cry again and yells, "I wanna pet the dog!"

"I know, but you can't run up to dogs or people that you don't know," Austin explains. "You need to have me or your mom or your grandparents or Montana with you." Montana's heart does a little flutter at being included in the list of acceptable guardians. "And you have to ask the person first if their dog is friendly, and if it's okay for you to pet it."

"Dog," Kalen pleads, sadder this time. "Please can I pet the dog?"

Austin puts him back on his feet. "We can go ask."

Kalen eagerly leads the way over to where the woman and the large brown dog are roaming in the grass. But when he gets closer, he hangs back, waiting for his dad before he approaches.

The woman smiles cautiously at the three of them.

Austin nudges Kalen. "Ask her."

Kalen's cheeks turn red, but then he says clearly, "Is it okay if I pet your dog?"

The woman's smile brightens. "Oh, sure! This is Sadie. She's very friendly."

That's all the permission he needs. He practically throws himself on the ground in front of the dog, whose tail starts wagging out of control. Rather than pet her, Kalen throws his arms around her neck, laughing when she licks a long stripe of slobber up his face. After a minute, Austin joins him, crouching down to pet the dog's back and scratch at her hips.

Montana wants to pet her, too, but for a moment all she can do is stand there, looking down at father and son, both of their faces lit up with joy at receiving the dog's affection. It's possibly the most adorable thing she's ever seen. Her heart can barely take it.

Austin tells her afterward how Kalen is obsessed with dogs, how badly he wants one. But they're not allowed at Austin's apartment. Montana couldn't have any at her apartment in L.A. either, but she loves dogs too, and she realizes it's been so long since she's had one. Since her family had to put Daisy down when she was in high school.

And at home that evening, when she's working on an article at the desk she bought and set up in what's supposed to be the dining room, the house suddenly feels too quiet and empty. She lived alone in L.A. too, but her apartment was so much smaller there. This house has too much space to be alone in.

What if she got a dog now? Kalen would like that. And she would too, but it's a huge commitment, one she's not sure if she's ready for yet. She's only recently gotten her life back together here. Maybe soon though. It's definitely something to think about.

Yeah.

A dog would be nice.

THEN

Standing in her backyard, Montana watched as Austin threw a tennis ball for Daisy to chase for about the hundredth time. She was expecting the black lab to eventually lie down in the grass and pass out from exhaustion, but Daisy kept bringing the ball back to Austin over and over again, tail wagging nonstop. At this point, Austin was surely her favorite human after Montana. (And Montana only came first still because she let Daisy sleep in her bed.) But who could blame the dog? Austin was so . . . *Austin*. Who could resist loving him?

Her dad was at the grill, cooking dinner for everyone, while her mom lounged in one of the Adirondack chairs with a book. It was a picture-perfect evening. Montana always loved summer, and now she even had a boyfriend to spend it with. He'd long ago charmed her parents, so he was welcome over here basically whenever he wanted.

Austin stepped closer and put his arm around her waist as Daisy came running back with the fuzzy green ball clenched between her teeth. Montana reached down to take it from her, but Daisy turned her head and dropped the ball right at Austin's feet instead. Traitor.

"Isn't your arm getting tired?" Montana asked, when Austin cocked it back and sent the ball flying again.

"Nah. This is fun."

Of course. He played baseball. He was probably enjoying this little game almost as much as Daisy.

Daisy retrieved the ball, but instead of returning it this time, she plopped herself to the ground, rolling onto her back with her legs pointed at the sky, ball still in her mouth. She wriggled from side to side enthusiastically, and Montana realized she was in a perfectly Daisy-sized dip in the yard that she'd obviously made for herself.

Uh oh.

It had rained yesterday, so when Daisy sprung to her feet again and came running back, she was covered in mud. It was immediately apparent how dirty she was, even with the black fur.

"Are you kidding?" her dad yelled, snapping his long pair of tongs in the air. "She dug another hole again!"

Her mom looked up from her book and frowned disapprovingly. "You need to give her a bath."

Montana knew she was talking to her, even though this wasn't at all her fault. But she and Austin *were* the ones playing with Daisy, getting her all riled up.

"And hurry up!" her dad added. "Food's almost ready."

Turning to Austin, she told him "Sorry. You can hang out here still, or up in my room if you want. It might take a bit." It was hard to tell if Daisy liked baths or hated them from how crazy she acted when you got her into the tub. Maybe a little of both.

Austin leaned in to kiss her forehead, then said, "Don't be silly, I'll help you."

"Are you sure? It's not easy."

"All the more reason for me to help."

She smiled and managed to grab Daisy by the collar. When she led the dog inside, she was careful not to let her near the furniture or to walk across any rugs. Though she'd still need to wipe the muddy paw prints off the hardwood later. Austin followed the pair of them upstairs to the bathroom and shut the door.

"Daisy, sit," Montana commanded, and Daisy was quick to obey. After turning the water on to start filling the tub, she glanced at Austin's white T-shirt and navy blue basketball shorts. "You're gonna get dirty. Or wet. Probably both."

He shrugged and pulled his shirt over his head, tossing it to the floor. And well. It wasn't like she'd never seen his bare chest before. She'd seen a hell of a lot more than that, in fact. But something about the bath water drawing, and the small, confined space made this situation suddenly feel hotter than it should have been.

Like he knew exactly what she was thinking, Austin smirked. Damn him.

She blushed, but two could play this game. "Lock the door."

He squinted in confusion but did it. When he turned back around and found her standing there in her purple bra, his eyes grew comically wide.

"What?" she asked innocently. "I don't wanna ruin my shirt either."

She'd been wearing an old gym shirt from middle school that she didn't care about at all, but so what?

He made a small noise—a whimper or a groan, she couldn't tell— and then yanked her closer to him so he could kiss her, his hand winding its way into her hair.

They only got caught up for a moment before Daisy let out a happy bark and jumped up, muddy paws landing on Austin's forearm.

"Daisy, down!" Montana shouted, but she was laughing too hard to really make it sound like a command.

Austin shoved the dog gently off him, and together they urged her into the tub. Montana got to work quickly with the shampoo while Austin attempted to hold Daisy still, but he ended up having to get in with her. And although Montana was grateful for his help, by the end of the dog's bath, she was almost equally as wet.

When they finally let Daisy out of the tub, she immediately shook out her fur, spraying them some more.

Montana took another long look at Austin, water droplets falling off his skin, and she wished they could take a shower together. That wasn't something they'd done yet, and she'd never given it too much thought before. The idea of it felt even more intimate than sex somehow.

But she wanted to do it now. Wanted to lather up his back with her loofah, massage shampoo into his hair like she did for Daisy. Rinse it out with one hand on his waist, sliding over his wet skin. If only her parents weren't right outside, expecting the two of them to hurry back down to grab their dinners.

That fantasy would have to be saved for another time, if they ever got the chance for some extended privacy.

As he squeezed out his shorts in the tub, Austin smiled jovially, like he didn't mind at all that he'd gotten soaked. Daisy whined, pawing at the door. She probably wanted to get back outside, not just out of the bathroom, but that was too bad. She wasn't running free out there again until the ground dried up. Montana put her shirt back on, and after shooting one last longing look Austin's way, she opened the door to get away from temptation.

Her parents hadn't waited for them to start eating, and Montana and Austin had to reheat their pork chops a bit, but they didn't care. No one cared all that much when Daisy stole a pork chop off the large platter on the counter either.

CHAPTER SEVENTEEN

NOW

*E*ventually, Montana's freelance writing is going so well that she's able to start pitching articles to magazines and websites ahead of time, and then work out deals with businesses that would like to be featured in order to cover some of her expenses. She's doing a lot of the leg work herself arranging things, but it's worth it because she finally feels like her writing career is getting somewhere again.

Especially after she scores a huge discount at a Vermont bed and breakfast when she tells them she's writing an article on romantic fall getaways for *New England Travel*. By some miracle, she and Austin manage to get coverage for both of them at work so they can take the weekend off. It's only a three-hour drive, but it's the farthest Montana has traveled since she's moved back to Massachusetts, so she feels positively giddy as they start the trip up there.

They're staying at the Hummingbird Inn, and Austin has made fun of the name three times already, but he's actually the more romantic of the two of them, so she's sure he's as happy as she is at the chance to take this trip together. Two nights in a beautiful room, just the two of them.

They stopped at Dave's Donuts for road trip fuel, and within an hour, they've finished their large coffees and the half-dozen box of donuts is empty. Austin grabs a napkin to wipe his hands, and then he reaches out for her hand, interlacing their fingers. But his fingertips are still tacky against her skin, so she pulls away.

At his raised eyebrow, she makes a face. "Sticky."

"Sorry that I'm not a heathen," he says, rolling his eyes, "and I didn't lick the glaze off my fingers like you."

His attention is flitting between her and the road, but she makes sure his gaze is on her as she brings her hand up to her mouth and pointedly licks the back of it to clean it off from his touch. She catches his small, amused smile before his eyes flick back to the road. But she's not done. She grabs *his* hand and slowly sucks each of his fingers into her mouth to clean them. His eyes are glazed over now as they stare at her longer than is probably safe.

"I'm not trying to turn you on," she says. "Pay attention to your driving."

He huffs. "Like hell you're not."

She shrugs innocently. "I only want to hold your hand without it being dirty."

"You're a menace," he tells her. But he wipes his hand on his jeans, then reaches out again, and they settle their joined palms over the center console.

When they get up into Vermont, Montana remembers why fall in New England is the best. They've come at the perfect time because the leaves are changing. She ties her hair back and rolls down her window, making hand waves as she takes in all the brilliant colors.

After a few minutes, Austin nudges her thigh with his knuckles. "I bet fall in California can't compete with this."

Turning to him, she takes in all his colors too. His blue jeans, black tee, red flannel shirt, dirty blonde hair, green eyes. Plus those dimples, *my god*. He has one hand wrapped tight around the steering wheel, the other settled on top of her leg. And what feels like a third, invisible hand wrapped around her heart. The scenery whips by as he looks at her, patiently waiting for her answer.

She bites her lip to keep from smiling too hard. Then she releases it and tells him truthfully, "No. It really can't."

◆

THE HUMMINGBIRD INN is a huge three-story blue house with a white wrap-around porch. The flowerbeds out front are filled with more types of flowers than Montana can name, showing off a vibrant rainbow of new colors. As Austin takes her hand, leading her up the steps and through the front door, it feels like they've walked into a fairytale. All that's missing is a white horse trotting across the lawn.

Once inside, they're immediately greeted by Linda at the front desk, an older woman who looks like she bakes the best pies and gives the best hugs. And when she happily informs them that she's upgraded them to the honeymoon suite at no extra charge, Montana has the urge to test the hug theory, but the counter in between them prevents her from enacting that awkward moment.

The wallpaper lining the hall upstairs is actually covered with hummingbirds. It's cheesy, but it makes her smile as she runs her finger across a tiny bird. Austin looks torn between smiling and groaning at it, but when he opens the door to their room, he gasps.

She nudges him over so she can step inside, and then reacts the same. A bottle of champagne sits chilling in a bucket of ice at the foot of the enormous bed, along with a dozen chocolate-covered strawberries lining a silver platter.

"I never want to leave this room," she declares, rushing forward to grab a strawberry and biting off the chocolate-dipped end.

"I think you'll have to leave at some point," Austin says pragmatically, setting their duffle bags on the floor. "Like Sunday morning when our reservation is up. Unless you can afford to book this room for longer. Which you know you can't."

With a half-hearted glare, she hands him a strawberry. "Fine, Mr. Reality. But we're not leaving here for the next two days. No hiking tomorrow."

"Seriously?"

She sighs. "No."

"Good. I'm looking forward to that."

Despite his words, he probably *would* stay in here with her for the whole trip if she really wanted him to. It's impossible not to smile at the thought.

Wandering over to check out the bathroom, she opens the door and finds herself staring at the largest and fanciest tub she's ever seen. "Oh my god."

Austin comes up behind her, curling a hand around her hip and peering over her shoulder. "I changed my mind," he says. "We're never leaving this room."

As she turns to face him, she winds her arms around his waist, and he pulls her in tighter. "We're definitely taking a bath tonight."

"Mmhmm," he says, leaning down to kiss her.

They move their kissing over to the bed, which is as soft as it looks. Things manage to stay PG, but eventually, they decide they should stop. Otherwise they really won't leave the room.

Montana wants to explore the small town, so they drive to the downtown area, park the Jeep in the first available spot on the street, and start walking. The street is lined with shops and places to eat. Like Hartley, but even smaller. It feels quaint, and she loves it. She also loves dragging Austin along as she pops in and out of stores, oohing and aahing over the merchandise, which ranges from kitschy to posh.

Ignoring Austin's groan of distaste, she ends up buying a set of salt and pepper shakers shaped like pigs and a coffee mug with a rainbow heart that says "I LoVermont." He buys a stuffed moose for Kalen and a green baseball cap that simply says VERMONT for himself (after Montana jams it on his head and insists it looks good).

Even though Montana's used to traveling now, she'll never get tired of buying touristy crap. It's nice having reminders of all the places she's been. She has her articles, of course, but she likes to have things she can see every day. Granted, when she lived in L.A., most of her souvenirs were tiny items like magnets, vinyl stickers, or keychains, since she didn't have much space for extra stuff in her apartment. But she doesn't have to worry about that now. Now she's got plenty of space—too much, maybe—and she's happy to start filling it.

At a tiny counter service place called Dos Amigos, they grab tacos and margaritas and enjoy them at a table out on the patio. Montana finishes her drink first and licks the remaining salt off the rim of her glass before eying Austin's hopefully.

"Do you want me to order you another one?" he asks.

"No. I don't want to get drunk and end up passing out before I can enjoy that bathtub. I just want some of yours."

He eyes her critically, fingers wrapped possessively around his glass, probably suspecting if he hands it over, she'll end up finishing it. Which is likely true, if she's being honest. "Why don't I go get one more and we can split it?"

She tries but fails to conceal her grin. "If you insist."

When he returns a few minutes later and passes her a new margarita loaded up with salt, she reaches for it eagerly and catches herself about to say *I love you*. There's a weird moment where her mouth hangs open before she recovers and says, "Thank you," instead.

Wow. Where did that come from?

While he finishes his tacos, she sips the second margarita more slowly, trying to keep the nervous feeling in her gut at bay. It's way too soon for the L word. They're not even officially in a relationship. It's just been a wonderful day, and she's happy. That's all.

Returning to the inn in the evening, they wander the grounds out back and discover a firepit surrounded by Adirondack chairs. They join one older couple and a family with two kids, making polite chit chat. That's something Montana's not a huge fan of normally, but it's all part of the bed and breakfast experience, isn't it?

The family goes back inside as it gets later, and she and Austin head off on a winding path that leads through some trees, eventually spilling them out into a clearing on top of a hill. There's a bench swing over-looking a small forest, and Montana gets the feeling again that they're in a fairytale.

They sit down beside each other, Austin wrapping his arm around her shoulders, and her tucking her feet underneath her on the seat, letting her knees lean over his thighs.

"This is nice," he says.

She rests her head against his chest. "This is perfect."

They talk about Kalen starting school and how much he likes it. About Montana's parents wanting her to come visit for Christmas, and whether or not she thinks she will. They talk about the time Austin tried to teach Montana to drive his truck, which was a standard, and how she'd come so close to making it successfully to her house until she crashed right into Mrs. Coulter's mailbox. And the time Andrea wanted to dye pink streaks in her hair right before her sophomore picture day, and Montana convinced her to do her whole head instead. It looked awesome, but the Adler's weren't too pleased about the yearbook photo, so Austin told them it was his suggestion.

As the sun sets, Austin plays with her hair while they watch two deer roaming in the grass below them. And she can feel those three words again, blooming inside her.

She blames the mood set by this romantic inn and the gorgeous honeymoon suite.

And the nostalgia.

And this perfect, perfect man beside her.

It's just too soon for that, right? The first time they said it, so many years ago, he'd been the one to say it first. It was so soon she didn't expect it, and she didn't say it back. Not right away. She'd been overwhelmed by the realization he felt that strongly about her so fast.

She doesn't want to overwhelm him now. Not when things are going so well.

But she does want to get him inside, where she can let her body try to communicate what she can't say out loud. Sitting up, she turns her head to him and says, "I'm ready for that bath."

He cups her cheek as he looks at her. His eyes are dazzling in the fading light. "I've been ready since the moment I saw it." He punctuates that sentiment with a kiss to her nose, making her scrunch it up in delight.

"Let's go then."

They make it back to the inn much faster than they made their way out here. He even squeezes her ass a couple times, calling her a slowpoke and telling her to hurry up. The teasing only makes her that much more desperate to get him naked and wet so she can glide her hands all over his hard body.

Inside their room, Montana draws the bath, pouring a packet of lavender bubble bath into the water and inhaling deeply as the relaxing scent fills the bathroom. She whines for Austin to hurry up, and a moment later, he appears in the doorway, carrying the bucket of champagne and the tray of strawberries. He sets them beside the tub, then puts his hands on her waist to pull her in close.

Their lips meet, and while they kiss, she grasps at his shirt, trying to tug it up, eager to get in the tub with him. But he pushes her hands away, taking his time kissing her instead, stubbornly refusing to be rushed.

Eventually, he lets his lips stray from hers long enough to remove both of their shirts before he goes back to kissing her. His fingers slide one of her bra straps down, and his lips trail kisses along the side of her neck and top of her shoulder until her knees feel weak.

She reaches out to undo his belt, but he stops her again. Her groan of impatience is cut off as he sinks to his knees, undoing her jeans instead. He gently lifts her legs one at a time, holding her steady as he frees her from the clothing. Then his fingers hook into the sides of her underwear, and he glances up, sending her a wicked grin as he tugs the thin material down, not even bothering to help her step out of it this time before he puts his mouth on her.

The first soft contact makes her gasp. She brings her hand to the back of his head for support, because she really doesn't trust her knees to keep working while he's doing this. But it also serves to keep him in place, and he seems to like that, if his small moan is any indication. As his tongue swipes against her, she curls her fingers into his hair, tugging just a bit, which makes him moan again. He sounds like he's devouring her. Maybe he is.

Maybe he already has.

"Okay, okay," she finally breathes out, using her grip on his hair to pull his head back. "We need to get in before the water gets cold."

The way he pouts up at her is insanely adorable. But he's still on his knees, which is so damn hot, and her brain is having trouble processing the dichotomy.

Then he stands, quickly removing the rest of his clothing without ceremony. He steps into the tub carefully and lowers down, keeping his legs spread so she can slot between them. After she gets in and fits herself in front of him, her back pressed to his chest, he leans over to pour them each a glass of champagne.

"We should toast," she says.

"What are we going to toast?"

"I dunno."

There are so many things, really, for Montana to celebrate. Reconnecting with him when she thought it completely unlikely. Her writing career going well enough to afford them this weekend getaway. The way he uses his tongue to send tingles through her whole body. The direction her life seems to be headed.

"To us," he says, kissing her temple as he clinks his glass against hers. She smiles. "To us."

Yeah. That about sums it up.

He wraps one arm around her as they finish their champagne, then he pours them each another glass. And another. Montana is most pleasantly buzzed by the time they put the glasses down on the side of the tub and he starts to massage her shoulders and upper back, leaving little kisses along the path of his hands.

She scoots forward just enough so she's able to reach behind her and wrap her hand around him. He hardens quickly in her grasp, and she gets to work, slowly stroking him up and down. The angle is awkward, but from the way he digs his fingers harder into her skin, she assumes she's getting the job done.

Soon he abandons the massage all together and reaches around to play with her nipples, squeezing them both into tight little peaks. Satisfied there, he moves his hand down, parting her thighs. Only holding him loosely now, she forgets her own task as he slides one finger inside her.

He's toying with her, thumb circling her clit for a few moments and then stopping, not giving her everything she wants.

"Bed," she pleads.

"Okay."

He stops all his ministrations, gripping the edge of the tub instead, and she whines at the loss of contact. But he urges her to stand, one hand on her hip as she carefully steps out of the tub, and then he does the same. He wraps her in a fluffy white towel before securing another around his own waist. Then he helps dry her, his legs dripping onto the tile floor as he takes his time patting the towel over every part of her body.

Once dry, they kiss their way back into the main room and tumble onto the bed together. Austin's delicate treatment of her has made her feel like a princess already, and this gloriously plush bed only adds to the fantasy.

They lie down and explore each other's bodies as if they hadn't already grown intimately familiar with them more than a decade ago. Finally, when neither of them can take it anymore, he guides himself into her, right where he belongs.

Most of the other times they've done this since reuniting have been hard and fast, and Montana's been so there for it. But this time, in this four-poster bed made for royalty, in this room with baby blue walls that smells like potpourri, they go slow. They hold eye contact practically the entire time.

Even when he flips them so she can be on top, she uses a smooth, slow rocking of her hips, her fingertips trailing down his chest. His hips raise off the mattress, meeting her for every thrust, but he lets her keep the pace, his hands squeezing with the perfect amount of pressure around her waist.

After a minute, he reaches up, smooths his palms across her mid-back, pressing her down gently until she's flush against him and holding her there. She doesn't have much leverage this way, but it doesn't matter. They move in an easy rhythm together back and forth.

She cards her fingers through his hair and kisses him, losing her rhythm a bit as his tongue takes the opportunity to explore her mouth. Then she pulls back and just watches his face as he watches hers. His lips are wet and parted slightly, curving up into a tiny smile under her scrutiny, and his green eyes look like they're trying to peer all the way into her soul.

It's there on the tip of her tongue again, but she bites it back.

I love you.

I love you.

I love you.

THEN

*A*re you sure?" Austin asked, his tone reverent as he gazed down at her.

Montana bit her lip, not with uncertainty, but to keep herself from grinning too hard. She ran her fingers over his shoulder and down his back, wanting to memorize every inch of him like this. "You know I am. I love you."

"I love you too."

It was their spring break, and Montana's parents were both at work, finally giving them this opportunity. Granted, her parents had no idea exactly what opportunity they'd given them, but she was pretty sure they wouldn't mind too much if they knew.

Growing up, she never imagined she'd be having sex at sixteen—she was the quiet bookworm, after all—and she was sure her parents hadn't imagined it either. But a little while ago, around her and Austin's six-month anniversary, her mom had given her the safe sex talk and supplied her with a small box of condoms.

"This isn't permission," she'd said. "It's only in case."

Montana suspected her parents could see clear as day how serious she and Austin were. Even though they were so young and hadn't been together that long, she just had this intensely strong feeling that this was it for her. That *he* was it. From the first time he kissed her, a part of her knew they'd end up here together.

Most people didn't find the person they were meant to be with when they were teenagers. But maybe she and Austin weren't like most people.

As he made love to her, checking in with her every step of the way, kissing her forehead, her cheek, her neck, her shoulder, she was certain they weren't. Neither of them really knew what they were doing, but it didn't matter because they were figuring it out together.

They could figure everything out together.

As long as they had each other, they'd have everything they ever needed.

Even with no experience, she knew when he was getting close by the way he sighed out her name. "*Ana.*"

She kept moving with him, helping him get there, as he repeated three small words almost like a prayer.

"I love you. I love you. I love you."

CHAPTER EIGHTEEN

NOW

The next morning begins with the most fabulous breakfast in the inn's dining room. Montana's enjoyed many a continental breakfast in the past, but this is nothing like that. The Hummingbird Inn takes the bed and breakfast title seriously. She could already attest to the pure bliss that comes from sleeping in one of their beds. Now she can say that the breakfast they serve is equally as divine.

Rather than a grab-and-go situation, they're handed small, laminated menus and led to a table where a waiter comes to take their orders. Montana's torn between the eggs Benedict and the cinnamon apple brioche French toast, so Austin suggests they get both and share. It's a great idea and both meals are delicious, but as it turns out, the food doesn't stop there.

After Montana is stuffed full of eggs, bread, and two glasses of apple juice, and grateful she's wearing leggings instead of jeans, the waiter returns with a basket of baked goods, offering them danishes, muffins, or scones to take back to their room. Austin shakes his head to decline, but she shoots him a look, so he takes a chocolate scone. She selects a cranberry lemon muffin, and upon discovering it's still warm, she has to resist the urge to break off a bite of it right now even though she has no room.

It's hard to believe this is all complimentary—although they do leave a generous tip on the table. She's going to make sure to give the inn a glowing review in her article. Honestly, she should be taking more notes. She's been all caught up in Austin and kind of forgetting the reason she's here. But the article is supposed to be about a romantic getaway, and she's certainly gathering plenty of inspiration by having him here with her.

She could write a whole page praising the romantic qualities of that bathtub alone.

Dressed in comfortable clothes, and with a backpack full of pastries that feel stolen even though they aren't, she and Austin hop in the Jeep to go check out a trail he researched online that's only a twenty-minute drive from the inn. It takes less than an hour to do, and the incline is supposedly gradual enough that he's assured her she'll make it to the top without dying.

As they head there, Montana still has a few doubts about this choice of activity. "I can't believe I didn't know you were a hiker," she muses, reaching out to lightly scratch her nails through the hair at the nape of his neck.

He leans back into the touch. "I'm not, not really. I've rarely had the chance to do it since Kalen's been born. But I got kind of into it years ago. There's something about standing alone or with a friend at the top of a mountain that makes you see the world differently, makes all your problems or worries seem like not that big of a deal."

When he shrugs, she lets her hand fall back to her own lap. Is it self-centered to wonder if those problems he needed an escape from had anything to do with her?

Regardless of if they did, though, she likes hearing about how he expanded his world in this way. There aren't any real mountains to climb in Hartley, so he must have started exploring a bit outside of his comfort zone after all.

Which is something she always wanted for him, as much as she wanted it for herself. Guess he didn't need her pushing him. He just needed to want it on his own.

She certainly appreciates a good view. But she prefers to get hers from jumping out of planes or walking up a winding ancient set of stairs in a foreign city, or at a rooftop party in Vegas. She's not sure how well she'll do with a mountain, especially since she's gotten a little out of shape since she moved. But Austin has faith in her ability, and she wants to have the new experience with him.

She wants to have all her new experiences with him.

So they go for a hike. It's not as easy as Austin or the trail reviewers made it sound, but Montana can appreciate hearing the birds chirping and spotting small animals scattering through the underbrush. Accidentally walking through spiderwebs and brushing against prickly briars, on the other hand, is much less appreciated.

Needing a break when her breathing becomes too labored, she directs Austin off to a small area beside the path where they can sit and rest on a couple of small boulders. She takes her time eating her muffin, thoroughly enjoying it, and has some water before she decides she's ready to keep trekking.

They don't run into any other hikers, and Montana takes advantage of that by groping him occasionally and pausing for kisses.

The view when they finally make it to the top is, of course, breathtaking. Almost as breathtaking as the smile Austin gives her as they stand there, holding hands, with the world spread out below them. And yeah, the effort to get here was totally worth it.

For the rest of the day, they relax, checking out the town some more and then taking advantage of the inn's magical ambience by just hanging around the property. They sit on the porch for a while, and Austin asks Montana to read to him from the book she brought, even though she's already a few chapters into it. It brings back so many warm memories.

They end up going into town again for dinner, picking up a pizza and breadsticks and taking them back to eat in their room while they watch a movie. After that, they take another luxurious bath, and then he gives her a full body massage on the bed.

She's so relaxed by the end of it, she's ready to fall asleep on her stomach with her head pillowed in her arms. But then he smacks her ass, and she yelps in surprise. He does it again a couple more times. And okay. At some point recently, that move has become an instant turn on for her.

Rolling over onto her back, she reaches for him, grabbing whatever she can to drag him down closer, because she needs to feel the weight of his body pressing into hers. "We can't do that here," she tells him regretfully. "People will hear us."

He shrugs like he really doesn't care if anyone hears them, but they've been treated so well here, and she doesn't want the owners to have to deal with complaints about them.

"I mean it," she warns.

"Fine. But they're gonna hear us anyway, because before I'm done with you, you'll be screaming."

Jesus. He can't just say things like that. She feels that threat—promise?—all the way down to her core. She squeezes her thighs together to stave it off. Or to get some friction, she really doesn't know.

"But if you wanna be safe," he says, one hand ghosting over her throat, "I could always gag you."

Jesus. Again.

She's practically panting, and he hasn't really touched her yet. His lip quirks up as he observes how her chest is rapidly rising and falling. Oh, he totally knows what he's doing to her, and he's clearly feeling smug about it.

Nope. Can't have that.

Jerking her hips up, she catches him off guard and uses that to knock him off her. She pushes him onto his back and climbs on top, leaning down to nip at the shell of his ear. She tugs a little harder with her teeth until he lets out the tiniest whimper. Then she whispers, "Or maybe I'll make you scream instead."

Since she's already naked and he's only wearing a pair of black boxer-briefs, his reaction to her words is evident as his cock grows even harder between them. She grinds down against him, but then pulls back when he tries to grab her hips.

"Nuh-uh. I'm in charge now."

"*Fuuuck,*" he breathes out.

This is fun already. Taking both his hands and moving them up over his head, Montana grips them together against the mattress. Her hand is barely big enough to fit around his wrists, and he could easily break free if he wanted to. But he doesn't.

His eyes immediately flood with lust as she wraps her other hand around his throat and applies a slight pressure. She raises her eyebrows to say, *Oh, I see.* And then she squeezes a little harder. He jerks his hips up, and she shakes her head.

"Don't move," she orders.

When he stills obediently, it gives her another rush. She rewards him by reaching her other hand down and wrapping it around the base of his cock, squeezing just slightly there too. As she leans down to kiss him, she releases his neck and swallows the gasp he lets out. That's almost like a scream, but not good enough.

While they kiss, she begins to stroke him in earnest, tugging on his hair at the same time. After a minute, he seems incapable of kissing her back. He's basically just panting into her mouth now. Taking pity on him, she slides down his body and settles herself between his legs. As soon as she gets her mouth on him, his hands fly to the back of her head.

She pulls off and gives him a pointed look. "Hands above your head."

His groan sounds pained, like it's physically hurting him not to be able to touch her, but he does what she says. And she's not going to lie, this is all doing wonders for her ego.

Now she gets to work on sucking him. But thanks to knowing his body and his reactions so well, she's perfectly equipped to torture him while she does it, bringing him right to the edge and then pulling back. She does this a few times until he's whining and babbling incoherently, something about *please* and *need to* and *fuckfuckfuck*.

That's good, but it doesn't count as screaming.

With a devilish grin, she climbs back on top of him, hovering her hips so she's positioned right above his cock. She grips him, rubbing the tip back and forth between her legs. She's already wet, and he feels amazing gliding over her clit. Biting her lip, she lines him up and starts lowering herself down ever so slowly.

He immediately looks relieved, but she's not done toying with him. She only takes the head into her, purposefully clenching her pelvic muscles tightly around it. His eyes fall closed as he moans loudly. Then he opens them and his hands twitch, like he wants to grab her and sink her down fully, but she gives him another pointed look and he stills.

God, this is amazing. Having him at her mercy, driving him crazy. And she didn't even need to physically tie him down to do this. To be honest, though, she's driving herself crazy too, because she's dying to feel him fully seated inside her. But she hasn't made him scream yet, and she's nothing if not determined.

So she keeps this up for a little bit, taking in just the head and squeezing him before lifting her hips back up. He's starting to sweat, even though she's doing all the work, and he looks like he might cry if he doesn't get to fuck her properly in the next thirty seconds. And since her thighs are starting to ache from the effort, combined with the morning's hike, she decides to take pity on them both. With no warning, she finally sinks all the way down his length.

"Yes!" he screams, thrusting up to meet her.

She grins down at him, because she won the game. But she's not done playing. "I didn't say you could move yet. Hold still or I'll stop."

He whimpers, and she lets out a pleased laugh as she braces her hands on his chest, using that for leverage so she can slide up and down his cock. She fucks him at her own pace, still enjoying being in control, because his reactions to what she's doing to him are so immensely satisfying.

He's watching her like she's the most incredible thing he's ever seen, and it does something wonderful to her. Not only to her ego, but to her heart. Sitting up straighter, she brings her hands up to her breasts and starts playing with her nipples, needing to make it dirty again so she won't be tempted this time to say anything too sappy.

"Fuck," he says, his eyes zeroed in on her fingers pinching her nipples. He loses control again and moves his hands to reach for her, but she slaps them away. "*Please*," he whines.

She shakes her head. But it's so much harder for her to keep her rhythm this way.

His whining turns absolutely desperate. "Please, fuck, please. *Ana*. I need to touch you. I need—"

"Okay," she relents, dropping back down to brace her hands on his chest again. "Pinch my nipples."

He wastes no time in following the order, and even when she allows him to start thrusting up into her roughly, she stills feels like she's the one in control. She did this to him. Turned him desperate and wild.

They're building up a steady rhythm together now, matching each other's thrusts. Then she lets him take over most of the work from underneath her, sitting upright more so he can see it when she reaches one hand down to play with herself as he fucks up into her. From there, it takes barely a minute before she's coming, her muscles squeezing involuntarily around him.

Suddenly, without warning, he's coming too. They both stay there, frozen in place when they're finished, staring at each other in awe.

"That was . . ." he starts but can't seem to find the words.

"It was . . ." She doesn't do much better.

"Amazing," he finally gets out.

"It's always amazing."

He smiles. "Yeah, but that was so amazing I felt like I might have a heart attack from it."

"That doesn't sound like a good thing."

"You know what I mean," he says, pulling her down to give her a brief, soft kiss. "I'm having some trouble with words at the moment, okay?"

As she kisses him again, she can feel him softening inside of her, so she starts to slide off him.

He grabs her hips, holding her in place. "Don't. Stay."

Gently stroking his jawline, she nods. She's not sure how long they can realistically stay like this, but sure. If he wants her to stay, she's not going anywhere.

Hopefully he wants her to stay forever.

GOING THROUGH THEIR morning routines together is so domestic. They brush their teeth side by side at the sink, Montana bumping her hip into Austin's to nudge him aside when she needs to spit. She leans into him as he hangs up their damp towels over the shower rod, pressing a firm kiss to his midback through his shirt. He plays with her hair, distracting her as she does her makeup.

Austin makes the bed neatly, despite the fact that the housekeeping staff will no doubt need to strip it anyway when they leave. Then they pack up their stuff so they'll be ready to check out after breakfast.

Breakfast is just as good today as it was yesterday. After eating quickly and snagging a couple pastries for the road, they return to the room to grab their bags. And that's when Montana finds herself moving reluctantly, absolutely not wanting to leave. Wishing they could stay in this room forever.

"Are you coming?" Austin asks, turning back to her by the door with his duffle slung over one shoulder.

"Yeah, of course," she says. But instead she drops her own bag back onto the bed, and he raises his eyebrows, confused.

It hits her in that moment. This all feels too real now. The two of them—they go on dates, they go on vacation together, they go to sleep together, they wake up together.

They're *together.*

At this point, it feels like they're only pretending this is still casual. Because it's so not. *It's real.*

"Are we really doing this?"

"What?"

Sighing, she sinks down to the edge of the bed. "We can't keep going along with 'whatever happens, happens.' We need to be clear about what we're doing now, and what we each want from this, so no one gets hurt."

It's probably her that's going to get hurt, because the last time they tried to do this as a casual thing, it eventually became too much for him, and he cut her off completely. She can't let that happen again. She'll do anything she needs to in order to make sure it doesn't.

He lets his bag fall off his shoulder and onto the floor as he crosses the room to stand in front of her. "I thought casual would be easier for us this time. Easier for you. I didn't want to scare you away by telling you how much I care about you, and how much I need you."

She looks up at him, wide-eyed. "I'm not scared."

His face does a little twitch as he reaches down to run his hand over her hair. "Well, maybe I am."

"What are you scared of?"

"Montana." He shakes his head. "You were *everything* to me before, but I wasn't enough for you."

"That's not true."

Sadly, he says, "I wasn't enough to make you stay, was I?"

"But that wasn't about you! It was about me." She reaches for his hand, gripping tightly, like she's afraid he might walk away right now. "I loved you more than anything. I never wanted to give you up. But you were talking about a four-year long-distance relationship, and then who knew where I'd end up after that? I couldn't make you sit around forever, waiting for me and whatever times I could get back to Hartley."

He slips his hand out of hers gently and sits down beside her. "But I would have."

"I know," she says, angling herself to face him. "That's why I couldn't let you. You deserved so much more than that."

"Well. I think it's what I did anyway."

She places her hand tentatively on his thigh. "At first. Then you moved on. And once you weren't in my life at all anymore, that's when I realized how much I'd given up." She realized it even before that, truthfully. "It *killed* me. It killed me to lose you."

"But you didn't lose me," he says softly. "I'm right here."

"But you're scared?"

"I just . . ." He hesitates, dragging his hand roughly through his hair, and she holds her breath until he speaks again. "I'm happy for you that you're rebuilding your writing career. And I feel like a total asshole for even saying this, but I guess I'm also a little scared that . . ."

"That what?"

He frowns slightly, and she wants to kiss the sadness right off his face. But she knows she needs to hear exactly what he's thinking, so she waits.

"I don't know." He covers her hand with his own. "That it's going to take you away from me."

The *again* goes unspoken.

"Austin. I'm here. You're here. We're twenty-eight, not eighteen, and you have a son. I promise I'm not taking any of this lightly. I *want* to do this. I'm not going anywhere." Whatever she needs to do to assure him of this, she will.

An eternity passes before he says anything.

And then—"Okay."

"Okay?" She has to double check before she gets her hopes up.

"Okay."

Feeling like she can breathe freely again, she smiles. "Okay."

"So," he starts, taking her other hand and lacing their fingers together, "we're really doing this? For real?"

"Austin, you and I are the realest thing I've ever known. I'm all in if you are."

He rushes forward, pulling her into a hug and then only moving back enough to smash his lips against hers, clumsy with happiness.

It's so easy to get swept up in him. He makes her feel like she's living in a lovestruck Taylor Swift song. He always has.

They kiss until she finally has to use every ounce of her self-control to remove her mouth from his and tell him that they're going to be late checking out. He looks like he wants to argue, maybe say they'll pay for another night, but then he sighs and stands, reaching down to help her up.

He hoists her bag over his shoulder and then picks up his off the ground, grasping her hand with his free one as they leave. Together.

Maybe neither of them was truly ready to be in this place together before. Maybe they needed the time and the distance. Maybe they were always meant to find each other again and be here together *now*.

Even though, logically, she never could have predicted this—*them*—happening when she moved back, a small part of her must have known. That part of her that she always kept hidden way deep down inside knew it. It wasn't only the first drunken kiss at the bar that had been inevitable. It was all of this.

They were inevitable.

Austin Adler and Montana Sinclair.

THEN

I can't believe your dad gave you this truck," Montana said, patting the worn vinyl seat underneath her.

"It's sweet, right?" Austin replied. "I know it's nothing fancy and it's kind of old, but it should last me through high school, at least."

He pulled into the empty parking lot of their school and parked the truck neatly in the farthest space from the road. It was a Sunday evening, so the school was closed, but they didn't really have anywhere better to go. He'd already driven them in a few laps around town, just because he could. His sister had begged him for a ride, but he'd told her he was giving Montana the first one.

He'd been driving very carefully, both hands on the wheel, which was cute. But now he relaxed, reclining his seat back a bit and reaching out to take her hand. She gave his a squeeze and smiled.

It wasn't long before they were making out, leaning awkwardly over the gear shift. They grasped at each other, wherever they could reach, and when his hands found their way under her sweater, clutching her sides tightly, her whole body shivered.

Pulling away, he asked, "Are you cold?"

Before she could say no, he was already moving to turn up the dial on the heat. It was surprising chilly out for spring, yeah, but her shiver was more of a reaction to him than to the cold. Lately, she couldn't even kiss him without wanting more, and when they fooled around, it was so hard to stop.

"I wanna have sex," she said, the words spilling inelegantly out of her mouth after she'd spent a bunch of time trying to think of a good way to tell him. Well. Guess that was as good of a way as any.

His eyes widened, and he asked, "Now?"

She shook her head. She was ready—emotionally and physically, with a condom stashed in her purse—but time and privacy were hard to come by. Hopefully it would be easier now that he had his license and his own vehicle. But she didn't want their first time to be rushed in a cramped pick-up truck where anyone could catch them. Her overactive imagination could just picture a cop walking up and tapping on the window with a flashlight like in a movie.

"Not here," she told him. "But I wanted you to know that I'm ready if you are."

A grin spread slowly across his face. "Hell fucking yeah, I am. As long as you're sure."

"I'm sure."

"Then that's perfect. But I agree, not here." He rubbed his hand up and down her thigh. "It should be special."

The urge to roll her eyes was strong, because that was such a cheesy line. But really, she couldn't help but think that no matter what, it would be special simply because it was going to be with him, which was equally as cheesy. So she smiled and said, "Glad that's settled."

He looked at her for a moment almost like he was in awe. Then he said, "God, I fucking love you."

And she would've said it back, but he didn't give her a chance with the way he hurriedly yanked her in for a kiss. They resumed making out, and more groping quickly followed, until by some unspoken agreement he was helping her crawl over the gearshift and into his lap. From there, they ended up grinding against each other until he was hard and, *dammit*, she was so ready. But she could wait for a better time.

It would happen. At this point, it was inevitable.

CHAPTER NINETEEN

NOW

C an we get one with sauce *and* one with sugar?" Kalen asks, tugging on Austin's hand as they wait in line in front of the fried dough stand. "And then can we get cotton candy? And the fried Oreos!"

"Woah, kid," Austin says. "One thing at a time, okay?"

"Okay, but after this can I go on the rides? I wanna go on the spinny one! And *then* we can get Oreos."

Montana laughs, but Austin just sighs in either exasperation or amusement. It's hard to tell.

They took off a Friday night from work to come to the carnival, which Montana can't exactly afford after missing a whole weekend for the Vermont trip, but she hasn't been to the St. Joseph's carnival in forever. They hold it in the spring and the fall, and it was a staple of her childhood and high school years.

And, like she told Austin the other day, she could always use another break from all the dude-bro types that come into Alan's Place on the weekends.

"Who else do you want to come in?" he asked her when she said this.

"I'd rather be selling expensive bourbon to hipsters," she said. Then she told him about one bar she worked at in L.A. that catered to that crowd. Granted it was hard not to roll her eyes at them, but they did tip well.

"I'm not sure you're going to find a hipster crowd in Hartley," Austin said. But then he told her they could try doing something new to bring in different people. He suggested an open mic night, and they decided to set it up soon. If it was a success, they could even do it once a month.

To be honest, Montana isn't sure there's too many artsy types in town either, but it's worth a shot.

Now the line moves up and there's only one person ahead of them. Austin looks to Kalen. "Okay, you've got to decide which kind you want."

Kalen gives him the puppy dog eyes. "Can't we please have both?"

"We don't need both."

"But they're both good!"

Austin turns to her as if she'll help. "You make the decision."

She grins. "What if *I* want both?"

He shakes his head. "You're the worst."

She shrugs sheepishly. Yeah, she knows she shouldn't be ganging up on him with his kid. It's not her place if he doesn't want Kalen to have too much junk food. But she and Kalen have been bonding over food, and maybe she's trying a little extra now to really make sure the kid likes her. Because Austin hasn't told him about the two of them dating yet, but he's going to. And she needs Kalen to be cool with it.

According to Austin, he just hasn't had a chance to have the talk with him, and he didn't want to do it right before they came to the carnival, in case it's going to be weird for him. But she suspects he's a little worried about it too.

He promised that tonight would be the last time they have to hide in front of his son, and she hopes that's true, because it's so hard not to show affection for Austin whenever she's with him. It's easier to keep it professional at work, but when they're out having fun like this, she's constantly fighting the urge to reach for his hand as they walk or kiss him when he does something cute.

Now that they made it official, she wants the whole world to know. She wants to hire a plane to fly a banner over the town. AUSTIN & MONTANA 4EVER!

But Austin's first priority is to make sure Kalen is comfortable. She doesn't come first with him anymore, and she's okay with that. She cares about Kalen too.

Though it doesn't hurt to score him all the gooey fried goodness he wants.

She and Kalen both pout at Austin until he gives in and orders one fried dough with sauce and parmesan cheese and another with cinnamon and powdered sugar. When she bends down to give Kalen a high five behind Austin's back, he turns and sighs at her the same way he did at Kalen. Exasperated or amused. Maybe a mix of both.

"We should have waited to eat until after he goes on the rides," Austin comments as they take their two paper plates to a free picnic table.

"But I was hungry now," Montana tells him.

"Me too," Kalen chimes in.

Austin rolls his eyes, but as he slides onto the bench beside her, he subtly runs his thumb across her thigh under the table. Once he's settled, she briefly presses her thumb into the side of his leg in return. Out of the corner of her eye, she catches him smile.

It's sort of fun having their own little secret. But she doesn't want to keep a secret from his kid for any longer than they need to.

Kalen digs into the sauced up fried dough first, immediately dropping a thick red glob onto his shirt. Montana rises and leans across the table with a napkin, trying to clean him off without rubbing it in more. When she sits back down, she notices Austin giving her a funny look.

"What?" she asks.

Smiling, he shakes his head and says, "Nothing."

After they're all stuffed with fried dough, they make their way over to the rides. Montana doesn't know if she's pleased or worried to find that none of them look like they've changed in ten years. Her favorite one with the giant spinning apples is still here, but her stomach gives a little protest as she watches the apples whip around. Definitely going to wait on that. Now she sees Austin's point about eating after the rides.

Kalen bounces his way over to a small kiddie roller coaster that looks like a dragon, and she and Austin wait off to the side while he gets in line.

"Your article was great," Austin says, bumping his hip into hers.

She smiles. "Thanks. But you already read it." The article about the bed and breakfast just came out, and he insisted on buying a copy of the magazine even though she'd emailed him the finished draft.

"I know, but seeing it in print is so much cooler."

She has to agree with him there. "The editor told me to pitch her my next idea when I'm ready."

"So what's your next idea?"

"I don't know yet. But I'm excited for it, whatever it is."

They watch Kalen squeal in glee as the metal dragon coaster goes down the first small drop. Austin takes Montana's hand and squeezes. She squeezes back. Kalen's too busy enjoying himself as the coaster careens around the curves, climbing up and dipping back down, to notice them standing here. Austin doesn't let go until the ride is slowing to a stop.

When Kalen gets off, he comes barreling through the gate and runs toward them. "Can I go on it again?"

Austin laughs. "Why don't we check out the other rides first? Maybe there's something Montana and I would like to go on with you."

"We have to go on the Ferris wheel," Montana tells them.

Kalen grimaces. "That's boring."

"Too bad," Austin says. "I think it sounds like a great idea. And it won't make any of us puke."

Despite his claim of boredom, Kalen appears to enjoy himself on the ride, sitting in between her and Austin. Austin's arm is slung casually over the back of their little cart, and he surreptitiously strokes her hair while Kalen leans as far forward as Austin will allow (which isn't much), trying to spot all the parts of town he recognizes.

"Grandpa's place is over there, right?" he asks, pointing to the left.

Montana's heart pings in her chest at him describing the restaurant like that.

Austin nods. "Yup. That's Main Street." He catches Montana's eye behind Kalen's head and gives her a sad half-smile.

Not for the first time, she wonders how much Kalen remembers about Austin's dad. He obviously remembers enough if he knows Alan owned the restaurant before Austin. Although, it *is* right in the name, so maybe he doesn't actually remember. Maybe it's just something he was taught.

The only thing that eventually draws Kalen away from the rides is the promise of fried Oreos. They each eat two, even though Montana is still full from the fried dough. But stuffing yourself with greasy fried foods is the whole point of a carnival, right?

After Austin has cleaned his hands with a pile of napkins, and Montana and Kalen have both licked the gooey chocolate and powdered sugar off their fingers and then grudgingly accepted the napkins Austin held out to them, they decide to play some games. They do the one where you shoot water guns into a clown's mouth, and Montana and Austin silently agree to let Kalen win.

He's clearly unimpressed by the stiff and puny stuffed monkey the attendant hands to him though. "I want one of those!" he exclaims as they pass a booth with giant stuffed bears hanging on netting from the top of the tent.

Austin takes one look at the game and grins. "You got it, bud."

When Montana sees that it's the milk toss one where you get three balls to knock down the whole pyramid of silver jugs, she grins too.

As Austin hands his money to the game attendant, the guy warns him, "It's not as easy as it looks."

Kalen looks nervous when Austin's first throw only knocks off the top jug, but Austin's confident expression doesn't waver. "Just warming up," he says, in a tone that borders on cocky.

He's almost never cocky, but he knows what he's good at. And sure enough, with his next throw aimed directly at the space in between the middle bottles on the bottom row, all the remaining bottles tumble off the platform with a series of loud clangs.

"Yes!" Kalen cheers.

"I see you've still got it," Montana tells him.

"You better believe it," Austin says, and the flirty look he gives her makes it clear he's not only talking about his throwing skills.

Even the attendant looks impressed. People must not win this game too often, but Austin's always been good at it.

Kalen selects the dark brown bear that's wearing a white bow tie with red polka dots. And when the guy passes it over the counter, he almost topples under the weight of it.

"Why don't I hold him for you," Austin offers.

"How'd you do that, Daddy?" Kalen asks, still in awe over his dad's win.

"I told you I played baseball in school."

"Can you teach me how to play?"

The proud smile on Austin's face when he says, "I'd love to," warms Montana's heart.

By the time they leave the carnival, she's ready to pass out in her bed, but as Austin pulls into her driveway, Kalen says, "Can we play a game?"

Looking to Austin, Montana shrugs.

"It's getting late," Austin says.

"Just one game, please?" Kalen asks.

Montana smiles because she can tell when Austin's going to give in.

"One," he says, undoing his seatbelt.

They go inside, and Kalen runs right over to the bookshelf in the dining room which holds a small pile of his games. They've somehow migrated to her house over the last couple months. He grabs Uno and heads into the kitchen to sit at the table. Austin brushes a hand across Montana's shoulder before they follow him.

A huge smile threatens to overtake Montana's face the entire time they're playing cards. The three of them already feel like a family. The transition from casual dating to a proper relationship should be easy.

THEN

*A*ustin's hand pressed into the small of Montana's back, gently guiding her, as they stepped down from the large apple ride and made their way out through the exit gate. Montana was a little wobbly, while Sloane walked past her looking steady as a rock. It only took another second for the spinning sensation in Montana's head to abate though.

Blake, on the other hand, looked the worst out of their group. Grabbing the top of the short metal fencing surrounding the ride, he bent over and clutched his stomach.

"Oh no," Austin said with alarm. His arm flew out in front of Montana, making her take a few steps back.

"He's not going to puke," she said. For the entire ride, Blake was the one trying the hardest to twist the wheel in the center of their apple which would make them spin faster.

Blake stood and let out a small laugh. "Nah, nah. I'm good."

"Should we go on the swings?" Sloane asked, already taking off in that direction without waiting for anyone's answer.

"That's wimpy," Blake complained.

Montana rubbed up and down her arms, trying to warm up. Technically, it was spring, but winter was sure doing its best to hold on. "I think the swings are fun."

"Me too," Austin said, shrugging out of his zip-up and wrapping it over her shoulders.

Blake rolled his eyes at them. "Fine, let's go."

They hustled to catch up to Sloane, but only made it a couple feet before Montana heard a horrible retching sound. She unfortunately turned her head just in time to see Blake throwing up all over the ground.

"Ugh, gross!" She ran a few feet away, putting some distance between her and Blake's mess so she wouldn't start gagging.

Austin bravely remained by Blake's side, gingerly patting his friend on the back. "I'm gonna take him to the bathroom to get cleaned up."

"Okay, I'll go on the swings with Sloane. Meet us over there?"

"Yeah," Austin agreed.

Pointing down at his pile of puke, Blake shouted, "Look, that's my corn dog!"

Austin shook his head as he started to lead Blake away. "I hate you sometimes."

"No you don't," Blake argued.

Austin's sigh was so loud Montana heard it even from a distance. She knew Blake was right though. For better or worse, Blake had been Austin's best friend since the third grade—when Austin forgot his lunch box on the bus, and Blake offered to share his peanut butter and jelly sandwich and his Jello cup.

She'd been surprised when she heard this story, considering how, in the short time she'd been hanging out with Austin, and therefore Blake, she'd already learned how much Blake loved food. Blake had seemed embarrassed when Austin told her, which only made it more endearing.

Finding Sloane by the swings, Montana got in line with her. "Blake threw up."

"I heard," Sloane said.

"And you just kept walking?"

"Absolutely." As they shuffled forward in line, Sloane turned to her, pulling her hair back into a ponytail. She eyed Montana's borrowed hoodie. "I know it's been a while now, but I still can't believe you're dating a jock."

Instinctually, Montana reached up to rub at the letters JV over her chest. She knew Austin was hoping to get on the varsity team next year, and she had no doubt he'd make it. Still she insisted, "He's not just a jock. Did you know he plays guitar?"

"So he's Zac Effron in *High School Musical*," Sloane quipped.

"Troy Bolton didn't even play guitar," she said, shoving her friend in the side. What a throwback though.

She wanted Sloane to like Austin. And it wasn't that Sloane *didn't* like him—she just didn't really know him. She'd known who he was before he and Montana started dating, of course. Their school was small enough that everyone pretty much knew each other. But Sloane didn't *know* him like Montana knew him now.

He'd turned out to be nothing like Montana expected. She wasn't judgmental enough to assume that, just because he was athletic, he was dumb or a jerk. But it had surprised her that such a popular guy would be so easy to talk to. And that he was equally as happy staying home watching Netflix with her on a Friday night as he was going to a party. She was surprised that he liked to play board games and card games with his family, and that he loved it when she played with his hair as she read books out loud to him.

"Sloane?"

"Yeah?"

"I'm ready to have sex with him."

Sloane's eyes grew wide. "Are you sure?"

"Definitely."

"Wow."

Montana grinned. "I know."

As they stepped through the ride's gate and found two swings next to each other, she was still thinking about it. They'd just had their six-month anniversary, and she'd thought he might ask her to do it then, but he hadn't. Austin was so respectful that she was starting to suspect she may need to be the one to bring it up, otherwise he never would. Even though he must be thinking about it as much as she was at this point. Right?

She really wanted to do it, but logistically, it was hard to find the time with a house to themselves. Especially when they were still relying on their parents to drop them off and pick them up from places. But at least she could let him know she was ready, and then hopefully they'd figure it out.

When the boys met back up with them, they all decided to take a break from the rides so that no one had to see the contents of Blake's stomach again. They headed over to the games area, where Montana and Sloane gleefully made fools of themselves by attempting to pop balloons with darts. After one of Montana's throws almost took out the attendant, they called it quits without winning any of the pathetically small prizes.

"Oh, sweet," Austin said, pointing across the way. "I wanna do that one."

The rest of them followed him over to a booth with pyramids of milk jugs set up on platforms.

"I think this is one of those games that are rigged so you can never win," Sloane said, as Austin handed a few dollars to the attendant. "The jugs are weighted."

"You just need to hit it in the right spot," Austin told her. He made a big show of winding his throwing arm to warm up, which made Sloane roll her eyes. But Montana could tell he was only joking around about it.

He wasn't joking about hitting it in the right spot, though. With his first ball, the entire pyramid clattered to the ground and Blake whooped obnoxiously. It happened so fast Montana almost missed it.

Austin was preening as the attendant congratulated him. "Which one?" he asked Montana, jerking his head toward the giant bear prizes.

She pointed to a tan-colored one that had rainbow hearts on his bottom paws, and the attendant turned to get it down.

Sloane caught Montana's attention behind Austin's back and mouthed, "*Jock.*"

Montana giggled. And when Austin turned and passed her the giant bear, she buried her grin in its fur. She totally loved her sweet, jock boyfriend. And she was *so* ready to have sex with him.

CHAPTER TWENTY

NOW

*M*ontana's pouring a couple of Sam Octoberfests Saturday night when Austin aggressively drops a case of beer beside her feet. She smiles and thanks him, but he just grunts before turning and walking away. He's been acting moody all night, which is totally unlike him.

She and Landon have been slammed behind the bar, so all she can do is try to catch his attention with her eyes as she's making drinks. But he seems to be avoiding her. If there was enough of a lull in customers, she could go corner him and ask what's wrong, but so far it hasn't happened. Good for her tips, bad for her anxiety.

Because something's wrong. She knows it.

It's all she can do to hold back her frustrated sigh as she slides the pint glasses across the counter to a guy wearing a retro graphic tee with a picture of Eminem flipping her off. He doesn't tip, and she slips his cash into the register and slams it closed a little harder than necessary.

As Landon's crossing behind her, he pauses to put a hand on her shoulder. "You okay?"

"Yeah, I'm fine."

"Girl, I know you're *fine*, but you don't seem fine. Know what I mean?"

What?

She catches his cheesy grin and rolls her eyes, though she appreciates him trying to make her laugh. That's not at all how he normally talks, but sometimes he'll joke around and lean into stereotypes. "Thanks, but I'm okay," she tells him.

"If you say so."

She forces a reassuring smile, and they both turn back to take more drink orders.

Landon's a pretty good work friend by this point. If they actually had time to talk, she could probably tell him how she's wondering what's going on with Austin. He'd be discreet about it. She and Austin haven't exactly been hiding their relationship at work, but they're careful to keep it professional. They can't bring any relationship drama here.

Not that this is relationship drama. Whatever he's upset about likely has nothing to do with her, but it's still distracting. Because she cares about him and doesn't like to see him upset. Whatever it is, though, it looks like she'll have to wait until after closing to find out.

Except after they kick everyone out and turn the lights up, Austin disappears immediately into the office. Montana's doing her best to focus on the closing sidework, but she's been staring into the beer cooler for way too long, trying to count what needs to be restocked, when a rag hits her in the chest.

Snapping out of her daze and straightening up, she turns to Landon, who's giving her a knowing look. "Sorry."

"Go talk to him."

"No, it's okay."

He steps closer, grabs the rag where it landed on the edge of the cooler, and gives her a tiny shove. "Just do it. You're being useless to me right now anyway."

"I'm sorry," she says again. "Thanks."

She heads over to the office and knocks tentatively on the closed door. All she gets is a "Yeah?" in response, but she takes it as permission to enter, slowly opening the door and stepping inside.

Austin is sitting at his desk, staring at the computer screen. He doesn't even glance up.

"Um . . ." she starts. "Is everything okay?" When he doesn't respond, she adds, "Because you seemed a little off all night."

"Don't worry about it," he says, typing something on his keyboard.

"Austin."

There's a beat. Two. Three. Then he looks up.

His face shows signs of exhaustion, which could be just a result of the busy night they had. But she suspects it's more than that. Is there a problem with the restaurant? Business seems to be as good as ever, but what does she know?

Her instinct is to cross the room and run her hand through his hair. Let him lean his head against her. But she waits.

Finally, he says, "I talked to Kalen this morning before I brought him to Brittani's."

Montana darts forward a step, worry souring into panic. "Is he okay?"

"Yeah, no, it's not . . ." He trails off, shaking his head. "He's fine."

"So what, then?"

"We can't—Let's not do this here, okay? Can you please finish up out there so I can get home? It's been a long day."

So *he* can get home. Not so they can leave together. She expected he'd spend the night at her place, or she'd spend it at his.

There's a chill in the air. Something isn't okay.

"Austin." She keeps saying his name like a plea.

"I'm sorry," he says, getting up and coming to stand in front of her. He presses his lips to her forehead, but when she tilts her head up for a real kiss, he's already stepping back. "Can we talk about this tomorrow? I'll meet you for brunch before I have to be in here."

"Sure," she says. Because what else can she say? She doesn't want to push and get into something he obviously doesn't want to get into with Landon right out there. "I'm gonna go finish up."

When she steps back behind the bar, Landon takes one look at her and asks again, "Are you okay?"

This time she answers truthfully. "I don't know."

He quickly moves the length of the bar and wraps one arm around her shoulders, pulling her into a side hug. "Do you want me to kick his ass?"

She huffs out a small laugh.

"Because he's pretty much the coolest guy I've ever worked for," he goes on, "but if he's being a dick to you, I'll do it. Or I'll try, at least. Pretty sure he would crush me. I mean, have you seen those biceps?"

Laughing again, she extends her arm to hug him back. "It's okay. Thank you."

As they finish their work, she does her best to ignore the uneasy feeling in the pit of her stomach. She'll talk to Austin tomorrow. Whatever it is, it'll be okay.

◆

SITTING ACROSS FROM Austin at a table at Bread & Brew—her bacon, egg, and cheese bagel half-eaten, and her spiced apple latte getting cold—Montana wants to scream. He still hasn't brought up what was going on with him last night, and she's five seconds away from demanding an explanation, but she's trying to restrain herself.

It isn't like Austin to hold something back from her. Something must really be bothering him, and she needs to let him get around to telling her on his own.

She takes a sip of her tepid latte, then sets it back down. "So are we just gonna sit here in silence until you have to go to work?"

Okay, or maybe she won't let him get around to it on his own time.

He crumples his foil sandwich wrapper into a tight ball and says, "I told Kalen about us."

"Oh!"

"He didn't take it well."

Oh.

Picking nervously at her cuticle, she asks, "What do you mean?"

Kalen loves her, doesn't he? She certainly thought so. She shares her junk food with him, and she's even been practicing doing the voices when she reads him a book. She's not going to win an Oscar, but she's gotten so much better.

Austin squeezes the foil ball in his fist. "I explained that we're more than friends, like me and his mom used to be. And maybe that was the wrong way to describe it, because he kind of freaked out." Another squeeze. "He said I'm happier when we're hanging out with you."

Her forehead scrunches in confusion. "Isn't that a good thing?"

"Yeah, but he said if it's like me and his mom, then that means you can leave too. And I'll be sad again, and he'll be sad too."

"But—"

"I told him you wouldn't do that," he cuts her off. "And he said, 'Do you promise?' and I—" One more hard squeeze, then he drops the foil onto the table, letting it roll to the edge. "I realized I couldn't promise him you'd never leave us, because you left before. You might again. If I promised him anything, I might be lying to him. And I realized maybe

I'm lying to myself a little too, thinking things will be different this time."

"Are you serious?" she says, voice raising a little too high for this quiet café, but she can't believe she's hearing this. "Things *are* different! I want to be here with you. *And* Kalen."

"But you're only here because you had no other choice."

She jerks back like he slapped her. That fucking stung. She's known Austin half her life, and in all that time he's never said anything to her that hurt like that.

It only takes him a few seconds to catch the look on her face, and then his own face crumples. "Oh my god. Montana. I'm sorry, I didn't mean—"

"No, you're right," she says, jaw tight. "I did only move back to Hartley this year because I had no other choice. But I thought about moving back a long time ago. When I had plenty of choices. I wanted to choose *you*. I was going to."

Feeling backed into a corner, she finally tells him how she was thinking about moving home to be with him after college. She says the words she should have said back then but didn't get the chance to. Or was too scared to, whatever. That afternoon in his bedroom, on her winter break senior year, when it felt like the world was the brightest when she was with him. A Massachusetts winter brighter than even a California summer.

"But then you wanted nothing to do with me, so I stayed in California," she finishes somewhat bitterly.

His lips part, but he doesn't say anything. It takes him a few seconds, then—"Oh."

She taps idly at her paper cup. "Yeah."

"I didn't know."

"I know you didn't."

A small commotion at the counter draws Montana's attention. It looks like the cashier spilled a drink on a customer. She's apologizing profusely as the man dabs at the brown liquid on his white shirt with a handful of crumpled napkins. And right now, Montana would almost prefer to be in either of their positions rather than sitting here having this painful conversation.

With a sigh, she refocuses on Austin. "I didn't get a chance to tell you because you made yourself disappear. And I'm not saying it's all on you. It was a huge decision, and I was going to talk to you about it, but I was nervous, so I waited too long."

Reaching across the table, he wraps his fingers around her wrist, the warmth seeping into her skin. "You still could have told me after."

She yanks her hand away. "After what? After you stopped speaking to me? Yeah, sure, I could have told you in a fucking text message, not knowing if you'd even read it. But you'd already made your choice to cut me out of your life, so I'm sorry if begging you to take me back would have made me feel a little too pathetic."

"I—"

"Look. It doesn't get us anywhere rehashing the past." Gazing down at the table, she swipes at a few bagel crumbs and tries to calm down. "You know, you can't guarantee anything in life. One of us could get hit by a car and die tomorrow."

"Jesus," he says, shaking his head.

"You could have promised Kalen that I care about both of you very much, and that I'm going to try my best to never do anything to hurt either of you. Like I said, I'm here now, and I want to be here with you. I think you could help him understand that. But it's never going to work if *you* can't believe it." As she says this last part, she realizes it's the truth. And that really fucking sucks. She takes a deep breath, struggling to fill up her lungs and not cry. She thought they were past all this, but apparently not. "Maybe I *should* leave."

She's not sure if she means the café or the damn town, but she can start with the café. When she abruptly stands from the table, Austin starts to get up too, looking panicked. But he hesitates when she says, "No." And then she walks out the door before she can change her mind.

This whole thing between them began again when he saw her in the café and ran out on her. Did it really just end with her walking out of the same place?

No.

This can't be it. It's not over.

They weren't over ten years ago, and they're not over now.

But clearly, he still doesn't trust her, and she's tired of it. She needs a break.

THEN

*C*oming out of the girl's bathroom, Montana almost ran right into Austin. Grabbing her upper arms to steady her, he said, "There you are. I've been looking for you."

She offered him a small, guilty smile. "Sorry."

They should be eating lunch right now, but she'd fled the cafeteria before getting her food when she'd heard her name being spoken by a group of people a couple feet ahead of her in line. It was clear that they were talking about her, not to her. And it only took a minute of listening to their not-quite-hushed whispers to get the gist of the gossip.

Last night she'd gone to Troy Gabler's house to work on a group project, but when she got there, she realized the third member of their group was sick and not coming. She and Troy didn't do anything but schoolwork, obviously. Yet somehow, it had gotten around that they'd hooked up. This morning in her homeroom, she'd heard his friends joking about something like that, but at the time, she hadn't realized she was supposedly the girl involved.

Running out of the lunch line and all the way into the bathroom at the end of the cafeteria's hallway was maybe a little melodramatic. She honestly didn't care what people said about her. And she likely wasn't interesting enough to her classmates for the gossip to last longer than a day. But what concerned her is what Austin would think when he heard it. Imagine minding your own business and then suddenly someone starts talking about how your girlfriend cheated on you.

He gently guided her into a corner of the hallway, hidden slightly by the giant trophy case on the wall. "I just heard . . . Do you know there's a rumor going around about you and Troy?"

All she could do was nod, trying not to cringe at the words.

"I can't believe he would make up something like that!"

Wait, what?

"I'm gonna kill him," Austin added matter-of-factly.

Oh. He didn't . . .

Managing to find her voice, she said, "I don't even think Troy started it. I'm pretty sure his friends were just joking around, saying dumb shit, and then someone else probably overheard and spread it."

He nodded. "Fine. I'll kill his friends then."

"You're not even going to ask me if it's true?"

Now he looked appalled. "Do I need to?"

"Of course not!" she assured him.

Laughing softly, he rubbed down her arms, his fingers lingering loosely around her wrists. "Then why are you surprised that I didn't ask?"

Oh. Well. "I don't know."

"Montana, I trust you. And I know you." He squeezed her wrists gently. "Come on. Would you believe it if you heard a rumor about me cheating?"

"No." She didn't even need time to consider that.

"Good." He tugged her in for a quick kiss. Then he pulled away and said, "Now, I'm gonna need the names of those friends so I can kill them."

Fighting a smile, she told him, "Stop it. No violence."

Even though she knew he wasn't actually the type of guy to start a physical fight with anyone, he might be inclined to say something to them. But she didn't need him to defend her honor, because she didn't care what some random people thought about her. All that mattered was what Austin thought.

He knew how she felt about him—knew she'd never cheat. And it was really nice knowing that he trusted her without question.

CHAPTER TWENTY-ONE

NOW

*A*ustin called on Monday, but Montana didn't answer. On Tuesday, she ducked out of work as early as possible after her lunch shift to avoid seeing him when he came in for the dinner shift. Wednesday, he texted, Please talk to me, and she wrote back, I will when I'm ready. Three dots appeared on his end, but they disappeared after a minute without him sending another message.

Now it's Thursday, and she's going insane. It's only been a few days, but the missing him feels like she's missing a limb. He used to feel like a part of her, and apparently, they've already gotten there again.

She wants them to fix this. Work things out. But every time she tries to come up with something to say to him, she remembers the sting of his words when he said she was only here because she had no other choice.

Ugh.

Flopping onto her stomach on the couch, she buries her face in a cushion. All she's done for days is mope around the house when she's not at work. If her life were a romcom, this would be the breakup montage sequence. A sad song plays as you flash from one pathetic moment to the next. She's eating a whole pint of ice cream in dirty pajamas with her hair a knotted mess. She's crouched down crying on the shower floor as the water runs over her back. She's refusing to get out of bed while her dog licks her face to make sure she's alive.

Except she doesn't have a dog. So really, it's just her, left all alone to wallow in her misery.

Her phone beeps, and she almost falls off the couch as she lunges for where she dropped it on the floor earlier. After she thought about texting Austin but didn't. She wanted the temptation out of her hands, but now she's quick to pick it back up.

It's a text from him. Please don't bail.

Scoffing as if he could see her through the phone screen, she types out, I'm not. I didn't mean it when I said I should leave. You're the one who's having doubts.

His response comes quick. I'm not! Then the dots to indicate he's typing more. I can't do anything that would hurt Kalen, but he only wants me to be happy too. He'll come around.

She already told him that. But how am I supposed to get past the fact that you still don't trust me?

The messages come rapid-fire now.

I do.

I trust you.

Montana.

I'm an idiot.

I just freaked out for a minute.

I'm sorry.

But I swear.

I trust you.

Trust ME. Please.

When he finally stops typing, she takes a deep breath and writes, I do. Then let me see you.

Her fingers hover over her phone, hesitating. She wants to see him. Oh god, does she want to see him. She wants him to wrap his strong protective arms around her, and she wants to run her fingers through his hair, and she wants to look into his green eyes as he leans in to kiss her.

So what's stopping her?

He's asking her to trust him, and it's not like she doesn't. She believes he means everything he says. Or that he thinks he means it, at least. But what if he only *thinks* he's forgiven her for leaving him once before, and he's wrong? What if he thinks he's over it when he's really not?

What if she's spent half her life believing the two of them were inevitable, but the only inevitable thing is that they'll continue to hurt each other over and over and over again?

She bites her lip as she types out her response. I just need a bit more time alone. But I'll see you at work tomorrow night.

The dots appear on the screen and stay there for a long time. But when he finally sends his message, all it says is, Okay. Tomorrow.

Sighing, she wonders if maybe she's not being fair by refusing to talk to him when he's trying to work things out. But he said some pretty hurtful things to her. Sure, he apologized and tried to take them back. The thing is, though . . . if he still has those thoughts in his head, then that's going to be a problem for them.

She gets how upset he was with her for leaving him, and how he didn't believe she'd ever come back to him. She gets why he wanted to move on, and she gets why he's afraid she might leave again.

But does he get how much it sucked that he held her wanting to go to her dream college against her? They've never addressed it. Their issues have all come back to what she did to him. But damn it, she was an eighteen-year-old girl moving away to go to college. Is that really such a horrible thing?

Still, she knows how badly her decision hurt him. So maybe she can cut him some slack for being weary of her doing it again now.

Her fingers twitch around her phone with the desire to give in and tell him to come over. Before she can either talk herself into or out of it, though, the phone rings.

Not bothering to sit up, she swipes to answer. "Hey, Mom."

"Hi, hon. How are you?"

The obligatory answer she gives practically gets swallowed up by her mom quickly launching into a story about how her dad thought he could fix their leaky sink himself, rather than hire a plumber. Apparently, he ended up flooding the kitchen floor, then twisting his ankle when he tried to stand up in the puddle. Montana utters reactions in the appropriate places while she picks at the black polish on the corner of her fingernail.

"So anyway, now he has to sit in the recliner with his foot elevated for the next few days."

"Isn't that what he does anyway?"

Her mom frowns at her. Montana can't see it, obviously, but she can just tell.

"You haven't gotten back to us about Christmas, you know."

"I've been busy," she says. Busy being with Austin, then busy avoiding Austin. Busy, busy, busy.

"Christmas is coming up soon, whether you're busy or not."

She groans. "It's not that soon."

Sighing, her mom says, "I don't understand why you aren't excited to come down here and be with us. It kills me to think about you spending the day by yourself in that house watching all three *Home Alone* movies."

"There's like five now."

"No, there's not."

"Pretty sure there is," Montana insists.

As if the fact actually matters, her mom says, "Well, that's even sadder."

"Mom."

"Yes?"

"I don't know. Let me think about it, okay?" That's the best she can do.

Her mom barely lets her finish her sentence before she's asking, "Do you have a better way to spend the holidays?"

Images hit her then. Spending Christmas Day with Austin. Watching Kalen unwrap presents. Drinking his mom's eggnog. Sledding down the hill behind the high school.

"Montana?"

She realizes she hasn't even told her parents about her and Austin getting back together. She could tell her mom now. Except . . . she's not sure what's happening with them right now. That's how fast they've messed it up.

"Just give me a little more time to figure out if I need to be anywhere for any articles I'm doing," she says. "I'll get back to you, I promise."

"Fine. But remember, plane tickets aren't going to get any cheaper."

Through gritted teeth, she says, "Yes, I know." Then she quickly scans her brain for an excuse to get off the phone. "Listen, I gotta go. I'm working on an article right now."

"Okay, let us know where it will be published."

"I will."

After disconnecting, she smushes her face back into the couch cushion. That sad movie montage comes to her mind again. A dog to lick her and force her to act like a functioning human would be really nice right about now.

Well, fuck it.

Jumping up, she grabs her purse, then runs out the door, slamming it behind her.

At the animal shelter a couple towns over, she wanders up and down the rows of cages, her heart hurting more and more as she sees all the faces of the lonely dogs. Some look sad, some look eager. She wishes she could bring all of them home with her. That's a guaranteed way to make the house not seem too big and empty.

Then she turns the corner and spots him. Sitting quietly right behind the bars of his cage like a perfect gentleman is a large, adorable golden-doodle.

"Hey, there!" she coos. She glances at the plastic nameplate affixed beside his cage. *Denver.* A place she's never been.

His tail begins to wag, but he's still sitting up with perfect posture. When she brings her hand to the cage, he leans in to sniff her, then lets out one small, happy bark.

"I'll be right back," she tells him, before going to find a shelter worker so she can ask to take him for a walk.

The dog is well-behaved on his leash, but when she stops and sits down in the grass to pet him, he wags his tail excitedly and nuzzles his head into her chest. She scratches her nails through his curly fur and gives his butt a few pats. Then he rolls over, exposing his belly for her to rub, and when she does, he cranes his neck to lick her hand in gratitude.

That's it. She's in love.

But can she really do this? Can she get a dog on a whim? What if she and Austin don't work things out—will she still stay at her parents' house?

Yes. She will. Her whole life doesn't revolve around whether or not she's with Austin. It can't.

Though if they're not together, who will watch Denver for her if she needs to go away on a writing trip? And can she even afford to take care of a dog?

She has to work all weekend, and she doesn't know how he'll handle being alone in a new place. The responsible thing would be to wait until she's better prepared for this. But as Denver nudges her with his head again, she melts.

"Give me a few days," she says to him. "I'll figure it out."

◆

SHE'S STILL THINKING about how much she wants the dog when she goes into work the next night. It kind of gave her a short break from stressing about her and Austin, but now she's still unprepared for what she wants to say to him.

It's the first open mic night, though, so he's running around frantic, trying to make sure everything is going smoothly. Which it seems to be. In fact, the place is packed, and Montana's seeing so many new faces. They must be college students from a few towns over. Austin did a good job in getting the word out.

They said hi to each other at the beginning of the shift, but they haven't had any time alone yet. Just seeing him makes it hard for her to stay upset though.

Maybe she's being foolish. Maybe they don't have their issues all worked out. But she's not going to bail. She only wishes he could understand why she needed to leave before—and why she wants to stay now.

She's busy making two spicy margaritas for a girl with pink tips in her blonde hair and another in a Harry Styles T-shirt with an arm covered in friendship bracelets, so she's not paying much attention as Austin gets on the stage to introduce himself and talk about how this is the bar's first open mic night. "We've got a nice list of performers signed up already," he says, "but there's still time to add your name if you're interested. And if it's cool with you guys, I'm gonna kick things off with a song of my own."

Wait.

Huh?

Montana whips her head toward the stage, sticky liquid sloshing over the rims of the margarita glasses as she haphazardly slides them across the bar. Austin is sitting on a stool now, his guitar in his lap.

"Hey, can you pour me two Stellas and a Guinness?" Landon calls out to her.

She nods, but even as she moves over to the taps, she's still watching Austin. He looks like a natural up there, strumming the opening chords of a song she doesn't recognize. She keeps staring as she lets the Guinness settle, but then has to tear her eyes away so she can deliver the beers to Landon. And then there's another three customers trying to wave her down, so she has to take more orders.

Maybe I held on too tight
Maybe I didn't trust you knew
What was right for you

As she's handing a guy his change, she catches the first lines of Austin's song and freezes.

Wish I tried harder to understand
It all back then
But believe me, I get it now

Completely ignoring the next customer in line, she turns and ducks underneath the closed top of the service bar. She pushes her way through the small crowd until she's standing directly in front of the stage, looking up at him. *Did he write this?* He must have.

He notices her and stares right into her soul while he sings the rest of the song.

If you need to leave
Then I can let you go
But I need you to know

That if you stay
I'll do anything
Give you everything
If you stay, stay, stay
All I need is to hear you say
Say that you'll just stay

Her mouth is still hanging open as the crowd starts clapping. Austin has the nerve to look embarrassed now, cheeks turning red as he ducks his head down. He mumbles a quick, "Thank you," into the mic, and then hops down from the stage, making a beeline to Montana.

"Don't you need to announce the next singer?" she asks in stunned disbelief.

"Oh crap." He rushes back up there and grabs the clipboard with the sign-up sheet. "Now let's all welcome up Annaliese Mascena."

The crowd claps politely as he hops down again, taking the list with him. He grabs Montana's hand and leads her off to the side of the room. For a few moments, they just stand there staring at each other.

She can still hear his song in her head. The fact that the one line echoes a Taylor Swift song doesn't go unnoticed. She wonders if he did that on purpose for her, but it doesn't even matter. "That was . . ."

"I'm sorry if it was awkward or embarrassing," he jumps in. "I know you're not one for public displays. I just . . ."

"It was perfect." She can't contain her smile anymore. "I thought you'd quit trying to write songs."

He shrugs. "Guess I finally had something important to say."

"Guess so. And so do I." Wrapping her arms around his neck, she leans in, head tilted up so her lips brush ever so slightly against his when she tells him, "I'm staying. Here with you."

He closes the tiny gap between their mouths so fast that she stumbles backward in surprise, but his arms reach out to catch her and pull her back in.

She loses herself in the kiss—in him, in *them*—until the girl on stage starts to sing, and she remembers where they are. "Shit!"

Austin laughs, and she pecks his lips one more time before rushing back behind the bar, where Landon only has time to spare her one exasperated and amused eye roll, because the customers are piling up on the other side. Physically, she stays here making drinks for the rest of the night. But in her head, she's off in the sky somewhere with Austin, floating on a cloud.

THEN

*M*ontana headed to her locker before homeroom, the small homemade card she'd made for Austin tucked safely underneath her arm. She hadn't seen him yet, and she didn't even know if she was going to give it to him. This was her first Valentine's Day with a boyfriend. What if he thought the card was silly? What if he thought the whole holiday was silly?

It was, actually. But Austin had been so sweet to her ever since they started going out, and she'd learned that he could be a bit of a romantic sap sometimes. He was always telling her the things he liked about her, from the way she spoke her mind in class, to the way her left pinky toe stuck out a little bit away from the rest of her toes.

Hopefully he understood how she felt about him too, but it was harder for her to say these kinds of things out loud. She was better when she could put something in writing, so that was what she'd done with the card.

Standing at her locker, she spun her combination into the lock and popped it open. An avalanche of pastel colors spilled out and into the hallway, making her jump back.

They just kept coming and coming. As she recovered from the shock, she got a better look at the cascading objects and realized they were candy hearts. There must have been a thousand of them, or maybe even more, because they were still spilling out and noisily hitting the ground.

Oh god.

Austin.

He knew her locker combination. They'd exchanged them so that they could both keep their books in whoever's was most convenient. She sometimes opened her locker to find little folded up notes from him, just saying he was thinking about her or that her shirt looked cute today. But this was insane.

By the time the last heart hit the ground with a tiny thwack, she'd attracted a small crowd in the hallway. Boys laughing as if this was so corny and girls expressing their jealousy. Not used to being the center of attention, Montana lets her hair fall forward to hide the flush she could feel creeping onto her cheeks.

Before she could figure out what to do, her old history teacher marched up to her with a stern look on his face. "Miss Sinclair, what's going on here? This is a hazard. I need you to clean it up right away."

"Yes, of course," she replied, cheeks heating further. "I'm sorry." She set the card in her locker and crouched, then began to pick up the candies one by one. She piled a bunch into her open palm, but not knowing what else to do with them, she unzipped her backpack and dumped the handful in, feeling ridiculous.

This really wasn't doing much good, and her cheeks were on fire now. As she bit her lip trying to calm herself down, though, she heard Austin's voice.

"I'm so sorry, Mr. Gibbons. This was my fault. I'll go get a broom from the janitor's closet and take care of it."

"That's fine, Mr. Adler. Thank you."

Montana heard the teacher walking away, but she didn't move to stand up.

Austin crouched down to her level. He was grinning at her, but when he saw her somber expression, his face turned serious. "Hey, what's wrong? Didn't you like it?"

"No, I did," she told him. "It was just . . . a lot. You didn't need to do all this."

He ran a finger over the ripped knee of her jeans. "It wasn't a big deal. I mean, I did have to hit up every CVS, grocery store, and Walmart in Hartley and three other towns to find enough boxes, but—"

"But that's not a big deal?" Despite herself, she was laughing now. "That sounds like a lot of trouble to go through."

"Nothing's too much trouble if I'm doing it for you," he said sincerely.

"You're a cheeseball."

He shrugged, apparently unconcerned.

When she stood, she took his hand so he'd stand with her. "I'm just not so into the big public displays, okay?"

"Oh." He frowned. "I'm sorry. I didn't mean to embarrass you."

"You didn't," she said. Although that wasn't exactly true. He had embarrassed her a little, but it was also really damn sweet that he'd thought of this and took the time to make it happen. "Maybe next year you could keep it simple though."

"Next year, huh?"

She blushed, realizing she'd implied they'd still be dating a year from now. But she hoped they would be.

Austin bent to grab a candy heart off the ground, and then held it out to her with a grin.

KISS ME?

Laughing, she leaned in to oblige him. She suddenly didn't care if people were still looking at them.

She was pretty sure they'd still be together next year, and for plenty more after that. He was her first Valentine, and if he was also her last, she didn't see a problem with that. She'd have to tell him she liked chocolates much better than these chalky candy hearts though. And next year she'd have to give him something more than a card.

CHAPTER TWENTY-TWO

NOW

*T*hankfully, Denver is still at the shelter when Montana goes back for him on Monday. She fills out the paperwork, forks over a small adoption fee, and the next thing she knows, she's got a golden-doodle sticking his curly head out of the backseat of her car.

When they get home, she opens the front door and unclips his leash, nudging him inside. He sits down right in the foyer, looking around like he's unsure what to do.

"It's okay," she tells him. "This is your home now."

He turns his head to her questioningly.

She nods. "Go ahead."

Apparently, that's all the permission he needs, because he suddenly bolts into the living room with the speed of a racehorse, sliding the area rug across the floor and crashing into the couch. For a moment, he looks confused about what just happened, but then he wags his tail and takes off exploring the rest of the house. He keeps stopping to look back at her, checking if he's allowed to do things like jump on the furniture and go upstairs.

After he's explored the whole house—including the basement, which he appeared somehow disappointed by—Montana lets him out into the backyard where he immediately begins running laps. She already bought a pack of tennis balls, and when she calls his name and throws one, he chases after it and brings it right back, dropping it at her feet. Then he wags his tail, eagerly waiting for her to throw it again.

So he definitely knows how to play fetch. She grins as she sends another ball flying for him. This is going to work.

Leaving him to sniff around the yard, she goes inside and calls Austin.

"Hey!" he answers, and she can hear the smile in his voice. "I miss you."

"You saw me last night."

He lowers his voice when he says, "I know, and I still have the scratch marks down my back to remind me."

She inhales sharply. Yes, she remembers vividly the way he fucked her so hard and fast she had to dig her nails into him to hold on. "Oh," she says dumbly, trying to recover from the flashback and get back on track. "Is Kalen there?"

He already had another talk with his son, and it went better than the first one. But she feels like she needs to talk to Kalen herself.

"Why do you think I whispered that?"

She laughs. "Do you guys wanna come over? I have a surprise for him."

"You do?"

"Mmhmm."

"Okay," he says. "I was about to make something for lunch, but how 'bout I pick up a pizza?"

"Sounds great. As long as you don't put nasty mushrooms on it."

He huffs and promises he won't, though before he hangs up, she swears she hears him muttering something about her having no taste.

When they arrive, Denver is still in the backyard, happily entertaining himself by chasing butterflies and digging small holes. He probably didn't get to spend enough time outside while he was at the shelter, but Montana's determined to give him the best life possible now, everything he was missing out on.

She opens the front door, and Austin steps over the threshold, leaning in to give her a one-armed hug while balancing a pizza box on his other hand. Kalen is lagging a couple steps behind. As he follows Austin inside, he looks reluctant, which breaks Montana's heart a little. He's always been so excited to come here until now.

"Hey, bud," she says, giving him her warmest smile.

Even though she always greets him that way, it feels like she's trying too hard. And he can probably sense it, because he gives her a look like he's sizing her up in a different way than he did when they first met. That day at the restaurant, he looked at her skeptically, like he didn't trust her to be a qualified babysitter. Today he's looking at her more like, *Eww, you're not even that pretty. Why does my daddy want to kiss you?*

And okay, possibly this is all in her head. She should not feel intimidated by a child. Austin assured her that they'll work it out and Kalen will come around. But she doesn't want him to feel weird or uncomfortable around her at all. They really need to have a talk, just between the two of them.

"I have something to show you," she tells him.

Austin nudges Kalen with his shoe when the boy doesn't respond, and then all she gets is a disinterested, "Okay."

Austin's the one looking more curious as the two of them follow her into the kitchen. He sets the pizza box on the counter and glances around the room, like maybe a clown is going to pop out of the corner with balloons. When his eyes widen, she figures he's spotted the dog out the window.

"The surprise is outside," she says, gesturing for Kalen to go out the back door.

There's a little more pep in his step now, his excitement for a treat possibly outweighing his distrust of her. As soon as he opens the door, he lets out a squeal of delight and takes off running into the grass. Austin and Montana follow at a slower pace.

"That's Denver!" Montana calls out.

Denver runs toward Kalen, tail wagging as if he's just seen his best friend. His enthusiasm knocks Kalen on his butt, and Kalen laughs like it's the best thing in the world. He wraps his arms around the dog's neck, letting him lick his face. When he doesn't turn his head quickly enough, Denver gets a good lick right into his open, laughing mouth.

Austin is smiling as he watches his son, but then he crosses the yard to him and crouches down, scratching Denver behind the ears. "Hey, kid?"

"What?" Kalen says through his giggles.

"You forgot to ask if it was okay to pet the dog."

"I'm sorry!" he claims, although it's the least sorry Montana's ever seen him look.

Austin shakes his head fondly. "It's okay, because Montana wouldn't have sent you outside if the dog wasn't friendly. But you need to remember for next time please."

"I will."

Leaving the two of them to play, Austin heads back over to Montana. "You got a dog?"

"I got a dog."

"I hope you didn't do this just for Kalen. Because I told you he'll come around. This is a big commitment."

Grabbing his hand, she holds on tightly and peers directly into his eyes when she says, "I'm committed." She's so committed. She's committed to them all. Hopefully, he sees that.

He probably does, because he's looking at her now like she's a better surprise than the dog. He reaches out his other hand to tug her a little closer, then runs a finger tantalizingly up her inner arm, from her wrist to the crease of her elbow. "He looks at home already," he says, turning his head to watch the dog and Kalen for another moment.

Montana nods. "He is home. Guess Denver and I are both here to stay."

"I want to kiss you right now."

Her breath catches in her throat. "Well, you can, can't you?"

He tilts his head as he considers her. "Yeah," he says slowly. "I guess I can."

And then he does. It's brief, but their lips slot together like they were made to be joined this way. When they separate, he glances over his shoulder nervously, but Kalen is too busy with Denver to be paying the two of them any attention.

"I didn't do this only for Kalen," Montana tells him. "I wanted a dog. I've been thinking about it for a while. But the fact that it's making him happy is a huge bonus."

"He's never going to want to leave here now."

Shrugging, she teases, "Maybe that was part of the plan too."

He wraps an arm around her and starts to walk them over toward the happy pair, but she stops him with a hand on his chest.

"I still want to talk to Kalen myself, if that's okay. Just to reassure him that things aren't going to change too much, and that I'm not going to hurt you."

Sighing, Austin says, "It's crazy, because he wasn't even old enough to really remember me and his mom being together. I don't know when he got smart enough to feel the need to protect me."

"Well, he's got a great dad. That's probably why he's smart."

He kisses her temple and lets her go, giving her a light swat on the ass as she steps forward.

She asks Kalen if she can talk to him for a minute, and then leads him back toward the house. Denver starts to follow, but Austin picks up the tennis ball, immediately diverting the dog's attention. Montana smiles, flooded with happy memories as she watches him launch the ball across the yard.

In the kitchen, she and Kalen sit across from each other at the table. Despite the fact that the kid's head is only about six inches above the top of the table, she feels oddly like she's about to be interviewed for a job she really wants. It's a struggle to find the words she needs to say.

"Can I play with the dog again?" he asks when she takes too long.

"In a minute, yeah, bud. I just wanted to make sure you and me are cool."

All she gets is a shrug.

"I know your dad's talked to you about how things are a little different now with me and him, but that doesn't mean things are going to be different with us. I still want to be your friend."

As if trying to detect a lie, he eyes her critically. Then he says, "Daddy hasn't dated anyone since he was with Mom."

She isn't sure if that's true, or if Kalen was just too young to be told about it. "Does it make you worried that we're dating?"

He shrugs again. "It's fun when we all do things together."

"I know it is. And that doesn't have to change."

"But what if you decide you don't like Daddy anymore? Then we won't get to have fun anymore, and he'd be sad."

Taking a deep breath, she places her hands flat on the table in front of her, ready to lay out her proverbial cards. "Sometimes when people are dating, they both decide they don't want to anymore, so they stop. I can't promise that'll never happen with us, and if it did, I'd be sad too. But the only way to find out if something's going to work is if you try."

"When I asked Daddy to let me try my bike without training wheels, he said I wasn't old enough."

Montana nods thoughtfully. "Sometimes that's true. Did you know your dad and I tried dating before, a long time ago?"

He shakes his head.

"Well, we did. But I think we were too young then."

"But you're really old now," Kalen declares.

"Gee, thanks, kid." She laughs at his perfectly innocent look. "My point is, we're ready to try again. We were good at it last time, but I think we'll be so much better this time. You know I love you, and I love your dad very much, right?"

He says, "Yeah," like it's simple, like that's something obvious. But Montana's heart jolts. She just told him she loves Austin before she told Austin.

"I . . . um . . ." She stumbles uselessly over her words. "So what do you think? Is it okay if we try?"

It feels like her fate is hanging in the balance as this small child stares at her, taking his time to think. Then finally, *finally*, he nods. "Okay. Can I go play with Denver now?"

"Yeah," she says, her emotions a confusing swirling mass in her stomach, threatening to spill out of her throat. "Yeah, absolutely. I'm going to talk to your dad, okay?"

"Sure." He's already striding to the door as fast as his little legs can carry him.

Austin turns when they walk back out to the yard, and a look of relief washes over his face, probably at Kalen's happy smile. Which has way more to do with the dog than Montana, but she'll take it. She catches Austin's eye, he raises an eyebrow, and a smile breaks out across her face too. Striding up to him, she grabs his hand, and then drags him quickly toward the house.

"Wha—" he starts to say.

"Hold on." Once they're in the kitchen with the door closed, she faces him. There's no reason to hold it back anymore. "I love you."

A quiet gasp slips from his lips. For a second, she fears a reversal of the time he first said it to her. Like maybe she got here before he did. But then—"I love you too."

Before she can express her relief and happiness, he's surging forward and kissing her. Lips never leaving hers, he pushes her backward until her lower back hits the edge of the counter. His hand tangles in her hair as he leaves open-mouthed kisses along her jawline. It's urgent, a little sloppy, but it's quite possible that nothing's ever felt better.

"I—You—" he pants out between kisses.

"Yeah?"

"Yeah."

Montana has no clue what they're saying. But it doesn't matter. Because she loves him. And he loves her, he loves her, he loves her.

THEN

*A*fter Austin walked Montana to her locker before sixth period and kissed her goodbye, he was about to turn and head off to his next class when he paused. She raised her eyebrows questioningly, and he smiled.

"I love you."

She froze. Her brain disconnected from her mouth, and her heart pounded in her chest like a trapped animal.

What?

It was the first time someone who wasn't a family member had said those words to her, and she couldn't process it. How could she have possibly expected that to come out of his mouth right here, right now? In the middle of the hallway about thirty seconds before the warning bell would ring.

Brrrrrrng.

There it was.

"I . . ." she tried, but no other words made it out.

"It's okay," he said, shaking his head. There was a slight wrinkle in his brow. "You don't have to say it back. I just wanted you to know."

All she could do was nod dumbly.

"I gotta run if I'm gonna make it to bio on time." He leaned in to give her another quick kiss, then took off.

She came back to her senses enough to grab her stuff out of her locker and head to her next class. But despite him assuring her she didn't need to say it back, she couldn't get his face out of her mind.

He'd looked disappointed.

Even though he didn't say it again, she couldn't stop thinking about it for the next three days. He loved her. He *loved* her?

Did she love him?

Maybe.

He was the person she wanted to be around more than anyone else. Sometimes when she wasn't with him, he was all she could think about. And whenever he looked at her a certain way, her heart did this silly fluttering thing as romantic Taylor Swift lyrics floated through her head.

But they hadn't even been dating six months. And were they even old enough to know what that kind of love was?

She wished she'd been better prepared to hear those words. It wasn't like she'd ever really pictured someone saying them to her before, but now that she was thinking about it, she supposed she expected the moment to be bigger. Maybe if it'd had some more buildup, like after an anniversary dinner or during a holiday—maybe then she could have seen it coming and been ready.

Who blurted out something like that for no reason in between classes?

Austin James Adler, that was who.

Was she overthinking this? Love wasn't supposed to be something logical, right? It was something you had to feel—and you either felt it or you didn't.

Now, day four since he'd dropped the bomb on her, they were watching a movie on her couch, and she was still thinking about it.

He'd pulled her legs over his lap and had been rubbing his hands up and down her calves for the last half hour. She kept stealing glances at him when she thought he was focused on the TV screen. He was gorgeous. And funny. And so kind and sweet and caring and—*Oh.*

She loved him.

She really did.

And this feeling wasn't only now hitting her for the first time. It had been there for a while. But now she was suddenly recognizing it for what it was. *Love.*

She opened her mouth to tell him, but then shut it again, biting her lip. What if it had taken her too long, and he'd changed his mind about it? Sometimes she hated the way she overthought things. Her need to make everything make sense. She had to tell him though.

Except every time she tried to release the words into the air between them, she got too nervous and couldn't do it. And the longer she waited, the more she was building the moment up in her head until it was too big to handle.

When the movie finished, she realized she hadn't been paying any attention to it.

Austin gave her thigh a squeeze and then gently scooted her legs off his lap so that her feet landed on the floor. "My dad will be here in a second."

"Okay," she said, feeling her last chances slipping away.

"Walk me out?"

"Sure."

She followed him out the door. They'd barely stood on the porch for thirty seconds—not enough time—when his dad's car pulled into the driveway.

Tell him. Say it. Just say it.

He gave her a kiss on the forehead, telling her goodnight. She said goodnight too, then watched him turn and walk away, down the porch steps and toward his dad's car.

"I love you!"

Oh crap.

She hadn't meant to shout it at his back like that.

But he turned around, eyes wide, and then a grin slowly spread across his face.

"I love you," she said again, calmer this time. Because she did, and he deserved to know it.

Suddenly he was running back up the steps and throwing his arms around her waist. "I love you too."

He kissed her then, his hands roaming up and down her back. As she kissed him back just as enthusiastically, she held tightly onto his T-shirt to keep him in place, not even caring if his dad could totally see them from the car.

They were in love.

CHAPTER TWENTY-THREE

NOW

*W*hat are you doing for Thanksgiving?"

"Huh?" Montana says, absentmindedly running her foot along Austin's bare calf under the covers. They're tangled up in bed after a round of mind-blowing sex, and she's not quite ready for words yet.

"You know," he goes on. "Pilgrims, turkey, cranberry sauce that nobody eats?"

Confused, she lifts her head off his chest to look up at him. "Sorry, I wasn't listening. What are you babbling about?"

He laughs. "Rude."

"Can't you just let me enjoy my blissful fucked out haze?" she jokes. "Gosh, what's with all the talking?"

His eyes soften as he tucks a strand of hair behind her ear. "I asked you what you were doing for Thanksgiving."

"Oh. Um. I dunno, I guess nothing really."

"Then how about you come with me to my mom's? Andrea and her husband will be in town."

Oh. She supposes she should've expected this. Couples do holidays together, duh. But somehow it's taken her by surprise. "Do they, uh,"— she lets her head fall back onto his chest—"all know about you and me?"

His fingers stroke her hair, rubbing soothingly over the nape of her neck and, quite frankly, doing the opposite of helping to draw her out of the post-orgasm bliss and into this serious conversation. But she won't tell him that, because she doesn't want him to stop.

"Of course they do," he says. "Didn't you tell your parents?"

"I did. Between dating you and getting the dog, they were pretty thrilled, actually. My mom said something about how it's good to see me settling down and living a normal life. Which is ridiculous. It's not like I was an international rock star or something before. By 'normal,' I think she just means suburban."

He jumps slightly when her toes tickle the back of his knee. "Well, you know what normal suburban wives do?"

Her heart leaps at his use of the word "wives" in the context of her life, and naturally, she tries to cover it with sarcasm. "Day drink and gossip about the neighbors while their husbands are busy cheating on them on their lunch breaks from the office?"

She can practically feel him rolling his eyes at the ceiling before he says, "No. They bake a pie and come to their boyfriend's family's house for Thanksgiving."

"Boyfriend? I thought they were married."

He jostles her off his chest as he sits up. Then he urges her up too and props the pillows against the headboard for them to lean on. "Can we be serious now?"

She shoots him a skeptical look.

"I was kidding about the pie, you know."

"Yeah, it's not about the pie," she says, shaking her head. If she set her mind to it, she's pretty sure she could bake the shit out of a pie.

But . . . "If I go with you, won't it look like we're making some kind of big declaration?"

"I'm okay with that," he says confidently.

And she believes him. If he's okay with it, then so is she. It's been six years since she's seen his mom or his sister, and she misses them. It would be less pressure if the reunion was more casual, rather than over a major holiday, but that's okay.

They're together. Finally. And they're happy. She wants the whole world to know that.

"If I say yes, can we get to round two?"

He laughs and squeezes her ribs, making her wriggle away. "I think I'm gonna need at least another fifteen minutes. I'm not eighteen anymore."

"I know," she tells him, rolling onto her side so she can run her hand down his abs, relishing in the way his muscles tighten at the attention. She's glad they aren't eighteen anymore. Back then, they got a lot of things right, but they didn't know how to make this work long-term. Now it seems like they've finally figured it out. "But I'm happy to spend the next fifteen minutes kissing you while we wait."

Beating her to it, he grabs the back of her head and pulls her in to press their lips together. His tongue slides against her bottom lip until she opens her mouth, and from there, it's all lips and tongues and teeth nipping hard enough to make her gasp.

She throws her leg around him and climbs into his lap. Cupping his face, she runs one thumb along his jawline and presses it gently into the side of his neck just underneath it. He responds by digging his finger into her sides, clutching her like a lifeline, and thrusting his hips. He might have overestimated his required refractory period.

But then he pulls back to look at her. "Montana." It doesn't sound like a question, though his eyes are unsure.

It takes her a few moments to realize what he wants. "Oh, yes! Of course. I'd love to spend Thanksgiving with you."

And hopefully every holiday after that for the rest of their damn lives.

♦

STANDING SQUISHED in between Austin and Kalen on the front step of Austin's childhood home, Montana wraps her oversized, chunky gray cardigan tighter around herself with one hand, because her other hand is balancing a pecan pie. The black tights she's wearing under her maroon dress aren't doing much to keep out the biting, late November chill. She's a little jealous of Kalen, bundled up in his puffy jacket, not having to worry about looking good or impressing anyone.

Just as she's thinking this, and her nerves threaten to rise to the surface again, Kalen reaches up and takes her hand, squeezing it with his much smaller one. She smiles down at him. This is going to be okay.

When Mrs. Adler opens the door, she beams lovingly at Austin. Montana could swear that when his mom's eyes flit to her, though, her smile assumes a fake, plastered-on quality. But it's probably her imagination.

"Come in, come in!" Mrs. Adler urges, moving back to usher them through the doorway.

Kalen drops Montana's hand as she steps inside the house, and she briefly wishes he didn't. But she's an adult, and she doesn't need a child holding her hand for encouragement, so she greets Austin's mom with a warm, confident smile. At least, that's what she aims for.

"Hi, Mrs. Adler. It's good to see you."

"Hello, Montana. My gosh, how long has it been?"

Is that supposed to be rhetorical? Doesn't everybody know it's been six freaking years? (She could probably tell you right down to the day if you give her a minute to do the math.) Or was Montana's absence from Austin's life not felt so acutely as Austin's absence from hers was?

Oh, for fuck's sake, it's just an expression.

"Uh, a long time, I guess," she mutters awkwardly.

Luckily, Kalen steps out from behind her then, and Mrs. Adler diverts all her attention to him. The woman bends down to pick him up in her arms and asks, "How's my little K-Cup?"

"*K-Cup?*" Montana mouths to Austin, unable to hide her amusement.

He shrugs good-naturedly.

Kalen allows his grandmother to hug him and peck him on both cheeks before he starts wiggling in his desire to be let down.

"Andrea's not here yet?" Austin asks.

"No, you beat her," his mom tells him. "But she and Marcos should be here any minute."

"Did he make empanadas?"

Mrs. Adler nods. "I think so."

"Sweet," Austin says. Then to Montana—"They're so good."

"Cool," she says with less enthusiasm, feeling mildly out of place standing here in this house that used to be almost as familiar to her as her own. She didn't even know the name of Andrea's husband thirty seconds ago, which is a reminder of how much time really has passed, and how Austin's family continued on with their lives while she wasn't here to witness it.

She would have loved to see Andrea walk down the aisle. She bets her wedding dress wasn't entirely traditional. Andrea's tastes usually aligned with what might be considered typically "girly," but she liked to put her own unique spin on things.

The house looks different too, Montana realizes, as she follows

Austin and his mom into the living room. Though, she suspects this is less a reflection of the natural progression of time passing, and more a result of Mr. Adler passing away. There's a very large, framed picture of him with Austin and Andrea hung above the fireplace that wasn't there years ago, but his old bowling league trophies aren't littering the mantle anymore. The wooden rocking chair that originally belonged to Mr. Adler's grandmother is also missing. She remembers how Mr. Adler spent a lot of money one time to have it restored after a leg broke.

He's only been gone two years. Do the Adlers still feel the pain of it on the holidays? They must.

God, Austin must feel it every single day. Or has enough time passed to shrink the wound to a small cut? The kind you can forget about until you reach for something acidic and get a stinging reminder.

Biting the inside of her cheek, Montana sits down next to Austin on the couch. She needs to get out of her head and refocus her concentration on making a good impression. It kind of sucks, though, because she already made that impression so many years ago, and now she has to do it again. But she can't fool herself into thinking Mrs. Adler still sees her as a part of the family the way she used to. Even in college, Austin's parents didn't exactly treat her the same. Breaking their son's heart changed things.

But now Montana desperately wants Mrs. Adler to know that she loves Austin and she's going to be so careful with his heart this time. She can't just blurt that out though—she'll have to make her see it somehow.

Realizing she's still awkwardly holding the pie, she raises it up and says, "I brought this for dessert."

Mrs. Adler smiles, but the smile is almost too big, making it a bit unnerving. "Isn't that thoughtful of you?"

"It's pecan," she adds lamely. "Austin said you would already have pumpkin."

"Yes, we do. But of course, you can never have too much pie on Thanksgiving. Let me take that into the kitchen for you."

Montana hands over the pie, and she swears Mrs. Adler gives the dessert a critical, inspecting look at she walks aways with it. But she's probably imagining things again.

Hopefully it tastes good though. Because it turns out that baking a pie is a little more difficult than she expected. She threw out her first attempt when it came out of the oven looking like a mess. Denver seemed to greatly approve of the few forkfuls she'd scooped into his bowl, so it might have been okay, but presentation is important.

Shit, she should have been making test pies all week.

Austin presses the back of his knuckle into her thigh, and when she turns her head, he offers her a small smile. His kind face is almost enough to make her forget where she is and what's going on here. He's like her human equivalent of a security blanket.

But then Mrs. Adler strolls back into the room, bringing the tension back with her.

"It smells wonderful in here," Montana says, trying again for some small talk.

"Oh, thank you," Mrs. Adler replies. "The turkey will be done shortly."

And then silence.

Thankfully, it's broken by Kalen climbing roughly onto Austin's lap—kneeing him in the stomach and causing him to let out an *oof* in the process. "But I'm hungry now!" he whines.

Montana fights a smile. She and this kid are so often on the same wavelength.

"Too bad," Austin says. "You're not spoiling your dinner."

"A little snack won't hurt him," Mrs. Adler says. "I could make him peanut butter and jelly."

Austin rolls his eyes and tells her that's fine. But once his mom leaves the room, he mutters under his breath, "Not really a little snack."

With his dad's permission, Kalen gets up and follows his grand-mother into the kitchen, leaving Montana and Austin blissfully alone.

Angling himself to face her, Austin asks, "How are you doing?"

"Oh, just peachy," she says in what she hopes is a light tone.

"Uh huh. And how are you really feeling?"

"Nervous," she admits, scratching at a sudden itch on her wrist.

He takes her hand and runs his thumb soothingly over the back of it. "You don't have to be."

"I sort of do."

"No," he says. "It's going to be fine. Trust me."

She trusts him. She just thinks he's maybe being a little naïve about the situation here. Before she can tell him that, though, the doorbell rings.

"Austin, can you let your sister in?" his mom calls out from the kitchen.

He gives Montana a brief, regretful look before releasing her hand and rising to get the door. She remains rooted to the couch cushion, eager to see Andrea, but not wanting to seem *too* eager. This is stupidly complicated.

"Hey, doofus!" Andrea's voice rings out cheerily from the entryway.

"Love you too, little sister," Austin replies.

Montana can hear a third voice that must be Andrea's husband, and then the three of them enter the living room, so she jumps up from the couch. "Hey!" She's about to step forward to give Andrea a hug, but the girl's completely indifferent face stops her in her tracks.

"Hi, Montana," Andrea says flatly. Then, at Austin's not-so-subtle nudge in her side, she adds, "This is Marcos, my husband."

"It's nice to meet you," Marcos tells Montana.

Compulsively smoothing down her dress, she replies, "You too."

"Where's mom?" Andrea asks.

"In the kitchen feeding Kalen," Austin tells her.

Andrea tilts her head questioningly. "Dinner's ready already?"

"Nope. She's just babying him."

"You have to tell her to stop doing that."

Montana sort of wishes someone would baby her right now. Feeling left out of the conversation again, she takes her seat back on the couch. This time she can't convince herself she imagined the look Andrea gave her before she forced her face into a more pleasant expression. And it hurts.

Andrea used to be like a sister to her. Back then, Andrea seemed so sure that they would *officially* be sisters someday.

They still could be. It's not too late.

"And Montana, what are you up to these days?" Andrea asks, tuning her back in to the conversation. "Still doing the little writing thing?"

She flinches. The way Andrea said it, so dismissive of her entire career, stings. She makes it sound like writing is just a hobby, instead of Montana's actual job that she used to get paid pretty damn well for. Andrea used to think her dreams were the coolest, but apparently that's changed too.

"Of course she is," Austin jumps in. "She's great. She's had a ton of articles published in the last few months."

A *ton* is an exaggeration, but she appreciates his pride in her.

"You're a writer?" Marcos asks.

"A journalist," Montana says.

"Yeah, and she travels *alllll* over the world," Andrea adds. But the pointed way she says it doesn't make it sound like praise. It sounds like a reminder.

Oh god, she's reminding Austin of how much travel Montana's job involves. And how she left him for it.

She wants to say something, but she doesn't know what, and she honestly can't believe this is happening. She expected things to be pretty awkward between her and Austin's family, but she didn't expect this thinly veiled hostility. Especially not from Andrea.

Andrea's watching her, a challenge in her eyes, and Montana cowardly breaks the eye contact to look up at Austin for help. She's afraid he isn't picking up on what's going down, but he cuts his eyes sharply to his sister, who glances to the floor.

"That's incredible," Marcos says, blissfully unaware of the silent war being waged in the room.

"Yeah," Montana says, recovering a little. "But I'm not doing that kind of traveling anymore. I want to stay close to Hartley."

And to Austin.

She isn't sure if she should add that. But Austin sits down beside her and slings his arm firmly around her shoulders, pulling her into him, so hopefully that makes the point for her.

"I'm gonna see if Mom needs any help," Andrea announces, promptly spinning on her heels and marching off into the kitchen.

Marcos sits down in the armchair, and he and Austin start to talk sports, which Montana tunes out. This is going worse than she thought it would. Granted, Austin doesn't seem too fazed as he rubs his fingers over her shoulder. But there's a really bad feeling sinking to the pit of her stomach.

Mrs. Adler's being overly polite, and Andrea's being . . . whatever that was. Maybe she should try to pull Andrea aside and talk to her privately. Or maybe she should cut her losses and run.

No. She's not giving up here. She's not running away. She's going to make this work.

Because Austin is worth it.

The two of them are meant to be together, she's sure of it. And his family felt that way at one point too. They'll come around again.

It's a relief when Mrs. Adler leads them all into the dining room to sit down for dinner. At least now they'll have something to do other than sitting around staring at each other, trying to make polite conversation.

Mrs. Adler takes her seat at one head of the table. Austin, Montana, and Kalen sit on one side, and Andrea and Marcos take the opposite. There's a plate and silverware setting at the other end of the table.

"Is someone else coming?" Montana asks.

Andrea coughs as Mrs. Adler lets out a strangled sort of a cry.

"That's for my dad," Austin says calmly.

Oh.

Fucking hell.

"Oh god, I'm so sorry!"

"It's okay, dear," Mrs. Adler tells her. But the pained edge in her voice betrays that it's really not.

A somber silence hangs over the table. As embarrassed and remorseful as Montana is, those emotions are overpowered by the sharp pain of Mr. Adler's absence. She thought about it when she first walked into the house, and now she's made everyone else think about it. Before she can help it, a tear spills over her eyelid and rolls down her cheek.

Austin reaches over, wiping it away with one finger. Then he takes her hand under the table and holds it in her lap. She squeezes. He squeezes back. She squeezes again. He does too.

"Should we eat?" he says.

"Yes, of course," Mrs. Adler agrees.

"Finally," Kalen says, and they all laugh, though it's awkward, nervous laughter.

The day doesn't get much better after that. Not for Montana, anyway. No one really seems to blame her for bringing up the subject of Mr. Adler, but Austin's mom continues to treat her like she's a formal guest, and his sister continues to treat her like a pariah.

Every time she's getting upset, Austin seems to sense it, and he subtly touches her to calm her down. It works a little bit—that whole security blanket thing. But she knows she can't hide under a blanket forever. And she just prays that this less than warm welcome from his family isn't going to affect the good place they've finally reached.

THEN

*A*ustin slapped three cards face down in a line on his bed, then waited for Montana so they could reveal their final cards at the same time. "*Ugh*," he grunted when her Jack beat his nine and she swept everything toward her. "This game is never going to end."

Grinning, Montana organized the cards and added them to her pile. "I was losing big time until a couple minutes ago."

"That's what I mean! We keep going back and forth. Right when you think someone's done for, things turn around, and then it just keeps going and going and—"

She leaned in, cutting him off with a hand over his mouth. "Pretty sure that's what war is known for."

He licked her palm, which made her squeal and jolt backward, causing both of their card piles to topple and splay messily across the comforter. Then he took the opportunity to ruin the game completely, using his hands to scatter the cards even more until there was no hope for reorganizing them.

At her disbelieving look, he shrugged innocently. "We should play poker," he suggested.

"Do you know how to play poker?"

"Sort of."

"We don't have anything to bet with," she told him.

Smirking, he eyed her up and down. "We could play strip poker."

"Or you could try not to get murdered by your parents," she said laughing.

"They're not here!"

That was true. Right after she got to his house, his mom had to run to the restaurant to help his dad with something. But his sister was there, so they weren't entirely unsupervised. The fact that their supervisor was two years younger than them was irrelevant. Montana wasn't going to fool around with him with Andrea in the bedroom right next door. It was too weird.

Not that they were doing all that much fooling around anyway. They hadn't been dating too long, and it still felt a little surreal to her that Austin Adler was actually her boyfriend. But they'd done some stuff—in only a few months, she'd had so many firsts with him.

Sometimes when she was alone in her bed at night, she started thinking too much, worrying about if she was doing this whole girlfriend thing right. But whenever she was with him, he had a knack for making her feel comfortable in any situation. Like when he was joking about playing strip poker.

She reached behind her for one of his pillows and whacked him with it, taking him enough by surprise to knock him over onto his side. But he recovered quickly, sitting up and then crawling his way up the bed toward her.

"You're bending the cards!" she cried as his knee landed right on top of one, folding it down into the mattress.

Apparently, he didn't care, because he just kept coming, a look in his eyes like a lion stalking its prey. When he got close enough, he began tickling her sides. She yelped and made a show of trying to squirm away. But you know what? She didn't really mind being his prey.

They were both giggling as she fell onto her back with him landing half on top of her. He kissed her then, his hands ceasing their attack and running gently over her ribcage instead. Her breath caught in her throat. As his thumbs brushed over the sides of her breasts, she had to remind herself again that there was only one thin wall separating them from his sister.

"Okay, okay," she gasped out, pushing his hands away as she sat back up, making him roll off her. "We can't."

He groaned. "I know, I'm sorry. I wasn't trying to push—"

"I know," she cut him off gently.

They shared an understanding smile, and then he leaned over to kiss her on the cheek. "You wanna watch a movie? Or I guess we could see if Andrea wants to do something with us."

She shrugged. It wasn't that she didn't like his sister—she just didn't know her well.

"You can decide," he said. "I'm up for anything. But I'm gonna run to the bathroom first."

In his absence, she debated with herself. She'd prefer to stay in his room with him, where she felt most comfortable. But would that make her look antisocial? Did he actually want her to spend time getting to know his family, or was he just trying to show that he's not only thinking about fooling around with her?

He returned quickly, before she could make a decision. "Andrea's in there."

They cleaned up the mess of cards on his bed and put them neatly back in the deck, and then he left again to see if the bathroom was free now. A couple minutes later, Montana heard him out in the hall pounding on a door.

"Come on!" he yelled. "Quit hogging it!" Reappearing in his bedroom shortly after, he looked irritated. "She won't let me in. I dunno what she's doing in there."

"Using the bathroom?" Montana offered awkwardly.

"No, she's not. She said something about being a girl and told me to leave her alone."

Being a girl? Uh oh.

"Maybe I should go check on her."

He shook his head. "You don't have to do that. I'm sure she's fine, she's just being a brat."

Maybe she was, or maybe it was something else that a thirteen-year-old girl would be too embarrassed to explain to her older brother. So Montana told Austin she'd be right back and went to knock softly on the bathroom door.

"I told you I need a minute!"

"Andrea?" she said. "It's me. Um . . . do you need help?"

A few seconds of silence passed before the reply. "I'm fine."

"Are you sure?" Montana pressed. "Because if it's something, uh, *girl* related, I'm a girl. I'll understand."

The silence lasted longer this time, and she worried she was over-stepping. She was about to turn around and go back to Austin's room when she heard the click of the doorknob being unlocked. The door opened slowly to reveal Andrea standing there fully dressed with her eyes cast down at the floor, looking miserable. "You can come in."

Montana stepped cautiously inside, closing the door behind her. She waited a moment for Andrea to tell her what was wrong, but Andrea just yanked her long sleeves down over her hands and kept staring at the ground. "Is it your period?" Montana finally tried.

Andrea's eyes shot up to look at her. "How did you know?"

"Just a guess. Is it your first time?"

She nodded. "I found a box my mom had in the back of the cabinet, but it's tampons. And I can't figure out how to . . ."

"Put it in?" Montana supplied.

"Shit, this is embarrassing."

"No, it's not. It's fine. My mom had to show me when I first got mine."

Andrea cringed, but then she sat down on the closed lid of the toilet and sighed. "Could you . . . I mean, not like . . . Can you just try to explain it to me?"

"Of course," Montana told her.

It was a little awkward, truthfully, but Montana took the box out of the cabinet, opened one package and demonstrated how to push the tampon out of the applicator. Then she turned to face the door to give Andrea some privacy and waited for her to attempt it again. There was a decorative sign on the wall that said FAMILY, which was a little odd for a bathroom, but she liked it.

It sounded like Andrea was getting frustrated, so she tried to help calm her down without looking at her.

"I'm freaking out that's it's gonna hurt," Andrea admitted.

"I promise you'll barely feel anything," Montana assured her, "but you need to relax to make it work."

She heard the sound of another wrapper being torn open, and then after a minute—"Oh my god, I did it!"

"That's great."

"You can turn around now."

She did.

Dressed again and standing back up, Andrea thanked her.

"No problem. I'm sorry your mom wasn't here to help you."

Andrea shook her head. "But thank god you were here. Because I sure as hell wasn't going to ask my doofus brother."

"I doubt he would have been much help anyway," she said, laughing. "So are you good?"

"Yeah," Andrea said. And then suddenly she launched herself at Montana, hugging her tightly. "I've always wanted a sister. Now it's kind of like I have one."

Montana was momentarily stunned. She barely knew this girl. She didn't normally get close to people so easily. But maybe a period crisis was enough to bond girls together. Or maybe all of Austin's family was simply as kind and warm and open as he was.

Smiling, she said, "I've always wanted a sister too."

They hugged again, and then both started to giggle.

Andrea jutted her chin toward the closed bathroom door over Montana's shoulder. "We should let Austin get in here to pee before he loses it."

"Definitely," Montana agreed, opening it. "Then do you wanna watch a movie with us?"

"Sure!" Andrea said brightly.

And it was that easy.

CHAPTER TWENTY-FOUR

NOW

*M*ontana wakes up with an uneasy feeling in her stomach and a goldendoodle sprawled across her midsection. Denver has his own dog bed downstairs, but more often than not, he nudges her door open at some point in the night and jumps into bed with her.

As soon as he realizes she's awake, he gets down and starts spinning in circles on the floor, tail wagging rapidly, ready to go outside. She'd love to burrow farther under the covers and not come out until next year, but she takes pity on him, getting out of bed and pulling on a pair of leggings before dragging herself downstairs.

Leaving the dog in the yard to search for the best spot to do his business, she brews herself a pot of coffee. She wishes she'd gotten to talk to Austin after dinner yesterday. But by the time they left his mom's house, they were about to fall into a food coma, and she didn't spend the night with him because he had Kalen. When he dropped her off at home, he acted like everything was fine. Like his family's reception of her didn't change anything.

But she still has a bad feeling.

While she drinks her coffee, she munches on a couple slices of toast at the kitchen table and tries to work on the crossword. But she can't stop thinking about how Austin's going out to breakfast with his sister and Marcos this morning. She doesn't blame him for wanting to spend more time with his sister while she's here—and after yesterday, she doesn't think she could handle sitting through another meal with Andrea subtly dissing her—but the fact that Austin didn't invite her makes her nervous.

She's trying not to take it as a warning sign. He deserves to spend alone time with Andrea. It shouldn't be a big deal. But tell that to her stomach, because her toast is threatening to make a reappearance.

He told her he'd stop by to see her afterward, so she's waiting for that. Hopefully everything will be okay, and she's just been freaking out for nothing.

After finishing the crossword, which takes her much longer than it should with the way she's distracted, she checks her email. She's waiting to hear back about a publication date for a recent article she wrote. There's no news on that front, but a familiar email address catches her eye. It's an editor for a website she wrote a lot of pieces for over the years while she was in California.

She clicks open the message and is surprised to find an offer to travel to New Mexico for the week of Christmas to cover some town's crazy week-long holiday festival. The writer assigned to the piece had to back out, so the editor needs to find a replacement quickly.

A lot of Montana's coworkers in L.A. didn't like to travel over the holidays because they wanted to spend time with their families. Did this editor think of her for the assignment because he likes her work that much, or because he remembers Montana doesn't have any of those family-related hang-ups?

That was before though. Things are different now. She has a dog. She has Austin.

At least, she hopes she has Austin.

No. That's ridiculous. She has him. Of course, she does.

Another thing she has is her parents wanting to see her for Christmas, so it's really not a good time to take a trip. It's pretty cool to be asked though.

She brings her laptop out onto the porch, along with a third cup of coffee and a heavy blanket to keep her warm, and she curls up on the loveseat. Then, just out of curiosity, she looks up the festival. The town's website boasts all about it. It looks like they go all out with the decorations, even shipping in fake snow to cover the sidewalks of Main St. and the town green. Each day of the week, there's a different contest or event. Cookie decorating, a giant group sing-along, speed gift wrapping, and— *a sandman building contest?*

The whole thing sounds hilariously fun.

But she's going to turn down the offer.

She's in the middle of drafting her reply to the editor when Austin's truck pulls into the driveway. Setting her laptop on the table, she stands to greet him, letting the blanket fall off her lap.

He looks tired as he climbs the porch steps. And even though he meets her lips when she leans in to kiss him, he barely meets her eyes. "I'm gonna grab a drink," he says, heading for the front door. "Do you want anything?"

"I'm okay, thanks."

Sitting back down, she curls her feet up underneath her to make room for him on the loveseat as she waits for him to come back outside. When he does, he's holding a beer bottle. And it's not even noon. She raises an eyebrow but doesn't say anything. It feels like a bad sign though.

But not as bad as when he chooses to sit in one of the chairs rather than squeeze in beside her. "Are you working?" he asks, nodding his head toward her laptop.

She reaches out to close the screen. "Not really. I actually got an offer to go on a trip to do an article for a website. I was just turning it down."

Austin is quiet, his lips pressing into a tight line.

It makes her nervous, so she keeps talking to fill the silence. "It's on this crazy Christmas festival in New Mexico. Obviously, I can't go spend Christmas in a random town, but it sounds like it'd be fun."

"Why can't you?" he says. And okay, she's *not* imagining the sharp edge in his voice. "If you want to take the trip, take the trip. Nothing's stopping you, is there? Don't say no on my account."

What the heck?

"I'm not saying no because of you," she tells him. Even though she is, partly. But that's okay. "I don't wanna go."

"You said it sounds like fun."

"Austin. No. I'm fine with turning it down. I don't want to work over Christmas, and I don't want to go to New Mexico."

God, she shouldn't have even brought it up. But she didn't know this kind of stuff would still be such a sensitive subject with him. She thought they'd moved past this.

He takes a sip of his beer. Then another, longer one. Slowly, he leans over and sets the bottle on the table. He doesn't say anything.

"Talk to me," she urges. "How was your breakfast?"

He frowns. "It was . . . kind of a lot."

"Tell me please." She's scared to hear what happened to put him in this mood, but she needs to know.

"I guess Andrea isn't entirely happy with the idea of you and me getting back together."

I could have told you that yesterday, Montana thinks. But she holds her breath and waits for him to go on.

Picking up his bottle again, he takes another long pull, leaving almost nothing left when he sets it back down. "I basically told her to mind her own business and assured her she didn't need to worry about me."

Good, that's good.

"But I dunno," he says, and Montana's heart sinks. "Maybe she's right, and we're only kidding ourselves here."

His statement hangs in the air, like the ringing of a gong that was struck.

It takes a few moments, in which he stares at his shoes, for her to find her voice and ask, "What do you mean?"

He scuffs one sneaker on the porch wood. "She said your dreams were too big for this town. You've always wanted the whole world. There's always going to be new experiences out there, and you'll always want to have them. It doesn't matter that you have people here who love you." He gestures to her laptop again as if it's a grenade about to go off. "This just proves that."

"Are you fucking serious right now?"

How dare he? Since her reunion with his family, she's been worried that things might feel strained with the two of them because of how it went. Worried that she still has an uphill battle to climb to get the rest of the Adlers to welcome her back into their lives. But she didn't actually expect *this*. Austin letting other people get in his head again.

"Are you really telling me," he says, "if you turn down this opportunity because of me, you won't regret it?"

"Yes, dammit!" she shouts. "There will always be new opportunities, but you have to trust me. So what if I like to see new places and try new things? It's not a crime to want to experience things. But it doesn't mean I'll leave you."

She can't keep doing this. She can't. *They* can't.

Glancing at her innocent laptop then back at him, she's suddenly exhausted. "You'll listen to whatever anyone else says to you, but not me. What do I need to do to make you believe me?"

He shakes his head. "I know you say you're not going to leave me, and I'm sure you mean it right now. But I'm afraid . . ."

"What?" she asks. And in the moments that she waits for his answer, her stomach ties itself in knots. It feels like this is it. This is the crux of it all.

"I'm afraid you could never be happy here forever, so you can't be happy with me."

"You're wrong." Her voice comes out steady, thank god, but *fuck*. How can he really think that after all this time and everything they've been through?

"Montana," he says. And she can suddenly hear her own heartbeat. The chorus to "You're Losing Me" starts playing in her head. She wants to beg him to stop. *Stop*. He could say he wants to take this whole conversation back. But instead—"You left me to see what else was out there. Those were *your* words."

"Yeah, and I did," she tells him. Getting off her seat, she comes around to kneel in the space between the table and his chair, the blanket coming too, tangled and trapped underneath her. And she *is* going to beg now. She shouldn't have to, but she will. Beg him to understand. "I saw so many incredible places and met so many amazing people. But I never, not once, met anyone as amazing as you."

He doesn't say anything. And her heart is breaking, because how does he still not get it?

"I said I wanted to see what else was out there," she explains carefully. "I didn't say *who*. Because I knew it was you. I always knew that."

"But you still left me!" he argues, standing abruptly and stepping away, leaving her to fight her way out of the blanket in her rush to stand and meet him. "How do I know you won't want to leave again one day?"

She sucks in a sharp breath as she finally makes it to her feet. That's it. Her heart isn't breaking—it's shattered. The grenade between them went off, exploding the most fragile part of her into a million pieces.

Gathering up those pieces, she reforms them into daggers and aims them his way. "Because I'm fucking telling you!"

He flinches. And maybe she should lower her voice, because out of the corner of her eye she can see Mrs. Coulter across the street with her grocery bags, pausing in her driveway to listen. This is the problem with small towns. The nosy woman might call her parents. Heck, for all she knows, one of her other neighbors could be friends with Austin's mom and might call to tell Mrs. Adler about their fight too.

But in this moment, it doesn't matter. Let the whole town hear about it if they want to. Who fucking cares?

"How many times are we going to go through this," she says. Not really a question, more like . . . This is the last time she's willing to go through it. Because it hurts too much, and at some point, her self-preservation needs to kick in.

"You're saying that like you're not the reason we went through it in the first place," Austin fires at her, his voice raising too.

He never gets angry. Never raises his voice, especially not to her. And somehow, that's what it takes for her to find her calm. She looks him in the eye and holds herself together enough to finish this.

"I know I left you once before, and I'm so sorry that I hurt you. Hurting you was the hardest thing I've ever done in my entire life. But I thought I was doing the right thing, and I can't believe that after all this time, after everything that's happened with us this year, you're still punishing me for it."

All the fire drains from his eyes. "Montana—"

"No." *It's too late. She can't find a pulse.* "I can't keep apologizing for a choice I made when I was eighteen. I can't keep trying to prove to you, and apparently everyone else in this damn town, that things have changed, that I've changed. *I can't.* I'm done."

The shock immediately registers on Austin's face, and yeah, she can't believe she just said that either. But she had to. And now she has to get away from him before she takes it back. So she storms inside the house, grabbing her purse and shoes at lightning speed. He tries to follow her inside, but she's already moving past him back out the door.

"Where are you going?" he asks as she rushes down the porch steps.

"I don't know," she tells him, refusing to turn around, only focused on getting to her car. "But I assume you won't be here when I get back."

Once she's safely locked in her car and reversing out of the driveway, she risks one glance at him through the windshield. He's still standing there on the porch, looking lost. The same exact way he looked at eighteen when she broke up with him the first time.

It probably would've been easier on both of them if she never came back to him. If they had both just fought the intense magnetic pull that kept drawing them together.

She feels the tug of it in her chest even now as she turns her car onto the street. She almost expects him to jump into his Jeep and follow her, but he hasn't moved. And as she drives away, leaving him in her rearview, she wonders if it was luck or fate that he parked beside her today instead of behind her like he sometimes does. Allowing her to make this escape. Letting her go, whether he wanted to or not.

◆

SHE'S BEEN DRIVING twenty minutes, listening to the saddest Taylor Swift songs on repeat, before she realizes she truly has no idea where she's going. She was on her own in L.A., in that giant city, but she never *felt* as alone as she does now. Here in the place that's more familiar to her than anywhere else.

But wait. Even without Austin, she's not totally alone here.

She calls Sloane, and the dejected way she says, "Hey," after Sloane answers prompts her friend to ask her what's wrong. "I think . . . Austin and I broke up."

"No, you didn't."

"Yes."

"Oh my god. Seriously?"

The last thing she wants to do is confirm her worst nightmare one more time, so Montana just asks, "Are you busy? Can you meet up with me?"

Thankfully, since schools are on vacation, Sloane is free and willing. And since Montana has no idea where she wants to go, Sloane makes the decision for her, simply giving her a town and the name of a store and saying to meet her there.

It occurs to her then that it's Black Friday. And boy, the name has never felt more fitting. She only hopes they're not going somewhere they'll be mobbed by crazy shoppers. That's the last thing she can handle right now.

She's already been driving in the right direction, so she arrives at the address fifteen minutes later, finding Sloane's car already in the small parking lot.

"Is this a bookstore?" she asks when she and Sloane both step out of their vehicles, her curiosity edging out over depression for just a moment.

Sloane nods. "It's got new *and* used books, and believe me, you could get lost in here for hours. I figured maybe you could use that."

"I absolutely could," Montana says as they walk inside. She knows Sloane will expect her to talk about what happened eventually, but she needs a bit more time to collect herself. So she takes a look around, breathing in the comforting smell of so many books. This is a perfect place to distract her from her misery.

There's a table of shiny new hardcovers right at the front of the store. She flips open a few of them to scan the jacket flaps. Then Sloane trails behinds her as they wind their way through the store, moving away from the new books and into the used section.

Now Montana sees how right Sloane was. This place is huge, with multiple rooms to explore. Small wooden signs categorize the books into genres, but the shelves aren't simply arranged in neat rows like most stores. They go off in every direction, with stacks of books sometimes even piled up in random places.

Montana finds the Classics section, and it's there, standing among hundreds of copies of familiar friends, that she's finally ready to talk. Trailing her fingers over the cracked spines of the old books, she starts to explain all about the horribly awkward Thanksgiving dinner and the resulting fight between her and Austin.

Thankfully, Sloane doesn't interrupt, letting her get the whole messy story out as quickly as she can. Once she's finished though, Sloane looks her dead in the eyes and says, very bluntly, "He's an ass."

Though she appreciates the way Sloane never holds back what she's thinking, Montana sighs. "He's not really, though, is he? I mean, he said some dumb things, and I was mad. I *am* mad. But I know he loves me, and . . . and I love him." *Fuck*, she does. She can't just stop because he hurt her.

Maybe there's still a pulse, after all.

"I thought the fact that we love each other so much would be enough to make it work," she continues, letting her eyes drift back to the rows of books as if they'll have the answers. Like they can share their wisdom. "But we keep circling around the same issues. Every time I think we've got it figured out and we understand each other, it turns out that we don't, and we're back where we started. It feels like we'll always be stalled in the past, unable to move forward. And I don't know if it's his fault, or mine, or if it's both of us."

"It might not necessarily be anyone's fault," Sloane says. "You two have a long, complicated, and sometimes painful history. With all those emotions coming up again, I'm sure it's difficult finding a way to make everything work. But if you want to be with him, you need to keep trying."

Montana turns back to her. "I *do* want to be with him. But I'm starting to think maybe that's not what's best for either of us. I can't keep fighting."

"Fighting with him or fighting for him?"

As she struggles for a reply, she wanders a few steps away, stopping in front of a bookcase that holds four entire shelves of Jane Austen titles. One of her favorite authors. She spots a very large, beautiful bind-up of all of Austen's novels and carefully pulls it down. With the tome heavy in her hands, she answers, "Either. Both. I dunno."

"Nope." Sloane's fingers wrap around her wrist, squeezing lightly before letting go. "I don't believe that. Look how many years have passed, and you guys made it back to each other. So you had a fight. It hurts, and it sucks, and I get it. But you can still make up. In high school, you guys almost never fought, but when you did, it barely lasted half a day before you were running back to each other."

She clutches the book to her chest. The weight of it is comforting, even if nothing else is. Shaking her head, she says, "Not this time. Maybe it's just easier to make things work when you're teenagers. Before all this other life stuff gets in the way. Maybe Austin was my perfect first love, and that's all he was meant to be."

"I don't buy that," Sloane says. "I don't think *you* believe that's all he is."

Unable to figure out what the heck she freaking believes anymore, Montana deflects. "I'm gonna get this book."

Before Sloane can say anything else, she turns and rushes back to the front of the store. She's already at the cash register by the time her friend catches up with her. And though it looks like Sloane wants to press her further, this time she does hold back. As they leave the store and say their goodbyes at their cars, Sloane just tells her that she'll be around if Montana needs to talk some more.

It's nice to know that she has a real friend again, someone who will be there for her. Driving home, though, she can't stop thinking about the one person who's been there for her more than anyone. Did she really lose him for good this time?

There's a giant ball of sludge rolling around in her stomach by the time she gets back to her house. When she walks up to the porch, she notices that the laptop, blanket, and coffee mug she left there have been put inside. But even though she couldn't have expected any differently, Austin is gone. And it feels like that's her answer.

THEN

*M*ontana used her fingertip to gather up a bit of the marshmallow swirl from her giant spoonful of Rocky Road and offered it to Daisy to lick off. Her faithful companion had been keeping her company on the couch all evening while she wallowed. Daisy couldn't understand *why* she was sad, but the dog had the emotional intelligence to understand that she was.

Though she'd planned to watch a movie, so far, she'd just been scrolling idly through the Netflix options as she shoveled ice cream into her mouth. It was a Friday night, and she was supposed to be having a movie night with Austin, but he'd bailed.

They'd had a fight.

Their first one.

And it was so dumb.

At school earlier, he'd mentioned that some guys from the varsity baseball team were having a party, and they'd invited the JV team. He'd clearly wanted to go, but Montana wasn't comfortable at parties or with big groups, so she told him he could go without her. Sure, she'd been disappointed that they wouldn't hang out together, but she wasn't mad about it. Yet somehow, he'd gotten annoyed with *her*, and it became a whole thing.

Now she was sitting here wondering if that was it. Did they break up? They'd just barely started going out, and she really didn't know how these things worked. Would he still want to date her now that he realized she wasn't nearly as social as him?

Probably not. He was probably at the party right now meeting an outgoing cheerleader who would be a much better match for him.

A knock on the front door startled her. Daisy immediately leapt off the couch and sprinted over there, but it took Montana a few extra moments to set her ice cream carton on the coffee table and work out the pins and needles in her foot when she stood up.

Opening the door, she was so shocked to see Austin that she almost wondered if he was some sort of sugar-induced hallucination. But nope. There he stood on her porch, holding a DVD, a package of microwave popcorn, and a bag of Starbursts.

"What are you doing here?"

He smiled. "Movie night, obviously."

"But—" She didn't see either of his parents' cars on the street. "How did you get here?"

"I rode my bike."

"All the way here?"

"Mmhmm." His smile faltered then, and he suddenly looked unsure of himself. "Is it okay that I came? I brought these." He handed her the bag of candy. "I know they're your favorite."

Montana couldn't believe it. She'd only mentioned that to him once. "What about the party?"

Holding up the DVD, he grinned at her. "Who needs a party when we've got this?"

"*The Notebook?*"

"I borrowed it from my sister," he said. "I know it's like a huge cliché of a chick flick, but she says it's a classic. And don't try to tell me you don't like Ryan Gosling."

"Everyone likes Ryan Gosling. And I've seen it." Unable to resist teasing him a little bit now, she added, "It's *very* sappy and dramatic. Might even make you cry. You sure you wanna watch it?"

Either he didn't notice or didn't care about the teasing, because he immediately gave her an affirmative.

From behind her, Daisy whined and headbutted the back of her knee, clearly wanting to push through and get some attention from the visitor. From *Austin*. Because he was here, and not at the party. Even after they'd fought.

"Come on in," she told him, stepping back so he could walk through the doorway.

He bent down to scratch Daisy behind the ears before following Montana into the living room. She slid the movie into the DVD player, and then they both sat on the couch, leaving a couple feet of space between them, which Daisy didn't hesitate to jump up and fill.

Montana was so happy he was here. But she didn't like him missing out on things he wanted to do because of her. As the DVD's menu screen popped up, she couldn't help but say quietly, "I'm sorry that I'm shy."

"You're not shy with me," Austin told her.

"That's different."

"How?"

Good question. It might not have made sense, but she gave him the only answer she had. "You're . . . *you*. You make it easy for me to be *me* around you."

Over the dog's back, he reached out his hand and held it palm up for her to take, so she did. "All I want is for you to feel comfortable

being yourself. Because I *like* you. And if you can try to let other people see you, I promise they'll like you too. Just not as much as I do." He accompanied that last part with a cheeky wink that made her almost laugh.

"I still don't really understand why you like me," she admitted after a few moments.

"Okay, stop."

"No, I don't mean it like I think there's nothing to like about me," she pushed on. "I only mean . . . We'd barely ever spoken, and then one day, you were standing at my locker asking me to hang out. What made you even notice me?"

His thumb swept gently back and forth across the back of her hand. "You called Blake an idiot in class."

"What? But he's your best friend."

"Yeah," he agreed. "And he was being an idiot."

She let out a real laugh at that. She remembered what he was talking about. Blake had made some dumb, borderline sexist comment about Jane Austen's writing, and she couldn't let him get away with it. And Austin had noticed that? And he liked it about her?

That made her feel . . . She didn't even know. Seen? *Yeah.* It made her feel seen in a way she never had before.

And she wanted him to know that she saw him too. That she appreciated him. That she understood how much he thrived around other people, how he was friendly in a way that needed to be let free. She didn't want to hold him back from doing things that made him happy.

"Next time I can try going to a party with you," she offered.

He shrugged. "We'll see. I'm not worried about what we do or where we go. I just want us to be together."

Montana grinned. So did she.

CHAPTER TWENTY-FIVE

NOW

*P*eering into the fridge, wineglass in hand, Montana tries to decide what to make for dinner. The never-ending struggle of being an adult. Denver sits a couple feet away staring at her, most likely willing her to just pick something, anything, as long as she'll share it with him. With a sigh, she shuts the door. She doesn't have the energy to really cook, so pasta, it is.

The last two weeks have been miserable. She can't afford to quit working at Alan's Place, because she still isn't making enough from free-lancing, but she's avoided seeing Austin at all costs. Switching shifts with Landon and Sabrina, begging them to cover for her when necessary. She even resorted to promising to dog-sit Freddie and Mercury for Landon and his boyfriend when they take a three-night trip to New York at the beginning of next year.

At least someone trusts her to stick around that long.

She turned down the Christmas assignment. Part of her considered taking it after the fight with Austin. Because why the hell not? But she

really didn't feel up to it. She still has Denver to think about, and she feels settled here in Hartley—as impossible as that may be for some people to believe. Saying no just felt like the right decision.

What confirmed that for her even more was when she got a call from *New England Travel* telling her about an opening for a full-time travel writing position and offering her an interview. She didn't hesitate to take it, but she's still waiting to hear back. And it's been a constant battle with herself to not check her email every five minutes of the day for the last week.

The interview went great, at least in her mind. Now she just needs to trust that things will work out the way they're supposed to.

As she boils a pot of water on the stove, she remembers she really needs to do laundry before work tomorrow. She ordered a brand-new washer and dryer a couple weeks ago, so she's been avoiding going to the laundry mat because she was waiting for them to arrive.

They were finally delivered yesterday, and she thought the purchase would make her feel like a responsible adult. Instead, she feels awful.

The two machines in the basement now stand as more proof that she's putting down roots here—or rather, rebuilding them. She's here for good. She has a washer and dryer. She may potentially have a full-time job. She has a dog.

She has a home, but she's going to be alone in it, because she doesn't have *him*.

It must really be over this time. The last time they argued, he was calling and texting right away trying to apologize. Maybe he doesn't think there's any point anymore.

Maybe there isn't.

She's pouring in the pasta when her phone rings on the counter beside her. The fact that she doesn't even jump to look hoping it's Austin probably says something. Like she's resigned herself to knowing it won't be.

Setting down the box of penne, she glances over. It's her mom. Montana ignored her last call because she feels bad. She messed up by waiting too long to make a decision about going to Florida, and it's too late now. A last-minute ticket would cost a fortune.

Driving is a possibility. But what about Denver?

Lethargically, she grabs the phone and answers. Might as well talk to her. She already feels awful about more than just not booking the flight. Her mom's disappointment can't make it much worse.

Or maybe it can. Because when her mom asks how she is, she lies through her teeth, saying she's fine. But then when her mom asks how Austin is, she snaps with no warning. "He's fine. Jesus, do you think I broke his heart already?"

"No . . ." The confusion and hurt are evident in her mom's voice. And *okay*, that was uncalled for.

She sighs, giving the pasta a little stir. "I'm sorry. Actually . . ." Here she goes. No point in putting off the confession. "We kind of broke up."

There's a long pause on the other end of the line, and then—"Oh. Well. That's awkward."

"*Awkward?*" Montana squawks, dropping the ladle against the side of the pot. Water hisses as it sloshes over onto the burner. "That's all you have to say? Are you kidding?"

"No, no, sweetie," her mom rushes on. "I'm so sorry things didn't work out. Honestly, that's taken me by surprise. I truly thought . . . Anyway, it's just that . . . Well, it was supposed to be a surprise he was going to tell you about later. He—"

"He *who?*" Montana questions impatiently, cutting her off.

"Austin. He bought plane tickets for me and your father to come up and stay with you for Christmas so that you wouldn't have to leave your dog."

Oh god.

He did?

Is this part of the reason he got so upset at the idea of her leaving for the holiday? He was trying to do a nice thing for her, and she could've ruined it by saying she was flying off to New Mexico.

"Is that okay with you, sweetie?" her mom asks. "For your father and I to come up there?"

"What?" she says, refocusing on the conversation. "Yes, of course. That sounds great."

"Are you sure it's still a good idea though? I'm not sure if Austin could get a refund instead."

"No, it's fine. I want you guys to visit." She'll pay him back for the tickets if she has to.

Sounding very pleased, her mom says, "Well then, that's wonderful. I'm excited to see you."

"Me too, Mom." Smiling to herself, Montana realizes she actually means it. She'll get the chance to show her parents what she's done with the house, making it her own. And it'll be nice to have some company for the holidays.

Later that night, after she eats her dinner and feeds Denver his, she can't stop thinking about how Austin did that for her. He obviously did it before their fight, but still. It was incredibly sweet.

She always knew he was one of the good ones. Maybe the best one. And she's lost him.

It's hard to say where she went wrong. If she could do it all over again . . . Was there one moment, one decision she could have made differently, that would have changed everything?

There are probably a lot of them. She could have chosen a college closer to Hartley. She could have gone to UCLA but not broken up with him. She could have told him sooner that she was ready to come back for him. She could have kept trying to call for months—*years*—after he stopped answering.

But everything happens for a reason. She may not be particularly religious, but she believes in the universe. Living their separate lives in that time they were apart was important so that they'd be able to decide if they truly want to be together now.

And, well. Her decision is easy. She wants it. She wants it more than anything. But finding out if it's too late might be the hard part, and she's not ready for that.

Going upstairs, she searches frantically through her closet. She's flinging shirts to the side, desperately seeking the comfort of one particular article of clothing. But when she reaches the end of the hangers, it hits her that Austin's old baseball hoodie isn't here. He went home wearing it that day he ripped his T-shirt, and she never got it back.

Fuck.

The loss of the hoodie is so small compared to the actual loss of Austin, but it's just one more loss she really can't take. When she didn't have him for all those years in California, she still had the gray zip-up that said HARTLEY HORNETS BASEBALL. And when she wore it, she was able to pretend just for a bit that he wasn't gone.

She needs to get it back. No, she doesn't have any idea how she'll do that, but she has to find a way.

For now, she's going to bed. Who cares if it's only eight thirty? It's not like she has anything better to do. Because just like when she first moved back into this house, she's alone.

◆

THE NEXT DAY, Montana's extra moody at work. When one customer is a little bit rude to her, she loses it and snaps back at him, unable to control her frayed emotions. Realizing her mistake immediately, she apologizes profusely, but the look on the old man's face is murderous.

She's on the verge of tears when Blake swoops in out of nowhere, adding his own apologies to the man and offering to comp his entire tab. It's only two drinks, but the man seems satisfied with the freebies.

Blake takes her by the elbow then, guiding her away from the customers. "Come on."

They stop by a table off to the side of the bar and Montana starts to apologize again, knowing he's going to reprimand her and that she deserves it.

But he holds up a hand before she can get a word out. "Look. That obviously wasn't okay, but I get that you're miserable. And Austin's miserable too. You two need to figure it out."

"Aren't you going to tell me off for hurting him?" she asks, disbelieving.

"No."

"Why not?" She remembers their conversation when she first moved back very clearly.

"Because I think you've *both* hurt each other in the past and again now. But you didn't mean to, and neither of you deserve it." Blake pauses and sighs before he adds, "And you're my friend too."

Those words are nice to hear, but instead of just appreciating the sentiment, she can't help but see the opportunity there. "I need to get something back from his apartment," she tells him. "If you're really my friend, then will you please find a way to get it for me the next time you're over there?"

"You could just ask him for it, you know."

"I can't do that."

Blake gives her a contemplating look. "Well, I'm not going to steal something for you."

"It's not stealing if—"

He holds up a hand to silence her again. "But I do have a spare key.

When he comes in to work tonight, you can go over there and get whatever it is yourself."

"Thank you."

Maybe she's being crazy, but she wants that damn hoodie back. She can't let it go.

After Blake tells her to get back to work, she quickly does, and now she's feeling a small sense of relief that's enough to help her serve the customers without another incident. As she's washing some glasses a little while later, Blake comes up to the bar and silently places a single bronze key on top of it, then he walks away with barely a glance at her.

Toward the end of her shift, she hustles to make sure she gets all her sidework done early. That way she can duck out as soon as Sabrina gets here and hopefully avoid running into Austin, who'll probably be coming in around the same time.

Even with the rushing, she only barely makes it. His Jeep turns into the lot a few seconds before she pulls out. But that's fine. She avoids eye contact as she drives past him, and he has no way of knowing that his key is tucked safely inside her purse.

She drives straight to his apartment, forcing herself to keep her speed down enough that she won't get a ticket. Unlocking the door, she creeps inside stealthily like a burglar. Because no matter what reasoning she was going to use with Blake, this essentially *is* stealing. But she doesn't care.

As she's heading for his bedroom, an odd mess in the living room catches her eye. There are papers strewn across the coffee table and a small cardboard box sitting on the floor in between the table and couch. She's not here to snoop—only to get the hoodie back—but curiosity draws her over. Austin's usually pretty neat, not leaving anything out of place, with the exception of Kalen's toys sometimes.

Standing beside the coffee table, she bends down and picks up a piece of paper. It's a page carefully torn out of a magazine, and when she gets a closer look, she recognizes it. One of her articles.

"The Wild Beauty of Montana" by Montana Sinclair.

The page slips from her fingers as she sinks to the couch. She remembers Austin asking her if she ever made it out to Montana that night they were drinking at the bar. *But he knew.*

Heart pounding, she takes a look at the rest of the papers on the table. They're all articles she's written. She opens the flaps of the box and starts going through it, pulling out article after article. And not just the ones she had published in magazines. He's even printed out the articles that were only published online.

Every article she's ever written.

He kept every single one.

She can't believe it. Doesn't know what to think. She may have forgotten how to breathe.

He's read all of her articles. She wasn't sure he'd read a single one until the first one she wrote when she moved back to Hartley. They weren't in contact all those years, and she assumed he wasn't thinking about her at all. But clearly, he was.

Still staring in disbelief at the piles of evidence in front of her, she doesn't hear the door open. So she jumps out of her skin when a gruff voice says, "What are you doing here?"

"I—" She looks up at Austin towering over her, and her fight-or-flight instinct kicks in, telling her to get up and run out the door. But no. Sloane was right. She's never going to quit fighting for him. "I thought you were at work."

"I was, but as soon as I walked in, Blake said he could stay longer for me because I needed to go home. It made no sense, but he looked possibly the most serious I've ever seen him, so . . . here I am."

Here he is. And here she is, uninvited, snooping in his apartment. He deserves an explanation, but she needs one first.

"What is all this?" she asks, eyes darting to the mess of papers she's left everywhere before she stands up to face him.

"Well." He clears his throat, running a hand roughly through his hair. "Isn't it obvious? I took the box out last night because I was upset. When you were gone all those years, whenever I missed you so much that I couldn't take it, I used to reread them. To feel close to you. It kept me from breaking down and calling you."

Holy shit.

"I wish you'd just called."

Nodding, he says, "Me too."

Hope blooms in her chest as she glances down at the table again, still trying to process. "I can't believe you have all these. You hated me for leaving you to do this."

"No, I didn't," he tells her, taking a stilted step closer. "I was hurt that you left me. But I was *never* not proud of you. And I could never hate you." Now he's the one who breaks eye contact, focusing on the damn coffee table between them. "I was an idiot for not being able to fully believe you every time you've said that you're here to stay. You've never lied to me. Not once in our lives."

Surely that can't be true, but Montana doesn't know what to say.

Looking up at her again, he continues, so she doesn't have to say anything yet. "It feels like my life wasn't even real all those years when you weren't around. Or like I was stuck in this mundane black and white dream. Then when I saw you again in the cafe, I suddenly woke up, and the screaming colors flooded back in."

Ho-ly shit.

"Yes, I have Kalen and he's the most important thing in the world to me. I've done everything I had to in the last five years to make sure he has the best life possible. But I'm a better person, a better father to him, when I'm truly happy. You make me truly happy. You always have. We may have gotten lost somewhere along the way, but we're here now. We're both here. And this is where we belong."

He pauses then, brow furrowing, before he adds, "At least . . . I hope it is. I don't want to sound like I'm saying you belong to me. You're not my property, I know that."

"I belong to you," Montana blurts out. "Or maybe not *to* you, but *with* you. I always have. And I'll always want to."

"Yeah?" he asks, eyes painfully hopeful.

"Yes," she breathes. Because it's the truth, and it feels so damn good to say it. She steps over the cardboard box and around the coffee table, coming to stand in front of him. "That's what I keep trying to tell you. I want to be here with you. There's nowhere else in the fucking world I'd rather be."

"Except I wasn't lost before," she adds. Now she's the one on a roll, and she can't stop. "I was where I needed to be then. But if you think you weren't with me all those years, you're wrong. Because everywhere I went, every road I took, every place I saw, you were with me. You were there beside me on my journey, and you were there when I arrived. You were everywhere."

She reaches out tentatively, taking his hand. "Don't you get it? It doesn't matter where I travel, or how far I go. It always leads to you. Every single road leads to you. You'll always be my destination."

His lip quirks up like he's amused. And, *hello?* She just poured her heart out here!

"What?" she asks impatiently.

His face breaks out into a full grin. "I'll always be your destination?"

"Don't make fun of me."

Squeezing her hand, he says, "I'm not. You're just such a fucking writer." Another squeeze. "And I love it."

"I love you," she tells him.

"Montana Rose Sinclair, I love you so much my heart may burst with it, and I'm okay with that."

Her own heart swells as he tugs her in closer. But after he kisses her, she pulls away. As much as she wants to let herself get swept up in the moment, she still has some valid concerns. "How's it going to work if your whole family hates me?"

"They don't hate you," he says, his fingers trailing delicately down her arm. "They just know how much it killed me losing you the first time, and they don't want to see me go through that again. They're only worried about me."

"Yeah, everyone's worried about you getting hurt, I know. But who's worried about me?" she asks a little bitterly.

He winds his arm around her back, holding her gently in place when she tries to step away. "*I* am. I'm going to do everything in my power to make sure I'm not an idiot and I don't screw this up again. I'm going to do everything I can to make you happy."

"You make me happy without even trying," she admits. "And when you do try, it's wonderful. Like buying plane tickets for my parents."

"I hope that's okay with you. You haven't seen them in a long time, and even if your mom drives you crazy sometimes, I know you miss them. And I figured this way you wouldn't have to worry about leaving Denver behind."

"Or you."

He shrugs. "Or me."

"You're incredible."

Pulling her in closer, he kisses her on the forehead before backing away only enough to look in her eyes. "No. I just love you."

"I love you," she says again. Because she could never get tired of saying it.

"When you came back it was impossible for me not to fall in love with you again," he tells her. "I mean, I probably never stopped loving you. But even so, I think I've been guarded. I was afraid of getting hurt again. But since we got back together, I'm the one who's hurt you. More than once. And I'm so sorry. I let my own insecurities get the best of me. It's not that I didn't trust you. It's that I didn't trust that I could be enough for you. But I'm not going to let my fears or insecurities get in the way of what we could have."

He sweeps some of her hair behind her ear, never breaking eye contact. "I'm ready. I promise you, I'm ready. No more doubts. You don't have to prove anything to me anymore. You already have. Now let me prove myself to you. I won't let you down again."

"I know you won't," Montana says with certainty.

They may have other miscommunications, other fights, but as long as she knows he's just as in this as she is, that's all she needs.

This time she's the one to close the small gap between them, kissing him like it's been years that she's been deprived, rather than two weeks.

He reacts just as desperately. One of his large hands wraps around her waist and squeezes tightly. She yanks on his hair, pulling his head back so she can get her mouth on his neck. When she sucks on the skin there, he lets out a sound that's half gasp and half moan. But he only lets her get away with it for a few moments before he's reconnecting their mouths.

It's hard and fast. They're both practically panting through the kisses, unable to catch their breath and unwilling to slow down.

He starts urging her backward. And when her calves hit the coffee table, he only stops kissing her long enough to carefully gather up all of her articles, setting them safely back in the box before shoving it out of the way. Then he lays her down on the couch, settling on top of her.

Suddenly, all the desperation and urgency are gone.

They take their time, savoring languid kisses that make her melt into the cushions. Removing articles of clothing one by one with care. Hands exploring over every bit of skin as if they didn't both already have each other memorized.

The fact that it's the middle of the day and he's supposed to be at work? Doesn't matter. The fact that she essentially broke into his apartment? Eh, who cares?

Because this, right here, is the culmination of a lifetime of loving each other. It's a promise of a future where they only love each other more and more. Being with him this way right now feels as necessary to her as breathing.

Even though the way he uses his tongue to lick over the most sensitive part of her actually makes it hard for her do that. He doesn't let up, pressing down on the bundle of nerves with the flat of his tongue, swiping the tip of it over her, sucking and releasing. The whole time, his fingers are inside her, playing her like a violin. And this treatment goes on and on, building higher and higher, until she peaks, intense waves of pleasure cresting over her.

He pulls out his fingers, letting her body return to Earth. But she's only barely managed to catch her breath when his hard cock is there, nudging insistently at her entrance until he slams inside, knocking the air right out of her again.

But who needs air anyway? All she needs is him.

And that's exactly what he gives her.

Afterward, they're spooning, her back pressed up against his chest, his arms wrapped tightly around her. Montana's whole body is still tingling. His face is buried in her hair, and she can feel each warm breath he takes against the back of her neck.

Neither of them speaks for a while, content to simply lie there together. Eventually, though, he readjusts, loosening his hold on her and bracing himself up on one arm. She rolls onto her back so she can look up at him.

"You know, my dad told me something that first year after you left for California," he says. "I was devastated, couldn't understand why you didn't want to try to make things work long distance. He said if you love someone you have to be willing to set them free, and then if they come back, that's how you know they're really yours."

Montana lets out a tiny laugh.

"I know, right?" He smiles at her. "Such a cliché. But my dad told me it's a cliché for a reason, because it's true. Then I asked him why you'd want to be free from me, and he said that everyone wants to be free, but freedom doesn't look the same to everyone. He said birds have to leave the nest eventually, but that doesn't mean they'll never come home again. And he said if you were the kind of girl who was too afraid to fly, then you wouldn't be the girl that I was in love with."

She doesn't know what to say to all that. But she sends a silent *thank you* to Alan Adler. Because he understood her.

"It didn't really make me feel much better when I was eighteen and heartbroken," Austin goes on. "Then after that first Christmas when you came home for break and we got together, I told him about it. He just gave me this knowing look. But I told him you didn't *really* come back, and it didn't feel like it counted. He said I'd know when it did count."

"Oh," Montana says softly, because she has to say something.

Austin cups the side of her face, sweeping his thumb across her cheekbone. "The moment I saw you in the café, that's what I thought of. I remembered my dad saying, 'If she comes back, she's yours.'"

"And then you ran away," she reminds him gently.

He laughs. "Well, yeah. I kind of panicked. When you suddenly know you're going to get everything you ever wanted, it's a bit overwhelming."

"You knew that just from seeing me again for a few seconds?"

"My dad was the smartest man I've ever known. So yeah. I knew this time it was going to count."

She strains her neck up to kiss him, and his hand moves to cradle and lift her head, making it easier. Tears well up behind her eyelids, both happy and sad at the same time. She misses his father. And she's sad for Austin that he lost him. But she's also indescribably happy.

Because this is it. They figured it out.

Even if she could, she wouldn't change the past, because it got them here.

She's so lucky. And maybe for the first time, she realizes she's not the only one. He's just as lucky to have her.

"Hey, wait," he says, starting to sit up and taking her with him. "What did you actually come here for? Before you found those articles."

It seems so silly now that she cringes. "I, uh . . . wanted to get your hoodie back. The old one that I had in my closet."

He laughs, loud and open and carefree. She should feel embarrassed, but she can't, because his eyes crinkle at the corners with uncontained happiness when he looks at her. "You can have it."

"I don't need it," she says, shaking her head. "I have you."

Tucking a strand of her hair behind her ear, he lets his fingers linger at her temple. "You do. But you still want the hoodie."

"Yeah, I do," she admits.

"Then it's yours. Anything you want. It's yours."

THEN

*M*ontana was enjoying a slice of greasy cafeteria pizza, joking with Sloane about their history teacher who was trying to grow a mustache—but so far it looked more like a caterpillar—when she caught sight of Austin jogging over to their table. She dropped the pizza, an excited flutter of butterflies in her stomach.

It had only been a week, and she was still sometimes surprised to see him approaching her with such a purpose. His bright smile, those green eyes, all his attention focused solely on her.

"Hey," she said shyly when he slid into the seat next to her.

He leaned in to give her a quick kiss on the cheek before saying hello.

Slightly embarrassed by the minor PDA, her eyes fell down to her plastic cafeteria tray. Again it was something she wasn't used to yet. "I thought you were missing lunch because you had to make up a test."

"I am. But I didn't want to miss seeing you first."

She looked up, trying to subtly meet Sloane's eyes across the table. Hopefully her friend could help her out here, because this whole thing with him was out of her element, and she didn't know what she was supposed to do. But Sloane just raised her eyebrows dramatically. So much for subtle. Turning to Austin, she said lamely, "You can't be late for your make-up."

"I know," he told her. "I won't be. I just wanted to say hi. And now I did, so I can go."

"Okay then." She couldn't help but chuckle at that. "Good luck."

"Thanks."

He leaned in and kissed her on the mouth this time. It was practically as innocent as the cheek kiss, but she felt herself blush. Then, just like that, he left, expertly weaving his way upstream through the crowd of students heading toward tables.

Looking back at Sloane, Montana found her grinning. "What?" she asked.

"I can't believe you're going out with him. He's so cute! Is he a good kisser?"

Oh. Was she supposed to share these kinds of things?

"We haven't kissed that much," she hedged.

"Uh oh, that's a no," Sloane said. But then her friend caught the dreamy look that must have crossed her face at the thought of kissing Austin. "Ooh, wait! He *is*! That look says everything."

Montana shrugged, but she really couldn't keep the smile off her face. All it took was a gesture as simple as that one from Austin to put her in a good mood for the rest of the day. Maybe she wasn't used to this dating thing yet—but if this was how it went, then she certainly wouldn't mind *getting* used to it.

CHAPTER TWENTY-SIX

NOW

*A*rriving at Austin's apartment the next day for dinner with him and Kalen, Montana's ready to burst with her good news. She got the job with *New England Travel*. She actually did it. No more searching for freelance work. A steady paycheck. Stability. She'll have to cut back on her hours at the restaurant, and Austin might need to find another bartender, but she knows he'll be happy for her.

Because this means she's here to stay. He told her she didn't need to prove that to him anymore, but she's happy to do it anyway, and maybe to prove it to herself.

It also means that her success in California wasn't a fluke. She's good at this. And she's grateful she gets to keep doing it.

Austin answers the door with a radiant smile, immediately pulling her in for a kiss.

"Eww, can you not?" Kalen calls out, sounding hilariously more like a preteen than a five-year-old.

They break apart laughing, and Austin says, Sorry, kid. Can't help it."

Kalen rolls his eyes—like *ugh, fine*—and Austin takes Montana's hand, leading her toward the living room.

"I missed you," she tells Kalen, squatting down to his level. "Can I have a hug?"

"Daddy was sad," he says, giving her a glaringly accusing look.

Crap. As much as it kills her to think of Austin hurting, it also kills her to know Kalen was hurt too because of that. She remembers their heart-to-heart, and how he was worried about what would happen if she and Austin split up, though he didn't know how to phrase it like that. But she still believes what she told him then—it's worth it to try, despite the risk of heartbreak.

"I know he was, and I'm so sorry," she tells him truthfully, hoping he can forgive her. "I was sad too. But you know what? We worked it out, and we're all still here together, right?"

He eyes her sharply, as if searching for a lie, and she nervously awaits the assessment. Then suddenly, he rushes forward, wrapping his little arms around her. She kisses the top of his blond head, overwhelmed with relief.

Letting go, he asks, "Do you wanna read to me?"

"I'd love to, bud." She really, really would.

"Only one book," Austin instructs them, "and then Montana's going to help me with dinner."

She stands, smiling at him. "I feel popular."

"You are." He leans in for another kiss, ignoring Kalen's groan.

As she reads Kalen a story on the couch, she's feeling particularly pleased with herself, because he's smiling the whole time. Not one complaint about her voices.

In the kitchen afterward, where Austin instructs her to chop vegetables, she only makes it through one carrot before she can't hold in her news any longer. Setting the knife down on the cutting board, she turns to him. "I have something to tell you."

He stops prepping the chicken. "Okay," he says, going over to the sink and washing his hands.

"What are you doing?"

"I don't know, that sounds kind of ominous. I feel like, whatever it is, I don't want to hear it with raw chicken on my hands."

She laughs. "No, it's a good thing, I promise."

"Tell me."

"I applied for a full-time staff writer position with *New England Travel* magazine, and I got it!"

"Seriously? That's amazing!" He throws his arms around her for a huge hug. "Congratulations!"

"You might need to replace me at Alan's Place," she tells him regretfully. "I'm sorry."

He's beaming at her now. "Don't be! I mean, I'll miss working with you, obviously. But this is your passion. You deserve it so much."

Still in his arms, she drags her nails lightly over the nape of his neck. "Thank you. This means I can still travel, but now I don't have to leave you behind. The travel will be close, so I can take you with me."

"I do have a son and a very demanding job myself, you know," he teases her.

"I don't mean you have to go with me every single time. Just that I'll never have to be gone for too long, and when you have the time, you can join me. And I want Kalen with us too. We can all see new places together."

He tilts his head down and kisses her nose. "We can. Any time I'm able to, I'll go with you. Wherever it is. Whatever adventure you come up with. I'll be there."

It means so much to her that he's willing to go with her. That he wants these new experiences too, and he wants to share them with her.

She kisses him, smiling against his lips as she thinks about all the ways they've both changed from those two fifteen-year-olds who first got together. They've grown up together, learned from each other, made each other better, stronger, happier.

When they pull apart, he chuckles. "But you've already said that I'm everywhere you go. So you don't really need me to come with you, do you?"

Unable to stop smiling, she says, "Shut up. I *want* you to. I don't want to share places with the ghost of you. I want the real you. The one I can touch." She illustrates this desire by placing her hand against his chest, right over his heart.

His hand comes up to cover hers. "You'll always have me."

♦

MONTANA GOT Andrea's number from Austin. Even though he isn't worried about what his family thinks of their relationship, she still cares about Andrea, and she wants to repair the rift that grew between them. She plans to be in Austin's life permanently, so hopefully someday she and Andrea will feel like sisters again.

She texted first, asking if they could talk, and when Andrea finally calls her, it's awkward for a minute. The two of them exchanging the required pleasantries while knowing this isn't going to be a casual conversation. Montana's prepared to plead her case, throw herself at Andrea's mercy. But before she can start, Andrea says, "I'm sorry for butting in."

Oh. She didn't expect to receive an apology. "No, I totally understand. You wanted to protect your brother."

"It wasn't just that," Andrea says. "Yeah, I was mad at you when you broke up with him, but I knew you guys still loved each other. For a long time, I thought you would get back together eventually. But then Austin decided he couldn't have you in his life anymore, and I had to respect that." She pauses, clears her throat. "But *I* never heard from you again, and that sucked."

"Wait, what?"

"Yeah, I mean, I know I could have called you, but I was afraid it would seem like I was betraying Austin or something. I dunno. Maybe it's dumb. But I was hoping you'd get in touch with me, and we could still be friends."

"I had no idea," Montana tells her honestly. In those years without Austin, she *did* think of Andrea. She just assumed she'd lost her too. "I would have loved to keep in touch with you, but honestly, I was so devastated back then. I was a mess. He cut me out of his life so completely, I don't think it ever even occurred to me that you'd still be open to talking to me."

Andrea sighs lightly. "It's okay. It doesn't matter now. I was nervous when I heard you guys got back together, because I didn't want Austin to have to go through all that again if it didn't work out. But as he reminded me over Thanksgiving, you can't know something's going to work until you try, right? I'm glad you guys are trying."

"Me too." Montana's so glad to hear that. "But I want to make sure you understand that you're important to me too. I know we're not close like we were before, but you can call me anytime. I'd love to hear about your life."

"You can call me too," Andrea tells her. "Even if it's to complain when my doofus brother does something stupid."

Montana laughs. Just for a moment, it feels like old times. Like nothing's changed.

THE NEXT MORNING, Montana's eyes open before her alarm goes off. Denver is whining from the floor beside her bed. "What is it?" she asks him.

Obviously not getting an answer, she rolls over to check the time on her phone. Eight twenty. *Ugh.* She stayed up late last night talking to Andrea. It felt so good though.

As she sits up in bed, her eyes drift to the window. Everything looks shiny and white. She can't see the ground from here, but she knows right away that it snowed. Was snow even in the forecast? She hasn't been paying enough attention to that.

Groaning, she flops back down on her pillows. She may be happy to be here in Hartley, but that doesn't mean she's mentally prepared herself for her first real winter in six years. *Shit*, she hasn't even bought a shovel. She doesn't want to deal with this. Hopefully, it'll just melt by the time she needs to go to work tomorrow.

Denver continues to whine until she says, "Okay, okay," giving in and throwing off the covers. She goes to the window to check out how bad it is, and—*Oh wow.*

Beside her, the dog rises onto his hindlegs, setting his front paws on the windowsill and letting out one strong bark, even though he probably can't see what she sees. Kalen is in her front yard, bundled up in a snowsuit, building a snowman. And Austin—wonderful, incredible Austin, with his red and black flannel coat and a maroon beanie on his head—is shoveling her driveway. She really shouldn't be surprised at this point.

She puts on the warmest clothes she owns (which makes her realize that she doesn't own much, and she'll need to go shopping for a winter wardrobe) and then runs downstairs. Denver wants to go out front to greet the boys, but she sends him into the backyard instead. As soon as she steps out onto the porch, the cold bites at her fingers and cheeks.

Austin stops and smiles when he spots her. "I didn't want to wake you up."

Shaking her head fondly, she thinks of how lucky she is. Something she's thought about more times than she can count in these last few months. Which is crazy, because when she lost her job in L.A., she thought her whole life was falling apart. But she was wrong. It turns out, everything was all just starting to come together.

"I love you," she calls to him. "But it's freezing. I'm gonna go back inside."

"Yeah, go ahead. This won't take long."

"Did you have breakfast?"

"Not yet."

Kalen runs over and asks if he can play with Denver, so Montana ushers him inside with her and then back out through the kitchen door. Then she starts a pot of coffee and grabs the carton of eggs from the refrigerator. She's got a pan of them scrambling when she hears Austin come in through the front. He's already taken off his boots when he appears, and now he takes off his jacket, draping it over a chair at the kitchen table.

She hands him a cup of coffee—two spoons of sugar with no cream, the way he likes it—and says, "You're the best, you know that?"

"Yeah, I know," he replies smugly, earning himself a smack on the arm that almost makes him spill the coffee. "Hey, watch it!"

She returns to the stove to make sure the eggs don't burn, and he follows, sidling up to her, his fingers grazing her hip.

It's hard to believe it's already December. The time has flown by. When she first moved back into her parents' house, she told herself it was only temporary. She promised herself she would only mooch off them for a year at most. And now, since she's staying, she's been thinking about what she should do come next spring.

She wants to start paying rent. It's not fair for them to lose out on all that income. But even with her new job, it'll be tight trying to pay them the same as what they could get if they were renting the house to someone else.

As she's plating up three servings of eggs and bacon, she nonchalantly voices this concern to Austin. And what he says almost makes her drop the last plate to the floor.

"I could just move in and we'd both save money."

He makes it sound like a joke, but one look at his face, with his earnest green eyes, and she knows he isn't joking.

Slowly, carefully, thoughtfully, she says, "Yeah. You should. But not just to save money. Only if you really want to."

"Are you kidding? I've never wanted anything more." He smooths her hair away from her face and tilts his head, like he's silently asking if *she's* sure.

Her heartbeat is steady, and she doesn't take her eyes off his. Maybe this moment should feel overwhelming, but it doesn't. It feels like one more piece of her life clicking firmly into place. "Yes. Let's do it."

"I'll have to talk to Brittani about it," he tells her. And she doesn't flinch at the sound of his ex's name. "We agreed a long time ago to put Kalen first, but as long as he's safe and happy, then we both also need to make ourselves happy. And we promised never to get in the way of that for each other."

"Of course you have to talk to her. I understand."

"Honestly, she's been wanting to get to know you better ever since I told her we were getting serious. I think it would make her more comfortable with the idea of Kalen living with you half the time if the two of you weren't strangers."

"I can do that," Montana promises. "But what about Kalen? Will a change like this be too much for him? We have to make sure we can get him on board too."

Austin grins. "You have a dog now. Every day he's with me, he asks if he can come over here. You've won."

"I really have, haven't I?" she agrees. "I'm getting everything I've ever wanted."

Grin growing impossibly wider, he says, "So am I."

His arm snakes around her waist to pull her closer, and it doesn't feel like their happy ending. This is only the happy beginning of the rest of their lives together.

And when he kisses her, it feels like the very first time.

THEN

*W*hile Montana and Austin stood against a wall outside of the movie theater, waiting for their parents to pick them up, Montana's brain worked in overdrive. This was their third date, but honestly, she wasn't sure if any of them had even been dates at all. Because he hadn't kissed her or anything. This time, at least, he'd finally held her hand during the movie. Her palm was still warm with the memory of his touch.

But would he really want to date her?

He was popular, and funny, and he played baseball.

And he was so, so hot.

He was also nice. He'd asked her about her family, her favorite foods, music. Didn't laugh when she obsessed over Taylor Swift for five straight minutes. Listened to childhood anecdotes about her getting caught reading past her bedtime or reading in unusual places, and he'd smiled like he thought all of that was adorable instead of just weird.

Whatever was going on here, though, still wasn't clear to her.

Breaking the silence, he said, "This was fun."

"Yeah, the movie was good," she agreed. Although she'd barely been paying attention to it, so hyper-focused on him sitting next to her.

"We should do something again."

"Sure."

Pushing off the wall, he moved to stand in front of her. "I wanted to ask you something."

"Okay . . ." She was nervous, making it hard to hold his eye contact. But his eyes were so gorgeous, it was also hard to look away.

He reached for her hand, holding it loosely, his fingers dancing with hers, and asked, "Be my girlfriend?"

"Yes."

The word came out before Montana had a moment to think about it. But if she'd thought about it, the answer still would've been the same.

And then he was smiling at her, and she was smiling too. His grip on her hand tightened as he leaned in. She knew it was coming, yet somehow it still managed to surprise her when he kissed her. His lips were soft against hers, with just the right amount of pressure. When he pulled away, he was grinning wildly.

"What?" she asked, a bit self-conscious, her hand reflexively moving up to her mouth.

He gently took it, brought it back down, and interlaced their fingers. "We're going to be so good at this."

Also by Tammy Subia

Heartbreak Honey

About the Author

Tammy Subia writes romances that are both sweet and spicy. While most of her stories are M/M, she sometimes spreads the love to other pairings too. If she's not writing or listening to filthy audiobooks, you can find her in New England spoiling her cat, drinking iced matchas, and watching *Gilmore Girls*.

Connect with Tammy: ⓞ tammysubiabooks